THE WAITING GAME

Outrage and apprehension were mounting within Kate, and, once again, the feeling that she must be dreaming all this. Then Calvin took her arm and she got a grip on herself.

'Now for it,' she said as they crossed the street and one of the car's windows was sleekly lowered.

'One moment, please.'

They stopped short on the cobbled road, impelled by the authoritative tone. The man who had addressed them was the driver. He switched on the light in the car and they got a glimpse of the man seated beside him, who had leaned forward and turned to look at them. If ever Kate had seen a candidate for the role of the china-smasher, this was him. If she'd met the driver in other circumstances, he could have fooled her that he was a nice, ordinary Russian. But his companion – well, Kate wouldn't want to find herself alone with him. The main reason was his snakelike eyes, she was thinking when the driver said:

'Would you tell me, please, to where you are taking that child?'

'Would you mind telling us,' Kate replied, 'where you took his mother to? And why are you suddenly so concerned about him, when you so patently weren't then?'

IMAGES

'Sympathetic, shrewd and witty, IMAGES exposes the mid-life crisis in all its painfully funny aspects'
Guernsey Evening Post

'Anyone who is going through the mid-life doldrums will chuckle at the wickedly amusing IMAGES . . . There's an abundance of witty jokes and scintillating dialogue. It really is hilarious, don't miss it'
Annabel

'This complex story is a shifting kaleidoscope of personal relationships, a complicated theme handled with considerable skill'
Huddersfield Daily Examiner

'Very much a novel with human insight, a strong sense of humour and realism, and the essence of success'
Wrexham Evening Leader

'A book which is bound to put the lonely and confused mind at ease – with a smile'
Northampton Chronicle and Echo

About the Author

Maisie Mosco is a Mancunian now living in London. A former journalist, she turned to fiction in the sixties. Her early work was for the theatre, and she is also the author of fourteen radio plays. She began writing novels in the late seventies and her compassionate, human sagas were an immediate success.

The Waiting Game

Maisie Mosco

NEW ENGLISH LIBRARY
Hodder and Stoughton

ACKNOWLEDGEMENTS

My editor, Carola Edmond; Rita Eker, whose guidance helped make this book possible; my sons, Maurice and Stephen, and my grand-daughter, Jane, for their supportiveness on a research trip to Moscow.

Though the theme of this novel is all too real, the story and characters are the product of the author's imagination.

Copyright © 1987 by Maisie Mosco Manuscripts Ltd

First published in Great Britain in 1987 by New English Library

First New English Library Paperback edition 1988

British Library C.I.P.

Mosco, Maisie
 The waiting game.
 I. Title
823'.914[F]

 ISBN 0 450 43122 3

Printed and bound in Great Britain for Hodder and Stoughton Paperbacks, a division of Hodder and Stoughton Ltd., Mill Road, Dunton Green, Sevenoaks, Kent TN13 2YA (Editorial Office: 47 Bedford Square, London WC1B 3DP) by Cox & Wyman Ltd., Reading.

. . . any man's death diminishes *me*,
because I am involved in Mankind;

John Donne

CHAPTER ONE

THE TWO airliners had taken off on opposite sides of the Atlantic, bound for the Soviet Union.

Aboard the British Airways flight from Heathrow a tall, slender woman was trying to concentrate on the *Guardian* crossword puzzle, and wishing that economy-class passengers were allowed more leg-room.

The attractive redhead on her left watched her fill in the answer to an anagram, and said with a smile, 'I wish I had the brains to do crosswords.'

'This is only the quick one, and it's taking me longer than it should.'

'I know. I've been timing you.'

'If only you'd do the same with my boiled eggs!' her husband quipped from the aisle seat. 'Now why don't we let her get on with it?'

But she doubted that they would. She was stuck with this chatty couple – and the journey had barely begun.

'I'm hungry,' the redhead said to her, 'aren't you?'

'Well, it does seem ages since I had my breakfast. But we'll soon be getting lunch.'

On the Pan Am plane from Kennedy, breakfast trays had just been set before the passengers in the first-class compartment, and a man whose face seemed too young for his greying hair was drinking buck's-fizz. Not until they reached their destination would Kate Starling and Calvin Fenner be in the same time zone. Meanwhile, the night-flight he had just put behind him was causing him to stifle his yawns. She, on the other hand, had never felt more alert; as though all it took to set her adrenalin soaring was the unknown quantity that stretched ahead of her.

Kate gave up on the crossword, adjusted her seat to the

reclining position and shut her eyes, hoping her flight companions would take the hint and leave her alone with her thoughts. The same tactic she'd employed on her one and only cruise, when someone or other disturbed her peace on deck. What had she done in the years that had slipped by since then? Gone on being a good wife and mother. Well, she'd tried to be, within the limits of the person she was still discovering she was.

'Better put your table down,' said the redhead. 'The food's coming, or I wouldn't have disturbed you. I'm Barbara Ross, by the way. And my husband's name is Howard.'

Kate felt obliged to introduce herself. At this rate, by the time the plane touched down in Moscow they'd be on visiting terms.

'Our food won't be the same as yours,' Barbara told her. 'We asked for a kosher meal.'

Howard divined Kate's thoughts. 'You don't have to say it. We know we don't look Jewish. Nor does our surname sound it, which, where we're going, is a help — '

'Watch what you're saying, Howard,' Barbara butted in. 'This isn't an Aeroflot plane.'

'I should think not! Why would we ladle out cash to the you-know-who that we don't have to?'

Howard said, 'And the same would go for our hotel room, if they weren't all state-owned.'

Kate asked if they knew which hotel they would be staying at. 'I haven't the foggiest where I shall be put.'

'Nobody has till they get there, but you'll probably be with us,' said Barbara, as their trays were put before them.

Kate hoped her reaction to the last bit was not evident on her face.

'I saw on your hand baggage that we're with the same tour party,' Barbara went on. 'We always use them for our trips to Russia, and they generally house everyone together.'

'This isn't your first time, then?'

'Oh no.'

'And each time we go, we think it could be our last,' Howard declared.

'So it could be, if you're not more careful,' his wife hissed, digging her fork into some smoked salmon that made Kate wish that she too had asked for a kosher meal. Her own *hors d'oeuvre* tasted of curry, but what its components were was anyone's guess.

'The you-know-who aren't always recognisable,' Barbara whispered to her, and added to Howard, 'When I went to the loo, I passed a man in the smoking section who stared at me.'

'That could be due to your shape.'

Kate agreed. But what on earth was Barbara so nervous about? She had sensed an underlying tension beneath Howard's banter, too.

'Would you mind telling me who the you-know-who are?' she said.

'For the moment we'll leave you to use your imagination,' Barbara replied.

Could they possibly mean the KGB? Kate was getting the feeling they had read too many spy novels. Or were they just a pair of nuts?

'That man – he was drinking vodka,' Barbara persisted.

'So what?' said Kate. People ought not to take holidays in Russia if they were going to behave in a ridiculous cloak-and-dagger manner. 'I sometimes drink vodka myself. So does my husband. And how do you know the man wasn't drinking gin?'

'I noticed the bottle.'

Like you noticed the tour-company tag on my flight bag. 'You're very observant, aren't you?'

'I also have a good memory for faces, and I'm sure I've seen you somewhere before today. I kept looking at you in the departure lounge and thinking wherever could it have been?'

Barbara's smile was so friendly, Kate chided herself for being churlish. I'm travelling alone, and they're being nice to me. It isn't their fault that I'm feeling – feeling what?

'I'm already missing my kids,' Barbara said to her. 'Have you got any? We have two boys and a girl.'

'I stopped at one of each.'

11

'Is that because you're a career woman? You look like one.'

How did one look like a career woman? Kate was wearing pants and a sweater, not a pinstripe suit. 'I do have a career of sorts,' she replied. Not the one she'd once hoped for, but she'd made her choice a long time ago.

'Shall we guess what she does, Howard? Or let her tell us?'

'Let' indeed: Kate was left with no option. Friendly this girl might be, but nosey wasn't in it! 'I write a column for a weekly paper.'

'Which one?'

'If you don't live in South London, you probably won't have heard of it.'

Kate got on with her meal, after which she returned her seat and her eyelids to the broad-hint position. Where was she when lunch intervened? Trying to sum up how she felt, setting forth to meet a man she had known only briefly; whom she had not seen since they said goodbye after the Black Sea cruise.

That man was at that moment engaged in a similar self-examination. Why was sensible Calvin Fenner making this damn-fool trip? He had a gallery to run, back in Boston, though he had left it in capable hands.

Since liquor in the first-class compartment was free, some of his fellow-passengers had been glassy-eyed before the flight was an hour out of Kennedy, and after their fitful night's sleep now looked distinctly hung over. The guy next to him was gulping a Bloody Mary mixed by a stewardess with incredible legs and a plastic smile. Others were helping themselves to drinks from the polished table that served as a bar, though it was only mid-morning. If business execs behaved this way on the ground, America would grind to a halt. It must be something about flying. Calvin didn't get to do too much of it, but when he did he invariably felt like an outsider at a party.

His first transatlantic flight had been to join the S S *Ocean Queen* at the Italian port from which it had sailed for the Black Sea, and he'd expected that if he ever flew to Europe again it would be to London. Meeting Kate and Alun Starling on the cruise had given him a taste for British company. But that didn't mean that when Kate said to him on the phone, almost half a decade later, 'I'm going to Moscow. Are you coming?' Calvin would find himself answering, without a second thought, 'Yes.' The second thoughts were coming at him thick and fast now.

There'd been no preamble to Kate's question, but that hadn't surprised him. What was it she used to say on board ship, during spats with her husband? – and Cal had seen them have a few. That she didn't believe in shilly-shallying. Directness was Kate's way. Impulsiveness, too, which couldn't be said about Cal. He had agonised over the biggest decision of his life for three whole years.

The only split-second one he had ever made was agreeing to meet Kate in Moscow, and he hadn't consciously made it. It was as if something begun on the cruise and left lying had to be settled and they both knew it. If not now, it would be next year, or whenever, so let's get it over. Sooner or later, a person's conscience would catch up with them. But how in the hell was this trip going to purge Cal and Kate of the burden they shared? One that others would shrug off, as they had the whole event when it happened. What were Cal and Kate hoping for?

Kate was still reclining with her eyes closed, appreciating the sudden quiet that follows a meal on a flight, when the clatter and chatter give way to the soporific effects of food and wine. Even her talkative companions had lapsed into silence, and her mind was finally allowed to wend its way circuitously back in time.

Her father was paying for her trip to Moscow. She had asked him to lend her the money, but he had insisted upon giving it to her. Peeping behind the Iron Curtain would not have been her husband's idea of a holiday.

Not for the first time, she pondered on the word 'if', and its influence, for better or worse, upon people's lives. There are some choices which Fate makes for us, but it is we who are afterwards left to grapple with the consequences, and so it was with the Black Sea cruise. The Starlings could not have

13

afforded the price of two weeks on a super-luxury liner, though Alun's job at the hospital, plus Kate's earnings from her part-time journalism, allowed them to live quite nicely.

It was my pen that got Alun and me aboard the *Ocean Queen*, she thought with satisfaction. I might have got to Fleet Street on a national daily if I hadn't settled for what I did. Kate had women friends who split their lives down the middle, between a high-powered career and their family. For her that wouldn't have worked. Well, not while the children were still very young. She had always been the single-minded kind, and that particular choice had been a case of 'me or them'.

She could no longer remember the pithy paragraphs that had won her first prize in a competition, though she had once known them by heart. Entrants were invited to write the copy for an exotic holiday advertisement. It had not taken Kate more than a few minutes to weave her words. She had entered for a lark, without telling Alun. Some months later, they were on their way to join the *Ocean Queen*, the children left with Kate's parents, as though they were off on a second honeymoon.

Kate was aware of the aircraft's engines gently thrumming, and heard again the slow throb ever present on board ship. She could see herself standing on deck with Alun, waving farewell to the receding figures on the quayside, as the liner set sail. So vivid was the recollection, Barbara's perfume, wafting from beside her, was overpowered by a remembered smell of brine . . .

'I feel like the poor relation on this boat,' she had said to Alun.

'And everyone will know you are, darling, if you call it a boat, instead of a ship!'

Kate had thrust her hands into the pockets of her white linen jacket – which wasn't hers; those of her friends who were her size had contributed garments to her cruise wardrobe – and glanced around at the elegant and bejewelled women with whom she would be rubbing shoulders for the next two weeks. Every night was going to be like a fashion show, and the same would apply on the sun deck.

'Which of your borrowed plumes shall you wear to make an entrance this evening?' Alun asked her with a grin.

'Audrey's long slinky dinner gown, since first impressions count.'

'Fortunately, all a chap needs to make the right impression is a tuxedo.'

But not on the first evening at sea . . .

'There should be a notice in the cabins, telling people the correct sartorial drill,' Alun said, red-faced with embarrassment, when they entered the dining-room.

'Why would they bother? Everyone knows but us.' Kate hid her chagrin and kept her gaze fixed straight ahead, as they made their way to their assigned table. If first impressions counted, so be it!

The tables were for eight, to encourage the conviviality that can either enhance the holiday, or make one feel like jumping overboard. Kate and Alun had filled in a shipping-company form, on which they were asked to state their age, occupations, and leisure interests. They found themselves seated with a septuagenarian couple from Amsterdam who spoke only Dutch, a stout Viennese and his exceedingly thin wife, whose English was minimal, and two American men of their own generation.

When the necessary self-introductions had been made, the Americans exchanged a glance, and one of them said, 'Will you tell 'em, or shall I, Sandy?'

Sandy laughed. 'Only the timely intervention of our steward stopped Calvin and me from showing up for dinner tonight in *our* glad-rags. Had to do a quick change, didn't we, Cal?'

'But don't let it bother you,' Calvin said reassuringly to Kate. 'That's a real pretty gown you have on.'

'It's kind of you to say so.'

'And to alleviate our embarrassment,' said Alun, fingering his bow tie.

Kate was glad that they were seated opposite the Americans, since communing with the others could be no more than a polite smile when one of them looked her way, or when Herr Weber screwed up his face in concentration and said something incomprehensible to her. 'In London you have der Big Ben, ya?' and Kate's answering nod, was the sole moment of real communication. She became fascinated by the Viennese lady's dewlap, trembling while she ate, and by the long gold chains the Dutch woman was wearing, which kept clinking on her plate.

The Americans, too, were treated to one comprehensible remark from the Austrian, 'In Vashington is der Vite House, ya?' and it was then that Kate and Calvin shared their first smile of silent rapport.

When the lengthy meal had ended, and they had escaped to their cabin to change into casual clothes, Alun said, 'I'm sorry for those chaps from Boston. I mean, fancy forking out what this cruise must have cost them, and being stuck for every meal without a girl to chat up.'

'Aren't you forgetting me?' Kate replied.

'Still consider yourself a girl, do you?'

'Twenty-eight is young enough to interest those two — '

'If they haven't hotfooted it to request a change of table,' Alun cut in. 'I'm thinking of doing so myself. They might at least have put us at one where everyone speaks the same language.'

'Shall we wait and see if the Americans do? It would be a bit of an insult to those elderly couples if all four of us cleared off.'

The Americans must have seen it from that angle, too, because they were standing by the table with smiles of mutual understanding when Kate and Alun took their places for dinner the following evening. Thus it was that the shipboard friendship between the Starlings and the two Americans began. They were pleasant and courteous to their table companions, but it was each other whom they sought out, or arranged to meet.

In the ballroom, Kate discovered that Calvin danced, but Sandy did not. Since Alun found dancing a bore, it was Calvin who, more often than not, partnered her on the floor.

'You're getting a great tan,' he said one evening, when they were waltzing together.

'You, too.'

16

'Sandy has to be careful. If I didn't watch him, he'd peel like an onion.'

'Like I have to watch Alun.'

Though Kate was fair-haired, the sun was not her enemy. Alun, despite his darker skin, had to plaster himself with barrier cream.

'We usually arrive home from a holiday looking as if I've been to the tropics, and him to the North Pole,' she added with a smile.

'I hope he doesn't mind my stealing you away to dance, like I do.'

Kate glanced to where Alun and Sandy were leaning on the ship's rail. The *Ocean Queen* had just sailed from Istanbul, where it had docked for a shore trip, and she could see the lights twinkling distantly on the bridges over the Bosphorus. After shore trips, passengers were not expected to dress for dinner, and dancing was an informal affair on deck.

'Alun's had me to himself all day,' she replied lightly. 'After we'd done the sightseeing trip, we went bargaining in the Bazaar.'

Calvin chuckled. 'When Sandy and I came back on board, all the ladies in the tea salon were showing each other replicas of *objets d'art* in the Topkapi Museum. Did you go see the real thing?'

'There wasn't time.'

'It was the first place we made for, and Sandy would've liked to take back everything we saw there, for the gallery! The same goes when we're on buying trips, but fortunately one of us is a businessman as well as an art lover.'

'That sounds like the way Alun has to keep *my* feet on the ground. I wanted to buy a big brass gong for the hall. He managed to talk me out of it.'

'But I did let Sandy buy an extravagant item for our home. From one of those little Aladdin's-cave shops near the docks,' Calvin said while whirling her around to the music.

'You live together, then?'

'We have for years, Kate, and make no secret of it. The vase we bought is an exquisite example of early Turkish . . .'

Kate kept a listening expression on her face, but was prey

17

to her own confusion. Fragments, unregistered at the time, fell into place in her mind. The way each used the pronoun 'we' more often than 'I', as couples do. The air of everyday ease between them, like there was between Alun and herself, that spelled a secure relationship. The numerous sexy women whom she had seen try to engage their attention on board, but neither had succumbed.

'Sometimes your eyes look green, and sometimes, like now, they're grey,' Calvin said looking down at her.

'That's why I put grey-green on my passport application.'

What was he doing gazing into her eyes when he was gay? She had men friends at home who were, and no undercurrents were present when she was with them. A woman who loved her husband ought not to be gazing back into Calvin's eyes, either, but that was no part of this puzzle. She would have sworn he was as attracted to her as she to him, hence her confusion.

Since that final thought was not included when she told Alun, his only reaction was relief.

They had just made love in the secluded luxury of their cabin, and Kate gently kissed a red-raw patch on her husband's shoulder. 'How did that bit of you escape the barrier cream?'

'You weren't there to spread it on for me. You'd gone off for morning coffee with Calvin, and I was starting to think you were falling for him.'

'He isn't as handsome as you.'

'That's what I kept telling myself, but I needn't worry any more. Sandy and I were saying to each other, while you two were dancing this evening away, that it's a good thing he and I get on so well together!'

Kate could find little in common with Sandy who, apart from his work, seemed to be interested in nothing but sport – unlike Calvin, who was a stimulating conversationalist. Now that she knew they were a couple, Kate found them an incongruous one, even in appearance. Calvin was tall and aesthetic-looking, and Sandy stockily built and freckle-faced, his crew-cut hair accentuating its babyish roundness. Though she knew nothing about their respective

18

backgrounds, she would wager that Calvin was born to wealth and privilege, but that Sandy's assured manner was acquired.

'Did you tell her?' Sandy asked Calvin, while they took their nightly stroll on deck, before retiring.

'Tell her what?'

'What she needs to know, so she won't go on thinking you're romancing her, and I won't have to take any more cracks from Alun about you fancying his wife. Alun's a nice guy. If you can't bring yourself to tell her, I'll tell him.'

Calvin halted to stare down at the sea. 'The matter is taken care of.'

On the plane now heading closer to the Soviet Union, Calvin was remembering saying that to Sandy, with the salt air blowing in their faces as they turned to look at each other; and the vulnerable expression in Sandy's eyes. The same expression was there when Calvin told him he was going to Moscow to meet Kate Starling, nor had it helped when Calvin was unable to explain why.

To Sandy's knowledge, their only contact with the Starlings since the cruise was the annual exchange of Christmas greetings. It had come as a shock to him to learn that Cal had recently spoken with Kate on the phone. Sandy was never going to accept that the trip Cal had arranged with her was not a pleasure jaunt. Far from it. But how could Sandy understand, more than four years later, what he had failed to at the time? And the same probably went for Alun Starling.

Calvin gazed through the aircraft window at the billowing clouds, his whirling thoughts a kaleidoscope of recollected sights and sounds. Anyone could have gotten deeply affected by what they saw on that vacation. But few had allowed themselves to, which, in a way, was a reflection of Western attitudes. As those aboard the *Ocean Queen* were a microcosm of uncaring affluence. The 'haves' have it all, and the hell with the 'have-nots', about summed it up. But one of the things the passengers on board that ship had, and took for granted, could not be bought. The freedom to come and go, and voice opinions, denied to those whom they had briefly

19

encountered in the Iron Curtain ports. When had Cal stopped taking it for granted?

Kate could have pinpointed the exact moment for him. She had not since that time bought a jar of the Bulgarian cherry jam her children loved, because the label reminded her of that day in the ship's dining-room, when her own good fortune had struck her forcibly, and she had known that Calvin was similarly moved.

The liner had docked at Varna to allow the passengers a morning ashore, and Kate and Alun rose early to make the most of it, though their cabin steward had told them that the town was nothing special. Since taxis were hard to come by, and buses infrequent, they walked to the town centre, a misleadingly pleasant-looking tree-lined square, bordered on one side by a park. Though it was a weekday, the stores were closed and the pavements thronged.

'Today must be a public holiday,' Alun remarked, as they headed toward the park.

'And something is going on,' said Kate, noting the loudspeakers fixed to the trees, and a preponderance of uniformed men. Were they police? Or soldiers?

'Maybe there's going to be a carnival.'

Anything less like a carnival atmosphere Kate could not imagine. She had never seen so many miserable – or was it impassive? – faces. And the uniformed men were toting rifles.

A strident, female voice cut into her thoughts. 'Hi, there! Ship ahoy!'

The *Ocean Queen* hold-alls Kate and Alun were carrying were as good as a badge, and people with whom they had not exchanged a word on board would accost them matily, ashore. On this occasion, it was a twosome whom they had privately dubbed Big Momma and Poppa, since their height seemed to equal their girth.

'Might as well get in line with us at the bus stop,' Big Momma advised. 'There'd be zilch to buy in this hick town if the stores were open. We're heading back to the ship. Did you believe it when you saw the shop windows?'

'They made me feel sorry for the Bulgarians,' said Kate.

'What you ain't never had, you ain't gonna miss,' Big Poppa replied.

'I was lookin' to buy me an amber necklace, to go with this outfit,' said Big Momma, smoothing down the skin-tight catsuit that made her look like a yellow balloon. 'But they say that in Odessa they're gonna take us to a store that's packed with goodies.'

'Which only tourists can afford.'

Alun led Kate away, lest she follow up her remark with one which even the thick-skinned could not fail to know was directed at them. 'It isn't their fault that there's poverty and shortages here, Kate.'

'But it is that they don't give a damn. If we hadn't got friendly with Cal and Sandy, I'd be thinking that all wealthy Americans are like that couple. As for our other table companions, whenever I nip up to the late-night buffet to get myself a cup of tea, there they are, stuffing themselves with everything in sight, as if they've never seen food before. Except that it's quite the reverse – in company with most people on the cruise. You haven't the foggiest what I'm on about, have you, Alun?'

'No, and I'm not going to let it spoil our holiday.'

They crossed the road toward the park, in the late-September sunlight. In England, this would be a rare, golden day, reflected in the people's mood, thought Kate, but all around her were men and women whose aimless demeanour matched their lack-lustre expressions. Shoddy was the only word to describe their clothing, and their pasty complexions bespoke a poor diet. It's as though they've lost hope of anything ever changing for them, Kate summed up her impressions. And why wouldn't they?

'By the way, Sandy isn't wealthy,' Alun said. 'It's Calvin who owns the gallery, though they run it together – which, given their relationship, isn't a position I'd like to be in. If I were Sandy, I mean.'

Their conversation was drowned by an announcement blaring from the loudspeakers. Evidently an instruction was being given, for the milling crowd began surging toward the roadside as if preparing for a motorcade to pass by.

Kate and Alun, about to enter the park, found their progress halted by a burly soldier who had planted himself in front of them, his rifle gripped in a horizontal position, as if he would, if necessary, use it to sweep them backward. He could not have looked more fierce, and a torrent of words they could not, of course, understand was issuing from his mouth.

Kate swallowed hard. 'Would you mind letting us pass?'

She had kept her tone level, though anger at being treated this way was coursing through her, and was aware that the incident was being watched by the Bulgarians at the back of the crowd – Lord help them if this sort of thing was a feature of their everyday lives. Why didn't Alun *do* something?

'The park seems to be out of bounds, Kate,' he said, recovering his equilibrium, and more lightly than he felt.

'But there's no need to make it clear so forcibly, is there? All he had to do was shake his head and point us away from here with a finger – '

The rest of Kate's protest was cut short by what had to be a curse in Bulgarian. The soldier had lost patience with them and Kate felt the length of the rifle butt in her midriff.

Alun grabbed her arm and tugged her away, and her anger boiled over. Menaced though she had felt by the rifle, and by the beetle-browed individual toting it, she wouldn't have succumbed to such treatment if Alun hadn't made her. How dare they treat tourists, whose money they were happy to take, this way!

'This is supposed to be a holiday!' Alun exclaimed. 'Why must you take everything so damn seriously, Kate?'

'Perhaps I'm not as capable of shutting my eyes to injustices as you are – and I don't just mean how we were treated by that oaf. We can get back on the ship and breathe a big sigh of relief, can't we? But what must it be like to live here?'

Men like the one who had just made his strength felt were now planted, feet apart and rifles well in evidence, behind the crowd lining the roadside, and people began lethargically raising paper flags, as if they had no option but to do so.

Alun spotted Calvin and Sandy heading toward them – he'd be glad of their company, with Kate in the mood she was in.

Sandy, who was not enjoying the heat, was mopping his freckled brow. 'We just met one of the ship's officers and he told us who it is who's in town today. The president no less!'

'They wouldn't have to rent a crowd if it was our queen,' said Kate. 'Only this rent-a-crowd isn't getting paid for it. On the contrary. Alun and I just had an encounter with a rifle.'

'We'll tell them about it later, Kate.'

'I don't hear any hip-hoorays, do you?' Calvin said as some limousines turned into the square and began streaming by.

Only a muted cheer had greeted the approach of the first one, and it had already petered out. There was not the slightest sense of excitement among the crowd, which afterwards dispersed in an orderly manner as if doing so was part of an accustomed procedure.

'I guess the president was showing off his power to some sheik,' Calvin remarked. 'Did you notice there was an Arab in the car with him?'

'Since I'm not a six-footer, like you, I can't see over people's heads,' Kate said crossly.

'You'll have to excuse her,' said Alun. 'She hasn't got over the rifle incident yet. We could probably take our walk in the park now, Kate – '

'No, thanks. Let's just go back to the ship.' Kate had seen enough of the effects of power upon those at the receiving end, for one morning.

Later, at luncheon, Kate noticed that Calvin seemed as low-spirited as she felt.

'Why aren't you eating?' Alun asked her.

'I was wondering how come *you* haven't lost your appetite.'

Calvin picked at some salmon in aspic, then put down his fork. Light from the ornate chandeliers lent added opulence to the crystal and silverware spread upon the heavy damask cloth. Dishes of succulent vegetables, and an array of exotic salads, tempted the palate. A mouth-watering mound of fruit, on a gilt stand, was the centrepiece.

He looked at Alun. 'What Kate means, I guess, is the contrast in lifestyles between here and ashore has killed her appetite. Mine, too. And did you and Sandy happen to glance out the window? If anything were needed to cap this morning's excursion, that does it.'

Alun mustered a smile, though he was feeling distinctly fed up. Tomorrow they'd be in Russia, and if Kate behaved there as she had in Bulgaria, she could end up behind bars. 'All I can see through the window is some friendly Bulgarians, standing on the quayside to bid us *bon voyage*.'

'Then take a better look at their faces.'

'Lay off it, Cal,' Sandy interceded.

'He can get how he feels off his chest so far as I'm concerned,' Kate said. 'And maybe I'll join in.'

Sandy said to Alun, 'Would you believe these two? I mean, what the hell! Everyone could let a place like this, which fortunately we're about to leave, get them down. But it wouldn't change a thing.'

Kate responded, ' "Fortunately", from our point of view, is the key word. What must it feel like to be standing where those Bulgarians are? With just a short stretch of water between them and a ship that spells the freedom they haven't got?'

Alun glanced at their stolidly munching table companions, and let his gaze rove around the restaurant. 'But I don't see anyone but you and Calvin letting it put them off their food. Fancy a game of deck quoits this afternoon, anyone?'

'How the heck can you think about deck quoits!' Kate exploded.

'Would it do those poor devils on the quayside any good if I spent the afternoon bemoaning their lot?'

Why hadn't Kate realised until now how differently her husband ticked from how she did? That he was capable of just shrugging off things he could do nothing about.

'Cheer up, Kate,' Sandy said to her, 'you, too, Cal.'

And Sandy was just like him. It wasn't that they were hard-hearted, but – A silent message was being telegraphed between herself and Calvin: 'They're not like us.'

Further evidence of this was presented during dinner that evening. By then, the ship had put to sea.

Kate and Calvin had joined in the deck game, loth, and as if by mutual consent, to cast the gloom they shared over the other two. They had got together as usual in one of the bars for a pre-dinner drink, the men comfortably attired in casual clothes instead of having to wear what Alun called their monkey-suits, and Kate in another of her borrowed outfits, a deceptively simple white cotton top and pants – that must have cost its owner the earth, she had thought whilst putting it on.

The atmosphere in the restaurant seemed even more festive than usual, as if the passengers were letting rip with relief, she thought, listening to the gales of laughter at the next table. The depressing port of call was now behind them. But if that was Bulgaria, what would it be like in the Soviet Union, where they were now heading? She would have liked to conjecture about it with Calvin – but Alun and Sandy would try to muzzle them! What was the point?

The first course – melon with Parma ham – had awaited them on the table, their waiter standing at a respectful distance while they ate it; Kate had not accustomed herself to being treated like a princess, and gave him a friendly smile. Like her, he was a Londoner, and she had got quite pally with him; he sometimes gave her a wink, as if he knew she had her tongue in her cheek, as he did, about the deference he displayed to people who were no better than him.

'I've got something to tell you, Mrs Starling,' he said when he came to clear away the plates. 'Rumour has it that there's a stowaway aboard.'

'A Bulgarian?'

'Well, I expect so, seeing as Bulgaria's where we've just set sail from.'

Kate felt a lightening of her heart. Someone had made a stab for freedom and had managed it.

Calvin had seen her smile of delight. He was feeling pretty chuffed about it himself.

'Anyone would think these two knew the stowaway,' Sandy said to Alun.

'Is it a man or a woman, Terry?' Kate asked the waiter.

'Oh, I should think it's a chap – but it's only a rumour among the crew, Mrs Starling, though I've never known smoke without fire, not aboard ship I mean. Don't you folk go spreading it any further, though, or you'll get me hung.'

'What would they have done with the stowaway?' Calvin inquired.

'Put him in the cell, Mr Fenner. What else?'

'Do you mean there's a cell on this ship?' exclaimed Kate.

The waiter hurried away without replying.

A short silence followed, during which Kate and Calvin stared thoughtfully down at the table.

Then Kate said, 'Imagine your first taste of freedom being getting locked up!'

'That sentence doesn't make sense,' said Alun.

'But you know very well what I mean.'

'Well, *I* certainly do,' said Calvin, 'and if there was something I could do to stop him being sent back to Bulgaria, I'd sure try.'

'Count me in,' said Kate.

'I'd like to remind the pair of you that this is only a rumour,' said Sandy.

'And even if it weren't, I wouldn't want you getting involved, Kate,' said Alun. 'If it's true, I'm as sorry for the stowaway as you are, and I'm sure Sandy is. But this has nothing to do with us.'

'If Sandy agrees with that last remark, why don't the two of you just resign from the human race?' Kate replied.

By the following morning, the rumour was being discussed by all the passengers, but was soon overshadowed by the formalities surrounding the *Ocean Queen*'s arrival at a Soviet port.

A posse of Russian officials boarded the liner. Tables were set up in one of the lounges, and at the point of disembarkation. Passengers were requested to wait in another lounge, while their passports, collected the previous evening, were scrutinised in their absence.

In the interim, one of the ship's officers drilled them – Kate could think of no other word for it. Since individual visas were not being supplied, nobody could disembark except with a group supervised by a Russian guide. Once ashore, on no account must they leave the group, and must return with it to the ship. This strict supervision would also apply to the visit to the Opera House, scheduled for that evening. If anyone had envisaged exploring Odessa on their own, day or night, they had better forget it.

The process of handing back the passports dragged on for what seemed like an eternity. Some passengers were eventually told that they would not be permitted to disembark, but were not informed why. One of these to Kate's puzzlement was a frail old lady who might have been her granny. By the time she and Alun were allowed to leave the liner, she was seething, and her mind boggling.

Before descending the gangway, her bag was searched and her countenance scanned by grim-faced officials flanked by armed guards. If they're trying to make us nervous, they're doing a fine job, she thought. Her descent to the quay was arrested by a stout gentleman in front of her almost missing his footing. The sight of more soldiers staring up at them, rifles well in evidence, was menacing to say the least.

Kate thought of the stowaway, now imprisoned in the bowels of the ship. What would be his fate if he was returned to his own country? Bulgaria was said to be the most hardline régime in the Soviet bloc, and she had experienced a graphic example of it yesterday.

'The stowaway would never have got aboard from *this* port,' Calvin said to her, when their feet finally touched Russian soil, and they were walking ahead of Alun and Sandy to where the tour buses were parked.

They were on the same wavelength, which she and Alun never had been. Then why had she chosen Alun? Her youthful passion for him had rendered her blind; and it had taken eight years of marriage for her to finally admit it. She hadn't stopped loving him, and they were still good in bed

27

together, but if Calvin weren't gay – you'd still be a married woman with two kids and a devoted husband, Kate.

'I'm not going to let the matter of the stowaway rest,' Calvin said.

'Count me in, like I said.'

'I knew I could.'

Kate was disappointed when they were directed to different buses. Though this was to be a sightseeing tour organised by the Russians, Calvin, like herself, would be mentally stripping off the gloss, putting his own interpretation upon the set-piece commentary supplied by the English-speaking guide, wishing he could get to meet some ordinary Soviet citizens. Alun, on the other hand, seemed satisfied to take in what was served up to him, and admire the historic buildings and monuments of this beautiful city.

Kate's request that they be allowed to travel in the same vehicle as their friends had been courteously received, but dismissed as not possible, even though a Canadian couple in the Starlings' bus had offered to change places with Calvin and Sandy. The lists had been made and the buses assigned, said the dimple-cheeked girl, while checking the paper in her hand. Mr and Mrs Starling were in her charge, and must travel in Bus Number 7.

Kate, who had bridled at the term 'in my charge', said, 'The hell with that!'

'The arrangements made are for your care and protection, Mrs Starling.'

It was the first of several exchanges between Kate and the Intourist guide, but not once did the Russian girl lose her smiling blandness. Not even when, after a walk-around during which she delivered a eulogy about the splendid architecture of some old buildings, Kate said, 'But your régime didn't erect them, did it?'

'This square is of historic value.'

'But that doesn't answer my point.'

'What point was that, Mrs Starling?'

This was Kate's first experience of what she would afterwards think of as the 'Soviet brick wall'.

Later, while they stood at the top of the Potemkin Steps taking pictures of the view, Alun expressed his growing uneasiness about Kate. 'If others can behave as they're expected to when they're in Russia, why can't you? I don't know – what with one thing and another – what's got into you. Stop playing the probing reporter, Kate.'

Her husband didn't really know her. Well, not the side of her that had recently emerged. Nor, to be honest, had Kate known it was there. She would not have thought of herself as a rebel of any sort. But when had she ever had to be? She had lived a sheltered life. An insular one, too. The only dilemmas she'd ever had to face were those of her own small domestic world. Like how was she going to cope with the family laundry, when her washing machine broke down and the repair engineer was booked up for three weeks. Could she really have considered that a dilemma – and with two launderettes around the corner? She had cursed the inconvenience, but at least she'd had a choice of action. But what of those who had no choice in the larger issue of their own destiny, for whom the regimentation Kate had rebelled against yesterday and today was a way of life?

The vista below was of a charming city, and those of its citizens she had passed on the walk-around had not appeared overtly oppressed, as the Bulgarians had. But Bulgaria had, in recent history, been a free society.

'I wonder if Karl Marx foresaw that all these years after the revolution, Russia would be the sort of society it is,' she said thoughtfully to Alun. 'I mean – well, his and Lenin's motives were good, weren't they?'

'I wouldn't know. And we'd better get back to the bus.' The rest of the party were already boarding it at the foot of the monument, and Alun could see the guide staring up at him and Kate.

'Well, they wanted to make things better for the people, didn't they?' Kate said, as if she had not heard him mention the bus. 'To rid them of Tsarist tyranny and all that it meant. Cal, who's a lot more clued up than I am, said Marx wrote a book called *The Dictatorship of the Proletariat* – '

'Is that what you and he talk about while you're dancing

together?' Alun took her arm and marched her down the steps.

'We talk about lots of things. What do you and Sandy talk about?'

'Sport, mostly. But Sandy's favourite subject is Calvin, and I sometimes get the feeling that, though there's no doubt in my mind that Cal's faithful to him, Sandy's privately petrified that Cal might leave him one day. Also that he's jealous of you, though you're the wrong gender. Could you go a bit faster, Kate – I can see Natasha tapping her foot.'

'I'd rather she tapped her foot than I broke my leg.' The flight of steps seemed endless and Alun was tugging Kate along, one step ahead of her and gripping her hand.

'About that book Cal told me about,' she resumed their conversation about Karl Marx.

To Alun it was less of a conversation than a monologue he had to listen to. 'What about it? And please don't go on like this in front of Natasha – '

'Cal said that to get the new society going the people would have to be told what was good for them. I suppose Marx thought they would eventually come to see it for themselves. But theories are never the same in practice, are they? Or there'd be no dissidents in Russia. I'd like to meet some of them.'

Natasha eyed them with undisguised disapproval as they reached the pavement.

'If you mention dissidents to that girl, Kate, I'm going to leap off the bus.'

Kate managed to refrain from doing so, but later asked the girl if tourists granted individual visas to visit the Soviet Union were allowed to move around without supervision.

'Those who visit our historic cities spend most of their time enjoying tours to our great museums and monuments, Mrs Starling. In Moscow, for example, is the Lenin Mausoleum, to where people journey from the far corners of the earth, to pay homage to the founder of the Union of Soviet Socialist Republics.'

Was it possible that the girl really believed what she parroted? If so, it said a lot for the way the Russian people had been deluded about how citizens of democracies viewed the consequences of Marxist-Leninism.

'Within the walls of Kremlin,' the guide went on, 'our visitors may admire our famous gold and silver domed cathedrals of the fifteenth and sixteenth centuries – '

'But your people aren't exactly encouraged to practise religion, are they, Natasha?' Kate interrupted her.

The question was neatly evaded. 'I still have not answered what you wished initially to know. Yes, there is always some time at leisure for those who hold visas to explore areas of our great cities. In Leningrad, I would recommend the shops and cafés of Nevsky Prospekt. In Moscow is our famous Gorky Park.'

And if Kate heard the words 'great' or 'famous' used one more time! National pride was one thing, but there came a point when it stopped being just that, and came over like a salesman spouting a hard-sell line of patter.

The final stop of the excursion was the *beryozka*, where tourists could, with hard currency, buy items to take home. Alun was watching Big Poppa hand over a wad of dollars for Beluga caviar, when he realised that Kate was missing. They had splurged on a set of *matroshka* dolls for their small daughter, then he had gone to look at some crudely-made trinkets while Kate admired the embroidery on a horrendously expensive blouse. But where was she now?

Big Momma, who was waiting for all her purchases to be wrapped, told him she had seen Kate leave the shop. 'Could be your wife's gone to find a john. I could use one myself, after all that Russian tea at the café stop.'

Big Poppa said, 'But I guess if my honey was the kind you're married to, *I'd* be kinda worried where she's taken off for. You sure must find that lady a handful.'

But Alun had not found her hard to handle until now, he thought after checking the bus. Some of their party had already returned to it – but not Kate! It was as if something about this holiday had brought out the worst in her.

With Cal's encouragement. Calvin and Sandy were, he saw, emerging from a grocery shop on the opposite side of the street – where they had no right to be. Alun could imagine

Cal striding off there, and Sandy trailing behind, hoping their guide wasn't watching them.

'If you saw what the women were standing in line to buy, you wouldn't believe it,' Sandy said when they joined him. 'Bottled fruit that looked grey with age, and vegetables you and I would consign to the trash can.'

'But if we hadn't strayed from the tour, we wouldn't have seen what they'd rather that tourists didn't,' said Calvin. 'Where's Kate, Alun?'

'Probably doing what you did. She's gone missing. What am I going to tell the guide?'

'That your wife is a free spirit.'

'And we know what happens to free spirits in this country, don't we!' Alun clutched at the straw Big Momma had handed him, and said, when Natasha came to tell him the bus must now leave, 'My wife went to find a ladies' room, and must be having trouble finding her way back here.'

Five minutes ticked by, during which Calvin and Sandy were obliged by their guide's insistence to leave with their group.

Then Natasha made a decision. 'Mrs Starling will have to return to the ship alone. Since I have not eyes in the back of my head, I cannot be held responsible, and this has never happened previously to me. It is usual for visitors to conform to Soviet rules.'

Alun could understand why. There was something in the air that told you you'd better. When Cal had said Kate was a free spirit, Alun had felt like swiping the smile off his face. Did Cal think the way he and Kate were behaving set them apart as something special? What it did set them apart as was a pair of damn fools, who didn't know what was good for them.

Recollection of Kate saying there would always be those who wouldn't be told what to do – or words to that effect – returned to him later, while he paced the deck at the head of the gangway awaiting her return. Was her going missing some kind of gesture that she was one of them? Her way of telling Soviet officialdom to go hang? Why couldn't she just be glad that she lived in a free country, and leave it at that? Like everyone else was – except Calvin.

He and Sandy had missed lunch to stay with Alun, as friends at home would rally round in a crisis; and if this were a free country, they'd all be out searching for Kate. But the menacingly silent individuals at the document-piled table wouldn't let him off the ship even if he suggested it.

Kate arrived back in a cab, and paid the driver, thankful that she, not Alun, had pocketed the few roubles they had thought it necessary to exchange for sterling on board the ship and take with them ashore. The gift for their daughter had been purchased with a traveller's cheque; only hard currency was accepted in the *beryozka*.

While she covered the short distance to the liner from where the driver had dropped her, she put a nonchalant expression on her face and kept her pace to a stroll, though her spine was tingling in anticipation of the consequences of her late return. Would they grill her about where she'd been? Meanwhile it was nerve-wracking to have to walk past the soldiers – or were they police? – who weren't staring at her because she had nice legs!

Those at the foot of the gangway made no attempt to stop her from ascending it – but that didn't mean she wouldn't have to account for herself when she got to the top. What the heck was she going to say? This was one occasion when telling the truth wouldn't pay, though she'd raised her kids to believe that it always did.

The first thing she did was give her husband a kiss, which presumably wasn't against the law for foreign tourists. 'Sorry I'm late back, darling.'

How could she sound so carefree, the way those officials were giving her piercing looks? Alun wanted to yell at her for what she had put him through. At the same time, a surge of love for her threatened to well up and choke him. Nor was she out of the woods yet. He watched her present her passport at the table – and step neatly into the role of the injured party.

'The bus ought not to have left without me.'

The nerve of her! Alun said to himself.

Kate had finally decided that attack was the best form of defence. But her protest appeared to have gone unheard. The officials were conducting a whispered consultation – and the way they kept shooting glances at her, it was no wonder her hands felt clammy.

One of them cleared his throat. 'The person in this photograph is you?'

'I don't recall that being queried when I disembarked.'

'For that, I am not responsible. I was not then on duty.'

'Nor can I be held responsible for a cheap picture of me taken years ago. I had a different hairstyle then.'

'That would not account for the difference in the features.'

Kate was trying not to lose her temper, and received a cautionary glance from the ship's officer standing nearby.

'Don't you have photography booths in Russia?' she inquired. 'Where you sit on a stool in front of the camera, put some money in a slot, and what comes out makes you think, "That can't be me!"?'

The official's response was silence.

'Look, she is definitely my wife,' said Alun.

'But is she the person whose photograph this is?'

More of the same followed, and eventually the chief purser was summoned to vouch for Kate's identity.

Afterwards, he accepted Alun's invitation to join them in a bar where sandwiches were available for passengers who returned too late for lunch on shore days.

When they were seated with a platter of what Calvin and Sandy called double-deckers on their corner table, and Alun had ordered the drinks he felt all of them but Kate deserved, the purser gave Kate a quizzical smile.

'It is not too often that passengers miss the restaurant lunch at this port of call, Mrs Starling, but occasionally I have been called upon to play with the Soviet Authorities the game I have played with them today.'

'It didn't feel like a game to me!'

'But I can assure you that it was, that you and I have just participated in a Soviet face-saving exercise, Mrs Starling.'

'You're going to have to explain that to me, please, Mr Svenson.'

'You had infringed their regulations and could not be allowed to get off – what is that English expression?'

'Scot-free,' Alun supplied.

'I guess what Mr Svenson means is that querying your passport picture was just to make you sweat,' Calvin said.

'It did, too!'

Mr Svenson drank some of his lager and set down the glass. 'What I am really saying to Mrs Starling is that in my experience, however insignificant the matter, Soviet officialdom must, in its own eyes, be seen to have come off best.'

'I pity those who have to live with it,' Kate said.

'But they know no different, do they?'

'That doesn't mean they necessarily enjoy it. I met a young chap while I was off the leash who made no secret that he'd like things changed.'

Alun, who had just picked up what was left of his sandwich, put it down again. 'If you'd got caught talking to him – I mean, supposing a guide from one of the buses had seen you, Kate?'

Mr Svenson's eyes twinkled behind his rimless glasses. 'Your wife is an adventurous woman, Mr Starling.'

But Alun hadn't realised it until now. How could Kate be behaving as she was, when at home she wouldn't chance crossing the high street until the traffic lights had changed to GO?

'By the way, Mr Svenson,' Calvin said casually, 'we hear there's a stowaway aboard.'

The purser finished his lager, and rose – but not before Calvin and Kate had noted his briefly masked expression.

'On board a cruise liner hearsay is best to be taken – how do the English put it?'

'Americans, too,' said Sandy. 'With a pinch of salt.'

'I have enjoyed your company, also the drink, but if you will excuse me I must now return to my office.'

With that, the purser departed, and they had the bar to themselves. The steward who had brought the sandwiches and drinks was nowhere in sight, but could be summoned by the bell on the bar's polished teak top.

Kate sat with the mixed odours of liquor and stale tobacco in her nostrils, reminded of the local pub she and Alun sometimes dropped into at home on Sundays, when the roast beef was in the oven and the kids out of mischief. Alun's mother always came for Sunday lunch, and enjoyed telling Emily and Jason tales about her own childhood, while Kate and Alun had their break.

'So much for *that* piece of hearsay,' she heard her husband remark to Sandy. 'If you're not going to eat your sandwich, Kate, I will.'

'I am. But not right now. And so much for why the purser beat a hasty retreat.'

'Are you calling Mr Svenson a liar, Kate?'

'No, since he didn't categorically deny the rumour.'

'He seems a nice guy,' said Calvin, 'but his face sure clammed up for a second when I mentioned the stowaway, and I'd say he did a passable job of fencing me off without telling an outright lie, which leads me to think – '

'*I* didn't see his face clam up,' Sandy interrupted. 'Did you, Alun?'

Alun's reply was, 'Why don't you and I go and have a dip in the pool, Sandy?'

'I could sure use one. Coming, Cal?'

'I'll keep Kate company, if you don't mind.'

'Why would I mind?'

But Kate had the feeling that Sandy did; that their lighthearted foursome-relationship had suddenly grown complicated.

She was gazing disconsolately at one of the seascapes which relieved the bar's wood-panelled walls and Calvin surveyed her expression.

'For someone who's had an exciting morning you sure look down in the dumps, Kate. Tell me about your encounter with the young Russian.'

Kate wanted to explain that it was Alun's disinterest that accounted for how she felt – all he'd done was tick her off! But you didn't tell things like that to someone you had only recently met.

She brushed such personal thoughts aside though not

before she had let herself compare Alun's attitude with Cal's, and told him, first, how the encounter had come about.

'I got fed up with hanging around in the *beryozka*, and thought what's the harm in my popping around the corner for a few minutes, that it was unlikely anyone would miss me. And I'd have been back on time if Alexei hadn't spoken to me on the street.'

Kate smiled at the recollection. She had halted to look at her wristwatch for the umpteenth time, irritated by this brief diversion from what was permitted being laced with uneasiness, when a youth had detached himself from a queue at a bus stop and approached her.

'What's all this?' I thought. 'I mean, there's supposed to be a black market here, isn't there? And we'd been warned by the officer who lectured us before we went ashore that tourists are sometimes accosted by Russians who want to buy the clothes on their back. Since the denim jacket I have on was loaned to me by a friend, I couldn't have sold it anyway! Then the boy introduced himself and asked if I had any English novels I could let him have. I was so taken aback, I said the first thing that came into my head: What kind of novels are you interested in? And I shall never forget the hungry look in his eyes.'

Taken aback doesn't describe it, Kate thought. Affected summed up her reaction to the request. 'Beggars are not that uncommon – but I've never encountered a book-beggar before!' she said with feeling. 'And I can't tell you what it did to me. While Alexei reeled off a list of contemporary titles available in the West – and Lord knows how he's learned of their existence – I thought of my local library, where all I'd have to do is walk in and find them on the shelves, or put my name on the waiting list. Also, I must look like a bluestocking, I thought, wanting to giggle, if this lad thinks I'm travelling with a collection of up-market books.'

Kate nibbled some of her sandwich before continuing. 'The reason I'm not too hungry, Cal, is he took me home to meet his gran, and she made me eat a pancake. It was filled with cream cheese, and absolutely delicious. We washed the pancakes down with lemon tea. I'd expected to see a samovar in the kitchen, but there wasn't one. The old lady made tea for three in the biggest pot I've ever seen – '

'What was the house like?' Calvin interrupted.

'It was a flat, and quite a big one. In an old building near to the Marriage Palace – did your guide show you the Marriage Palace? When our party was crossing the square it's on, there were several wedding parties walking alongside us, with the brides' veils flapping in the breeze. I asked Natasha if anyone in the Soviet Union ever got married in church, but she pretended she hadn't heard me, and began describing the architecture – as if she didn't want to get involved in discussing religion – '

'You were telling me about the young guy's home. What sort of family does he come from?' Calvin, envying her the experience, wanted to know.

'His parents are academics. Since it's Saturday, I might have met them, but Alexei said they'd gone to a weekend seminar in Moscow. It was the sort of home you'd expect people like them to have, Cal, only Russian-style; there were rugs hanging on the living-room wall. And no shortage of *Russian* books. The furniture was dark and heavy-looking, lots of carving – '

'How I'd love to have seen it!'

'But I only got a glimpse as we walked down the lobby – which I remember had a black-and-white check floor. I think it was marble. Alexei took me straight to the kitchen, where his gran was up to her elbows in flour. The pancakes were already made, keeping warm in a big, black oven. Alexei said his mother had wanted to get a gas cooker installed, but his gran wouldn't have it, and it was she who did the cooking. It seems the flat is his father's family home, and the old lady – who looked about eighty – doesn't like modern kitchen equipment.

'Like her grandson doesn't like the régime. I asked if his parents felt as he does, and he replied that they both had good jobs and wanted to keep them. But back to the books! Afterwards, Alexei walked me to where I could get a taxi, and I thought, how am I to tell him that all I have with me is a couple of whodunits? Also, how *could* I get some books to him, when I'm not permitted to go ashore? Then I thought of all the paperbacks people leave lying around the ship after they've read them, and heard myself tell him to be at the Opera House car-park at interval time tonight. Have you got anything describable as a good novel with you, Cal?'

'I'm re-reading *To Kill A Mockingbird* – '

'And didn't I see you with *Catcher In The Rye*?'

'Since I've already read it twice, Alexei is welcome to that, too.'

Kate visualised herself sneaking out of the theatre in the dark, tonight, and shivered at the prospect of making the delivery she had promised. Supposing she got caught? As on the morning excursions, passengers would be under strict supervision for the evening entertainment ashore.

'You won't mention this to Alun, will you, Cal? He'd try to stop me.'

'So would Sandy, with me. But I'm not letting you do it alone.'

'Thanks.' Kate ate some more of her sandwich, and paused. 'You're probably getting the impression that I don't care how I upset my husband. Believe it or not, that isn't so. It's just that – '

'There's no need to explain, Kate.'

Not to you, there isn't – and if only it were that way with Alun.

'Though I have to say I can understand Alun not wanting his wife to take risks in a place like the Soviet Union,' Calvin added. 'But a cruise ship is the only way most Westerners would ever get to see a bit of it, and all we get shown is what the Soviets would like to be our lasting impression, which will send us home telling everyone they're wrong about how things are in Russia. Those Intourist guides are sure trained in the art of promotion! Now a trip to Leningrad, or Moscow, on an individual visa, would be something else – '

'I wouldn't mind doing that, one day.'

'Me, neither.'

But who'd have imagined us ever actually doing it – and together . . . though Leningrad won't be included, thought

39

Kate, when the friendly redhead's voice returned her to the present.

'Sorry to disturb you again, but the seat-belt sign's come on.'

'We're passing through some turbulence,' her husband remarked, as the aircraft bumped up and down.

Which describes what happened to me on the cruise, Kate said to herself. Afterwards, as events and impressions receded, she had settled back into her routine. Taken the children to school, fetched them home again, and done the everyday things that needed doing in the hours between. But she had not lost her awakened interest in the Soviet Union and its people. Her one day in Odessa had ensured that she never would. A TV documentary about Sakharov and his wife in exile had upset her. And when Anatoly Shcharansky was finally freed to live in Israel with the bride from whom he had been parted since their wedding day, it had meant a good deal more to Kate than it had to Alun.

It was that evening that Calvin telephoned her. Alun was playing in a squash match after work. Emily and Jason were upstairs doing their homework, when the telephone rang in the hall.

'Kate?'

'Yes?'

'How've you been?'

'Who's speaking?'

'Calvin Fenner, of course.'

Why had she felt the need to stall? His voice was unmistakable. 'How nice to hear from you.' What a useful word "nice" was.

'I just watched Shcharansky's showcase-release, on my office TV. It's a real victory and every one counts. Watching that little Russian cross the dividing line – well – '

'It brought everything back to you,' Kate finished the sentence for him.

'Didn't it for you?'

'I don't get to watch the news until after my kids are in bed.'

'It's lunchtime here. Sandy's gone out for a burger.'

40

'And you're not feeling hungry.'

'How did you guess? I was reminded of that other lunchtime.'

Of the Bulgarians on the quayside. Was it one of *them* for whom temptation to make a bid for freedom had proved too much?

'Well, Kate, it was good talking with you.'

'Same here.'

But what did we actually say? Kate thought, replacing the receiver. Except by implication.

Calvin's call from the blue left her feeling as if an unwelcome breeze had ruffled something she would rather let lie. It must have been the same feeling that had evoked in him the need to make contact with her. She was the person with whom he had shared a risky act of kindness on that wet night in Odessa. They had slipped out of the Opera House during the interval, while Alun and Sandy were being buttonholed by some fellow-passengers, and were back before the curtain rose for the second act. Only the black-clad old woman selling caviar in the theatre's magnificent marble foyer saw them return and remingle with the crowd. And how good Kate and Cal had felt about what they had managed to do.

They could not feel good about what they had later resolved to do and left undone.

Kate found Calvin's business card in her desk drawer, picked up the receiver, and impulsively called him back. The ensuing conversation was no more than a lengthy exchange of excuses for their sin of omission, which was how Kate now saw it.

Come on, hadn't she always? she thought while Calvin reeled off *his* list. There were still times when the matter of the stowaway rose to haunt her.

She had returned from the cruise to family chaos. The children had gone down with chicken-pox, and her mother had discovered that Kate's father was seeing another woman. And now she learned that Calvin had arrived back to find his gallery had been burgled and vandalised in his absence.

But all it amounts to, Kate thought after that second telephone conversation, is we both let our own lives take precedence over the fate of another human being. When two attempts to call Amnesty had found the number engaged, Kate had not made the time to try again. The stowaway's existence had gone unregistered by those who might have helped him, and Kate and Calvin were to blame.

A few days passed during which Kate was beset by restlessness. Television and the papers were dominated by the Shcharansky story, and by his appeal not to forget those whose rights were still being denied. Her journalist friend Audrey rang up to say she was flying to Israel to try for an exclusive interview with Shcharansky's wife. And here Kate was, sitting and writing her little column about what went on in her tiny corner of South London, stringing together words that epitomised her own narrow horizon.

Only then did she admit that there was more to her restlessness than conscience alone. But if she let it get a hold on her — ?

She already had, or she wouldn't be reaching for the phone as if it were a lifeline. Calling Cal yet again.

'I'm going to Moscow,' she heard herself say. 'Are you coming?'

Alun did not try to prevent her from going. The subtle separateness that had begun on the cruise had never righted itself. Though they were as affectionate to each other as ever, their relationship had shifted to a different balance. One in which, when Kate sat deep in thought, Alun never bothered asking what was on her mind. He had discovered on the cruise, as she had, that there was a side to her he was never going to understand.

CHAPTER TWO

KATE'S SECOND entry into the Soviet Union proved no less onerous a procedure than her first, and the welcome – if such it could be called – was decidedly chilling. A barrier of raised cubicles greeted the arrivals. Two uniformed officials stood in each, only their heads and shoulders visible behind a screen of thick glass. Since their plane was a small one, Kate had not expected a lengthy wait to pass through immigration, nor had she reckoned on each person being subjected to a nerve-wracking, silent scrutiny which, when her turn came, she thought was never going to end.

While one of the officials stared down at her from his elevated position, the other was apparently referring to some papers below her eye level, and, his lips barely moving, saying something to his colleague not intended for her ears. She wanted to smile at them, make a perky remark, pretend she didn't feel intimidated, but the atmosphere they exuded had stiffened her face and stilled her tongue.

When her visa was finally stamped, and her luggage claimed, she joined Barbara and Howard in the queue to clear customs.

'Get ready to have those magazines and newspapers you're carrying confiscated,' Howard said to her.

'But I haven't finished my crossword – '

'Try telling that to the Russians.'

'What the heck are they so scared of!' Kate flared.

'Western corruption is what they'd call it. And at this point in time – well, the people probably haven't been told about Shcharansky's release yet.'

Barbara glanced nervously over her shoulder. 'Watch what you're saying, will you, Howard!'

Kate wondered again why the couple chose to holiday in the Soviet Union if it had this effect upon them.

She shrugged off the thought. 'Are they likely to confiscate my paperbacks, too? I've got a couple in my suitcase.'

'That depends on what kind of books they are,' Howard replied, 'and you might not be asked to open your case.'

'*We* should be that lucky,' said Barbara. Then Kate saw her blanch. 'Where are they taking that man, Howard?'

A passenger whose luggage had been carefully searched was now being led away by two officials. Not led, hustled. They had him by the arms, and Kate could hear him gabbling in German.

'For a body search, probably,' Howard answered.

They had reached the head of the queue and he lifted his suitcase on to the scanner and walked to where the customs man awaited it.

'Those scanners are the most powerful in the world,' Barbara whispered. 'They can pick out even the thinnest slip of paper. Even if it's folded inside a heavy garment.'

Kate wondered how she knew, and was aware of her increased tension when Howard was asked to open his luggage. Why was Barbara so nervous if she and her husband had nothing to hide? And, come to think of it, why did each of them have a huge suitcase when they were only here for a week?

She watched the contents of Howard's being dumped, item by item, on the customs counter. Judging by the number of pharmaceutical items – Kate could recognise the Boots labels from where she stood – he must be either a hypochondriac or a vitamin freak.

He was allowed to repack his case without anything having been confiscated, and Barbara heaved a sigh of relief. Neither her luggage nor Kate's was searched, and Kate's newspaper and magazines were not taken from her, though those Howard and Barbara were carrying were; which struck her as odd, given that her reading matter, like theirs, included *The Listener* and *The Guardian*. They made no comment when she remarked upon this, but the inconsistency lodged in her mind.

Howard led the way to where the Intourist representative was waiting to shepherd their party to a minibus.

'My name is Olga, and I shall be your guide for the journey to your hotel,' the girl said brightly. 'En route, I shall show to you some of our great and famous monuments.'

Kate managed not to laugh. 'Great' and 'famous' both in one breath, and she'd only just arrived in Russia.

'During the time you shall spend in my native city, I shall also be your guide for the most interesting tours for which you have paid in advance. Those not included, I would advise that you arrange for yourselves at your hotel excursion desk. I would especially recommend to you . . .'

Kate shut out the brisk recitation of an inventory of museums. She and Cal might visit some of them, but that wasn't all they'd come for. What exactly had they come for? If Kate knew the answer to that by the time she got back on the plane, she'd have travelled far on many levels.

Olga's voice impinged on her thoughts: 'At the hotel you shall all take your meals together at the same table.'

'I beg your pardon,' said a frosty female voice from the rear of the bus. 'My daughter and I are not accustomed to boarding-house dining.'

'Don't make a fuss, Mother – '

'Kindly leave this to me, Daphne.'

'It is the usual arrangement,' the guide replied. 'But since the group is, on this occasion, few people, and the hotel tables are intended for many, those who wish to do so shall have the space in which to isolate themselves.'

'That is not the point,' the woman persisted.

Barbara whispered to Kate, 'If she doesn't isolate herself from us, we'll have to isolate ourselves from her!'

Kate agreed. But nor was she looking forward to eating all her meals, for a week, in Barbara's edgy company. And if, by chance, Calvin was allocated to the same hotel, would the rules and regulations that appeared to apply to absolutely everything in the Soviet Union, mean they couldn't eat together? If so, she just wouldn't stand for it.

Meanwhile it was no wonder, with one thing and another, that she felt like a rag doll. It was sensible of Cal to have

suggested that they didn't meet until tomorrow morning –
his longer journey, plus jet-lag, would surely have rendered
him fit for nothing but sleep this evening.

She gave her attention to the view through the window.
They had reached the outskirts of the city and the bleakness
she had noted in the earlier part of the journey, common to
most of the journeys from airports she had experienced, gave
way to a wooded ambience she had not expected to
encounter in Moscow. Great clumps of tall trees stood
between the buildings and the pavements – and must surely
have been there long before pavements were thought of.

'Shortly, you shall have your first glimpse of our famous
Kremlin,' the guide intoned.

'My wife and I have seen it before,' said Howard
brusquely.

'Please to excuse me for assuming that you had not.'

Had Olga given him a narrow-eyed glance? Or was Kate,
by now, infected with Barbara's 'melodramania'?

'Is the American Embassy near to our hotel?' she
inquired, and received such a glance, herself.

'You are not a *British* subject?'

'What has my nationality to do with it? Please answer my
question.'

'I am curious why you wish to know.'

But Kate was damned if she would explain it was where
she had arranged to meet her American friend. 'I'm not here
to satisfy your curiosity. Your job is to supply us tourists with
information.'

If Kate's sharpness had got Olga's back up, there was no
sign of it in the girl's expression. But nor was the answer to
Kate's query forthcoming. Only a silent smile. Kate was
coming to think that silence was employed by the Russians
as a tactic; given how the immigration officials had intimidated her with theirs, who wouldn't?

Later, after a shower had revived her, and she was
unpacking her case, her thoughts turned briefly to home.
Was this really Kate Starling, away on an adventure without
her husband? An adventure was what it felt like. How had
she had the nerve to do it? Would her easy relationship with

Cal be the same, nearly five years on? Or would there be the awkwardness of strangers between them? His plane would have landed by now, and he was probably on his way to his tour group's hotel. Perhaps he was feeling as uncertain as Kate suddenly was. When she'd called to ask him to join her on the trip, the misgivings now flooding her mind had not so much as occurred to her.

It struck her, now, that on a personal level strangers were what they were; though it hadn't seemed that way in the heady atmosphere of the cruise, when she had seen holiday friendships blossom which had afterwards doubtless wilted with equal speed. An ocean liner is like a world unto itself, where people seek out their own kind, as they do at home. But those who became your intimates on board are, in truth, nothing of the sort. What did she and Cal know of each other's everyday lives or of what had gone into the making of the person the other was? Getting to know someone on that level took time. Kate's picture of Cal as a person was like a jigsaw puzzle not yet completed, based upon fragmentary impressions and her own instincts.

Artificial flowers can neither blossom nor wilt, she corrected the imagery that had set her mind on this track. And shipboard socialising and its easy alliances are artificial. Would she soon discover that this was so with herself and Calvin? That all remained of their rapport was a shared guilt about the stowaway, that others would find ridiculous? If so, they were in for an uncomfortable week.

Kate glanced around her room, about which there was nothing remotely Russian. It could pass for a hotel room anywhere in Europe. Yellow bedspreads and matching curtains. An innocuous tweed carpet and a single armchair of the same muddy colour, beside which was a reading lamp with a chromium base and a parchment shade. Impersonal described it, she thought while deciding which of the two dresses she had with her to wear for dinner, but so what? Hotels usually were, and she wouldn't be spending much time in her room. Which hotel you got put in seemed to be a matter of pot-luck, and at least this one was the sort that Westerners were used to. Some of the pictures of rooms in other hotels, which Kate had seen in the travel brochure, had looked ethnic, but a lot less comfortable.

On her way to get the lift downstairs, the same black-garbed Russian woman she'd noticed earlier was still there, this time talking to a couple of maids – she must be a housekeeper – and replied with a polite nod when Kate bade her good-evening.

The lift was full of tourists who seemed to know each other, and one of the men looked Kate over, which, for some reason, gave her a lonely feeling. But she had not since her marriage stayed in a hotel without her husband. You've forgotten what it's like to be a female on her own, Kate! Though she had a working life, such as it was, her social one included having a man at her side.

She followed the other tourists, who'd been talking in French, to the restaurant, still feeling unsure of herself, and thankful that what the Intourist girl had said about tour parties sharing a table ensured that on her first night away from home she wouldn't be seated conspicuously at a table for one.

The restaurant seemed out of key with the hotel's opulent foyer, where marble and leather abounded and from which a broad, open-tread staircase curved upward to the mezzanine floor. Instead, the large room in which tourists ate their three-meals-a-day had a utilitarian appearance. The symmetrically placed and overlong tables, clothed in bright red, partly accounted for it. The walls were painted grey, their starkness unrelieved by any form of adornment, and Kate's overall impression was of a place designed for people to hurry into, swallow their food, and quickly vacate.

Instead of being received by the headwaiter, Kate was shown to a table on the far side of the room by the Intourist girl who had escorted her from the airport, who ticked her name on a list and led her away, reminding Kate again of her day in Odessa. But this time I've got a visa, I shan't be on a leash when I go out.

She was the first to arrive at the table and Olga said to her, 'You may, of course, sit in any place you wish.'

Kate put her tongue in her cheek, said, 'Thank you,' and sat down at the near end.

'Please to excuse me. Two others of your party have I see arrived.'

While Olga went to greet the frosty Englishwoman and her daughter, Kate surveyed the big dishes of salad on the table. One was green, and mostly thick wedges of cucumber; the other looked like chopped egg and potato in sour cream – or was it yoghurt? Whichever, it looked delicious. And maybe they'd serve pancakes one day, like she'd had at Alexei's home. Kate liked her food, and was lucky her figure didn't show it!

The Englishwoman's approach was heralded by her complaining voice.

'Are you quite certain it isn't possible for my daughter and me to have a table to ourselves?' she was haranguing Olga.

'The arrangements for parties are as I have told you,' came the implacable reply. 'But on this occasion, as I have also told to you while in the bus, the number is such that you may isolate yourselves if you so wish.'

And isolate herself the woman pointedly did. After giving Kate a nod, this example of snobbery at its worst seated herself at the far end of the table. Her daughter had no option but to follow and sit opposite her, though she did give Kate an apologetic smile.

'You look like you could use some company,' Barbara Ross said when she and Howard arrived.

Kate had not imagined herself welcoming theirs, but suddenly she did.

'Looking forward to your first meal in Russia, Kate?' Howard inquired.

'I'm not expecting cordon-bleu food.'

'But you can bet on it that what tourists get given is a lot better than the Russians eat. Excluding the élite, of course.'

'Howard!' said Barbara, glancing over her shoulder.

'When I first arrive here, I find it a bit difficult to control my feelings, dear.'

'Also your tongue.' She turned to Kate. 'I had to kick his ankle at least three times, while we were in our room.'

'Like you always do. But we've never yet managed to locate the bug.' Howard read Kate's sceptical expression. 'It's one of the facts of life here.'

'So I've heard, but I don't have to believe it.'

Barbara glanced over her shoulder again. 'Why don't we change the subject?'

'Encountered your floor-lady yet?' he asked Kate.

'That's practically the same subject – '

'And it'll do Kate no harm to know it.'

Between them, they were making her flesh creep, as they had once or twice on the plane. She hid it with a laugh. 'You two have read too many spy novels!'

Howard ignored her quip. 'You're a writer, aren't you? If you wanted to, you could go home with plenty of material. But you'd have to file it in your head. It'd be too risky for you to make notes – '

'Howard!' Barbara was all but wringing her hands.

'Unless the pepper-pot is a bug, Barbara – '

'Which it could be.'

'Who can hear what we're saying, with all this chatter going on around us?' he finished.

The dining-room had filled up since they entered, and a large noisy party of Spaniards was occupying the table directly behind theirs.

Howard patted his wife's cheek. 'You're letting things get to you, dear.'

'Who, me?'

'Want me to take the pepper-pot apart?'

'Now you're making fun of me.'

This brief private exchange was for Kate, like seeing a small drama enacted, in which the dialogue was double-talk, but a definite layer of meaning lurked betwixt the lines. What were the 'things' Howard had said were getting to Barbara? Some crisis at home that she couldn't put from her, though she was now miles away? Though the smile remained on Barbara's face while Howard bantered on, her right hand kept closing and unclosing, where she had rested it on the table, and her left was toying with her jacket button. Kate had thought her the sort who would dress up for dinner, but she still had on the tweed suit she had worn for the flight.

When the waiter brought their first course, Kate was surprised to hear Howard speak to him in his own language.

'My clever husband got a First in Russian,' Barbara explained while they helped themselves to the salads. 'Also in French, but he only gets to practise that on our *au pair*; it's years since we went to France. Me, I just managed a Lower Second,' she added with a self-deprecating chuckle, 'in Hebrew and Arabic.'

'Did you meet at college?'

'Howard went to Oxford. Do I strike you as that type?'

But nor could Kate visualise Howard capped and gowned amid the dreaming spires. Was there such a thing as a type? Outwardly, yes – but it could be misleading.

Barbara's fork clattered onto her plate.

'It's just hit me where I remember you from, Kate. The last time I saw you, before today, you were a slinky sixth-former, up on the school hall platform, receiving the English Lit. prize. And I was a pudgy third-former, sitting wishing I had your looks and your brains.'

Kate pictured Barbara with a pair of fiery pigtails and an orthodontic brace. 'You weren't that awful kid everyone called "Gingernut"? Who, among other things, got caught chalking a rude word on the lavatory wall?'

'None other, I have to confess.'

'What were the other things?' Howard wanted to know.

Kate laughed. 'Let's just say your wife was known for her daring.'

'She hasn't changed. We met when we were both working at the UN, and the first time I was in Barbara's company, she was telling an Israeli she thought the Arabs had a case.'

'That was brave of you,' Kate said.

'I don't have to agree with everything that Israel says and does, just because I'm Jewish. And there must be plenty of Israelis who question some of their government's policies –'

'But they don't get called dissidents, like they would here,' her husband cut in.

'Howard!'

He picked up the pepper-pot and wagged a finger at it. Then the waiter came to remove their plates, and laughed at something Howard said to him in Russian.

Howard glanced at a nearby table, where the main course had already been served. 'It's fish and chips, Barbara, we won't have to make do with just the vegetables. Shall I ask the waiter to wrap ours in newspaper, since we're Brits?'

Despite Howard's clowning, Kate was increasingly aware that, like Barbara, he was under some sort of strain. The vibes she had got from them on the plane weren't imaginary, and were still coming at her from both of them.

While they ate, they told her about their stint at the UN and how they had quickly come to see it as little more than a talking-shop. By the time dessert was put in front of them, she was wondering how she could have thought them a none-too-bright couple – though Barbara's intelligence seemed at odds with her melodramatic behaviour.

'Nevertheless, it was an interesting interlude,' Howard summed up their time in New York.

'And we might still have been there,' Barbara added, 'if my dad hadn't died and left me his business. What do I know about textiles? I thought. But to Howard, it was a challenge and he leapt at it.'

'Given what the rewards were, who wouldn't?' he said. 'Oh well.'

Kate felt that the 'Oh well' implied that he wasn't enjoying his change of career, and wondered if Alun enjoyed the way he spent his days. She had eschewed college in order to be a trainee-reporter, and had never regretted it. The paper on which she had cut her writer's teeth was the one for which she now wrote a column, and its parochialism hadn't stopped her from getting the practical grounding which cannot be taught. Kate had the know-how – and the confidence – to pursue an important story, nor had she quite lost her big ideas in that respect. Call them dreams, which was what, over the years, they had become.

Had Alun forgotten *his* dreams? He might as well, since he would never now become a professional rugby player. He was considering dropping his pharmacy studies and pursuing that path when he met Kate. But she was pregnant with their first child before they married, and that had taken precedence for both of them. People opted for the sure thing when they had reason to –

'About those notes I said it'd be too risky for you to make –' Howard said.

'Howard!'

'I was thinking of inviting Kate to spend the evening with us. If the pepper-pot wants to come too, it's very welcome.'

'But it wouldn't be if it weren't just a pepper-pot. Are you out of your mind, Howard?'

More double-talk – and Kate's flesh was prickling again. There was also Barbara's insulting reaction to her husband's invitation. 'I wouldn't dream of imposing my company on you.'

Barbara gave her a warm smile. 'Howard and I are long past the wanting-to-be-alone stage, Kate, and your company is delightful. It isn't that.'

Howard said, 'If you ladies wouldn't mind forgoing the Russian tea we're sitting here waiting for, why don't we all take a walk where there aren't any pepper-pots?'

Kate would never see a pepper-pot again without remembering this weird couple. 'I intended going for a stroll by myself,' she said as they went to collect their coats.

'Maybe we should let her do that,' Barbara said to Howard. 'It isn't fair to involve her.'

'Involve me in what?'

Kate received no reply. Her curiosity – no, it was something more than that – impelled her to agree to meet them in the lobby, which resembled a busy terminal through which people of many nationalities passed to and fro. She waited for Howard and Barbara on a velvet banquette, beside a veiled Arab lady whose bulk occupied most of the seat, and who cast not a glance at the two men hovering beside her. A group of Australians, their accents unmistakable, was beside the reception desk. She could hear Spanish – or maybe it was Italian? – being spoken by some women who had just walked by, and a party of Japanese was heading decorously, like a school "crocodile", for the revolving door.

'Got your pass to get back in, Kate?' Howard said when they joined her. She checked her handbag to make sure that she had, noting the guard standing beside the hotel commissionaires.

'Wouldn't they let me in without it?' she asked while they were walking down the hotel steps.

'Nobody's allowed in the tourist hotels without one,' Howard explained. 'If you had Russian friends, you couldn't invite them to come and have a drink with you – '

'That's absolutely ridiculous!'

'Nevertheless, the only Russians you're likely to encounter in the hotel are the staff, Kate.'

Howard took her arm and Barbara's and ushered them down the incline that led from the forecourt.

'It's so cold, I think perhaps our plane landed in Siberia by mistake!' Kate joked.

Her companions' reaction was to say in unison, 'Please don't mention Siberia to *us*.' Then Howard added, 'But all I'm going to tell you, until we're well away from here, Kate, is that Barbara and I haven't come to Moscow for a holiday.'

Nor, in the usual sense, had Kate. And the Rosses were even more weird than she had thought them. She turned up her coat collar against an icy wind that was threatening to blow her beret off her head. April had been colder than usual in England, but without the bite that was stinging her cheeks. Though the hotel was a good deal more luxurious than she had expected, it was not situated in the city centre, and all around her stretched vast areas of space. The street lights at the bottom of the incline did little to relieve the bleakness. What was she doing here?

Again she was beset by the doubts from which Barbara and Howard had diverted her at the dinner table. Though she could remember Calvin's personality she could no longer picture his face, which added to the absurdity of their spending a week together. She cursed her impulsiveness. Then her attention was riveted to what Howard had begun saying.

It was an explanation of why he and Barbara 𝚒̣ Moscow, delivered while they circled a block of shop for the night. Except for a solitary passer-by they ha̲ stretch of pavement to themselves when he halted, and sa̲ with feeling, 'The campaign to free Shcharansky turned him into a *cause célèbre*, Kate. But he's only the tip of the iceberg, the one everybody got to hear about. His friend Vladimir Slepak, though he's no longer exiled in Siberia, hasn't been allowed to leave the Soviet Union, nor has his wife – '

'Others are still exiled,' Barbara put in her own emotional word. 'You don't know the half of what's going on, Kate – all Howard gave you was a précis.'

'What's the difference between a dissident and a refusenik?' Kate inquired. Howard's use of the latter word during his explanation was somewhat confusing. 'The papers referred to Shcharansky as a dissident, didn't they?'

'But they'd got it wrong, like most folk have,' Howard answered. 'Dissidents want to change the régime. Refuseniks are just Jews who've applied for exit visas because practising Judaism is, to put it mildly, discouraged here. It's as simple as that.'

'When I think of the form the discouragement takes – ' said Barbara. 'Well, you'll see what I mean, Kate, if you come with us to visit the family we're on our way to see – one of the anonymous many.'

'The number who would like to leave, though not all have dared apply for visas, is around 400,000,' Howard supplied. 'We'd better get moving, Barbara. Kate can walk us to the metro while she makes up her mind if she's coming or not.'

They began walking toward a lit-up, blue 'M', visible in the near distance, and Howard added, 'But, for just one day, the people Barbara mentioned weren't anonymous, and I took off my hat to Tom Stoppard, who *gave* them their day. Did you see on TV that demonstration he organised, Kate? Outside the Soviet Embassy in London, when Shcharansky's release hit the headlines.'

'I did, as a matter of fact. A lot of famous actors and actresses were strewing red roses in the snow, while a long list of names was read out. Jane Asher was one of those taking part.'

here was a rose for every name. And Tom Stoppard will be my favourite playwright from now on,' Barbara declared.

'Do a lot of Jewish people come here to do what you're doing?' Kate asked them.

'Not enough,' Howard answered.

'Well, not in our opinion,' Barbara added. 'What we do when we come is little enough, given how lucky we are and they're not. Howard and I call these trips comfort visits, but the shortage of those prepared to come means that many families here are left feeling forgotten by their fellow-Jews in the West. The most important thing our visits do is help keep up their spirits, Kate – '

'The minute you apply for an exit visa to go to Israel, you lose your job or you're downgraded, so their standard of living has dropped to rock bottom,' Howard explained. 'To put it in a nutshell, Kate, all they have left is their hope.'

'And it beats me how they manage to hang on to that,' Barbara capped it. 'Last time Howard and I were here, we went to see a family where the eldest child had had her head split open by some Russian lads – anti-Semitism is rife in the schools.'

Kate went cold, but Howard said in a matter-of-fact voice, 'How wouldn't it be, when the curriculum includes lectures about the dangers of Zionism, and the two antis invariably go together.'

Despite the grimness of the subject, Howard managed to smile. 'If you're wondering why my wife looks shapeless tonight though she isn't, Kate, we never visit a family without taking them things we know they need. Barbara's wearing two bulky extra sweaters under her coat, to be given away. And I have on two sets of Marks and Spencer's thermal underwear, though I wouldn't be seen dead in longjohns at home.'

Weird they might be, but there was something about Barbara and Howard Ross that made you warm to them – hard though you fought against it, and Kate had. Nevertheless, the way they were going about things struck her as unnecessarily secretive.

'Is there a law against your visiting refuseniks and taking them gifts?' she asked.

'Suffice to say it's frowned upon,' Howard answered. 'And the more discreetly it's done, the less chance there is of causing trouble for those we're here to help. It's them we're protecting, by being careful, not ourselves. The KGB are experts in finding pretexts to make their lives unbearable, and the woman we're seeing tonight has enough on her plate. Her husband's in prison.'

They were approaching a lit up area bordered by trees. Kate could see a tramcar in the distance, and a crowd of people waiting to board it. Though the open spaces that characterised this part of Moscow still prevailed, there was here the bustle of life to be found in any big city. Ordinary folk – or so they seemed – were streaming in and out of the metro station; off somewhere for the evening, or returning home. Yet beneath the surface of this unremarkable scene was an aspect of life in the Soviet Union unthinkable to those from a democracy. Kate had come here with no illusions, but having it spelled out for her –

'Why don't they just let those Jews who want to leave, go?' she said hotly.

Howard replied, 'That question is too political for the likes of me. Meanwhile, tonight we must be extra careful. Families of imprisoned refuseniks are treated to special supervision. Hence my wife's extra nervousness, which you must have noticed.'

'I'm not really the jumpy sort as a rule,' Barbara said.

Kate was no longer sure that her own edginess was entirely due to present company. The preconceptions with which she had grown up were lent credence by the wall of officialdom you had to scale before they let you into the Soviet Union. A person would have to be totally insensitive to be impervious to the atmosphere Kate had been conscious of in Odessa and was prey to again now.

Howard fished in his pocket for a cigarette and put it into his mouth.

'If he lights it,' said Barbara, 'we'll know that it has got to him, too. We both seem to change character on our trips to

57

Russia. Believe it or not, my husband isn't really the jokey sort, and he did stop smoking at home some years ago, though he seems to find it necessary here.'

'I've never got back on the plane with nicotine-stained fingers, yet,' he said when she paused for breath, and added, 'Great-grandfather Rossinsky would turn in his grave if he knew that the same thing was happening all over again, under a different label. I remember him telling me he had nightmares about the Cossacks, when he was a kid. Now it's the KGB. And there's a child where we're going tonight. Are you coming, or not, Kate? No hard feelings if you don't.'

It was evident that they trusted her, and she was not unmoved by that. But did she want to be drawn into a network she had not known existed, which might lead to her never being allowed into the Soviet Union again? She now knew why Barbara hadn't wanted to involve her. But involvement began inside oneself, and Kate's had begun on the cruise, when she witnessed ashore the oppression under which some must live. Add to that the stowaway, and what she and Calvin had on their conscience, and her writer's need to observe and delve, that had lain dormant for so long, but was dormant no more.

'I'm coming,' she said.

They had halted beside a line of telephone booths, and Kate stood shivering, Barbara too, while Howard went into one of them and dialled a number.

'I can't get through, but that's no surprise,' he said after several attempts. Since the booths were open to the elements, he too was now stamping his feet to try to warm them. 'We'll just have to turn up at the door, but it won't be the first time.'

'One of the more pleasant harassments, for refuseniks, is putting their phones out of order,' Barbara told Kate. 'And we haven't thanked you yet for being prepared to come with us.'

It was not like Kate to have hesitated, but the Rosses couldn't have known that, she thought on the way into the metro. They probably thought her a conventional woman, who happened to have gone to the same school as Barbara – an opinion they would doubtless revise when they learned that her American friend was male. Since Cal didn't wear a 'Gay Rights' badge on his lapel – unless he now did – the Rosses would put the wrong interpretation on Kate's relationship with him. *And you're more conventional than you thought, or you wouldn't care what interpretation they put on it,* she was telling herself when Howard handed her and Barbara a coin each, and instructed Kate to put hers in the slot at the turnstile and follow them through.

'Don't wait for a ticket, there aren't any,' he called, leading the way.

Kate could not have paused had she tried to; there were too many people behind her, jostling her on a wave of rushing humanity onto an escalator so fast moving, she almost lost her balance. Howard and Barbara gripped her arms, one on either side, as they reached the lower level, or she might have landed spreadeagled on her face, as she stepped off.

'You should see it in the rush-hour,' laughed Howard.

'Sorry, we forgot to warn you,' said Barbara.

'Could we make the return journey by cab!'

'If we can find one,' said Howard, 'as far out as we're going.'

'Remind me to repay you for my fare.'

'We wouldn't dream of it.'

'I should think not,' Barbara added. 'It's enough that you were prepared to come, without it costing you, too.'

Kate hid her embarrassment – not on account of Howard's paying her fare, but because they seemed to construe her accompanying them as a favour.

'Are the churches in the West doing for their people what you're doing?' she inquired.

'Well,' Howard answered. 'We did meet a Baptist when we went to Leningrad, and – '

'Please, Howard! This place could be crawling with you-know-who. How d'you like the interior decoration in the metros, Kate?' she babbled on, drawing Kate's attention to the striking murals.

'Are they all like this?'

Howard nodded. 'But it's a false front, like the rest.'

'Howard!'

'It bespeaks a cultured people, which Russians in general undoubtedly are, and makes the barbarity of the régime the more incongruous. Would you rather I lit my cigarette, Barbara, or let off some steam?'

'There're people walking right behind us, aren't there? Also, this place is like a marble mausoleum, and voices echo.'

'You're making me want to reach for my lighter.'

'But you won't. Compared to me, you're made of steel. Would you mind glancing back, Kate, to see if there's a man in a dark coat and hat behind us? We passed him on our way to the turnstile, and I saw him look at us. I can't bring myself to turn round to see if he's there.'

'I didn't notice him.'

'Please don't aid and abet her wild fancies,' Howard requested, as they stepped onto another escalator. 'At this stage of the proceedings, she starts seeing the you-know-who everywhere. When we get back to the hotel, the first thing she'll do is look inside the drawers, to check if anything has been disturbed.'

'I couldn't look over my shoulder now if I were paid to, Howard.' Kate was clinging tight to each of them, dizzied yet again by the swiftness with which they were transported downward. But once off the escalator she could not resist glancing backwards. Then Barbara linked her arm and they began giggling, which they were still doing when the train came in.

Howard said, 'The funny thing is that none of this is funny, which proves, I suppose that laughter is a useful way of relieving tension.'

The seating on the train was similar to that on the London tubes and they managed to find themselves seats in the far corner of the carriage. The air was redolent of unfamiliar smells mingled together, but Kate became aware that one of them was body-odour overlaid by a sweet perfume wafting from the girl next to her, who was reading *Pravda*. Other passengers were eyeing them curiously, as Russians do with Western tourists, and Howard embarked upon a safe conversational topic.

'I wonder if the kids are asleep yet, Barbara? Think your mother will've remembered to give Danny his cough medicine?'

'If she didn't, he'll have reminded her. With his gran, he knows he'll get given a sweet to take away the taste. How old are your kids, Kate?' Barbara asked.

Kate pictured them in their pyjamas and dressing-gowns, employing their usual delaying tactics which worked better on Alun than on her. 'Emily's thirteen, and Jason's ten.'

'Who's standing in while you're away?'

'Emily's very capable, and wanted to prove it.'

Barbara smiled. 'Leave them enough burgers and beans and they'll get by!'

'That's what my husband said, when I insisted on freezing lots of homemade meals.'

'But you still felt you had to do it. So would I, if my mum weren't with them. It's the feeling that dogs us all, when we put whatever before our children. My mother never did. She leaves that to my generation, she once declared, when Danny had measles and I asked her to sit with him while I went to a meeting.'

Kate's mother had never had to say that to her, she reflected, while Barbara talked about the treats her children would be getting from their granny in her absence.

'Do Emily and Jason have a favourite cake, Kate? Mine are mad on anything with raisins in.'

'My two like chocolate-chip biscuits. I've got an American recipe that's easy to mix, if you fancy trying it.'

'Thanks, but Danny's allergic to chocolate, and I try not to put on the table what he can't have.'

'Where am I? At a mother's meeting!' Howard interrupted their conversation.

A silence followed, and Kate thought, while the train sped on, how unreal their conversation seemed, given the circumstances in which it was taking place. No, the unreality was the other way round. It was hard to believe she was on her way to visit people denuded of all but hope.

A pang of homesickness assailed her; nostalgia for the normality of her own life. Emily would have stacked the dishwasher, while Jason fed the cat, then both would join their dad in the living-room and try to persuade him to let them watch TV. Kate imagined the three of them seated around the hearth, the firelight playing on their faces, and the room all scrumpled cushions and scattered magazines. The picture stayed with her as she followed the Rosses from the train, and into the cold darkness above ground.

The seediness of the district – this was an old and run-down area of Moscow – subdued even Barbara as they made their way to the address Howard had memorised, lest he should be found with a refusenik's address in his pocket.

'It's for their sake, not mine,' he said again. 'And if we do manage to get a taxi back to the hotel, Kate, all we'll talk about while we're in it is the weather. A lot of cab-drivers are said to be ears for the KGB.'

'Said by whom?'

'Those who make it their business to know.'

Kate marvelled at the efficiency of the network, and at the nerve-wracking experience people like the Rosses were prepared to undergo, though it was not their own hide at risk.

The address proved to be a crumbling old building on a side street, whose appearance was more that of a rooming-house than of a block of flats. There were no labelled bell-pushes at the entrance, nor was it locked.

'I shouldn't think the people who live here have anything to pinch,' said Barbara as they mounted to an upper floor, the stench of stale cabbage strong in the air.

'Well, you can be sure,' said Howard, 'that by now the Smolenskys will've had to hock everything they'd got.'

'Is it really all right for us to just walk in on Mrs Smolensky?' said Kate. 'Supposing it's an inconvenient time?'

'There's no inconvenient time for friends from the West to call on refuseniks,' Howard replied. 'You can count on her being pleased to see us – and don't be surprised if that includes a tear or two.'

The heavily pregnant girl who opened the door received Howard's introduction with a dazed expression on her face. Then she ushered them in, as if with new-found strength, before bursting into tears, as Howard had predicted.

The living-room in which Kate found herself was also a bedroom. Though the Rosses had explained that loss of livelihood was a punishment meted out to Jews who applied for exit visas, she was unprepared for the degree of poverty that met her eyes and for the cramped conditions in which Irina and Lev Smolensky, once well-paid librarians, now had to live.

Irina dried her eyes on a corner of her apron. 'Please to excuse me. I am overcome.'

'My husband was looking forward to practising his Russian on you,' said Barbara with a smile.

'My mother, she speaks only Russian. Also my son.' She gazed down at the small boy who was clutching her skirt, but he hid his face against her.

'Children are often shy when they first meet people,' Barbara said gently.

'Shy, he always was. But tongue-tied before strangers is how Yuli has been since he saw his father dragged from this room. Afraid also. And if the KGB are listening, I would like they should know, though how would they care?'

'That's something we didn't mention to you, Kate,' said Howard. 'With respect to the pepper-pot.'

'He means with regard to the pepper-pot,' said Barbara.

Kate would have had to be dim-witted not to have registered that Irina thought her home was bugged.

'Now, Yuli clings day and night to me,' the Russian girl went on. 'But please to sit. I shall offer to you the tea, and you must to eat something. First, I must explain your presence to my mother. She has heard of visitors from the West, but, like me, did not expect ever to receive them.'

They seated themselves on one of the two divans which also served as sofas. While Irina spoke in Russian to the frail old woman occupying the sole and shabby armchair,

Howard said quietly to Kate, 'See what we meant now? About the dearth of volunteers to do what we're doing? If they saw for themselves what learning they're not forgotten does for these people – '

The old lady's face was lit by a beaming smile. Irina's, too.

'My mother, she would like to stand to receive and embrace you, but she is very sick with the heart disease. I myself have not yet embraced you!'

Irina came to kiss each of them in turn, the child still hanging on to her skirt.

'Please to excuse me while I make for you the small repast.' She went into a tiny kitchen, which was but a stride across the small vestibule through which they had entered, and called to Howard, '*Matushka*, she would be pleased you should converse with her in Russian.'

Howard went to chat to the elderly invalid, leaving Kate and Barbara to talk quietly between themselves.

'That kid could do with some of Danny's cough medicine, Kate.'

They could hear Yuli coughing, and Irina cast him an anxious glance while she filled a dented kettle at the sink.

'And that's not all,' Kate replied. 'He looks as if a good meal wouldn't do him any harm. When I think of my laden freezer – '

'Don't,' Barbara advised. 'These visits are always upsetting. Many of the refuseniks are ill from undernourishment, and that's only the half of it. If I let my feelings get the better of me, I couldn't keep coming.'

But Kate could not help making comparisons between her own lot and Irina Smolensky's. Though Irina had obviously done her best to make this room into a home for her family, a claustrophobic box was what it remained. The beds occupied most of the floor space, and except for a rickety-looking table set against one of the walls there was no other furniture. The floor was uncarpeted, and the window which overlooked the street was curtained in the same faded folkweave that camouflaged the two divans for daytime use. There wasn't an ornament in sight. Just a bright red feather, which must once have adorned a hat, sprouting from a bottle on the table, and so incongruous was it in this setting, Kate wondered if it represented for Irina a gesture of defiance amid her gloom. Or was it just something that reminded the Russian girl of happier times?

'How could they have managed for sleeping accommodation, before Irina's husband was arrested?' she pondered aloud to Barbara.

'That's a question I've asked myself before, when visiting refuseniks, Kate. But somehow they get by. The same goes for their eating arrangements. Irina will probably fetch that table to where we're sitting, and apologise to us for there being no chairs.'

'Given her circumstances, there's no need for her to apologise to *us*.'

'And I always think that when they do. But living like this is a comedown for them, and one tends to forget that they still have their pride.'

Irina's entrance with the supper tray followed the pattern Barbara had said it would, though Howard insisted upon moving the table for her.

'I am sorry that you must sit so low, though the table it is high. Please to take some bread, and help yourselves to my simple salad. I will pour for you the tea.'

'What beautiful cups and saucers you have,' Kate remarked. The huge cups were gilt-edged, and the china a translucent blue.

'*Matushka*, she would not allow me to sell them. They are all she has left of her home, and appear on the table only for honoured guests. But please to eat.'

'Aren't you and your mother going to join us?' Howard asked.

'We are too full of pleasure that you are here.'

Also filled with emotion, Kate noted, but trying to hide it. Irina had just blinked away another tear. Kate made herself swallow down some of the coarse black bread, along with a little of the salad, which was largely of cold potato and raw onion, with some slivers of carrot that lent it colour and sweetened it.

'This is delicious, Irina,' said Howard.

'What's in the dressing?' Barbara inquired appreciatively.

'The dressing?'

'What did you toss the salad in?'

'Toss? Like a ball, perhaps?'

Howard explained to her in Russian, and they all shared a laugh. When was the last time Irina and her mother had laughed? Kate wondered.

'I have put on to the salad a little yoghurt, which is how my Lev prefers it.'

How fleeting the moment of levity was. With the mention of her absent husband, Irina's gaze had dropped to her little boy, whose face was still hidden against her skirt.

When she raised her head, she saw Kate studying a wall poster from which two apple-cheeked children smiled down, and said after a pause, 'I look at that picture and say to myself, "One day we shall be where my Yuli can be happy and well, like that boy and girl, who are Russian but not Jewish."' She rested a tender hand on her abdomen. 'Also the child I am now carrying.'

Irina was one of those whose spirit couldn't be broken, thought Kate, recalling her conversation with Alun at the top of the Potemkin Steps.

'Before we applied for exit visas to join our cousins in Israel, we did not live like this,' Irina said. 'But of what use are the material things, if a person is not at peace with himself, nor with his God?'

She sat down on the unoccupied divan and set the child beside her, her arm around him, staring briefly into space. 'Some Russian Jews, as you must know, are content to remain in their native land, and Lev and I were once among them.'

She paused again, and stroked Yuli's hair. 'It was not until this little one was born to us that our Jewish feeling was revived, though "Jew" had always been stamped upon our passports.'

'If they did that with British Jews, *I'd* want to emigrate,' said Barbara.

'But here, we are accustomed to being singled out. Then one day, when Lev was watching Yuli playing on the floor,

66

he said to me, "A Jew must have a Bar Mitzvah. How shall we ensure that for our son, in the Soviet Union?"

'Also, I would fear to send Yuli to school,' she went on. 'It was when Lev heard that our children are sometimes mistreated by their classmates that the boil of injustice festering within him burst.'

She said no more, but rose to refill the teacups, her head held high, and a quiet grace about her movements despite her advanced pregnancy. She must have been pretty, once. Her hair had lost the sheen of health, but was still the colour of ripe wheat. The little boy's hair, too, and he'd inherited his mother's huge, dark eyes. But how was Irina able to muster a smile, with Kate and Barbara sitting at her table in their stylish clothes, and herself in this terrible plight? Expecting another child, her husband imprisoned, and a mother who looked as if she was not long for this world.

Howard took a bar of chocolate from his pocket. 'May I give this to Yuli, Irina?'

'You had better to give it to me, and I shall feed him a little at a time!' she said with a laugh. 'His stomach is unaccustomed to such riches.'

'We have one or two other things for you, too,' said Barbara, taking off her coat and divesting herself of the two extra sweaters. 'One of these is for you, and the other for your mother, Irina.'

'It is too kind of you. But shall you not be cold when you step outside?'

'The one I still have on will be fine.'

While Howard went to the bathroom to take off the thermal underwear he had brought for Lev, Irina put one of the sweaters on her mother, and the other one on her child.

'We'll be back with one for Yuli, tomorrow evening,' Barbara told her, 'together with some other items you might find useful.'

'It will be sufficient that I and *Matushka* shall have your company once more.'

The picture of that tiny boy, wearing a size-fourteen

jumper, would be etched upon Kate's memory for all time. She wanted to laugh at what he looked like, but she also wanted to cry.

When they left the building, it had begun raining, and a man was sheltering in the doorway. Barbara was sure he was the one she had noticed beside the metro turnstile, and said so at length as they strode through the puddles.

'She's at it again!' Howard exclaimed.

'And one of these days,' Barbara snapped back, 'I could be proved right.'

'What would you suggest we do about it?'

'There's nothing that can be done, now. My instinct, at the time, was to make the journey by a more roundabout route, try to shake him off.'

'My dear Barbara, if we followed your instincts in that respect, we should never have got to where we were going on any of our trips here. If you gave your attention to remembering to put in your handbag the bits and bobs you forgot tonight – '

'I was thinking about Danny, and the way I've left him for Mum to look after. And I thought of him again at Irina's. Her little boy reminds me of Danny, there's that same delicate look about him. Is that fellow following us, Kate?'

Kate wiped a raindrop off the tip of her nose, with the back of her hand. 'Not unless he's wearing carpet slippers. All I can hear is you two letting off steam.'

'You'll have to excuse us.'

'I do. How you can go on putting yourselves through this strain beats me.'

'Wouldn't you?'

'I'm not sure I'd have the stamina. And I'm not surprised that you're suffering from the cumulative effects, Barbara.'

'But it's a shot in the arm to me – and Howard – whenever some more refuseniks are granted visas. D'you think the number they've let out already would've been achieved if people like us didn't make a nuisance of ourselves? And I'm not just referring to these visits.'

'But sticking with the visits, that's what we are, Kate,' Howard put in. 'A thorn in "their" side – and the more the merrier. As for Danny being delicate,' he harked back, 'that's another figment of my dear wife's imagination.'

Barbara retorted, 'And your refusal to accept it is another example of your being an ostrich when it suits you. Danny gets every childhood ailment that's going.'

'So did I, and I'm hale and hearty now.'

'Only because your mother's an even bigger fusspot than you think I am, and probably kept you wrapped in cotton-wool.'

Another sharp exchange followed, and again Kate was assailed by a sense of unreality. What was she doing, plodding through a Russian downpour and listening to a couple she'd met only that morning air their intimate family grievances? Had she really been where she had tonight? Seen what she'd seen, and been moved to near-tears by it? The taste of raw onion, clinging to her tongue, proved the experience was real.

When she interrupted the Rosses' tiff her voice sounded as sharp as theirs, perhaps because her beret felt sodden and her toes were freezing. And maybe she, too, needed to relieve her pent-up feelings. 'How on earth will Irina manage, with a new baby, in that flat?'

'I'm not letting myself think of it,' said Howard.

'His head's in the sand again, Kate.'

'No, it isn't, Barbara! But what we're able to do for them is, unfortunately, limited. Did you notice how cold it was in that room?'

'Why do you suppose I kept my coat on? But buildings here are usually overheated, aren't they?'

'Exactly. And Irina's mother mentioned a few things her daughter didn't tell us. Like how all the other flats in the building are still nice and warm, but they can't get the janitor to come and fix whatever's stopping *their* heat from working. The old lady thinks it was fixed on orders from "them". The day after Lev was arrested, Irina took her mother to try to get her some medical treatment. When they got back, the heat was off, and it hasn't been on since.'

'What a pig that janitor must be!' Kate exclaimed.

'Or maybe he's just afraid of the KGB,' Howard said as they entered the metro station. 'Who wouldn't be?'

Barbara glanced over her shoulder. 'Watch it, will you, Howard!'

'Did the old lady get some treatment?' Kate asked him, when they were aboard the train. This time she had negotiated the escalators without assistance, and was feeling quite proud of herself.

'It seems that she needs a pacemaker, Kate. And I don't see a refusenik qualifying for one.'

'If there were anyone sitting near us, I'd muzzle you, Howard!'

'And if we had some tranquillisers with us, I'd make you swallow one.'

The Rosses lapsed into a silence that lasted for the remainder of the journey, and for much of the walk back to the hotel. Nervousness was still emanating from both of them, but Kate need no longer ponder why. What they are, thought Kate, conscious of Howard's bespectacled ordinariness on one side of her, and Barbara's glamorous presence on the other, is a pair of unlikely crusaders.

'It's stopped raining,' Howard remarked.

But Kate felt chilled to her bones. A hot bath would thaw her out, but she longed for the familiar comforts of home. Like the cosy robe she wrapped herself in on winter evenings, before making a cup of Ovaltine to sip by the fire. Alun always chuckled about the Ovaltine, but it was part of Kate's reassuring memories of a childhood with parents she could not have envisaged ever getting a divorce. Her father was the laconic sort, but her mother had made up for it, never lost for a word to fill the conversational gaps. Mum had always seemed the spokesperson for both, and Dad amusedly tolerant, puffing his pipe. This was how Kate remembered her years under their roof, and she had gone on seeing them that way, through the eyes of a child, long after she was grown up. Not till her father walked out on her mother did Kate pause to wonder what he had been thinking, all that time, behind his smile.

Barbara cut into her reflections, as they neared the hotel.

'What are you and your American friend planning to do tomorrow?'

Kate had momentarily forgotten about Calvin. 'I hadn't given it a thought.'

'If the two of you would like to join Howard and me on an excursion – '

'Not that our doing the excursions fools "them",' Howard interrupted.

'Then why do they keep giving us visas if they know what we're here for?'

'I have two theories on that, Barbara. One is that they're sadists, who enjoy playing cat-and-mouse games. The other is that if we step out of line in some way, it could help them to take it out on the people we've visited.'

'And you're probably correct on both counts! If I thought our visit to Irina could land her in more trouble than she's already in – '

'There's always that chance. But not taking it would leave people like her and the others completely isolated from the outside world. You can never be absolutely safe and sure, whatever you do. Barbara doesn't want me to take Danny swimming, Kate, but I'm going to,' he added obliquely.

Or was it just an attempt to return all three of them to the safe realities they had briefly left behind in England? Whichever, it led to another bout of bickering which continued in the hotel lift.

When they reached Kate's floor, Barbara remarked meaningfully, 'Aren't you lucky to be taking a break with a girlfriend?'

Kate had stepped out of the lift, and the doors closed before she had time to correct Barbara's assumption. For the second time that night, a paroxysm of mirth shook her shoulders. When had she last had a fit of giggles *before* tonight? Not since her schooldays.

She turned around and came face to face with the floor woman, and almost jumped out of her skin, her laughter petering out. Why did she have this once-removed sensation, as though she were outside this little scene, looking on? It had to be part of the 'I must be dreaming this' feeling that

71

had dogged her throughout the evening, though the scene in that poky flat was all too real to Irina Smolensky.

Kate pulled off her soaking wet beret, smiled at the woman, and glanced at her watch. Midnight had passed, and the floor woman must be wondering what had kept an English tourist, female at that, out in the rainy streets of Moscow so late. Why did Kate feel the need to provide an excuse? Because she'd done what 'they' frowned upon, hadn't she? A few hours in the Rosses' company, and she too was unwilling to use those sinister initials, even in her mind, she was thinking while the woman asked whether she required anything.

Kate yawned ostentatiously. 'Only some sleep, thank you very much. Do you ladies work around the clock?' The broad face regarding her wasn't the same one she had passed by on her way out.

'I am sorry? My English she is small.'

'Round the clock means all the hours there are.'

'Thank you, madam. I wish to you good night.'

Kate returned the greeting, and walked along the corridor leading to her room. Her query had remained unanswered – but in the nicest way. She was coming to think that fending off questions must be taught in Russian schools! Or was that kind of training included in courses for those whose work brought them in contact with people from the West? Not all of the questions she had asked the tour guide, Natasha, in Odessa, had been the loaded sort, but all had been dealt with in the same way. The least that could be said about Natasha's answers was that they were carefully blurred.

Kate had almost reached the end of the corridor – was the floor woman watching her? – when a devilish impulse made her do an about-turn and retrace her steps.

'Madam?'

'You didn't tell me your name.'

'You did not ask it, madam.'

'I'm asking now.'

'Why, please, do you wish it to know?'

'In a British hotel, guests often ask the staff what they're

72

called. I'm here for a week, and if there's something I need, it would be impolite for me to yell, "Hey, you!"'

Kate's impishness was increasing by the minute. Given that the Rosses believed that the floor women were fronts for 'them', Barbara would have a fit if she knew. But the heck with it! Kate was going to get a direct answer to *this* question – how could she not? – and it would help her to feel less intimidated.

'I am known as Babushka, madam.'

'Isn't that the Russian word for grandmother?'

Their eyes locked, the woman's like twin currants staring out from a suet pudding. She nodded.

'But you still haven't told me your name.'

'For the purpose you wish it, the one I am known as will serve.' The suet pudding creased into a brief smile. 'Goodnight, madam. It is very late.'

When Kate turned away, the woman was taking a pencil and pad from her apron pocket. To intimidate me further? Or was the pad just an innocent laundry list, and Kate Starling in the throes of an attack of auto-suggestion? Why, outside the pages of a spy novel, would the Soviet authorities station watchdogs in the guise of housekeepers, or whatever, to check up on the comings and goings of foreign tourists?

By the time she reached her room at the far end of the long corridor, Kate's mind was awhirl with probabilities and possibilities, but how much was born of imagination she had no means of knowing.

She shut the door and locked it, briefly wishing she had not met the Rosses. *Was* her room bugged? Alun said she sometimes talked in her sleep.

Meeting Barbara and Howard had led her to see for herself what the Soviet authorities preferred to keep hidden: the harrowing consequences for those who dared seek permission to leave.

Would the thermal underwear ever reach Irina's husband, still being held on a trumped-up charge of 'hooliganism' in Moscow's Lefortovo Prison? Howard thought it unlikely, but had brought the warm garments for Lev nevertheless. The Rosses' attitude was that anything that might help their victimised co-religionists was worth a try. Kate had been surprised to learn that Howard and Barbara rarely attended synagogue services, but there were more ways of practising your religion than a formal way. How you lived your life, and what you did for others; wasn't that the essence of Christianity, too? Kate could remember her late grandmother telling her that.

She controlled the urge to search the room for a bug, and wondered, while she was getting undressed, if some device was providing a peepshow for an unknown voyeur.

Take your bath, then go to bed and pull the blankets over your head, Kate! But which bed to choose? She'd been allocated a double room, which emphasised the absence of her husband.

She obeyed her own command, but was unable to shut out the events of the evening. When sleep finally claimed her, Irina Smolensky and the frightened child flitted, like pale ghosts, across the canvas of her dreams.

CHAPTER THREE

THE FOLLOWING day began for Kate with a pleasant surprise. She was at the breakfast table when Calvin entered the dining-room.

She did not immediately recognise him; he had grown a moustache since she last saw him. But, like the remembered timbre of his voice when he phoned her, there was no mistaking that upright carriage, and those finely chiselled features. He walked toward her.

'Kate!'

'None other.'

'It took me a minute to pick you out.'

'And I wondered who the distinguished-looking bloke was, hovering near the doorway.'

'I checked at the desk in case you might be staying here.'

'And I am.' How fatuous that sounded.

'Given the small number of hotels for foreigners, the odds weren't too long that you could be.' Did those words sound as stilted to Kate as they did to Calvin?

They were still shaking hands, which added to their awkwardness. Kate disengaged hers.

'Are the empty places at this table reserved?'

Kate glanced at Daphne and her mother who were maintaining their isolation policy. 'There are only five of us in the party, and I'm the odd one out. But a couple I met on the flight, and spent the evening with, said they'd join me for breakfast. Haven't you been allocated a table, Cal?'

'How d'you mean "allocated"?'

'Everyone is supposed to eat with their own party.'

'Mine's over there.' Calvin indicated a table across the room, and called, 'Hi!' to a young man and woman who waved to him. 'But here is where I'm going to sit,' he said taking the place opposite Kate.

'Now the Rosses will have to squabble across the table,' she said with a smile. 'And Barbara will probably put herself beside *me*, for moral support.'

'You seem to've got to know them well, for such a short acquaintance.'

'One can't help noticing, can one?'

'I wasn't accusing you of anything, Kate. Just remarking.'

'Remarking what?'

'I guess that couples don't ordinarily squabble in front of those they've just met.'

'Are we into one of our deep discussions already?' she quipped.

But on the cruise, their topics had never been the personal kind. Except for that night when they were dancing on deck, and Calvin had, though not in so many words, carefully informed her that he was gay. Casual though his revelation had appeared at the time, in retrospect it no longer seemed so. Had he had to steel himself to tell her? No, she hadn't felt that then and still didn't. It was more as if he had put off telling me something that he'd said he and Sandy made no secret of – which was a puzzle in itself. Nor had it led to discussion. On the contrary, when Kate looked back on it now it was as if a door had been gently shut in her face.

Calvin drank some of his juice and grimaced.

'What in the hell is this stuff?'

'It smells of acetone, doesn't it? But if you don't let that bother you, the taste isn't too bad.' Kate surveyed the hot mushroom-and-egg concoction a waiter now placed before them. She had expected to breakfast on cucumber and sour cream, or the like, and suffer indigestion for the rest of the day.

'Why did the waiter bring your new friends' breakfast when they're not down yet?' Calvin said, digging into his. 'They'll get here and find themselves confronted by con-gealed eggs – '

'Which could be the way tourists get punished if they're late for meals!'

'Come off it, Kate.'

But they were to find that the dining-room drill – and such it was – never varied. The meals for which tourists had paid in advance were placed on the table whether or not they were there to eat them. In their absence, course after course would accumulate on the table, the service proceeding like clockwork and with the cheerless efficiency of a machine.

Calvin glanced at the mother and daughter. 'Those two don't look too friendly.'

'The daughter seems positively cowed, to me.'

'Still the observer, aren't you, Kate? Remember those excruciating mealtimes on the *Ocean Queen*?'

For several minutes, while Calvin ate bread and plum jam, and Kate drank another cup of coffee, it was, 'Remember, remember . . .' What do we talk about when we run out of recollections? she was asking herself.

Calvin was thinking further ahead, contemplating a whole week in the company of a woman with whom all he had in common was a Black Sea cruise he often wished he had not experienced. The aftertaste had lingered on, or he wouldn't have come to Moscow. Nor had he been able to fool himself that the shutter he'd lowered on what he had put behind him years ago hadn't been briefly raised on that vacation.

A penny for your thoughts? Kate wanted to say to him. But she sensed that they were personal, on a level that had better be avoided. At the same time, it struck her that there had always been something unspoken between them. Only by skirting around it had their shipboard alliance been possible. Kate and Cal against their less-sensitive partners was how they had played it. But could that same relationship be re-established now the two of them were alone?

Their eyes met across the table, and what had once been there was *still* there, call it what they might.

'It's good to be with you again, Kate.'

'Same here.' And she would just have to play it by ear.

'Shall we go take a walk, to work off our breakfast?'

'I'm surprised I woke up feeling hungry – '

'Did your night out leave you with a hangover?'

77

'Not the alcoholic kind. I'll tell you about it later.' Kate managed not to glance over her shoulder. 'The Rosses suggested we go sightseeing with them this morning, Cal. I must call their room, they've probably overslept.'

Calvin experienced a pang of disappointment – which didn't jell with his doubts of a few minutes ago – and said, as they left the dining-room, 'Is this trip going to turn into a foursome deal, Kate?'

'Would you rather it didn't?'

'Apart from being squabblers, what are the Rosses like?'

'They tick like you and I do, Cal, though you wouldn't guess that when you first meet them.'

Calvin followed her to a house-phone in the lobby, and was left to make what he would of her reply, while she made the call.

'All I'm getting is a crackling noise,' she said.

'Try again.'

'I have.'

'Then why don't we go check it at the front desk?'

'Is the phone in Room 504 out of order?' she asked one of the receptionists, who seemed to her a near-replica of Natasha.

'It would be best to ask that to the telephone operator, madam.'

'Would you mind doing it for me?'

'I have other duties, madam.'

'And it would probably be quicker, instead of going through the correct channels, to go up to the fourth floor and knock on the door!'

'As you wish, madam.'

'Why did you let that girl have it?' Calvin inquired in the lift.

But Kate could not find the words.

'And how did you manage to memorise the Rosses' room number? I usually have difficulty in remembering my own in a hotel, when I go collect my key.'

'You won't have to remember it. They won't give you your key without your showing them your pass, and the room number's written on it.' What Kate couldn't put into words was her feeling that the receptionist, like the floor woman, was someone behind a mask, whom you couldn't get to.

'"Room 504" is the title of an old love song,' she said to Calvin, 'and Howard made a crack about them being put in it. His humour can be astringent. And Barbara is easy to bait.'

'Ever seen a play with offstage characters who influence the action, Kate? That's what this couple seem to me.'

They were destined to remain so, and a few minutes later it was for Kate and Calvin as if they were part of such a play. The door of Room 504 was opened by a man whom Kate had never seen before, who smiled at her blandly, shrugged his shoulders, and said something in German before closing the door again.

'Where are you going?' Calvin asked as Kate shot like a bullet along the corridor.

'To ask the floor-woman a few questions. Not that she'll give me a straight answer to any of them!'

Calvin caught up with her and brought her to a halt. 'What exactly is a floor-woman?'

Kate gave him Howard's interpretation of that nomenclature.

'Why was it necessary to whisper that in my ear?'

He received no reply.

'What's the matter with you, Kate?'

'I can't tell you now.'

'And before you go raising the dust, wouldn't it be wise to check that there isn't a simple explanation to the Rosses vanishing in the night? Maybe they were bothered by street noises, or whatever, and requested a change of room.'

'They've gone from the hotel, Cal. I feel it in my bones. And with the benefit of hindsight, I think Barbara had a premonition last night of something going wrong.'

'Are you telling me that Kate Starling gives credence to premonitions? Why don't we go back to the front desk, and check the facts?'

'You're under the disadvantage of not yet being in the picture, so I'll forgive you for doubting my instincts and do as you suggest.'

After two hours of being passed from person to person, with long waits in between, they were finally told by the assistant manager that the Rosses had been summoned home suddenly. By then, they were seated in an austere office, Calvin chewing his third cigar, and Kate tapping her fingers on the large expanse of desk.

'Were they summoned by telephone, or telegram?' Kate inquired.

'To establish such technicalities, it would be necessary for you to investigate at the hotel switchboard.'

'And who will *they* refer me to?' Kate gave the cherubic-looking little man a scathing glance. 'The Soviet equivalent of British Telecom? Or an operator who is not on duty? I wish to know *now* what has happened to my friends.'

'Happened, Mrs Starling?'

'Someone who speaks English as well as you do, Mr Kropotnikov, doesn't require a dictionary to understand the meaning of that word.'

Kate's eyes had sparked with anger. It's a wonder the guy doesn't back away, thought Calvin. This was the gutsy female he remembered. Kate Starling had more character in her little finger than all the women of Cal's acquaintance put together.

'Well?' she prodded the man seated opposite her.

'I can tell you no more than I have.'

'And what if I don't believe you?'

His smile became even more implacable. 'That is your privilege, Mrs Starling.'

Kate stormed out of the office with Calvin at her heels. 'That chap is a bloody liar!'

Calvin was closing the door, and had the satisfaction of seeing Mr Kropotnikov loosen his tie – as any guy would feel the need to do, after a clash with Kate. 'How are you going to prove it, Kate?'

'Time will prove it. If I had the Rosses' phone number, I'd call them from here, tonight. Find out if they've arrived home, or not – though getting a call from Moscow, if they haven't arrived, would terrify Barbara's mother.'

Kate paused for breath and made herself simmer down. 'But I shall get to the bottom of this the minute I'm back in

London, Cal. Ring up every Ross in the phone book, if necessary, till I'm through to Howard and Barbara. I have to make sure they're all right.'

'I hope your determination lasts, Kate.'

'Is that a crack?'

'I'm hardly the one to make it, am I?'

They were crossing the lobby, and halted to look at each other in what felt, to Kate, like an islet of silence in a sea of activity. Tourists were returning for lunch after the morning's sightseeing. A babel of languages was buzzing around her. She heard the whine of the lift, and a clank as it came to rest on the ground floor. Someone whistling a tune brushed past, and guffaws of laughter from a group beside the reception desk assailed her ears.

'Why is it,' she said to Calvin, 'that you and I don't have the capacity for carefree enjoyment that most other people seem to have? It's as if we're somehow cut off from the mainstream by the sort we are, and I felt that on the cruise. I mean – well, we might never get to Moscow again, and there's so much of interest to see and delve into. But here am I, spending time on two people who entered my life only yesterday. And you're doing it with me.'

Calvin gazed down at her and noted that her eyes, when she was thoughtful, were more grey than green. 'You might well ask why we're here together, Kate, and come up with the same answer.'

'I don't *know* the answer.'

'Me neither. Maybe it's best left that way. Let's go get our coats and we'll take that walk now.'

'Which floor are you on?'

'The same one your friends were. And I didn't hear any shots in the night!'

Others joined them for the ride upward, or Calvin might have received a piece of Kate's mind. Instead, she avoided looking at him. He thought she was being melodramatic about the Rosses' disappearance. But hadn't she thought that about Barbara's behaviour, before learning the reason for it? Kate was now convinced that something had got Howard and Barbara kicked out of the Soviet Union, at the double. They weren't the kind to have involved her in what they had, and then take off, for whatever reason, without leaving her an explanation. Not if their departure was voluntary.

'Shall we make for Red Square?' Calvin suggested when they met in the lobby.

Kate stalked to the hotel entrance and out to the forecourt. 'I'm in no mood to saunter beside the Kremlin!'

'Then let's take a cab to Gorky Park.' Calvin set the fur hat Sandy had given him for the trip more snugly on his head, and turned up the collar of his overcoat against the ever-present biting wind both he and Kate would remember as part of their sojourn in Moscow. 'On a day like this, we'll probably have the park to ourselves.'

'You look like a Russian in that hat.'

'And you look like a mademoiselle in that beret.'

'Berets are the only headgear that seem to suit me.'

'I have to say that they suit you very well.'

And that, thought Kate, is as personal as we're likely to get. The word 'personal', in that respect, was cropping up in her thoughts too often! – though it hadn't on the cruise. She had not then felt what she was feeling now after only a morning in Calvin's company. The rapport they'd shared had been rekindled, but it wasn't enough. Just as her life with Alun was no longer enough; and she had Calvin to thank for opening her eyes to its limitations. If she'd never met Cal, would her own true self ever have been released? And if he weren't gay – You've reached stalemate again, Kate. Time to switch off and remember a wedding ring is still on your finger.

She saw Calvin glance down at it as she took off her gloves in the cab, and remarked, 'It's engraved, on the back.'

'So was mine.'

Kate was too taken aback to reply. By the time she had recovered, he had changed to a different topic, and again it was as though a door had been shut in her face; but on this occasion less gently. Nevertheless, another piece had clicked into place in the puzzle of their relationship.

It was a good deal less puzzling to Calvin, who was increasingly aware of a stirring within him no other woman had aroused since he chose the path he had. Since he was bisexual, it had to have been choice both times. When the first didn't work out, he had considered himself lucky to be equipped for the alternative, and had thrown in his lot with Sandy. Not until later had it struck him that a guy capable of swinging both ways was less secure than those whose instincts kept them pinned to one path. They were never going to falter and lose their way, be hit with the urge to double back. Calvin wasn't the sort to enjoy leaping back and forth from one path to the other, as some did. He was the all-or-nothing kind, and that went for how he lived with whoever he lived with. He and Lori – how long was it since he'd let himself think of that chapter of his life? – had been great together between the sheets. But in other respects –

The taxi drew to a halt and the driver returned him to the present. 'Our Gorky Park is very famous, no?'

Since the only possible reply was yes, Kate agreed. 'Do many people go to the park on weekdays?'

'In the Soviet Union, every person has the work to go to,' he replied, and added defensively, 'Just as in your country.'

Kate refrained from saying, 'If only that were so.' But she doubted that Britain's unemployed, hard though their lot was, would swap it for a life that included employment in a closed society. One thing they would never be deprived of was the right to try their luck outside their own country, or to vote for a government that might bring change.

'Ever think of the stowaway?' Calvin asked while they strolled through the imposing main entrance to the park, where the sound of piped music immediately blasted their ears.

We're back with what we have on our conscience, she thought before replying. 'He's been stalking me, on and off, Cal, since you called on the day Shcharansky was set free. Every victory counts, you said, and I didn't sleep a wink that night.'

'That makes two of us.'

They were crossing a spacious paved area, wooded slopes on either side of them, making their way past an open-air ice rink were Muscovites skated in winter, its disused appearance adding to the general air of desolation. Two giant ferris wheels were standing idle, and the brightly hued pennants on a line of flagpoles had abandoned themselves to the wind. Ahead was a rustic avenue which seemed to stretch endlessly into the distance.

'I'd heard that Gorky Park was a fun place,' Kate remarked.

'But we're here between seasons, and we haven't come on the weekend,' Calvin pointed out. 'What the hell kind of music are they hitting us with, Kate! It sure isn't the Moscow Symphony Orchestra – '

'If Howard were here, he could translate the vocal bits for us.'

They entered the avenue, still pursued by the same few phrases of Russian, over and again, or so it seemed, interspersed, at the climax of each strident rendering, with the words 'Gorky Park!'

'D'you think it's a device to stop people who come here to talk privately from concentrating, Cal? If so, it's working with me!'

Calvin was not sure if she was joking or not. Though there were not many folk around, he had noted her glancing surreptitiously at a man walking a dog.

'Getting back to the stowaway,' she went on, managing to shut out the sound effects, 'my worst moment was when I finally emerged from the preoccupations that grabbed me the minute I got home, and had to face up to what I hadn't done. That I'd left it too late. I kept hoping to hear that you'd done something.'

'The same went for me. And all it would've taken to set the wheels in motion was – '

'You don't have to tell me. I know.'

'One phone call,' they said in unison.

'Did you try to tell Alun how you felt?'

'What was the point?'

'Exactly my sentiments about unburdening myself to Sandy.'

'What I mainly recall them both saying to us repeatedly, on board ship, was, "If there *is* a stowaway."'

'But if it was just a rumour, why was even our friend Mr Svenson, not to mention the other ship's officers, so cagey with us about it? None of them ever actually denied it point-blank, did they?' Calvin recalled.

'Which didn't help me to rid my mind of the picture of a tall, thin Bulgarian, in a pullover and a peaked cap, penned in below decks, while we were living it up,' said Kate.

There was now another mental picture to add to it, one which required no confirmation. Of Lev Smolensky gripping the bars of his prison cell.

She brushed that harrowing image away. 'Remember the night of the fancy-dress ball, Cal? When Alun and I didn't speak to each other for the entire ghastly evening? It was because I couldn't bring myself to dress up, and Alun accused me of ruining his holiday because of a non-existent stowaway.'

'I noticed that your eyes were red-rimmed that night.'

'It was the first time I'd cried since my gran's death. I wanted Alun to understand how I felt about the stow-away, and not just that. About what we'd seen – and I'd sensed – on some of the shore trips – oh, you know what I mean, Cal – '

'That you wanted Alun to understand *you*.'

'But he wouldn't – or couldn't. Nor was he prepared to try. And I found myself looking at him in that ridiculous King Neptune outfit he'd concocted for the ball, and thinking, "I don't know you. And you don't know me." It came as a shock.'

'Have you recovered from it?'

Now who was getting personal? But Kate had left herself wide open for it.

They had halted beside a bench, and Calvin saw her expression. 'You don't have to answer that question.'

'Let's just say my recovery isn't complete.' Kate wrapped

her camel coat tighter around her and sat down. 'But before we leave the subject of that night, I'll just add that I wasn't surprised, when we got to the ballroom, to find that you weren't in fancy-dress either. I felt like setting fire to all the streamers everyone was merrily flinging around, and I had the feeling that if I'd suggested it, you would have struck the match for me. It was also the night I discovered a violent streak in myself!'

Calvin sat down beside her. 'Like you said before, Kate, we're a pair of outsiders, in an "I'm all right, Jack" world.'

'I didn't put it that way, nor would I. There are others like us, though they seem to be thin on the ground. I just wish you could've met Howard and Barbara, have been with us last night.'

'Isn't it time you filled me in on that?'

When Kate had done so, Calvin said, 'The way you told it, your newspaper stories sure must be good, Kate.'

'They could be, if the subjects were more worthwhile.'

'Why did you say that so angrily?'

'Perhaps because I'm angry with myself,' she said after a pause, 'for letting what I know I'm capable of go to waste. I have friends in Fleet Street, people who began like I did and when I did, and that's where they are now. And they're not all men. Some are women who didn't settle for what I did. That evening gown I had on, when Alun and I made the gaffe of dressing for dinner the first night at sea; it was lent to me by one of those friends who's now at the top of the heap.'

'So you have the right connections to get there yourself, don't you?'

'It'd take more than that. But first I have to make up my mind.'

Kate switched her pensive gaze from a woman playing ball with a toddler, beneath a tree, to a raincoated figure approaching along the path, his ungloved hand clutching his Homburg hat to prevent it from being swept away.

'I'm sure I saw that chap in the hotel lobby this morning,' she said – reminding herself of Barbara.

Calvin replied, 'He doesn't look particularly memorable to me.'

'You haven't been glancing over your shoulder; but now you know about last night would you say there's no reason to? There's no doubt in my mind that the Rosses were under surveillance, and I was with them, wasn't I? The same could now apply to me.'

The weedy-looking man was drawing near. Calvin was fascinated by his bounding gait. 'Anyone less like my idea of the KGB I've yet to see.'

'They come in all shapes, sizes, and outfits,' said Kate, out of a corner of her mouth.

The man paused by the bench and the Homburg was raised to her.

'Mind if I tek the weight off my feet?'

A Northern accent in Gorky Park was the last thing Kate expected to hear, and she wanted to giggle. Oh, the relief! 'Please do.'

'I'm Joseph Peabody, an' I'm a Baptist lay preacher.'

Why was he presenting his credentials?

'Would you mind telling me *your* name?'

Kate introduced herself and Calvin, and Calvin said, 'There's one of your churches close to my home in Boston, Mr Peabody, and I hear the congregation singing when I pass by on my Sunday morning stroll.'

The preacher gazed down at his highly polished black boots. 'Would that the same could be said over here, Mr Fenner.' He collected himself, and briskly cleared his throat. 'I've been following you all day, Mrs Starling, hoping to get you on your own.'

'Why, Mr Peabody? And if you knew who I was, why did you ask my name?'

'Mind if I answer one question at a time? Is she allus like this, Mr Fenner?'

'It's part of her charm,' Calvin answered, while Kate sat impatiently tapping her fingers on the bench, as she had on Mr Kropotnikov's desk.

'Are you sure you don't mean part of her temperament?'

87

'I'm still waiting for the replies to my questions, Mr Peabody.'

'Well, let me put it this way, shall I? Folks as are engaged in what me an' that nice Jewish couple come to Russia for has to be careful. Though our doings are no secret.'

'Howard Ross said that to me – it's him and his wife you're referring to, isn't it?'

'An' as I said to him, when the good Lord fetched us together on a previous occasion, the KGB turn a blind eye to it, like they might to flies on the Kremlin wall; but every so often they'll swat one, to frighten the rest away. An' there's only once to get swatted.'

Mr Peabody turned from contemplating his boots, to look at Kate. 'Any road, I had to mek sure as you *were* Mrs Starling. Though Mr Ross described you to a T, he said as you'd be wearing a brown beret, not a green one.'

'Was that why you weren't certain? My brown one got soaked last night.'

'Well, I weren't sure what to do, at first. Then I thought mebbe as Mr Ross might be colour-blind, since the rest of you matches his description. He said as you had ankles like a racehorse. An' so you have,' Mr Peabody added with unexpected impishness, exchanging a wink with Calvin behind Kate's back. 'But I'd best mek the delivery an' be on my way, or I shall miss my flight to Leningrad.'

'What delivery?' Kate felt a prickling at the back of her neck.

'The one as has been burning a hole in my pocket since Mr Ross put it there. That's the answer to your second question, my dear. Or was it your first? No matter. He asked me to pass summat on to you, and tell you to tek it to where you were last night, if you can manage to find your way back there. I was hoping not to have to do what I promised till I got you by yourself, but you'n Mr Fenner's stayed glued to each other, so I reckoned as how he couldn't be such a friend of yours if he weren't trustworthy. An' it's now or never.'

Though Howard and Barbara were gone, the network of people like them was still operating, and this kindly-eyed man, whose shabby coat seemed several sizes too big for him, was a part of it. 'Howard and Barbara Ross were deported, weren't they, Mr Peabody?'

'Well, I don't know what else you'd call what I witnessed at six o'clock this morning. I'm an early riser, an' I like to start the day with a brisk walk, breathe some fresh air, before all the traffic starts spouting out fumes. A body has to keep themselves fit, to do the Lord's work – '

'You were telling us what you saw,' Kate interrupted.

'She hasn't much patience, has she, Mr Fenner?'

'It's never been one of my virtues,' Kate said.

'But I reckon as how you've got a few others, to mek up for it. Mr Ross said as you're one of us. Now where was I?'

'Taking an early-morning walk,' said Calvin with a smile. If Mr Peabody's preaching was as long-winded as his conversation, the message of his sermon would be buried beneath a mountain of words.

'Oh yes,' he gathered his thoughts. 'An' when I got back to the hotel – I'm stopping at the same place as you two – there was this big black car parked outside. The sort with curtains covering the back window, that you see, among other places, parked by that building that teks up one side of Dzerzhinsky Square.'

'We haven't yet done the city sightseeing excursion,' Kate told him.

'But if an' when you do, Mrs Starling, they'll drive through the square without mentioning that the building is KGB headquarters.'

'Several of those limos overtook us on our way to the park,' Calvin recollected, 'and I wondered why our cab driver moved out of their way to let them pass.'

'They all do, Mr Fenner. On the main roads, there's a traffic lane reserved for them, an' it's woe betide the motorist that gets in their way. I were once in a taxi on the street where the Ministry of Culture is, an' the chap behind the wheel was made to pull over and stop by a policeman – or mebbe it was a militiaman, I have trouble sorting out the uniforms, what with them all seeming to have red on their caps – any road, as I was saying – '

'Please tell us what you saw this morning,' Kate cut in.

'What I saw was what I said. Them fancy cars're in an' out of the Kremlin all the time, used by the top Party officials, an' all. Needless to say, I thought the one outside the hotel had come for *me*. Call it guilt, if you like, though the good Lord knows as I've nowt to feel guilty about.'

That's the feeling that finally got to Barbara, thought Kate, drumming her fingers when Mr Peabody paused.

'The driver was standing beside it,' he went on, 'an' gave me what Mr Fenner'd call the once-over. By the time I'd stepped inside the hotel, I was praying, "Dear Jesus, don't let them stop me from bringing Thy comfort to my Russian brethren whose faith in Thee hast landed them in a pickle."'

Though Kate found the preacher's blend of archaic and down-to-earth language amusing, she found it moving also. 'Weren't you scared on your own account, Mr Peabody?'

'The worst that could happen to me, I reckon, was what happened to Mr and Mrs Ross, but I can't say as how my flesh didn't go goosey. Then I near tripped over a couple of big yellow suitcases, by the entrance.'

'Belonging to the Rosses.' Kate had recoiled from their gaudiness, which had helped her form her totally wrong impression of their owners.

'An' there the two of them were, being escorted from the lift by two gents I wouldn't call lightweights.' Mr Peabody resumed his tale. 'Then Mr Ross spots me, an' I hear him say that he's sure the friendly KGB won't mind him bidding me farewell. An' over he comes – to give me a bear hug, whisper in my ear, an' transfer to my coat pocket summat he says got overlooked in their hasty packing, so he'd popped it into his. Included in the whispering was his message for you, Mrs Starling, an' how I was to pick you out. It wouldn't've done for me to be asking for you at the desk, or phoning your room.'

Kate could imagine the panache with which Howard had carried off his final gesture of defiance. 'Did they

try to intervene, Mr Peabody? Lay ⌐   ⌐
mean?'

'It were over an' done with, an' him back linking ⌐.
arm, before those two goons an' me got our breath back. ⌐.
laying a hand on him – *or* on me – is more than they'd dare
do. Everything has to seem amicable, even when all
concerned know otherwise, in their dealings with foreign
tourists.'

'Even with those who get picked up and taken in for
questioning?' Kate asked.

'Those I know who it's happened to tell me so,' Mr
Peabody replied, 'which isn't to say they enjoyed the
experience.'

Calvin said, 'Remember what Mr Svenson told us on the
ship, Kate? About Soviet officialdom?'

'He didn't say it was amicable.'

'But he did say they'd go to any lengths to save face.'

'Whoever this Mr Svenson is, he knows what he's talking
about,' said Mr Peabody. 'As for Mr Ross's quick-wittedness,
well, I'd never've dreamt it of him. He struck me on our
previous meeting as the slow but sure sort; p'rhaps because
of them big, horn-rimmed specs he wears, an' him having a
bit of a paunch. From now on, the only book I shall judge by
its cover is the Bible.'

Kate felt something being transferred to *her* pocket, then
Mr Peabody rose and doffed his hat, in the old-fashioned
way he had when he halted by the bench.

'Good luck to you both. An' Jesus bless us in our work,' he
said, returning the hat to his balding head, and was gone
before they had time to bid him goodbye.

Calvin noted the 'us' and the pensive look in Kate's eyes as
she watched the preacher's ungainly figure recede along the
path. 'You've been roped in, I guess.'

'At the moment, I feel as if I'm playing "pass the parcel".
Only this isn't a game.'

'But that's exactly what it *is*, Kate.'

Calvin's reply was a statement to which Kate's mind
would later have cause to return. Meanwhile she rebuked
him.

In case it hasn't seeped through to you, Cal, people like Mr Peabody and the Rosses don't do all this because they get a kick out of it!'

'That wasn't what I was implying.'

'Then what were you implying?'

'I guess, that they're gambling against the odds. And in the full knowledge that the authorities are smiling contemptuously at how little material impression these visits of theirs are able to make.'

'I wouldn't be too sure about that. And limited assistance is better than none. I'd like to join that organisation Barbara works with. She says it's run by married women, and many of their husbands are active in it, too. Maybe they wouldn't mind having a Christian member,' Kate mused aloud.

'Would that leave time to expand your career?'

'I didn't say I was going to expand my career.'

'But I'm hoping you will. You're very special, Kate.'

'Thank you, but what has that to do with my writing?'

'It's bound to shine through, and someone with your sincerity, who can also write, could say a lot to a lot of people. If your work ever brings you to the States – '

Kate interrupted with a laugh. 'You're jumping the gun, aren't you, Cal? At present, I'm lucky if it takes me to a local fashion show – and that's only when the Women's Page editor goes down with flu, which she does every winter.'

Kate's mouth is too wide for her face, Calvin noticed for the first time. But she was beguiling all the same, and more so when she laughed.

'We've digressed from the point even more than Mr Peabody did, and it's you who keeps doing it,' she said, her expression serious again.

'I can't remember what the point was.'

'In a nutshell, it concerned my being what you call roped in to deliver something to Irina Smolensky. But I was roped in, in a manner of speaking, on the cruise, wasn't I? When Alexei stopped me on the street in Odessa, and I did what he asked me to. It was fortunate I had that big handbag with me, that we put the books in. That was the night I realised Alun no longer noticed my clothes and accessories, since I had on an evening dress, albeit not ankle length, and silver shoes, and the bag was not only big, it was black patent.'

'What was that remark about Mr Peabody and me digressing?' Calvin said. 'And some nutshell!'

'I haven't finished yet. My agreeing to deliver the novels to Alexei was my first practical involvement in what I'd already become emotionally involved in, is what I'm trying to say. And if I live to be ninety, Cal, there'll still be moments when the thought of the stowaway comes between me and my knitting,' she added.

'Did you knit the sweater you have on today?'

Kate shook her head. 'It's from the store those that Barbara took to the Smolenskys came from.' Remembrance of little Yuli in the size-fourteen woollie returned to her. 'Since the package in my pocket couldn't possibly be the jumper intended for Yuli, he won't be getting one. But there's no way I'm not going to deliver it.'

Kate was still clutching it, and it felt like a small paper bag. She put it on the bench between herself and Calvin, who said when he saw it was not sealed, 'Shall we take a look at the contents?'

When they did so, Kate had another of her uncharacteristic giggling fits; and Calvin gaped.

'All that pass-the-parcel business over a packet of multi-vitamins!' he exclaimed. 'I expected some forbidden Jewish phylacteries at the very least.'

Kate managed to control her mirth. 'Howard would never ask me to deliver anything as incendiary to the KGB as that, in case I got stopped entering Irina's building with it.'

'Nevertheless, the idea of Mr Peabody following you all morning to make a secret handover – !' Words momentarily failed Calvin.

Kate paused reflectively. 'A packet of vitamins might seem trivial to us, Cal, but if you'd seen the people they're for, you'd wish you could give them a barrelful. And even if it were just a note of good wishes, I'd deliver it.'

Kate tucked the vitamins into her shoulder bag, and

glanced up at the darkening sky, as they rose to leave. 'We could be in for some more rain.'

'Did you bring an umbrella along on the trip?'

She shook her head.

'Me, neither. D'you think you *can* find your way to Irina's? And we'd better get some food inside us, before we set off.'

'Then you *are* coming with me?'

'Did you doubt it?'

No. Of course she hadn't.

'We can't read the Russian street names, Kate. Have you thought of that?'

'I wouldn't know the name of the street if we could. But I know which metro station the Rosses and I started out from, and I should be able to pick out the route to the right platform. I have a good memory for that sort of thing, and a good sense of direction in general. Alun once said I must be a reincarnated homing pigeon.'

Why, when she pictured Alun, was he always wearing the white coat he wore in the hospital dispensary?

'In our ménage Sandy's the one with the sense of direction,' said Calvin, 'and I hate it when I'm driving and he tells me I've taken the wrong turning.'

What would Sandy be doing now? Wondering what Cal was doing, no doubt – and if I've remembered to put on my warm hat.

We've moved apart, thought Kate. She could feel it – and just when they'd seemed to be drawing closer in a way the presence of Alun and Sandy on the cruise had prohibited. Calvin's revealing remark in the taxi, apropos wedding rings, had confirmed that a woman is rarely wrong in the matter of a man being attracted to her. Think of something else, Kate!

'Once we're on the train, I'll just have to count the stations,' she said. 'I remember counting six – or was it seven? – last night, and thinking it was quite a long journey.'

'We'll get there, Kate.'

They were passing beneath the Imperial Roman arch that made the main entrance to the park so impressive, and shared a smile as they went to find a taxi.

The closeness is back, thought Kate, and all it took was that smile.

Calvin was thinking, Why does this woman make me feel that together there's nothing we can't achieve? But they were only going to be together for a week, and a day of it was almost gone.

Chapter Four

When Kate and Calvin went to collect their keys on their return to the hotel, Calvin was told that his room had been changed.

'Would you mind telling me why?' he asked the girl at the desk, whose expression was as maddeningly bland as when she stalled their initial inquiry about the Rosses.

'A minor plumbing problem, I understand.'

'I can live with a dripping faucet,' said Calvin.

'And wouldn't it be simpler,' said Kate, 'to fix whatever it is, than for Mr Fenner to have to repack all his things?'

'Mr Fenner's things have already been transferred to Room 300.'

'Without his permission to touch them? No hotel would do that where we come from,' Kate declared.

The girl silently handed Calvin a key.

'What would one have to do, I wonder,' Kate flared as they left the desk, 'to make that smug, stuck-on expression of hers crack?'

'Forget it, Kate.'

'Among other things, I don't like being presented with a *fait accompli*.'

'It's me who's been presented with one.'

'We both have, Cal.'

Kate waited until they were inside the lift, which, since it was nearly dinner time, they had to themselves, before showing him the number-tag attached to her own key.

His reaction was a thoughtful, 'Hm . . .'

And why wouldn't it be? she was thinking, while he tried to work out why she viewed his being put in the room next to hers as a *fait accompli* for them both.

'Let's not discuss this till we're out of here,' she said lest the lift was bugged.

'You're giving me the heebie-jeebies, Kate!'

That described her own unfailing response to the sight of the floor-woman, who was, as usual, stationed where the comings and goings of guests were visible.

'Good evening, Babushka. Had a good day?'

'It is so kind that you ask, madam.'

Even that platitudinous inquiry could not elicit a direct answer! 'A good day off, I mean.' A less motherly-looking version had watched Kate's departure this morning, while pretending to supervise the activities of the chambermaids.

'Thank you. Is there something that you now require of me?'

Kate shook her head and gave up. Gave up on what? Trying to prove that what the Rosses had told her about the floor-women's true function was a myth. You still don't want to accept that nobody's what they seem here, do you, Kate? Being spied on was too repellent to contemplate – but you'd better believe it, she counselled herself, as she and Calvin headed toward their rooms.

'Why do you suppose they contrived this, Cal?'

'What makes you think they did?'

'I've been trying to convince myself it's coincidence, but I doubt it. I'm the woman who badgered them about the Rosses' sudden departure. You're the man who backed me up. For my money, that girl at the desk was lying through her teeth, like she did this morning. Plumbing problems in your room my foot!'

I wasn't left in doubt about why she made that *fait-accompli* remark for long, Calvin thought quizzically. Had he hoped the reason was other than cerebral?

Kate shifted her shoulder bag to a more comfortable position, conscious of the package inside it. Since the contents were innocuous, why did she feel as a drug smuggler surely must? Was it the burden of responsibility that Barbara and Howard had mentioned? Born of the necessity to protect refuseniks one visited from repercussions? Not just that.

'Brief though my experience of Soviet officialdom is,' she mused aloud as they neared the far end of the corridor, 'I'm coming to realise that cunning tactics are something they excel in. I mean, here we are, conjecturing about why they want us in adjoining rooms. Given what preceded it – my friendship with the Rosses, and all that – it's obvious.'

'What, exactly, are you saying, Kate?'

'That we're being wordlessly warned. As surely as if a serum of apprehension were being injected into our minds.'

'We're not that important to them.'

'But, like Howard and Barbara said about themselves, we're thorns in their sides. Anyone who comes here and doesn't behave strictly according to the rules is in that category. One explanation for their moving you is it simplifies their surveillance of a pair of nosey parkers. Another is they're making it convenient for us to have private conversations where they can tape them.'

Calvin watched Kate insert her key into the lock of Room 302. 'There's such a thing as injecting *oneself* with apprehension. Couldn't that be what you're doing?'

'I've already had that debate with myself, Cal – and they'll be counting on that, too. There's nothing like uncertainty for reducing the nerves to shreds.'

'I'd forgotten how a woman always manages to get in the last word!'

Calvin was gone before Kate had time for a reply, nor could she have thought of a suitable one. He had made the quip ruefully, and a moment later had secluded himself inside Room 300, as firmly as he had kept his past from her.

Nevertheless – and unexpectedly – an additional flavour had crept into their relationship, like the subtle introduction of a spice into a dish that had formerly lacked it. No, the spice had been there from the start, its presence tacitly denied by both of them, deepening the enigma Cal was to her.

But he's less of one now than he was on the cruise, she thought while tossing her coat onto one of the twin beds. What their rapport had lacked was a vital element now easing its way in – if gingerly on Cal's part. Little by little they had begun opening up with each other, via a comment of his, here and there, or an unintentional confession of hers, like the one about her dissatisfaction with her work. And Cal's remark about his wedding ring was a confession of sorts, his way of telling her he was once married, without actually saying so. It must be painful for him to talk about it, and Kate would do no probing though she longed to know all there was to know about him. Because she couldn't bear mysteries? Or was the true reason that he interested her more than any man she'd ever met? Leave it at that, Kate! Time to switch off.

She sat down at the dressing-table and took the package from her bag. Where else in the universe would supplying someone with vitamins, and that person accepting them, be, under any circumstances, construed as subversive? It was no wonder that a sense of the ridiculous kept causing Kate to giggle about what wasn't funny – which was not to say that tension played no part in the tremors suddenly shaking her shoulders with mirth again; Howard had been right about that.

The thought of the girl for whom the vitamins were intended was sufficient to sober Kate. Irina would have to decide whether to take some of them herself, for the sake of the child she was carrying, or feed them all to the one whose need was before her eyes. What a choice to be faced with. But the choice that had led to the Smolenskys' penurious situation had been made when they decided to apply for exit visas to go to Israel. Once a Russian Jew took that step, there was no going back; ostracism was the price, and persecution and poverty the punishment, the Rosses had told Kate. But she couldn't have envisaged the effects in human terms. You had to see it for yourself.

Since Lev's arrest, some weeks ago, how had Irina got by without even the pittance her husband had earned by stoking boilers, or by doing this odd job, or that, for those who ceased to employ him immediately they learned from informers that he was a refusenik? The pawn shop had to be the answer, but Irina, by now, had little left to hock. When she and the Rosses ate at her table, last night, Kate had felt that they were taking the food from the family's mouth. But

Howard had prepared her in advance for the hospitality displayed to them, and had instructed her that it must be accepted.

Faith and hope were *not* all that the refuseniks had left, she thought now. They still had their pride. Memories, too, and how extra-precious those beautiful cups and saucers must now be to Irina's mother. Had they perhaps been a wedding gift, like the Crown Derby teaset Kate's grandmother had kept in the parlour cabinet, and only used on Sundays, for forty-odd years? Though the word "parlour" had gone out of fashion before Kate was born, she could not recall her gran ever referring to the room where the china cabinet and a piano stood stiffly facing each other by any other name. Kate had only ever had one set of grandparents, since her father was orphaned when he was a child, and could recall being envious of her playmates who had two sets – but why on earth was she recalling it now? She'd had a happy childhood, hadn't she? A far cry from little Yuli Smolensky's lot, which didn't include any playmates.

Nobody in the building wanted to be seen talking to them, Irina's mother had told Howard, and the only neighbour whom they felt they could trust was the man next door, though they didn't trust his wife. How could such rejection not leave one scarred? thought Kate. But Irina had not stopped holding her head high.

Kate's heart was still aching for Irina when she went to freshen herself with a quick shower. She could hear Calvin moving around in his bathroom, and was momentarily peeved with him for his cautious response to her deductions. But she'd noticed on the cruise that though his compassion was as strong as hers, he was less inclined to give full rein to it. Cal was more controlled in general than she was. He could weigh up a string of facts without leaping to immediate conclusions. Maybe he just wasn't burdened with a fertile imagination.

Kate might not have thought so, had she known he had heard the gush of water in her shower, and was visualising her soaping her breasts. But his treacherous imaginings – for so they seemed – had begun when he saw a door in the wall

100

between his new room and Kate's. A convenient arrangement for a family. Also for an illicit affaire. Had that occurred to Kate? Shoot back the bolts and . . .

But why would it occur to a devoted wife and mother, who thought herself on a vacation with a platonic friend? Though Kate now knew that he hadn't always eschewed the opposite sex, she had not known it when the trip was planned. Nor had her husband, at whom Cal's treachery was directed; as well as at Sandy, who no longer entirely trusted him, and hadn't since the cruise, though they never talked about it.

But Cal's real problem, the one from which all this sprang, was that he couldn't trust himself with Kate Starling. What had begun as a meeting of kindred spirits was becoming for him more biological by the minute.

He wiped the steam off the bathroom mirror, and said to the man staring back at him, 'Now you've started being honest with yourself, why not go the whole way?' A spark had shot from Kate to him the moment they met on the ship, and was now threatening to cause a major conflagration. He hadn't let it ignite then, why had he now?

The answer was he'd tried to stamp it out and failed. Or maybe he'd thought he'd succeeded, until they met again today, and a tiny tongue of flame flickered where he'd vowed – after Lori, and all *that*! – no woman was ever going to set him alight.

He dried himself savagely with the scratchy bath towel – hadn't the Russians heard of fabric-softeners? – as though it were a penance for his own folly. Which particular folly was that? Looking back, his history was peppered with them, though those that figured largest had seemed, at the time, the right move to make. Like taking a girl he'd known all his life for his wife, and learning, later, that he hadn't known her at all.

Would the time ever come when Cal really knew *himself*? Or was a bisexual guy a kind of split personality who would never get himself together? It was all fine to opt to live one way or the other, but what did you do when your hormones called the tune? As mine are doing right now! On account of one particular woman – but that made things no easier.

101

What made him assume that if he'd married Kate, not Lori, neither man nor woman could have come between them?

By the time he'd met Sandy, there was nothing left of his marriage to come between. But that couldn't be said of my relationship with Sandy when I met Kate, he reflected while combing his wet hair. He hadn't brought a hair dryer; had Kate? He strode to the bedroom, to knock on the door between their rooms and ask her, decided that the door had better remain symbolically closed and bolted, and began dressing for dinner.

Then Kate knocked on the door and called that she would be ready in a few minutes.

Think about Sandy, he ordered himself, who's as devoted to you as Alun is to Kate. Be grateful for the sure thing. But could it still be called that when one of the partners was no longer sure of himself?

While Calvin knotted his tie in a Moscow hotel room, what would Sandy be doing, on the other side of the world? To figure that out would require some mental juggling with the time-zone difference, and Cal was still too jet-lagged to make the effort. But, whatever the time now was in Boston, Sandy would be engaged in what always engaged him at that particular hour. If we didn't drink our nightly Martinis at seven, and eat dinner at seven-thirty, Sandy would probably suffer withdrawal symptoms, Calvin thought with a smile. A creature of habit was Sandy. The plants on their roof patio were watered the moment the sun went down, even when they had guests, and the brass *objets d'art* in the gallery were personally polished by Sandy each morning, before they opened for business. Their apartment being situated above the gallery made it possible for him to blend his domestic activities and his work into one strict routine.

Thinking of him never failed to produce in Calvin a mellow feeling, though it was tinged with guilt right now. Time, and sharing a life that embraced both earning their living, and home, had welded them solidly together. If Cal had to sum up their bond he'd call it mutual respect and affection. How many hetero men do you know who could truthfully say that of their marriages? he asked himself.

Calvin sometimes thought that his and Sandy's alliance had to be successful because passion could not wane where it had never existed. They had found a comfortable peace together, after their separate traumas. One of Cal's was going to be with him always, but this was no time to let it come flooding back full force. How had he got into taking an inventory of his gains and losses? And ended up making himself count his blessings?

Another knock on that insidious door provided the answer. 'See you in the corridor in a minute, Cal!'

Kate.

While they ate the *borsch* their late arrival for dinner had rendered tepid, and were eyeing without enthusiasm the second course placed in readiness for them, one of Kate's deductions was confirmed by their table companions.

'*I* found nothing wrong with the plumbing, Daphne.'

'So you keep saying, Mother.'

'That's extremely impolite of you, dear.'

'But it's true.'

'And also true that I'm now on a different floor from you. What am I to do if I need you in the night?'

'Ring my room, and I'll come up.'

'This is Moscow, Daphne dear, not London. A lady hurrying along hotel corridors in her nightwear could arouse suspicion.'

Kate exchanged a glance with Calvin. 'Did you hear the bit about the plumbing?'

'How could I not? They may be at the other end of the table, but they both have piercing voices.'

Daphne's response to her mother was, 'I recall your ticking me off for popping from my room to yours, in my dressing-gown, when we stayed at Brown's Hotel, the weekend of Martin's wedding.'

'I daresay I did, though my memory is not what it was, and your brother has been married for years.'

But Daphne is still at your mercy, thought Kate, surreptitiously studying them. Though the mother was seated on

Kate's side of the table, and only her profile visible, her determined jawline made her seem formidable. As for Daphne, her attempt to stand up to her mother had sounded like a lamb bleating at a lion, and her drooping posture lent her a downtrodden look. Both women were expensively clad in cashmere twinsets, Kate noted, and each wore a single strand of pearls. But elegance would always escape them; there was about them that genteel frumpiness peculiar to some Englishwomen whatever they wear. My great-aunt Harriet's one of them, Kate reflected – but she wouldn't be my favourite relation if her resemblance to Daphne's mum didn't end there.

'I needed you to help me do up my cardigan buttons, this evening, Daphne,' the dreadful woman resumed.

'It's good for your rheumatism to exercise your fingers occasionally, Mother.'

'The doctor didn't say so.'

'He probably thinks you do a lot more for yourself than you do.'

'Are you hinting that I am a burden to you, Daphne?'

They gave their attention to the ice cream they were eating – as if, thought Kate, they had now reached the point on a familiar conversational path where Daphne dared go no further, and her mother knew it.

'If ever there was a classic, invalid mother and long-suffering single daughter, set-up – ' Calvin said in an undertone.

'Is the mother really an invalid?'

'That had occurred to me. But since I'm not a professional observer, like you, I don't intend mulling it over.'

'What I'm mulling over,' said Kate, 'is that remark about the plumbing.'

'I knew you were mulling something over. Your eyes have changed colour.'

Kate averted them to her plate. 'You said something like that to me on the cruise.'

'While we were dancing on deck. I remember every detail of that evening, Kate.'

She looked up and met his gaze.

'Why do you suppose I chose the moment I did to fill you in about Sandy and me?'

'I haven't the slightest idea.'

'Really? Maybe you hadn't then, but in the light of your new knowledge – '

'What knowledge is that?'

'Don't fence with me, Kate. It isn't like you.'

'No, as a matter of fact it isn't.'

'Then why are you doing it? If I can come clean with you, why can't you with me?'

'I wouldn't call what you've said so far coming clean. You're trying to get me to help you do it, and I won't.'

After a pause, Calvin said, 'That's what the shrink I went to for a while used to say.'

'But his reason for saying it was less personal than mine.'

'Returning to *my* reason – for telling you what I did on that particular evening – the ambience was so goddamn romantic, I was liable to succumb to your charms and the heck with Sandy.'

Kate reached up to finger the crystal beads she usually wore with this dress, and found she had forgotten to put them on. What on earth must she look like, in unrelieved grey? 'Are you saying you were frightening me off, Calvin? And for your own good? I'm as tied as you are, may I remind you.'

'Since when did that make a dime's worth of difference?'

'It always has to me.'

'Yes. We're two of a kind in that way, as well.'

'But one of us isn't as forthcoming as he should be with the other.'

'Nevertheless, it's you being my kind that's the trouble. Shall we pretend this discussion never took place?'

Discussion? To Kate it had felt more like a verbal ping-pong match – which neither had won. 'Pretending isn't my style, Cal. Any more than it's yours.'

A sudden commotion at the other end of the table intervened.

'Why did I let you persuade me to come to Russia, Daphne?'

'You could have dripped soup on yourself anywhere in the world, Mother.'

Daphne had risen from her chair and was dipping a table napkin into a jug of water.

'Kindly do not pile insult upon injury, my dear! Anywhere else, it wouldn't have been beetroot soup, would it? Since you're seated opposite me, you must have seen it happen, but said not a word.'

Daphne, stiff with embarrassment, was trying to remove the stain from her mother's beige cardigan with the damp cloth.

'If I were her,' said Kate, 'I'd be tempted to chuck the jug of water over that old harridan's head.'

'What's the betting she *will* rebel, one day?' Calvin replied. 'She sure has the incentive to.'

There was more to come.

'It really is too much; I'm upset enough with having to change rooms. Room 300 was quietly situated, as I'd requested our accommodation should be, though why they put you next door but one to me, instead of next door, I failed to understand. As for Room 519 – well, I shan't be able to sleep for the traffic noises.'

Since the tirade was rapidly delivered, it took Kate and Calvin a moment or two to take in the significance of what they had heard. Daphne had helped her mother rise, and they were making their way out of the dining-room, before Calvin said, 'Okay, Kate. You were right.'

'But *you* had to have proof, didn't you?'

He stared down at his dish of melted ice cream – they had found the dessert lined up with the rest of the courses. 'Not from here on, I don't! But since I have indisputable proof on this, why don't I get the lady who provided it to join forces with me at the front desk?'

'Ask them why they moved her to your room, and you to hers, you mean?'

'I guess we know why.'

'But we're never going to get proof of *that*.'

'Nevertheless, Kate, confronting them with what they can't deny would put them over a barrel. A straight room-swap, like they've done, exposes the plumbing-problem excuse for the out-and-out lie it is. And I don't like the idea of them smiling behind my back, thinking they've got me fooled and where they want me.'

Kate observed his steely expression. 'At last something has got you going.'

'It sure as hell has.'

Kate sat absently crumbling the remains of some bread, the buzz of lighthearted chatter going on all around her in stark contrast to her own mood. But it was good that Cal had finally stopped thinking her paranoid.

'That couple who waved to you this morning from the table you should be sitting at look rather nice,' she remarked to him. She noted the man's dark suit, and that the girl was wearing a simple black dress, with an elegant scarf. 'They remind me of a couple I know at home who both work in a bank.'

'They were on my flight.'

'Did you sit beside them?'

'Not on the plane; they were across the aisle from me on the bus from the airport. They were in clipper class, I was up front.'

'With the celebrities and tycoons.'

'I can't say I've ever thought of it that way.'

'But you always travel first, like I travel cabin class.'

'What's this all about, Kate?'

'Well, it sort of confirms what just struck me. That people take their own lifestyle with them wherever they go. Clipper class is how I'd expect that couple to travel – '

'But I'm neither a celebrity, nor a tycoon,' Calvin cut in. 'Are we talking income brackets, Kate?'

'Only in passing.'

They heard a snatch of conversation from a table occupied by a party of elderly Australians.

'How did the Kremlin grab you, Peggy?'

'I was fascinated, Jack. It'll be something to remember when Joe and I get home.'

Kate said to Calvin, 'I feel like asking them if they've given a thought to what they're *not* being shown.'

She poured them each a cup of lukewarm coffee and stirred some sugar into hers. 'Before the cruise, I was as complacent as those I'm now criticising, Cal.'

'That's hard to believe.'

'But true. And I'm not exactly criticising them.'

'Remember Big Momma and Poppa?' Calvin reminisced.

'Who could forget them? They were larger than life in every way. But I've grown up some, since then. At twenty-eight, I thought I knew everything. My lips used to curl about almost everyone on that ship.'

Kate stared into her coffee, thoughtfully. 'But who was I to grudge them their carefree holiday? What did I know about what they'd left at home and would be going back to? Maybe Big Momma and Poppa run an equally big, fast-food restaurant, and two weeks' holiday, once a year, is what they look forward to, and the only time off they get.'

'Think their specialty is clam chowder, or chilli con carne?' Calvin said with a grin.

'For my money, it's doughnuts, and they eat their fair share of them! But what I said could apply, give or take the details, to most of the tourists in this room. Hence my observations not being criticism, Cal. It just strikes me as strange that people from free countries can spend time in the Soviet Union without letting it leave a mark on them.'

' "Letting" is the operative word – and can we get back to where we were when you went off at your usual tangent, Kate? We were deciding whether to enlist Daphne's mom's aid at the front desk.'

And how quickly you and I have settled back into being "we", thought Kate, elbowing away a vision of Alun, when Calvin said, 'Do we, or don't we?'

'Why give "them" the advantage of knowing we've proved what we have?' she replied. 'We're now one step ahead of them, which includes the probability that we're under surveillance. If they're looking for an excuse to swat us off the wall, as Mr Peabody would put it, because of my association with the flies they did finally swat, so be it.'

'It isn't the hotel management you're talking about, is it?' Calvin said, as this seeped through to him.

'According to my friends-the-swatted-flies, the hotel management and those I'm talking about are in cahoots. And if Daphne's mum knew her room-change was part of some skulduggery, she would now be hammering on the door of the British Embassy.'

Calvin thought of the delivery they were planning to make tonight, that had to be cloaked with secrecy as if it were a microfilm of state secrets. The pettiness of bureaucracy was legendary, but this went far beyond that, into the realms of the bizarre. Why would the Soviet Union, ostensibly afraid of nothing and nobody, go to such lengths to crush the spirit of small fry like the Smolenskys, whose presence in, or absence from, the vast population of Russia would not make a mite of difference either way? Was the Israel connection, with its close ties to the other Superpower, Calvin's own country, the one thing they did fear?

Calvin would have liked to discuss the wider political implications with Kate, but this was neither the time nor the place. Briefly, he was prey to the feeling of unreality that was affecting her. Himself and Kate talking about swatted flies; the way the preacher had tailed her to make the handover; the crafty room-swap.

It was small wonder Cal was sitting here thinking, What have I gotten into?

CHAPTER FIVE

KATE PROVED to be less of a reincarnated homing pigeon in
Moscow than in London. Or had the tension gripping her
from the moment they left the hotel sent her instinctual
compass haywire?

Though she personally had nothing to fear – deportation
was the worst that could happen – anxiety was making itself
felt. She could feel her heart thudding, and had to will her
hands to relax. The Rosses' nervousness had rubbed off on
her last night, but she hadn't felt like this. There was a
difference between being an observer and a participant.

'Made up your mind how many stations along the track it
was?' Calvin said to her on the train.

Kate was trying not to look at a stout man seated directly
opposite, who had boarded immediately behind them and
seemed to be having trouble balancing his document case on
his lap beneath his overhanging belly. It was also necessary
to try to ignore being stared at as if she and Cal were exhibits
– which she supposed they were – by people in their carriage.
Just like last night, she recalled. Our clothing is so superior
to theirs – well, Kate felt positively stylish, though her coat
was only the warm one she wore to go shopping on a chilly
day at home; or when her work entailed trudging around
outdoors to talk to people – like the time she'd done that
article about the Sunday morning market a reader had
written in to complain was turning the locality into a
Petticoat Lane. And that was about as controversial as
Kate's column ever got!

She cast aside her growing discontent with her part-time
career, tried smiling at a woman of about her own age who
was eyeing her from a seat beside the carriage door, and was
pleased when the smile was returned. Nevertheless, her

unease persisted that among the passengers might be someone from the KGB. They came in all shapes, sizes and outfits, Barbara had said; and Kate no longer needed telling.

'You didn't answer my question,' Calvin prodded her.

'What question was that?'

'I asked if you'd decided how many stations along the track the one we want is.'

'To tell you the truth, Cal, I'm not even sure we boarded at the right platform.'

'Now she tells me!'

The Russian with the document case gave them a reminiscent grin. 'When once I was in London, I had with myself the same problem. It was with a trade mission I was there, and could not find back my way to Highgate by the Underground. I had been for my wife to buy something nice to wear, to take home to Moscow. It was a – how do you call it? With the buttons?'

'A cardigan?' Kate supplied.

'So clever that you should know.'

'Not really. Everyone who visits Britain takes home knitwear. It's one of the things *we're* famous for. Did you get it at Marks and Spencer, in Oxford Street?' When Kate went there to buy the sweater she had on now, she had seen some Arabs buying them by the armful, and it had struck her as somewhat incongruous since the sweaters were labelled Made in Israel.

'Oxford Street I do not recall,' he answered eventually. 'It was in a district called the Knightsbridge that I bought for my Tamara the how-do-you-call-it. She has kept for a souvenir the wrapping bag – '

'And it probably has "Harrods" written on it,' Kate cut in, with false bonhomie.

He slapped his knee, with an enthusiasm that ricocheted his document case to the floor. 'That was, yes, the store! So clever again! And also so kind you Britishers are,' he added when Calvin retrieved the case and handed it to him.

Why is he flattering us? Kate wondered warily.

'I happen to be an American,' said Calvin.

'I am so sorry to make such a mistake.'

111

'It isn't an insult to be thought British,' Kate informed both of them.

The Russian sidestepped her remark smartly and with a chuckle. 'Of the special relationship between your two countries everyone knows. But this kind gentleman does not speak with the same accent as the Ewing family, whom I have on the television watched each week, in London. I would have liked to find it out if the father, Jock, has returned himself from the jungle, dead or alive.'

'I'm afraid his death was established,' Kate replied. 'But Miss Ellie is now happily remarried.'

'So soon?' The Russian looked shocked. 'To whom?'

Kate spent a minute or two bringing him up to date on the storyline of a soap opera she would, at home, be loth to admit she occasionally watched. But when your choice of entertainment was limited to that seen fit by the State for its citizens, and you'd briefly tasted the varied flavours of programming in the West — That had to be why this unlikely *Dallas* addict was avidly drinking in her words. Also why Soviet society was kept so tightly closed against influences the Kremlin deemed corruptive.

Calvin was amused by the turn the encounter had taken, and joked to the Russian, when Kate had finished speaking, 'Maybe you should give her your address, so she can keep you informed.'

The man proved that he, too, was not without wit. 'That would deprive me of a topic for conversation with some other charming English lady I might meet on a train. But it is not too often I would have such a pleasure. Our foreign visitors are much occupied by our official excursions. At night, they go perhaps to our internationally known concerts and theatres, for which they would take a taxi.'

And he's wondering what we're doing, all on our owney-oh, thought Kate, noting the word 'official'. Rattling to he'd liked to know where, on a train. Ought she to say, casually, that they were going to visit some friends? But he hadn't actually asked, had he? That didn't stop the auto-suggestion from doing its worst again. Keep your trap shut, Kate!

'You were a student of Yale, perhaps?' he asked Calvin, chattily.

'No.'

'Columbia University?'

'Harvard, as a matter of fact. Until I dropped out.'

Was that last bit of information for Kate's benefit? Another of the snippets of his past he'd begun tossing into the near-vacuum their knowledge of each other's background was? And the more so, it seemed, when yet another revelation, minor or major, came along.

' "Dropped out" is not an expression I have before heard.'

Calvin explained what he had meant.

It was received with raised eyebrows. 'Young people in the West do not always wish to complete their studies? In the Soviet Union, such could not be the case. It would constitute the ingratitude to our great educational opportunities.'

'Where we come from,' said Kate, 'gratitude doesn't enter into it.'

'Enter into it?' The man looked nonplussed.

'I guess what she's telling you,' said Calvin, 'is that students, like everyone else, can do what they think is best for themselves. Make their own choices.'

'And what better choice,' said the Russian, 'than the fulfilment of your own potential, for the betterment of society? This is something which every Soviet citizen believes. Even those who sweep our streets are proud to be the citizens who keep them clean, and will do so to the best of the ability.'

Better return this little foray into Soviet-versus-the-West attitudes to safer ground, thought Calvin. There was no way a guy raised to accept that the State came first could comprehend what Kate and Cal were trying to explain to him. That in their countries, the right to do your own thing, for better or worse, was valued above all else.

'I hear you have a big store in Moscow called GUM,' he said to the Russian.

'To which I must recommend you, but not that you should go there on the weekend, when every Muscovite and his family is out to do the shopping. There is, too, Petrovka

113

Street – it is near to the Bolshoi Theatre – where is a small and interesting market with produce, in addition to fine stores. Also, if you will tell to me where you are wishing now to go, I will check that this is for you the correct train.

'It is the losing of the way in a foreign city that began our conversation, and I am wishing only to be helpful,' he added when the wheels ground to a halt, and Kate sat staring at him blankly.

'And you are being! Tremendously!' she sprang to life. 'We really do appreciate it. But this is our stop. I remember now. Thank you and goodbye!'

She grabbed Calvin's hand and leapt with him from the train, with but a second to spare before the doors slid shut.

'Thank heavens for that,' Calvin said.

Kate was waving gaily to the Russian, as the train pulled out. 'I wish I could say the same.'

'Does that mean you've mistaken the station?'

'No. It means I knew this wasn't it.'

'Then why are we off the train?'

She thrust her hands into her pockets and gave him a withering look.

'If I weren't wearing a hat, Kate, I'd be standing here scratching my head over how you're behaving. You are definitely not yourself tonight.'

'Nor are you, since I credit you with some intelligence. How could we have told that Russian – when he finally got around to asking – that we haven't the foggiest where we're going to?'

'So you panicked and ran.'

'I didn't hear you come up with a credible reply, that could have kept us *on* that train. Nor did I trust that man. He must be from the Soviet élite to have gone abroad with a trade mission, and to cough up for Harrods cardigans for his wife – '

'He only bought her one,' Calvin cut in.

'Kindly don't split hairs. And everyone knows that trade missions are often fronts for something else. Why did I bother thinking, when we got proof that your room change was skulduggery, that you'd trust my instincts from now on?'

'In this instance, they probably extend to convincing yourself that the guy on the train had a walkie-talkie along, and could be setting whoever on our trail, right now!'

'Poke fun at me if you wish. But would you have believed, when we left the hotel this morning, what we'd return to? This is a country where anything can happen.'

'And I'm here with a woman who seems to *make* things happen.'

'That isn't fair!'

'Okay, I'll withdraw it.'

'But this could be the right time to remind you you're not chained to my side.'

Brief though their first quarrel was, it had run the gamut from irritation to a spurting crescendo of anger, and down from that peak to the anticlimactic moment of depression that followed the cool finale. Nor was it easy to set matters right. Their relationship was still a tentative and tenuous one, with the added disadvantage of neither being sure whither it was proceeding.

Kate made herself break the strained silence. 'Are we going to stand here gawping at each other all night?'

'Gawping,' said Calvin, mimicking the Russian, 'is not an expression I have before heard.'

'It's a word I got from my grandmother, up north. Gran used to let me lick the froth off the top of her glass of stout, when I was little – '

'One of my grandmothers lived in the deep South. She showed me how to make mint juleps when I was a kid, but never let me take a sip.'

'Now we're standing here discussing our grannies! What's the matter with us, Cal?'

'Nothing's the matter with *me*. But when I think back to that leave-taking performance you put on for the Russian – right down to the "Thank you and goodbye" – I am still asking myself that question with regard to you. Maybe we'd just better beat it from here fast, before he gets some possible action going, with his possible walkie-talkie!'

'Beat it to where?'

They burst out laughing, and at last their small personal crisis was over.

'I'm glad you're able to see the comic side of us not knowing where we're going,' said Kate, 'despite the seriousness of what we're into. Or I should begin thinking there's something very wrong with me.'

'I have to tell you, Kate, that I wanted to laugh when I saw my grandfather in his coffin. Grandmother had selected what he would wear for his burial, and he had on a tie she'd given him that he'd refused to wear when he was alive.'

'That has the makings of a black comedy.'

'I can think of better places to discuss theatre than a subway platform, when we still have the delivery to make. And I guess there's no comic side of anything, right now, for the folk we're making it to. Shall we toss a kopek, to decide if we return to our point of departure and start over from a different platform?'

A train was now pulling in, and passengers awaiting it were moving to throng the edge of the platform.

'Let's stay with this line,' said Kate, 'and hope it turns out to be the right one. I'm pretty sure that one of the murals we passed on our way to the train was one I'd admired last night.'

Calvin smiled. 'I guess it must be a culture shock for members of Soviet trade missions and the like, when they visit New York and see the wild artistic expression on the subway trains there. I never saw one where the exterior wasn't adorned by graffiti that offends my sober tastes, but is nevertheless an art form – and it doesn't cost the city a bean.'

'I've heard say it gets done at the railroad yards, after dark, and even New York's finest haven't managed to stop the kids from doing it,' Calvin continued when they were aboard the train. 'My guess is the cops don't try too hard; that they maybe view it as a better way for teenagers to let rip than some of the other ways now prevalent in US society.'

'British, too, Cal. But I wouldn't like to contemplate what would happen to a kid who let rip in *any* way, here.'

Kate switched her gaze from two soberly clad lads to some

116

youngsters at the far end of the compartment, talking and laughing together, who had emulated the blue jeans and bomber jacket image they probably associated with the West. Since none of them sported a Mohican hairdo, and the girls each had on a *pair* of earrings – Emily now left one ear-lobe naked when she did herself up for the youth club disco – they were somewhat behind the times. But Kate applauded their rebellion against the drab uniformity she had observed. The time to settle down and conform came all too soon for all young people, but in the Soviet Union, where citizens couldn't even travel to another town without a passport – well, 'restriction' seemed the word that governed people's lives.

'I hope you're trying to decide which station we get out,' Calvin said.

'The sixth, or the seventh, like I said.'

'When we started out, which would leave us now with only three – or four – to go.'

'How useful to have a mathematician on the team.'

'I was lousy at maths, and it did me no good with my father since we're a merchant banking family and I'm his only son. It remains to be seen if *my* son will turn out to be the right material for the Board.'

Another piece to fit into the jigsaw puzzle – this time a major one – and as casually divulged as those that had preceded it. So Calvin had a child. Or possibly more than one; if so, did he intend revealing the existence of the others to Kate one at a time?

'Let's do this methodically, Kate. Try the sixth stop first, and see if the platform there strikes a chord with you.'

Why didn't she just ask him if his son was an only child? Given his reticence, it would seem like prying. And his immediately switching to a different subject was becoming part of a pattern, as if he didn't want to dwell, or couldn't bear to, on what he had allowed to emerge.

'I shall need to see the street outside,' she said when they were alighting from the train. 'There was a café opposite the station.'

That useful landmark was not in evidence and they had

to re-enter the metro and again negotiate the escalators, Kate's vertigo vying with her impatience, before boarding yet another train.

And there the café was, facing the entrance at the next stop.

'Where now?' Calvin asked.

Kate stood with a crossroads confronting her, which she couldn't recall being there last night. 'Your guess is as good as mine, I'm afraid.'

'And it isn't inconceivable,' he replied, 'that a lot of Moscow subway stations have cafés opposite them.'

'That's the same café I saw, Cal. With the same miserable-looking dog sitting outside. Barbara remarked that it looked neglected, and that in England its owner would be reported to the RSPCA for making it stay outside when its tail must be stiff with the cold.'

'Okay, let's go. If the first route proves wrong, we'll retrace our footsteps and try an alternative one.'

'That sounds like a philosophy for life,' said Kate, as he linked her arm and they set forth.

Too true, thought Calvin. Well, it sure had been *his* philosophy. He was aware of Kate's slim figure moving side by side with his, matching his stride – which only a long-legged woman could do – and of her purposeful profile, its purity not diminished by being so. Would he ever again see a woman wearing a simple beret, without thinking of Kate as she now was? Her looks were the kind described as 'English rose', and on the cruise that was what she had seemed to him, but with an extra-special radiance that came from within. There'd been a youthful eagerness about her then, a zest for life, that had calmed down in the years between. As she had said at the dinner table, Kate, who at twenty-eight had struck him as somewhat naïve, had grown up some. But she's the kind who'll go on growing as a person with each new experience that comes her way, he was reflecting when she halted and clutched his sleeve.

'You picked the right road, Cal! I remember that cinema beside a clump of trees.'

He would have liked to think that his picking the correct route was some sort of omen for them together, but superstition wasn't his style. Nor had he the right to hope for that, since utter selfishness wasn't his style, either.

Kate quickened her step until she was almost dragging him along. Attracted to me she may be, he thought, and he was sure she was, but Kate Starling wasn't the one to take her eye off the ball. Only Irina Smolensky and her child were in Kate's mind right now.

She halted him again, with the same sleeve-tugging movement, on a street corner opposite a cheerless looking apartment house. A man was standing by the doorway. If it weren't so dark, Cal would see how pale she'd just gone. She'd felt the blood drain from her face and the prickle at the back of her neck this time had goose-flesh on her arms to keep it company.

'There was a man loitering by the house last night, Cal – '

'That didn't stop the Rosses from going in.'

'Nor will it stop us.'

They crossed the street and entered the building without the man so much as glancing at them.

'Was he the same guy as last night?' Calvin asked, grimacing at the odour as they climbed the stairs.

'I don't know. I was too scared to look at him.'

'I have to confess the same. Whatever you've got must be catching, Kate!'

'I thought that when I caught it from Barbara.'

When they reached the first floor, the Smolenskys' door was slightly ajar. There was no response to Kate's knock. She peeped inside and saw only the grandmother, who appeared to have fallen asleep in her armchair.

'I don't see Irina slipping out somewhere and leaving the flat open to whoever,' she whispered to Calvin.

'You're making with the apprehension-syringe, Kate! Like we *both* did downstairs – '

'Kindly don't snap at me!'

'I wasn't snapping. But *you* are.'

They stood eyeing each other uncertainly, not a sound to

be heard, nor a soul to be seen on the ill-lit landing; only their two figures casting shadows on the wall.

Calvin tried to pull himself together. 'I guess I'm not cut out for this.'

'Me, neither. But we're going in.'

He followed her, feeling like a trespasser. 'Now, what?'

Three candles were flickering on the table, standing in a baking tin that looked as if it had been scoured until it shone bright. The table was where Irina had put it when she fed her guests last night, and was now covered by a white cloth. A loaf of bread was peeping from beneath a square of linen embroidered with the Star of David. Beside it was a goblet and a bottle of wine.

There was something holy about the picture it made and Kate could not tear her gaze from it.

'Have you never seen a table laid for the Jewish Sabbath Eve before, Kate?'

'No, as a matter of fact.'

'Well, it's Friday night, isn't it? And that's what you're looking at. Sandy has a Jewish brother-in-law and his sister converted. We sometimes get asked there for Friday-night dinner. We gave them the candelabra they use.'

'I bet the Smolenskys once had one, too,' Kate replied, 'but not having one now hasn't stopped Irina from lighting the Sabbath candles, has it?' Seeing them stuck in a baking tin – well, for Kate, that said it all.

They were whispering so as not to waken the old lady, the necessity to do so an added strain.

'Irina must have taken her little boy with her, Kate – '

'And she must have left in a hurry.'

Kate was now looking at the two glasses of tea on the table. They looked freshly made. She felt them, and they were icy cold, like the air in the room. You're behaving like Miss Marple in an Agatha Christie whodunit, Kate! But alarm was mounting within her. Who done what?

'Why don't we just leave the package where Irina'll find it when she gets back, and tiptoe out of here, Kate?'

'Make ourselves scarce, you mean? Consider our job done?'

'That would be the sensible thing to do.'

'But I'm not going to do it.'

Calvin hadn't expected her to. That Kate had emotionally involved herself with Irina's plight was plain whenever she spoke of the Russian girl and one glance around this place was enough to deepen Calvin's compassion for the family. But if he didn't keep Kate's feet on the ground about all this, who would? What could she hope to achieve in the short time he and she would be in Moscow? Or, indeed, if they were here for longer. What they'd gotten into was Soviet internal affairs, and they could find themselves on a plane out of here pronto.

'Irina can't afford to make tea, then let it go to waste,' Kate said. 'Nor would she voluntarily have taken Yuli out on a bitterly cold night.'

The sound of coughing drifted towards them from the kitchen. Kate was there in two seconds flat, Calvin at her heels.

'Oh dear God, Cal – '

The child was cowering in a corner between a cupboard and the sink, his teeth chattering with cold, and beneath him a pool of urine, as if fear had caused him to wet himself, over and again.

It was then that Calvin too became emotionally involved. 'What in the hell's been going on here!'

They had to pick their way through broken crockery on the floor to get to the little boy, who cringed away, his hands in his mouth, when Kate tried to lift him up. It was Calvin whom he eventually allowed to do so.

'If I could lay my hands on whoever – !' Kate's outburst ended in mid-sentence. An ageing man with a resigned expression on his face was standing in the doorway.

'Please permit me to answer your question,' he said to Calvin, 'after which it would be best you should leave.'

Kate bristled. 'Are you threatening us? Come on, Cal, let's find something to wrap Yuli in.'

'I am not one of those whom you have doubtless heard so much about,' the man said, following them into the living-room.

Kate grabbed a faded patchwork quilt which was lying, neatly folded, at the end of one of the divans, ready for bedtime. What a tidy person Irina was. In her position Kate wouldn't've cared how her home looked. She unfolded the quilt, but Yuli wouldn't let her wrap him in it. If Kate had never seen real terror before, she was seeing it now. In this kid's eyes.

She gave the quilt to Calvin. 'Maybe he'll let you do it. Are you a refusenik?' she asked the man.

'I am not even a Jew. Just someone who lives next door, who would like to help, but must turn the blind eye to the troubles of his neighbours,' he said with a sigh more eloquent than words.

This must be the one person in the building whom Irina's mother had said they could trust.

'I have tried to bring Yuli from the kitchen, but the poor little one, he would not permit me. I could not take the risk that he should make a noise to attract the attention to me.'

While he plucked at his stringy beard, Kate noted his stooped stance, his old carpet-slippers, and his kindly eyes.

He glanced at the grandmother and emitted another long sigh.

Since returning to the living room, Kate and Cal hadn't bothered whispering, though they'd kept their voices low and so had the neighbour. Irina's mother must've taken a sedative after whatever had happened. Kate put a hand on the old lady's shoulder. 'It's a shame to waken her, but I'm going to have to.'

'From that sleep she will *never* awaken.'

Kate took a step backwards, registering simultaneously her own involuntary reaction to the presence of death and that Calvin had wrapped Yuli in the quilt and was gently stroking his hair. Another part of her mind was finding it remarkable that Yuli was letting him.

'There was nothing to be done when I came an hour ago to say to her my sympathy,' said the Russian. 'I had heard her screaming, and waited until it was over, and the car gone from outside. It was not for me easy, too, to listen to the bumping on the stairs – and to Irinshka's voice – ' He broke off abruptly, with a sharp, sideways movement of his head as if trying to shake off the memory, then glanced again at the old lady. 'Who would be surprised that her sick heart stopped beating when they took away her dear daughter?'

Kate stood with her fists clenched in the silence that followed, her knuckles white as the tablecloth, staring at the flickering candles. What had Irina done to deserve *this*? While anger and compassion in equal measure churned within her, the Russian began speaking of practical matters.

'I would take Yuli into my home,' he said, 'if he would permit it and if losing my job would not result from it. Also, my wife she is not strong.'

Kate remembered that the Smolenskys' trusting him had not extended to his wife. 'Your English is very good,' was all she could manage to say, with a picture of Irina being dragged from the flat shutting everything else out.

'I was, when younger, a taxi driver, and met visitors from the West. But I am now driving a bus.'

Kate eyed him warily. 'What made you give up taxi driving?'

'I had not – how do you say? – the constitution for that work.'

And if he meant he hadn't the nature to do what the Rosses had mentioned was expected of cab drivers here, that went with the Smolenskys' impression of him. She couldn't imagine many British cabbies being prepared to tape the conversation of their fares, but supposed there was no shortage of Soviet citizens who would swallow their misgivings for, as the Russian on the train had pronounced, 'the betterment of the State'.

Calvin had set Yuli, a pathetic, swaddled little bundle, on the bed by the window and was gazing down at him. He turned to look at the Russian, who was hovering in the doorway. 'We understand your problem, sir. But it isn't your responsibility to care for the child. Do the family have any friends who might?'

The man shrugged. 'At first, others like themselves used to visit them. When first they came to live here, that is. But Lev – it is hard to like him. The sound of his own voice is what he

123

likes best to hear. Soon, nobody came any longer.' Another of his sighs followed. 'I have always been sorry for Irinshka.'

And he must be fond of Irina, Kate registered, or why had he called her by a pet-name?

'If you will now to excuse me, I must return to my wife.'

He was gone before they had time to reply, leaving them with no advice other than his initial warning that it would be best for them to leave.

Best for whom? thought Kate, looking from the dead woman to the pitiful child. She exchanged a glance with Calvin who was still stroking Yuli's hair, and knew that he, too, was thinking that in their countries, if you found a body you'd call the police; who, when necessary, would arrange for the temporary care of a child. But none of this could happen at home, nor were the police a front for what they were here. And the last thing Irina would want was the KGB "caring for" *her* child.

Kate knelt down beside Yuli. 'Nobody is going to hurt you, sweetheart.' What would he do if she kissed his cheek? She'd better not try. But he let her touch it. 'I noticed a wardrobe in the lobby, Cal. See if you can find anything warm in it for Yuli to wear. When I left here last night, he had on a sweater Barbara had brought for his mum, but it's probably on the back of some KGB man's girlfriend by now. I hope she's allergic to Shetland wool and is covered with a rash when he strips it off her!'

'Your imagination knows no bounds.'

'But not about why we found Yuli shivering in his vest.'

They dressed the little boy in an assortment of shabby garments, which, with touching docility, he allowed them to do, noting his spindly arms, and that his bottom was sore from the urine.

'We ought to've washed him, Cal – '

'When I tried the hot tap it ran cold. We'd have had to boil up some water and there isn't time.'

Urgency on the child's behalf was affecting both of them, and it was as though something sinister hovered in the air. While they each put a sock on Yuli's feet, Calvin broke the silence which was becoming unbearable.

'When I saw all that broken porcelain, Kate – But that is the least of it.'

Kate was unable to reply. Those smithereens were all that remained of the beautiful teaset she had admired last night, and it must have been done deliberately. Had the cups and saucers been dropped, one at a time, before Irina's eyes, and then ground underfoot? Like saying: So much for what you treasure, and we'll do the same to your hopes.

While they were rewrapping Yuli in the quilt, Kate fondled the child's cheek again, and said to him, 'This will keep you cosy on the journey, sweetheart, and help you not to be too homesick.'

'He can't understand a word you're saying, Kate.'

'Nor can my cat, but it knows when I'm saying something kind to it from the way I say it. We can't help your poor granny, Yuli,' she added, glancing compassionately at the frail corpse, 'but we're not leaving you here all alone.'

'Come on, Kate!' Calvin led the way with Yuli in his arms, and said, as Kate shut the door behind them, 'Have you thought how deep we're getting in?'

'Thought doesn't come into it.' She was doing what her heart told her to. And so was he.

They made their way down the creaking stairs without exchanging a word. Was the man they had passed on their way in a KGB operative watching to see who entered and left? He was not there when they reached the street. But a young Russian in a black leather jacket was leaning on the wall, picking his teeth, and Kate saw his steel toothpick flash in the streetlight when he clamped it for a moment between his lips and glanced at a motor-cyclist seated astride his parked bike. The glance had been accompanied by a barely perceptible nod.

The motor-cyclist too was young, and was wearing an anorak, but their casual appearance did not deceive Kate. And right opposite the building was a limousine that matched Mr Peabody's description of the car used to collect the Rosses.

Yuli stared, wide-eyed, at the vehicle, then buried his face against Calvin. Had he stood with his nose pressed to the apartment window, watching first his father, then his mother, being driven away in a car like that one? He had still not recovered from the initial shock; how much more damaging would the second one be to his bruised mind? It would be remarkable if his tongue were *not* paralysed with fear when strangers approached him.

Outrage and apprehension were mounting within Kate, and, once again, the feeling that she must be dreaming all this. Then Calvin took her arm and she got a grip on herself.

'Now for it,' he said as they crossed the street and one of the car's windows was sleekly lowered.

'One moment, please.'

They stopped short on the cobbled road, impelled by the authoritative tone. The man who had addressed them was the driver. He switched on the light in the car and they got a glimpse of the man seated beside him, who had leaned forward and turned to look at them. If ever Kate had seen a candidate for the role of the china-smasher, this was him. If she'd met the driver in other circumstances, he could have fooled her that he was a nice, ordinary Russian. But his companion – well, Kate wouldn't want to find herself alone with him. The main reason was his snakelike eyes, she was thinking when the driver said:

'Would you tell me, please, to where you are taking that child?'

'Would you mind telling us,' Kate replied, 'where you took his mother to? And why you are suddenly so concerned about him, when you so patently weren't then?'

Typically, both questions were evaded, and the evasion served up with a smile. 'If you would be so kind as to hand him to us, we shall attend to his welfare.'

Kate retorted, 'Our interest in him has evidently made you decide that you better had. Since the story of his being left to stew – along with his sick grandmother – would do Mr Gorbachev's image no good in the foreign press.'

'An ambulance will be sent to transport the grandmother to hospital,' came the pat reply.

But the mention of Mr Gorbachev had sent the smile

126

briefly askew on the man's florid face, and his companion had paused in the act of lighting a cigarette.

They've boobed and they know it, thought Calvin, though it wouldn't be construed that way if Kate and I hadn't got into the picture. 'Make that an undertaker,' he said to them.

'A Jewish one, please,' Kate requested, 'if it's still possible to have a religious funeral in the Soviet Union.' Irina would not want her mother to be buried without the appropriate religious rites.

The driver cleared his throat, straightened his tie, and said something in Russian to his partner, before pasting the smile back on his face. 'You have my word that I shall try to arrange it.'

'And what is your word worth?' said Kate.

There was no reply, and the men in the car now embarked on a heated discussion between themselves. What this pair were now concerned with was their own skins, Kate and Calvin sensed.

They must be the officials assigned to the Smolensky case, hence the limo, Calvin thought, and the two casually clad operatives mere minnows in the KGB pond. The guys in the car were wearing overcoats and trilby hats, and they're the ones who'd have to answer to the upper echelons of their organisation if this affair did the damage Kate implied that it could.

Kate was reflecting how vast and far-reaching their organisation must be. And how faceless it *could* be. The young chap on the motor-bike reminded her of her friendly milkman at home, right down to the blue anorak; and dumpy Babushka, the floor-woman, looked no different from the housewives Kate had seen queuing for groceries in Odessa. Who, in the Soviet Union, was it safe to trust? And why are these men having such a long discussion while *we* stand here in the road! Kate wanted to tell them that they couldn't treat British and American citizens like this. But Calvin had a Russian child in his arms, and that was what the confrontation was all about. Until Yuli's fate was settled to her satisfaction, she would trust nobody.

She moved closer to Calvin, hugging her coat around her

as a gust of wind came tearing around the corner, aware of the vehicles passing behind them keeping their distance, though it was a narrow street – so would Kate if she were a Muscovite, given what a car like this, parked and with two men in it, could mean here.

Calvin interrupted the rapid flow of Russian issuing through the car window.

'It's time this little boy was in bed.'

'Then please to hand him over.'

But the spokesman's smile had gone missing.

'That is out of the question,' Kate declared.

He interpreted this for his partner, who seemed astounded, then turned as if to get out of the car. The driver put a restraining hand on his arm and a short debate followed, after which the one with the snake eyes – whom Kate had privately named Beefy Boris, since he was built like a bruiser – hid his impatience behind a cloud of smoke, while some false charm was ladled out.

'If you would like a ride to your hotel, we would gladly oblige.'

And the name for this one was Cunning Caspar. 'Not on your nelly, mate!'

It was a message which even the non-English-speaking Russian could not have missed. A moment later, the driver's window glided shut and the limousine slid away.

'They can't even drive off in a car without it seeming sinister,' Kate said with a shiver. 'But we won, didn't we, Cal?'

'For the moment.'

Kate followed his gaze. The toothpicker and the motor-cyclist were watching them, still stationed outside the apartment house.

'Let's go find a cab, Kate. I noticed one around the corner when we left the building.'

'And possibly by design. We're taking no chances, Cal.'

The taxi was still there when they turned the corner, the green light on the windshield indicating it was available; the driver was munching a sandwich, his shiny-peaked cap tipped back on his head, they glimpsed as they walked past it.

Was it there by design? 'Possibly' was the key word, and it struck Calvin then, as it had Kate a few moments ago, that they were into a situation where they would have to think twice before taking anyone or anything at face value.

'We'll forget cabs and go back by train,' he said to Kate.

'At least this time we know where we're going to,' she replied with a shaky laugh. 'But the station is a long trek for you to make carrying Yuli – '

'Do you think I give a damn about that?'

'Is he asleep?'

'Yes, I guess he is.'

They fell silent, their compassion for the child vying with the tension gripping them. Neither was fooled by the way the confrontation with the KGB men had terminated. It was not going to end there. Calvin had felt cold sweat break out on his forehead when he interrupted their discussion – and this was only the beginning. Meanwhile, they were plodding along this dark street toward the main road, their footsteps echoing as they strode the pavement, affected by the ghostly patches cast down by the meagre lamplight, keeping their eyes fixed straight ahead when they passed a clump of bushes tall enough to hide a watcher, and every passer-by, though there were few people around, serving to heighten the strain. Someone carrying a child bundled up in a bed-quilt could not be a familiar sight even in a country whose authorities had created this situation, Kate was thinking when a man getting into a car paused to look at them. Then a cat ran from a doorway and she almost jumped out of her skin. Would they never reach the metro? The street hadn't seemed this long the last time. Stop expecting someone to appear from nowhere and try to grab Yuli, Kate! But if they were going to, this would be the right setting for it. It would be over in a flash, Yuli whisked from Cal's arms and into a vehicle and we two left standing there with only our word against the KGB's about how we found him.

'There's only our word against theirs anyway,' Calvin answered when she shared her feelings with him. 'But they didn't try to grab him there and then, did they? One of them would have, but the other didn't let him – which gives food for thought, Kate.'

'That isn't stopping me from feeling scared stiff.'

They quickened their pace, Calvin painfully aware of the child held close against him, and on more counts than one. How long it now seemed since he'd felt responsible for a child. Was the guy with the toothpick following them? If so, he had let himself drop a long way behind. Neither had dared look backwards to check, as if by tacit agreement they preferred not to know, and no footsteps other than their own had been audible for some time. A black van approached and sped by.

'Do you think it was a mortuary vehicle going to collect Yuli's grandmother, Cal?'

A picture of the dead woman in the chair returned to them, and with it the feeling that they were experiencing a nightmare not yet over.

'If it was, the KGB have worked fast,' Calvin said grimly. Then a motor-bike whizzed by in the direction of the metro, whose lit-up M they could now see in the distance. 'But I'd expect them to, wouldn't you? That motor-cyclist might equally well've been the one outside the apartment house, ordered to be there when we get to the station. The two in the limo looked like they'd just have to snap their fingers to get things moving. Did you see the expression on that big guy's face when you said handing Yuli over to them was out of the question?'

Kate told him her names for them.

'And that won't be our last encounter with them, that's for sure. Nor, Kate, do I see how things can be sorted out for Yuli by you and me. His father is still awaiting trial, isn't he? Under this régime, that could go on indefinitely – '

'But they might let Irina out after a day or two,' Kate interrupted. 'When the Rosses were telling me what goes on with the refuseniks, they mentioned that the KGB sometimes do that just to frighten people. Give them a taste of prison, I mean.'

Calvin was by now prepared to believe it, but Kate had to

be made to face facts. 'I'd leave the hoping to Irina, if I were you, Kate. Meanwhile, we're taking her child to our hotel, though we haven't made it there unimpeded yet, but you had better stop kidding yourself that you can make things come right for Yuli.'

They were nearing the main road, and saw the motor-cyclist astride his parked bike outside the metro. When they entered it, he went on chewing gum without giving them a glance, though Kate had expected him to get off the bike and follow them.

'This not knowing who's going to do what, and why, is giving me the creeps, Cal!'

'Try not to let it.'

But Calvin's firm reply was at odds with his glancing around for the toothpicker, while he waited for Kate to fish in her purse for the fifty-kopek coins they must put in the slot to escape to the trains. His own hands were occupied in holding on tight to Yuli. After that nerve-wracking walk to the station, escaping was how this felt. To Kate, too; she forgot vertigo and wished that the escalators would carry her faster.

'I've never been so relieved to get on a train!' she exclaimed when they were finally aboard one, and with nobody whom they recognised in the compartment. 'It looks as if we *are* going to make it, unimpeded, to the hotel, Cal.'

'Why not let's wait and see what happens at the other end?' Calvin settled the sleeping child more comfortably on his lap. 'It isn't fair, is it, Kate? A kid is entitled to a stable homelife, and the way things're looking, this one isn't going to have one.' He paused before saying, 'I once had to make a decision in that respect. Well, given that stability covers many things, that is – '

Kate sensed from his expression that what he was recalling had been distressing and still was.

'The conditions attached to my being granted visitation rights to my son were such that I couldn't accept them. What it amounted to was I could have Gary with me on alternate weekends provided I kept my "tendencies" from him. By then I was living with Sandy, and my ex-wife made sure the custody court judge knew it. And how I saw it, Kate, was if a

131

guy can't be honest with his own son – well, what chance is there for their relationship when the boy reaches the age of perception? I turned the offer down.'

Another snippet of Cal's past, thought Kate. And what a choice for a father to have to make.

'I haven't seen Gary since he was Yuli's size,' Calvin said brusquely. 'It wasn't too long before Lori married a Texan, which made it easier for me not to see him.'

'How old is he now?'

'I was twenty-three when he was born. I guess that makes him thirteen.'

'The same age as my Emily, and I can already chat to her about anything and everything.'

'If that's your way of telling me that Gary is now old enough to accept the truth about his dad – well, he hasn't been raised by a mom like you, Kate. On the contrary. My guess is that by now his mother's attitudes will've rubbed off on him. But there's nothing I can do about that. The crazy thing is that I took the decision I did with my eye on the future relationship he and I are never going to have. What Lori plants in him will have killed the chance.'

Though Calvin's tone was somewhat bitter, Kate did not get the impression that he hated his ex-wife, and wondered why, in view of what he was bit by bit revealing. She eyed his profile and noted again its well-bred quality, and his air of quiet strength. Cal was reliability personified, but without the dullness that sometimes went with it. He was caring, too, and perhaps incapable of hatred. A person who weighed up everything as carefully as he did, be it past, present, or future, could not fail to see the overall perspective, including his own contribution to success or failure. With regard to his broken marriage and consequent separation from his son, there was no way he wouldn't hold responsible, in some part, his being bisexual – even though *he* could not be held responsible for how Nature made him.

Briefly the tension had gone from them and they exchanged a smile.

'Feeling power-drunk, Kate, because we've got this far?'

'I am, a bit.'

'Me, too. But it won't be allowed to last.'

Kate glanced around at their fellow-passengers, in whose hearing she was careful not to utter the dreaded initials. 'What are you expecting *them* to do next?'

'A better question would be what do *we* do next? What you said about thought not coming into us taking Yuli with us mustn't be allowed to cloud *all* your reasoning, Kate.'

Kate brushed a lock of Yuli's hair from his forehead. Irina must be beside herself with anxiety about him.

'Reasoning involves facts,' Calvin went on, 'and fact number-one is – '

'Asleep on your lap,' Kate cut in, 'a child who has nobody but us right now to look after him. I shall ask to be allowed to visit his mother, though I doubt they'll let me, to tell her we've got him. Meanwhile, and even if I manage to see Irina, I am not handing Yuli over to the people responsible for his plight!'

'Cool it, Kate.'

'I'm seeing this a lot more coolly than you suppose, and looking ahead to what would probably happen to Yuli if they got their hands on him. Where else would they put him but in one of their Children's Homes, where the kids are raised to be perfect Soviet citizens; and that would, by my reckoning, include instilling in him contempt for his religion – '

'Okay, you've made your point,' Calvin interrupted, 'but don't the Smolenskys have any family who would take care of Yuli?'

'Only some relations in Israel. And from what their neighbour said, nor do they have any close friends here. So fact number-two, Cal, is that if Irina and Lev are imprisoned for long enough, a great deal of damage could be done to their son – and I don't mean physically. If I can find a way to prevent it, I shall. Shcharansky was held prisoner for about nine years, and it took pressure from the entire free world to get justice for *him*, though he'd become a household name. Who's even heard of Irina and Lev Smolensky? Have you ever been to a Bar Mitzvah, Cal?'

'Sure. Sandy's nephew had one, last year. How did Bar Mitzvahs get into this conversation?'

'Irina is hoping for Yuli to have his in Israel.'

Kate noticed that the curious glances of others in the compartment were lasting longer than those she had received on her other train journeys here, and averted her gaze from the middle-aged couple seated opposite who were surveying Yuli's quilt. As she'd reflected on the walk to the station, the picture they presented was no ordinary sight. Tension gripped her again. Even if nobody stops us from getting that far, how are we to get Yuli into the hotel?

'There's something we hadn't yet thought of, Cal: Yuli hasn't got a pass.'

'If you'll forgive the cliché, we'll cross that bridge if and when we come to it.' Calvin launched into a description of Sandy's nephew's Bar Mitzvah party to distract Kate from the anxiety he could see in her expression, and said finally, 'It was one of the fanciest parties I've ever been to.'

Kate made herself smile. 'It's a good thing Alun and I shan't be required to make that kind of splash for Jason; we couldn't afford to. Not that I'm pleading poverty, but we don't have cash to toss around. I was against our moving to a larger house – we'd be paying off the mortgage till we're old and grey if my gran hadn't died and left me a surprising windfall – but Alun had just got a rise, and delusions of grandeur with it!'

Why am I telling Calvin all this? she was asking herself when he dropped a pebble into the pond. For thus it seemed; and the pond was Kate's complacency.

'Alun told Sandy that if he had the cash, he'd go into business for himself. But you probably know that one of the women he works with suggested they might one day open up a pharmacy together.'

'As a matter of fact I didn't.'

And how odd it was to find out from an American, on a Moscow train. Kate sat listening to the rumble of the wheels. Ought she to ask Alun about it when she got home? What was the point, when he was never going to have enough money to do it. The train slowed, and halted at a station. Her gaze shifted to the door, as it had at the previous stop; passengers got off and others boarded, but again there was nobody recognisable among them; a young couple sat down opposite as the journey was resumed, their curiosity as evident as that of the older people they had replaced, Kate registered with her mind still on what she had just learned about Alun. Why hadn't he told her? Owning a chemist shop was poles apart from what her husband's dream had once been. A vision of the lad in rugger togs she had in her youth watched running with the ball at a match was vying with the one that Calvin's revelation conjured up, of Alun penned in behind a counter. It wasn't a life Kate could imagine for him, though apparently *he* could. Was that proof that he had changed out of all recognition from the person she'd married? Are you still the same person *he* married, Kate? Of course not. But for both of us, that's probably the harvest you have to reap when you sow your seeds too soon and too young, she reflected while casting her mind over the range of Alun's female colleagues. Only two of whom had been there long enough to have suggested what he had repeated to Sandy on the cruise. Both were attractive, one unmarried and the other recently divorced. Which of them was it – and what was she really after?

Yuli coughed in his sleep, returning her mind to a matter more pressing than the one to which Calvin had innocently alerted her, and she thought of the Sabbath candles still burning bright when they left the flat, like Irina's hopes for her son and for her unborn child. Was there any chance of those hopes materialising? Though Calvin thought not, Kate wouldn't allow herself to share his pessimism. Why was he nudging her?

The train had reached another station. Kate froze. Among those who boarded was the toothpicker.

'Think the bloke on the motor-bike zipped to get him and he rode pillion to catch up with us along our route?' she said with bravado. He had remained beside the door and she was trying not to look at him. Ready for when we get off, at the next stop.

'Whatever,' Calvin replied, 'we're dealing with experts,

Kate, and we had better not forget it. Also, the looking ahead you said you were doing, and went on at length about, seems to have leap-frogged over the immediate future. How do you intend playing things if they let us hang on to Yuli overnight?'

'Off the cuff.'

When the train stopped, Kate brushed past the KGB operative with her gaze fixed ahead and Calvin directly behind her, prattling away nonchalantly about how she'd had to get her kitchen ceiling repainted after a burst from the bathroom pipes, above.

'In England the worst of the winter came in February this year, Cal,' she chattered on, while they made their way to the escalators.

Not many people had alighted at this stop. It was necessary to walk through a long tunnel, as at some stations on the Tube at home, its hollowness compounding the eerie echo of footsteps, and the harsh lighting seeming, right now, no less sinister than the darkness through which they had plodded earlier.

'Do you get bad winters in Boston, Cal?' He had not said a word and was tramping beside her, his expression set, the child in his arms and a corner of the quilt trailing to his knees. The toothpicker was behind them and they both knew it. And the tunnel seemed endless; like a scene in a film when you sat biting your nails till whoever it was got to the other end, Kate thought, while she went on proving that the weather was a useful topic when you couldn't bear the silence.

'The crocus in my garden seem able to withstand the frost if the sun lures them into sprouting too soon,' she was saying when they turned out of the tunnel and made for the ascending escalator. Her shoulder-bag felt sticky from her hand sweating while she held on to it. Some nonchalance, Kate! And we're not where we're heading for *yet*.

While they walked from the metro station to the hotel, aware of the man behind them, Calvin was not sure whether to envy Alun Starling, or pity him. What must it be like to live with someone who met whatever came along with Kate's

136

devil-may-care verve – and relied upon you to serve as ballast when your good sense deemed it necessary? Kate being the cautious one about putting down mortgage cash had to be the exception that proved the rule.

Cal was coming to realise that 'off the cuff' was how Kate played most things; the opposite from how he did, and, it seemed, a deal more successful. Apart from her discontent professionally, which it wasn't too late to set right, she appeared to have sailed painlessly through life. The difference he had detected in her since they last met seemed but added bloom on the rose, with nary a sign of blight, he thought lyrically. Was he falling in love with her? Too true he was. And if a single day with her had led him to that conclusion, what would his sorry state be by the end of the week?

The toothpicker followed them as far as the hotel entrance, from where he watched them present their passes to the porter, who cast not a glance at the child Calvin was carrying. The guard standing by seemed equally unobservant.

'That's one hurdle over,' Calvin said as they made their way toward the desk, where a group just returned from an evening at the theatre was queuing to collect room keys. 'And I guess those guys on the door had to've been primed for our arrival.'

'It tells us something about how "they" are playing it,' Kate replied. 'They could have stopped us from bringing Yuli in, and all three of us would've been without a place to sleep. I wonder why they didn't.'

'Don't let's get *too* power-drunk.'

They sat down on one of the velvet banquettes, in what seemed an oasis of affluence in a land of austerity. Calvin aired that opinion to Kate.

'To me it's more like being in a leper colony,' she replied, conscious of Yuli coughing while he slept, and of how fragile the little boy looked. 'But it's freedom the Kremlin would say we're suffering from and Soviet citizens must be protected from.'

Kate glanced at some people who were waiting for the lift

and eyeing them as the Russians had on the train. One woman met Kate's gaze and quickly averted her own. Were those in the key queue staring at them, too? Yes, they were – but why wouldn't they? This was a tourist hotel and they didn't expect to get back from the theatre, or wherever, and see two of their fellow-tourists sitting on a banquette with a child dressed like a ragamuffin, whom they had just unwrapped from a shabby bed-quilt. Kate smiled at an elderly Australian woman whom she had seen at a nearby table in the dining-room, and the smile was returned, but seemed cautious. Steering clear of anything out of the ordinary was an instinctive reaction for foreigners in the Soviet Union. And these people didn't know what had happened to Yuli, did they? Kate could imagine the motherly looking Australian woman having tears in her eyes when she found out.

'Let's go tag on to the end of the line,' Calvin said, rising as the queue for keys decreased.

'I was about to come over and say hi to you,' a friendly voice greeted them. 'I was just saying to Brad that one person handing out keys isn't enough when a large party gets back at night from an outing.'

The girl at the desk overheard the remark, and replied, 'It is usual that two of us are here for the convenience of our guests. But this evening has occurred a small emergency.'

Kate exchanged a glance with Calvin: was the small emergency the child he was carrying? At whom the receptionist had carefully not looked. Was it 'all hands on deck' for whatever the KGB were up to? Kate wondered, while Calvin introduced her to the young American couple she had assessed as bank clerks or something of the sort.

'Going to tell us who the cute kid is, Cal?'

'Allow me to, Connie,' said Kate. 'His name is Yuli, and his mother's a nice Russian Jewish girl the KGB have just arrested. His father's been in prison for a few weeks.'

'Who is next please for their key?' said the receptionist, as if she hadn't heard what Kate had said and did not know why a sudden hush had fallen beside the desk.

'Without going into details too distressing to describe,'

138

Kate went on, 'no decent human being would have left Yuli where and how we found him. He now has nobody to take care of him but us, and that's what we're doing. Would *you* have let the KGB have him, Connie, after what they've done to him and his family?'

'I sure wouldn't, nor would Brad.'

'This isn't our business, honey,' her husband said uncomfortably.

'But did you ever see a more pitiful sight than that kid?'

Brad remained silent, but the Australian woman said to her husband, 'Poor little shaver needs fattening up with some of my cooking, doesn't he, Jack?'

'Let's just get our key and call it a night, shall we, Doris?'

As if by common accord, all but Connie and Doris had returned their attention to the desk, where the receptionist was carefully scrutinising passes before handing out the keys. Kate saw Brad take Connie's arm and turn her away, as the Australian had done with his wife, and the two men began chatting about their evening at the Bolshoi Theatre, though their wives remained silent.

'How did the ballet grab you, Brad?'

'It isn't my scene, but I guess I was impressed.'

'Mine, neither. The missus's never managed to get me inside the Sydney Opera House, but us going to the Bolshoi'll be something to tell the grandkids, won't it, Doris? 'N stop turning to look at that poor little Russian, will you, love?'

'I can't help it, Jack.'

'I know what you mean,' Connie said to her, glancing again at Yuli.

'Not that us two looking at him will do him any good,' Doris said compassionately.

'My motto is play safe,' her husband declared, ''n that means minding my own business 'n keeping my lips buttoned.'

The Australian would wait till he and his wife were safe at home before voicing anything that could be construed as criticism of the Soviet régime, though an aspect of its inhumanity was plain from Yuli's presence. But Kate was

139

wrong to consider him unsympathetic, and the same went for Brad and the others who had listened to her brief explanation. Nevertheless, their message to me and Cal is loud and clear: Only a foolhardy foreigner would step out of line in the Soviet Union.

Do they think we don't know it? she thought, watching the lanky old Australian escort his tiny wife to the lift. But there were times when you didn't stop to consider the possible consequences of your actions, and tonight had been like that for Kate. Nor did she intend thinking of it now. Cal and I, after all our talk about the stowaway, let things slide, but this time the future of a child is at stake. Kate didn't know how far Cal was prepared to go, but she would fight tooth and nail.

Connie and Brad said goodnight and left. Kate and Calvin were next at the desk, and with nobody but themselves now waiting to collect their key. Or to hear the receptionist tell them that Yuli couldn't stay here. Was this what the KGB had instructed her to do? Was the plan, and the men in the limousine surely had one, to let them get this far and think they'd got away with it, then present them with the prospect of having to spend the night, with Yuli, on a bench in Gorky Park – if they didn't give in? There was only one way to find out, Kate thought in the split second she hesitated before addressing the girl at the desk.

'I had better inform you that the second bed in my room is about to be occupied,' she said, showing her pass while Calvin was still fishing in his pocket for his. 'Would you like me to take Yuli while you do that, Cal? What a lot of junk you carry around with you,' she made herself remark casually when he shook his head, and his hand emerged clutching several slips of paper and a couple of luggage labels with strings attached to them. She took the hotel pass from between the luggage labels and put it on the desk beside her own.

The girl went to fetch their keys from the board behind her.

'I presume you heard what I said to you?' Kate said when she returned with them.

'All the furniture in your room is at your disposal,' was her reply.

'Then if you'll hand me a pen, I'll sign the child in. His name is Yuli Smolensky,' she added crisply, because the receptionist was still avoiding looking at him, 'as I'm sure you already know.'

'Only official guests of the hotel are required to register.'

'Then let's make it official,' said Calvin. 'He'll be eating with us in the restaurant, too, and you may charge his meals to me.'

Though this was not the girl with whom Kate had clashed this morning – if clashing with someone in whom you evoke no reaction could be called that – her demeanour might have been cloned from that of her colleague. Once again, Kate wanted to swipe the charming mask, or stick a pin in it to make her yelp, though she doubted that it would raise blood.

'In the Soviet Union, foreign visitors do not pay for the board and lodgings of Soviet citizens,' she replied to Calvin.

This was the first direct answer they had received from anyone employed at the hotel, and, delivered so smoothly, it must have been rehearsed.

'You seem to have been prepared for us bringing the child,' Kate tried to provoke her.

'And do you mean the extra expense will be waived?' Calvin inquired.

'It is not possible to charge for someone who is not here, Mr Fenner.'

Another direct answer, and one that told them how the KGB intended handling the matter. For the moment. But Kate was not going to play this their way. 'How can you say someone isn't here, when you can see that they are?' she demanded.

'Did you not hear me before say to you that only official guests of the hotel are required to sign in?' came the bland rejoinder. 'The child, he is not *officially* here.'

'And that's the word that counts, is it? Well, I have to tell you that Mr Fenner and I have never in our lives encountered anything quite so chilling as Soviet officialdom and its consequences for mere human beings. And you may rest

141

assured that we shall be enlisting the aid of our two embassies, with regard to *this* little human being,' Kate added, though the idea of doing so had just entered her head.

'I am just a hotel receptionist, Mrs Starling.'

'But if you'd care to relay my sentiments to the KGB – which you surely would without my requesting it – I'd be much obliged.'

'I, personally, am very fond of children.'

Kate and Calvin exchanged a glance. Was it possible that she was telling them she was only doing her job?

'All Soviet citizens are fond of children,' she seemed to think it necessary to correct herself.

Kate looked her straight in the eye. 'Then why is this child in the position he is?'

The girl busied herself with some papers on the desk. 'To me, he appears comfortably asleep.'

They were back with the evasiveness. But, though Kate was reluctant to admit it, it had just been revealed to them that a flesh-and-blood person, with feelings like anyone else, lived behind the mask.

The foyer was by now entirely deserted, and all about them, as they picked up their keys and left the desk, was an air of late-night desolation peculiar to large hotels. Kate could hear the clack of her heels in the silence, which heightened the feeling that she and Calvin were alone in a vast arena where sinister foes lurked on every side, girding themselves for a battle there was no way of winning.

'What we're doing amounts to banging our heads on a brick wall!' she exclaimed.

'Let's stick with the Kremlin wall, and prepare ourselves to be swatted,' Calvin replied.

Kate stepped into the lift ahead of him and pressed the third-floor button. 'Our being deported is certainly on the cards, Cal. But I'd say we've increased in importance from the nuisance category Mr Peabody talked of. We've seen an aspect of Soviet society few Westerners see for themselves. And we're in possession of the evidence,' she added, tucking the quilt, which was trailing on the floor, tenderly around it.

In repose, the terror was gone from the small, wan face, but sorrow seemed to be with him while he slumbered.

'He looks like a weary little old man,' said Kate. 'Nobody has the right to do that to a child. And I'm not going to give him up till I'm sure that he won't just be dumped. They'd have to shoot me first.'

Kate's expression was steely, and she was again clenching her fists.

'I guess the guys in the car had time to figure you're no pushover, Kate. And me neither. That we don't frighten easily.'

'I was petrified.'

'But you didn't show it. And I have the feeling that Cunning Caspar, who struck me as the brains tempering his partner's brawn, would like to keep their assignment as low-key as possible.'

'Well, they wouldn't want it getting into the international press, would they? – though I admit I made that remark about Mr Gorbachev's image off the top of my head. Think of the headlines, Cal: "American man and British woman kicked out of Russia for – "'

'I can fill in the rest myself,' Calvin cut in. 'And that has to be why they didn't just snatch Yuli and put us on a plane out of here.'

'Why they're lying low.'

'Biding their time, you mean. Playing cat-and-mouse with us.'

Kate managed not to shudder. 'Could we stay with the swatted-fly analogy, Cal? Horrible though it is, I think I prefer it to what you just conjured up,' she said, trying to smile. The need to ask herself if this was really happening was gone. She only had to look at Yuli to know that what had rendered him homeless was for people like the Smolenskys a fact of life.

'But all this is only theory, isn't it, Kate? The sole certainty is that the crunch must eventually come, one way or another. In the meantime, they may sit tight and hope we'll hand Yuli over without a fuss.'

Kate glanced again at the Russian child, for whom she

and Calvin could be but a temporary haven. 'What assurances could they possibly give us about Yuli's welfare that we could believe?'

'Then we're talking deadlock, Kate.'

'And I am as capable of sitting tight as they are.'

The lift juddered to a halt. As they stepped out Babushka shifted her gaze to the spittoon-like ashtray.

Kate commanded her attention. 'Had a busy evening, Babushka?'

'Sleep well, madam.'

But would they be allowed to? Apprehension had its way with Kate again. The deathly quiet as they began treading the long corridor to their rooms did nothing to assuage it. Caspar and Boris could be behind one of the doors we have to pass, couldn't they, ready to open it and grab us, while everyone else is asleep. Stop it, will you, Kate!

She was aware of Calvin plodding along silently beside her. Was he thinking what she was? 'Your arms must be numb from holding him all this time, but you've said no each time I've offered.'

'Suffice to say he's re-aroused my paternal instinct.'

Since his tone was brusque, Kate said no more, and it struck her that his way of dealing with inconvenient emotions was to wrap them up so tightly that they were in danger of being strangulated. Was he doing so with what *she* aroused in him, after allowing it to briefly emerge? If so, it was just as well, and she must do the same with regard to him.

'That sentinel-in-a-skirt acted like she hadn't seen Yuli, which has to mean the hotlines must've been buzzing all around the hotel tonight, relaying the current strategy,' he remarked.

Kate stifled a yawn, her body at odds with her mind, which she doubted would allow her to sleep. 'You've finally accepted what Babushka is, have you?'

'Too true I have. Like the female functionary downstairs, she's what one might call a minor cog in a wheel within wheels. Did you meet anyone yet, in this whole bizarre exercise, beginning with our inquiries about the Rosses' sudden departure, who struck you as having a mind of their own?'

'Taking it at face value, no,' Kate replied. 'But I had to ask myself why the girl at the desk inserted into her set speech that she's fond of children. It was the nearest thing to a personal opinion about what's happened to Yuli that she'd risk voicing.'

'I guess "risk" is the right word. I am coming to believe, Kate, that if what oils the wheels of the system is ideology, it's something else that keeps them turning. Bigger cogs than those we've encountered are known to've been removed. When you mentioned Gorbachev to Caspar – who must know a thing or two about Soviet methods of cog-removal – for a split second fear was written on his face, and there's no more powerful fuel.'

'You seem to have forgotten what makes the world go round.'

And this was a good time to let love slip his mind, he thought as they entered Kate's room.

She watched him put Yuli gently on the spare bed, and take off his outdoor garments.

'He needs kitting out with warm clothes, Cal. Tomorrow, we'll go and buy him some. You don't have to come shopping with us if you'd rather not.'

'Let's get one clear, Kate. You're not venturing anywhere with Yuli without me until all this is resolved. Bright and brave you might be, but built for heavyweight action you're not.'

'Nobody could call that a character assassination. And given the picture you just conjured up, it might be a good idea to open the connecting door between our rooms, in case I get an official visit in the night.'

Calvin inspected the door to the corridor. The lock was the usual swivel kind which could be opened with a master-key. But in this hotel, there was no accompanying chain or bolt for extra security against the uninvited, he noted.

'Don't forget to unbolt your side,' Kate said as he dealt with hers, 'and we'll keep the door ajar. Anyone who's interested is welcome to know they have you to contend with, as well as me, twenty-four hours a day,' she added. She had not forgotten the possible bug – and why not make use of it?

'They're equally welcome to know I'm a light sleeper,' said Calvin, appreciating the irony of the situation. When he'd let himself imagine their opening up that door, the purpose was far removed from the present reality.

After settling herself in bed, Kate lay looking at the child whose future hung in the balance. It would be foolish of her not to accept how heavily the scales were weighted against him; and how wrong it seemed that Life should be so cruel to him and smile benevolently upon her own children. Barbara had warned her against making such comparisons, but it was easier to say than to carry through, as Barbara herself knew.

Nor could Kate stop herself from thinking of Irina, lying awake in a prison cell, without even the comfort of knowing that a friend was looking after Yuli, and would go on doing so for as long as she could. As long as I can, sums it up. When Kate's visa was no longer valid, time would have run out. What could be done between now and then? Sitting tight needn't also mean standing idle. There were the British and US embassies to appeal to, for a start – which I haven't yet discussed with Cal since tossing the idea like a ball at that girl. Needless to say, she didn't pick it up.

Kate's thoughts continued back and forth, dizzying her mind until sleep allowed her some peace. When Yuli suddenly cried out, she had no idea where she was or, momentarily, who he was. Then Calvin was in the room, switching on the lamp and comforting the child.

Neither was surprised that the first sound they had heard issue from his lips was a scream.

Chapter Six

Kate had wanted to take Yuli into her bed for what remained of the night, as she had with Emily and Jason when they were small and had occasionally suffered childish nightmares. But the little boy had clung to Calvin, and had ended up in *his* bed.

The next morning when Kate was shepherding him towards her bathroom, he indicated by pointing in Calvin's direction where his preference still lay.

'I think you've just been elected to bath and dress him, Cal,' she said, through the doorway between the rooms.

The door had been wide open since Yuli's scream brought Calvin to his bedside and, given the new circumstances, was likely to remain so. Meanwhile, both were suddenly conscious of their attire – or lack of it.

Why do I feel more undressed in my nightie than I did in my bikini, when we sunbathed alongside each other on board ship? thought Kate.

'Without make-up, and the way your hair's all rumpled, you look about seventeen,' Calvin remarked.

'And your chest is a lot more hairy than I remember from when we swam together.'

'Well, you're now seeing it minus sun lotion and pool water.'

Calvin felt like reaching for his pyjama jacket, and Kate for her dressing-gown, hairbrush and eye-liner. Then Yuli stationed himself in the doorway and glanced questioningly from one to the other.

'If he could understand English, I'd think he was wondering why we were standing here having that absurd conversation,' said Kate.

'And I guess the answer is we're not used to living *en famille*.'

That's one way of putting it, thought Kate. 'Think you can cope with bathing Yuli?'

'I'm somewhat out of practice, but here goes!'

He lifted the little boy and set him astride his shoulders, then galloped off with him to the bathroom as if they were playing horse-and-rider. Was that a hint of a smile she had just seen on Yuli's face?

For Cal, this must feel like being catapulted backward in time, to when a kid was part of his life, she reflected while she was showering. As for Yuli, this morning, though still unnaturally silent, he was behaving like a child; picking and choosing who he wanted to attend to his needs, like our children once did, with Alun and me. For the moment, that pathetic, little-old-man look was gone. Kindness from the strangers now caring for him, and the warmth and comfort of his new surroundings, must be responsible. But he would not be restored to normality while the element of long-term security remained missing.

When would this child see his parents again? And they see each other and him? Splitting up refusenik families was a KGB tactic employed to break their spirit. Nor was this inhuman device applied only to those considered trouble-makers, like Lev Smolensky; or arrest the sole method of ensuring the damaging separation.

Howard and Barbara had spoken of the broken families they had sometimes visited, Kate recalled, while she dressed in the privacy of her bathroom, though Calvin hadn't yet emerged from his with their small charge. What was he doing in there, all this time? Floating a sponge, or his soap-box, in the bath to try to make Yuli really smile? If such a thing was available in the stores outside this artificial oasis of plenty, they must buy Yuli a celluloid duck, for the bathtimes that were part of family life for parents and their young children. One of the children the Rosses had mentioned was still too young to bath himself when his mother and sister received exit visas and were obliged to leave for Israel immediately. He was now ten, and he and his father were still waiting. Their visas, though promised, had not been granted.

Kate returned to the bedroom to brush her hair, and found herself doing so with angry strokes. Yesterday, in Gorky Park, Calvin had referred to what they'd been drawn into as a game; and a cruel, waiting game was what Kate now knew it to be, one in which the authorities held all the cards but one. Though the lengthy separations they had engineered for numerous refusenik families had, in a few cases resulted in divorce, hope continued to burn in those who waited. Kate had found it remarkable that Irina was able to sustain hers without her husband's support, and she would surely find it even harder to do so now she had been parted from her child.

Kate willed herself to stop thinking about Irina, and set her mind to practical matters. The best that Cal and I can do for Yuli is try to get him settled in the care of compassionate people. But if, as their neighbour had more than implied, the Smolenskys were loners, how were such people to be found? Kate had never been more afflicted with the feeling that her hands were tied. Howard had said the refusenik community did what they could to help each other, but that was no help to Kate, since he wasn't here to contact those of them he knew. And what made her think the KGB would be amenable to her idea of a suitable home for Yuli? That would be letting you win, wouldn't it? Don't ever forget the face-saving element, Kate.

But if the embassies were to intervene — A child was a child, whatever crimes its parents had been accused of, and if Western diplomats kicked up a fuss . . . On Soviet soil the answer, like the if, was a great big question mark.

Calvin brought Yuli from the bathroom cocooned in a towel, and put the clothing he had taken off him on a chair. 'Though I'm going to have to temporarily, I hate to put those things back on him, Kate. Not only has he slept in them, they're a disgrace.'

We've begun bobbing in and out of each other's rooms without a second thought, she registered, while folding Yuli's quilt which she had found lying in a heap beside

Calvin's bed. 'But it won't be himself he's disgracing, when we take him into the dining-room for breakfast,' she replied. 'Nor us because he'll be with us, wearing the clothing Irina's done her best to make wearable. What it's a disgrace to is the "great Soviet society" that friendly man on the train was spouting about – to a couple of tourists he didn't know were up to their necks in the unseen side of it.'

'I wouldn't say we were up to our necks at that stage. And you've decided to give him the benefit of the doubt about the possible walkie-talkie, have you?' Calvin added with a reminiscent grin. 'You no longer suspect he was on official business?'

'I don't think one can ever be sure about that with anyone here, Cal, though I wish I could believe he was just a nice portly Russian on his way home from the office. And that I'd had the nerve to ask him how he could be so proud of a régime that inflicts the hardship it does upon those it impels, for religious reasons, to want to say goodbye to it.'

'There must be lots of decent, ordinary folk here who are sickened by what goes on in that respect,' Calvin replied.

'But they're never going to raise their voices and say so, are they? – given what might happen to them if they did. You were dead right about what keeps the wheels of the system turning, Cal. Aren't you going to comb Yuli's hair?'

Calvin fetched a comb from his dressing table, but Yuli took it from him and handed it to Kate.

'What's the betting his dad never did it as gently as his mom did?' Calvin said. 'And that his mom didn't let him splash water all over the place when he was in the bathtub?'

'Are you saying he's begun seeing you and me in those roles?'

'Association is how I'd put it, Kate.'

Kate sat Yuli on Calvin's bed, and combed his hair more gently than she bothered being after she had shampooed Jason's.

'I've changed my mind about just sitting tight,' she told Calvin. 'And while you two were romping in the bathroom, I did some practical thinking. Last night, I was too shocked and zonked to muster any useful thoughts.'

Calvin still felt in no state to do so. Attending to a small child again had set him privately licking his reopened wound. It brought home to him forcefully that Gary's childhood was almost gone, without his father having shared in its ups and downs. A boy going on fourteen would, in no time at all, be a young man.

He was ordering himself to stop mourning those lost years when Kate interrupted his thoughts.

'Yuli hasn't been coughing as much this morning, Cal; have you noticed?'

'Well, he's in a warm atmosphere, isn't he?'

'Too warm for me.'

'Don't you have central heating in England?'

'England isn't still in the Dark Ages! But we don't keep our homes like hothouses, and nor are public buildings kept as hot as this.'

'I did hear the phlegm rolling around on Yuli's chest while I was bathing him, Kate. Think we should try to get a doctor take a look at him?'

'If we weren't where we are, that's the first thing I'd do with a child in his state,' Kate replied, surveying the small, pale face and the dark shadows beneath the eyes that had a dulled look in them. Giving him vitamins would help restore their shine, but it would take more than that to brighten his expression. 'There must be some English and American doctors in Moscow whom tourists can consult if they fall ill, like anywhere abroad,' she went on. 'Jason once got a tummy upset in Spain that the medicine we had with us didn't put right. It wasn't an English doctor the hotel called for us – but when he arrived we didn't have to ask ourselves was he the real thing, or if what he prescribed for Jason might be – '

'Okay, Kate. Say no more – though that last bit sounds far-fetched even in these circumstances.'

Kate wanted to explain that she wasn't implying poison,

that she wasn't *that* melodramatic, but was inhibited by their being in a room they knew must be bugged – and whose imagination wouldn't run riot in the situation they'd got themselves into? Yet she wouldn't put it past the KGB to dope Yuli, so they could cart him off without his screams rending the air.

'And what makes you think a doctor from your country, or mine, would let themselves get dragged into this?' she asked Calvin. 'They're foreigners, like us, and I don't see them getting on the wrong side of the people we've been dealing with.'

'Then what do we do about Yuli's cough?' Calvin returned them to the point, as the little boy again illustrated that he needed medication.

'I noticed some honey among the little packs of jam on the breakfast table, yesterday,' Kate recalled, 'so when we go down to the restaurant, we'll pinch a few, and help ourselves to a lemon from that big basket of fruit I saw people taking apples from, last night. I thought, Who's going to take a lemon, that they must be there for colour, but we are. A piece of lemon with honey on it was what my gran used to give me if I had a cough when I was staying with her.'

Kate was gently massaging Yuli's shoulders, while she spoke, and said when the child's lengthy coughing bout was over, 'Immediately after breakfast, I'll call my embassy, and you must call yours, Cal. In the meantime, everyone in the dining-room will be faced with the evidence. Connie and Brad, and that Australian couple are bound to spread the word about why we're looking after him.'

'I don't recall the stowaway rumour having any lasting effects.'

'But Yuli will be before their eyes, won't he?'

'If you're expecting a protest march to Red Square, Kate, you're due for a disappointment.'

They became aware that Yuli was again glancing from one to the other of them, but this time more anxiously than questioningly, as if he sensed that something serious concerning himself was being discussed.

Kate gave him a hug, to reassure him. 'Nevertheless, Cal, ruffling the complacency most people from free countries wear like a second skin, as I used to, wouldn't come amiss.'

If they had rehearsed Yuli's entrance it could not have been more effective, and an entrance in the theatrical sense it was, since they were late for breakfast and their fellow-tourists already seated. While they led him to their table at the far side of the room, he kept glancing trustfully up at them.

Was Yuli's timidity as upsetting to the onlookers as it was to Kate? Or were those she saw put down their cups and stare at him merely noticing his poverty-stricken appearance? Why can't I just take him home to England with me? Look after him myself, until he gets his mum and dad back? Or, since Irina would want him to stay with a Jewish family, hand him to the willing arms of Barbara Ross? Though Kate hadn't known the Rosses for long, she had no doubt that they would take him. The answer to your emotional 'Why?', Kate, is that this is the Soviet Union, or Yuli would still have his mum and dad.

Daphne's frosty mother dropped her fork to her plate, when Calvin put a chair for Yuli at the head of the table, set him in it, and took his own place opposite Kate.

'Where did you get that child from? He's surely not British!'

'No, as a matter of fact,' said Kate. 'Though given the unemployment at home, especially up north, there must be plenty of British kids whose diet is deficient, and who never get new clothes.'

Daphne fiddled with the string of pearls she was again wearing, though with a different cashmere twinset, and said apologetically, 'Mother never watches the television, nor does she read the newspapers.'

'My life is depressing enough.'

'Then be thankful,' said Kate crisply, 'that ours is a country where nobody loses their livelihood for the reason this child's family did.'

While Kate explained that Yuli was homeless, and why, Calvin fed him cottage cheese and hardboiled egg, and watched him get through all the milk in the jug. By the time Kate had finished speaking, during which she ate not a bite herself, and nor did Calvin, Yuli was tucking into bread and butter, thickly spread with jam.

'One would think the child had never seen food before,' said Daphne quietly.

'Well I doubt that he remembers the last time he ate what we'd call a real meal,' Kate replied.

Calvin was too affected by the little boy's enjoyment of this treat to speak. Nor was he unaware that the Australian couple, seated nearby, were trying not to see it.

Before she and her daughter departed, Daphne's mother introduced herself as Mrs Caldwell, and wished them luck in their endeavours.

'From that lady, that was really something,' said Calvin.

'And, in a way, it makes me feel stronger,' said Kate.

A moment later, Connie came to their table. 'Brad is going to have to accept some time that I'm a liberated woman,' she said without preamble, 'and it may as well be now. If you need anything, call me, okay? We're in Room 609.'

When she had gone, Kate said to Calvin, 'Not just stronger, Cal. Warmer. As if a breath of the air I'm used to breathing has softened the chill. Write that room number down. You never know.'

She wiped the jam off Yuli's chin and poured them some coffee.

'Don't let him overdo it, Kate,' said Calvin, when Yuli picked up a spoon to help himself to more cottage cheese. 'We don't want him getting sick to his stomach.'

'I think I'll let you do the disciplining.'

'Like Lori used to, when Gary needed the iron hand.' He took the spoon from Yuli and patted his cheek.

'Some iron hand! And I must say you have a way with children,' Kate remarked, while registering that this was the first time he had spoken his ex-wife's name. It was one that conjured up an exotic woman. What had she done to turn Cal *off* women? Kate couldn't imagine him not being a

154

devoted husband. But there were some women for whom devotion spelled boredom. Kate's friend Audrey was one of them, and was now being led a dance by the philanderer for whom she had divorced her husband.

Calvin changed the subject. 'If there's still a synagogue in Moscow, Kate – '

'There is, like there are still some church services. I noticed its address in the official guidebook, along with where the churches are situated – but who do they think they're fooling? Not me!'

'All the same,' said Calvin, 'the synagogue could be a useful point of contact.'

'But not necessarily a trustworthy one.'

Kate stared thoughtfully at the pepper-pot, which continued to remind her of the Rosses. Much of what they had told her was distressing but this was something she hadn't wanted to believe.

Calvin had paused to take it in. 'Are you telling me there's a Judas in the camp?'

'Isn't there always? Even the concentration camps had them. We daren't take the risk.'

'Did your source provide any back-up information?' Calvin inquired, making Kate feel again like a character in a spy novel.

But spying was part of this all-too-real matter. In a country where nobody, least of all the refuseniks, could be sure their own home wasn't bugged, anything was possible. The subdued little boy seated between them was here to prove it. Her careful reply to Calvin was: 'Ask yourself why the synagogue hasn't been closed down.'

Calvin removed the napkin he had tied around Yuli's neck, and stroked his hand. 'Feeling better, little guy?'

He was rewarded with a hesitant smile.

Kindness was a language everyone understood. 'If we found it hard to forget the stowaway, Cal – and I never shall – how shall we live with *this*, if we can't help Yuli?' Kate said as emotion again welled-up in her.

'At least we'll have tried.'

'Much good that will do him, if we don't succeed.'

Yuli glanced from one to the other of them, as was becoming his habit when he heard his name mentioned. It had not taken long for them to perceive that he was acutely sensitive to the moods of the adults around him. To Kate it was as if she had just pricked a bubble she and Calvin were trying to keep intact, depressing herself and him, with a resultant effect upon the child.

Even if they could speak Russian, what could they say to reassure him? "Everything's going to be all right, love," could turn out to be a lie and a let-down, and she had never lied to her own kids. Not even during the only real crisis they'd had to face, when Alun got meningitis, and his condition was touch-and-go for several days. Jason was then about Yuli's age, and Emily looking forward to her eighth birthday party. Kate could remember returning from the hospital, night after night, to two little figures in pyjamas sitting anxiously on the stairs, and her mother, who had taken over during the crisis, hovering beside them.

Kate had longed to say something which would remove the anxiety from their faces, but her reply to the nightly question, 'Daddy will be coming home again, won't he?' was, 'We shall have to be patient, and keep our fingers crossed.'

Kate sipped the coffee she had allowed to go cold, recalling her mother's disapproval of her failure to cheer up the kids. But Mum didn't know about the let-down Kate herself had suffered as a child though it was she who caused it. It had concerned a bird, not a person, yet the effect of having her hopes falsely bolstered, and afterwards shattered, had been devastating to a nine-year-old. She had found a sparrow unable to fly, on her way from school, and had brought it home cupped in the palm of her hand, weeping buckets, she still remembered, because it had been hurt. Her mother had told her that all it needed was rest, and had even helped her make a nest for it in a shoe box. Kate could see that shoe box now, with the tiny bird lying in it. They had put it beside the kitchen hearth, and she could remember her father saying the bird's days were numbered – and hating him for it. But when he proved to have been right, it was her mother whom she could not easily forgive for lying to her.

Was it then that she'd moved closer to Dad? And stopped believing in Mum? A time had certainly come during her childhood when some kind of change in the way she viewed her parents had taken place, and it could have been then. Or was that when I suddenly began seeing each of them as a person, not just as my mother and my father? she was musing, when Calvin rose and lifted Yuli from his chair.

'You were miles away,' he said as they left the dining-room.

'And if I told you where, and how I got there – '

'The same keeps happening to me. One thought leads to another,' he answered with the brusqueness she was coming to associate with *his* remembrance of the past.

But it could only briefly take your mind off the present, Kate thought, conscious of the small hand she was holding, and of people in the crowded lobby turning to look at them.

They had just reached the lift when the assistant manager accosted them, his manner as ingratiating as it was yesterday, and evoking for her now, as it had then, a picture of someone giving you a friendly smile while they spat in your eye.

'Mr Fenner and Mrs Starling. Good morning! A word or two if you please.'

He led the way to a quiet alcove but did not suggest that they sit down.

'How convenient that I should find you together,' he said in the same unctuous tone.

'But hardly a coincidence,' said Kate. 'As us suddenly finding ourselves in adjoining rooms was no coincidence. Had you known that events would make it a most useful arrangement for us, you might not have done it.'

'Useful? How so?'

'Our accommodation is adaptable for a family suite, and we now have a child with us, don't we, Mr Kropotnikov?'

Yuli was clinging to Calvin's knees, a reversion to the frightened state in which they found him, as if he sensed that

Mr Kropotnikov definitely was not a friend. He did that with Irina, clung to her skirt, when I was there with the Rosses, Kate recalled – but he didn't look at us the way he's looking at Mr K.

'Aren't you sorry for this little boy?' she challenged him.

'I have children of my own,' was all he was prepared to say.

'And I'm sure you love them to bits, don't bother telling me. I'm prepared to accept that Russians in general love kids, but that's hard to relate to the double standards you seem capable of applying with regard to *some* children.'

'My dear lady, I am but a hotel assistant manager.'

'And your receptionist said last night that she's just a receptionist. I am beginning to view that kind of talk as some sort of defence. What you actually are, and the same goes for her, is a puppet on a string.'

Calvin could see beads of perspiration on Mr Kropotnikov's brow. Anyone but a trained, Soviet up-fronter would surely have capsized by now under the force of Kate's attack. Once she got the bit between her teeth, off she galloped and the hell with the consequences. For Alun Starling, it must be like having a potential runaway horse by your side as you journeyed through life, he was thinking when Kate won the staring-down match she was silently having with her current adversary.

Mr Kropotnikov, seemingly unable to furnish a suitable reply to being told he was a puppet – which he probably knew – averted his gaze and chuckled, as though he had finally decided to treat it as a joke.

Puppets or cogs, it's the same difference, thought Calvin. One had to feel sorry for such people. Since they had no choice but to carry through the function dictated to them, Calvin's initial outright contempt for them was becoming tempered, albeit reluctantly, with understanding of the inner conflicts they must surely on occasions be prey to. Mr Kropotnikov and the girls behind the front desk couldn't be compared with those prepared to do the real dirty work; the arresting, interrogating, and intimidating, carried out by men like Caspar and Boris. Nor with the toothpicker, who was probably outside the hotel entrance right now, in readiness to tail Kate and me wherever we might go with Yuli.

Kate returned the momentarily vanquished Mr Kropotnikov to his purpose. 'What was it you wished to speak to us about?'

'If you've found a faulty faucet in my new bathroom, forget it,' said Calvin. 'I'm staying put.'

Mr Kropotnikov kept his veneer in place despite the cutting edge to Calvin's voice. 'Representatives of your embassies have arrived to see you. I have put at their disposal, and for your convenience, my office,' he added.

The telephone calls they had planned to make had been forestalled.

Too true we've progressed beyond the nuisance stage, thought Calvin. The KGB would not have found it necessary to seek diplomatic assistance to deal with mere flies on the wall.

Kate was allowing herself to hope that this unexpected development might lend strength to her elbow. But there was no time for her to discuss it with Calvin. They followed Mr Kropotnikov in a semi-stunned state, each of them holding one of Yuli's hands, as he led them behind the reception desk to his office.

'I shall engage myself elsewhere, in order that you may have the privacy,' he said, opening the door, and closing it behind them.

Privacy, with a bug to ensure the opposite, thought Kate, as they were affably greeted by the two young men standing behind the desk, their backs to the window. Kate could not recall her hand ever having been quite so enthusiastically shaken, and Calvin was being subjected to the same.

Subjected? Come off it, Kate! But why had that word sprung to her mind?

'Harland Arbington, United States Embassy,' Calvin's bloke was introducing himself. Kate's announced in the same hearty manner, which didn't match his languid appearance, that he was Charles Farringdale.

159

There was much during those first few minutes that set Kate on edge, including that the element of reserve she had sensed immediately she entered their presence seemed somewhat at odds with the matiness of their greeting.

A moment of silence followed, during which Arbington gazed at the light-fitting, and Farringdale stood with his hands in his trouser pockets contemplating the door knob.

Though neither could have been older than thirty, there was about them both a world-weariness that probably came from dealing with too many insoluble situations, Calvin thought, studying them. Arbington was fresh-complexioned and built like a hockey player, nothing like Cal's idea of how an embassy aide would look if he ever came face to face with one. The other guy, though, had to be everyone's idea of a British Embassy type, right down to his tie, which Cal would bet was his old-school one.

Farringdale's most noticeable feature, so far as Kate was concerned, was his Adam's apple, which even when he was silent kept bobbing up and down.

As if by prearranged signal, Arbington switched his gaze to Calvin, and Farringdale removed his hands from his pockets and smiled at Kate.

'Moscow is an interesting city, isn't it, Mrs Starling?'

'Though us guys are kept too busy to go see the sights,' Arbington told Calvin.

Had they really let a silence gather in order to break it with those damn-fool remarks? Calvin was sure it had been deliberate. Meanwhile, he was all too aware that the child about whom they had come, yet whose presence they hadn't so much as acknowledged, was clinging to his leg ever more tightly, almost as if Yuli had divined that these guys might be instrumental in parting him from his benefactors. That they were here to eventually talk what they would deem 'sense' was a certainty. But it wouldn't have hurt them to have displayed the human touch to a kid whose predicament was way beyond their sphere of influence. And if this was diplomacy, it could go hang!

Calvin's face reddened with anger, and Kate was not surprised. She was seething.

'Forgive me, Mrs Starling,' said Farringdale. 'Do please sit down.'

'I prefer to stand.'

'As you wish. I'm afraid that in an office which isn't one's own, one tends to forget to play the host.'

And the embassy men remained standing behind the desk – even the hand-pumping had taken place across it – with Kate and Calvin side by side in front of it. Not only was there a distinct air of formality about this little get-together, there was an atmosphere of protagonists facing each other – and so much for enlisting the aid of our embassies, thought Kate.

'Shall we get on with the interview?' she said.

'I wouldn't call this an interview.'

'Then what would you call it, Mr Farringdale?'

'May we say it's a friendly visit?'

'That isn't how it feels to me. Nor have you yet so much as mentioned its object, let alone come out with what's on your minds.'

'A technique, if I may say so, that smacks of our encounters with Soviet officials,' Calvin added. 'If you wish to take that as an insult, you're at liberty to do so. Now may we get down to discussing the welfare of Yuli Smolensky? I am sure getting sickened by the way guys like you apparently can't say pass the salt without pretending it's sugar.'

The embassy men exchanged a glance.

Then Farringdale squared his shoulders. 'Very well.'

'If you want it straight, we'll level with you,' said Arbington. 'Would you care to take it from here, or shall I, Farringdale?'

'Which of us makes the point is immaterial, Arbington. But if you wish me to – '

'I don't recall saying that.'

'Then forgive me for assuming you may have been implying it.'

'Look, I've never been the guy to pass the buck – '

'Or I to mind having it passed to me – '

This deferential exchange was a lesson in diplomacy for

their impatient listeners. If this is how joint negotiating is usually handled, heaven help my country and Kate's, thought Calvin. Then he felt a sudden dampness on his socks, and saw a small pool on the floor.

'While you guys have been trying not to step on each other's toes, this kid has wet his pants! Could be he's trying to remind you he isn't just a case for your files.'

'And we sure feel for him,' said Arbington.

'That goes without saying,' Farringdale echoed.

'But what does it mean in practical terms?' Kate inquired.

'The practicality of this situation,' her own country's representative informed her, 'is plainly and simply that a Soviet internal matter cannot concern us.'

'Nor can it actively concern our visiting citizens,' said Arbington.

They had finally made the point between them, and it was no surprise when it came.

Farringdale then cleared his throat so violently, Kate thought his Adam's apple must be threatening to choke him. 'If I may address just you for a moment, Mrs Starling. You have, if I may say so, created a precedent by taking upon yourself responsibility for a Russian child.'

'Did whoever asked you to lecture me tell you why it was necessary for me to do so?'

'Be that as it may, I must strongly suggest that you hand over the child.'

Kate gave him the reply she had given to the men in the limousine: 'Not on your nelly, mate,' and received a look which told her he was reassessing her.

Arbington said quietly, 'Does the same go for you, Fenner?'

'You bet it does.'

Again the embassy men communicated with a glance. Behind them, the obelisk that dominated the horizon in this part of Moscow was silhouetted against a sky as gloomy as Kate now felt. She was aware of Calvin soothingly stroking Yuli's hair, and of a tugging at her heartstrings that was like a physical ache. Get yourself back on a cerebral plane, Kate.

'There is only one condition under which I'd be prepared to hand Yuli over,' she said.

'Would you mind telling her she's in no position to talk conditions?' Arbington said to Farringdale.

'I see no reason to say what you have already said. Only that I endorse it.'

'Nevertheless,' Kate countered, 'if it could be arranged for me to see Yuli settled with a suitable Jewish family, instead of being put into an institution, I would regard the matter as satisfactorily settled.'

'That sure isn't a suggestion *we* could make,' said Arbington.

'Indeed not,' Farringdale agreed, his Adam's apple wobbling precariously at the mere idea. 'It could be misconstrued as a criticism of how Russian children are treated in such institutions.'

'And our embassies wouldn't wish to give that erroneous impression,' Arbington declared to the unseen bug.

Calvin waited for Kate to blow a fuse, and was not disappointed.

'Since I've never visited one of their Children's Homes, I have no idea of how the kids are treated,' she blazed. 'Nor do I give a tinker's about how my suggestion is implemented. The only thing Mr Fenner and I are concerned with is what is best for the child.'

The embassy men had visibly recoiled from her ire. Arbington left it to Farringdale to fend her off.

'There is absolutely no point, Mrs Starling, in your letting *us* have it,' he said with the air of a man who knows he is on a losing wicket.

'Then would you kindly make an appointment for me to see the Head of the KGB?'

'She has to be joking,' said Arbington to Calvin.

'I wouldn't be too sure of that.' And nor was Cal.

'I would also like to visit Yuli's mother,' Kate followed it up.

Farringdale removed the monogrammed handkerchief from his breast pocket, eyed it for a moment, and carefully reinserted it. 'Do forgive me for saying this, Mrs Starling, but I can't make up my mind if you are what Arbington would call a nut, or a lady too intrepid for her own good.'

'What I actually am,' she answered, 'is a woman with two children of her own, who can't just stand by and see someone else's child victimised. And there's one more request I have to make. We would like to take Yuli to his grandmother's funeral, since he's the only member of her family at liberty. And please make sure it's a Jewish one.'

Kate picked up Yuli and swept from the room. Calvin had to move fast to catch up with her.

The embassy men were left to recover their equilibrium and stare down at the pool on the floor.

'Fortunately, mopping-up operations do not fall within the diplomatic scope,' Farringdale said with a smile.

Arbington contained himself until they were away from the listening device and heading toward the hotel car park. What he and Farringdale had envisaged as delivering a few words of advice to put the fear of God into their delinquent tourists had, instead, left Arbington feeling distinctly uneasy. And what would the Russians make of Farringdale's final, and damn-fool quip? – since they wouldn't know it referred to piss, and it sure had military overtones. As for the incendiary material Mrs Starling had tossed into the ring – Fenner, too – any further meetings with them would have to be held in an open space.

'Who does that lady think she is, Charles!'

'An Englishwoman, I'm proud to say. And one who reminds me of my mother, I might add. Hang on a minute, would you, Harland?'

Arbington tightened the belt of his trench coat and watched Farringdale unfurl and raise the rolled umbrella he had never seen him outdoors without, not even in high summer. Nor was it like him to have walked a few yards in the rain without putting the damn thing up. Why was Farringdale so preoccupied? And that reply he made to me expressing my feelings about Mrs Starling didn't smell good, Arbington thought as they resumed walking. Could he be hatching a plan to tie up their joint assignment so all the credit would go to the Brits?

164

'Was that remark meant to be some sort of compliment to your mother, Charles?' he asked with a blandness Mr Kropotnikov would have applauded.

'It most certainly was. When a cause is worth fighting for, Mother is not the one to give up – or there might now be a motorway through our village green. She spearheaded the campaign.'

Arbington blotted out a vision of a large woman in tweeds, carrying a banner, and allowed one of Kate Starling storming into KGB headquarters to briefly rise in its place. If they didn't do something to stop her, she'd be hotfooting it to Dzerzhinsky Square. 'Was the lady serious about getting the kid's granny a kosher funeral, Charles?'

'I think it would be wise to accept that everything she said was seriously meant.'

Arbington booted a tin can off the pavement, an action for which Farrington thought him eminently suited. It was unusual to encounter litter on a Russian street, and he said irritably, 'Our tourists will be getting us blamed for this sort of thing, next!'

'But it would be more in keeping with the small infringements in which they occasionally involve us.'

'And even they have to be handled cagily, given the touchiness of our hosts!'

'You *are* in a bad mood, Harland. If I may say so.'

Arbington was trying to figure out what Farringdale could find to smile about, since the ringleader in what they'd been landed with was a Brit. Though Fenner had dug in his heels as deep as she had, he came over as a guy who, without her along, could be made to see reason – and that was worth a try. If Arbington could manage to extricate Fenner, Farringdale would be left to do as he might, and with the smile on the other side of his face.

'If we could swing it for her about the funeral, Charles, we'd be doing her a favour, and she may then see things our way,' he said when his pipe-dream had receded; if ever a man was in a woman's clutches, Fenner was. 'Tactically speaking, that's how it would have to be put to the Russians.

165

We should have to let them think they were doing the favour, of course.'

'That goes without saying.' But if Farringdale's assessment of Kate Starling was correct, she would consider a religious burial the dead woman's right, not a favour to herself. Nor would it bring her to heel.

Calvin followed Kate into her room and watched her set Yuli down. It was hard to believe that the woman now kneeling beside the little boy, gently removing his wet pants, was the same one who had dealt so peremptorily with the embassy men.

'Thanks to *them*, we can't take Yuli shopping for new clothes this morning!' she exclaimed. 'Since these are the only ones he has here – '

'His socks must be damp, too,' Calvin interrupted.

'Of course they are!' Kate sat Yuli on the bed, to unlace his scuffed little boots.

'If you'd done that first, you wouldn't have had to struggle, getting his pants off over them,' said Calvin.

'Instead of remarking on my inefficiency, fetch me a towel to wrap him in.'

Yuli dug his knuckles in his eyes, as if about to cry, but no tears came.

Kate did her best to comfort him. 'It's all right, sweetheart. Nobody's cross with you.' She gave him a reassuring cuddle. 'I could shoot those embassy blokes, Cal!'

Cal brought a towel before replying. 'But your letting off steam isn't helping our little friend. We're going to have to watch it in front of him.'

Kate paused. Calvin was right. 'But if that interview was a sample of what we're in for, it won't be easy.'

'Meanwhile,' said Calvin, 'why don't I go dunk Yuli in a nice, warm tub, while you rinse out his pants and socks?'

Cal is the practical one of the two of us, Kate thought, though that wasn't to say she couldn't get to grips with practicalities when needs be. And the main practicality of this situation was that they had a child to look after.

She ran some water into her bathroom handbasin, to wash the pitiful little pile of garments. Pitiful because they were those of a child cruelly bereft, for however long, of the parents he loved. And they of him and of each other.

Kate lathered a small blue sock, and a surge of protectiveness for its owner welled up like an ache in her breast. If you saved a kitten from drowning – and Kate once had – you then felt responsible for it. The tabby she had rescued from her garden pond was now the family pet, and old and sensible enough not to risk its life trying to get at the pond's occupants. If only it were that simple to ensure Yuli's welfare. While Kate had him with her, she would give him the same loving care she'd given her own kids when they were little. It was afterwards, the shadowy unknown with which his future was shrouded, which filled her with foreboding. What she wanted was a guarantee that the child would be kindly treated if she handed him over to the KGB.

When you hand him over, Calvin would correct her. But she couldn't envisage ever doing it. Any more than she could have envisaged throwing the kitten back into the pond.

While she rinsed and wrung out Yuli's clothes, she visualised her husband and children, who, right now, would be engaged in their usual Saturday morning pursuits. Alun was probably in the greenhouse, fiddling with the tomato plants he nursed each year; and Jason would be glancing at his watch, lest sweeping the garden path make him late for the football match. As for Emily, Kate thought with a smile, she'll be going through her wardrobe, deciding what to wear for the youth club tonight. In my absence, she might even be going through mine! I can imagine her thinking that my white silk blouse would look good with her jeans.

Suddenly, in the midst of her anxiety about the child she had taken under her wing, Kate was overwhelmed by a longing for the son and daughter she had left at home. And for home itself, as she had been last night. For Alun's familiar presence. Safety was what home and family spelled, and never more so than now. It summed up what Yuli had been forcibly deprived of. But there was no reason for Kate to feel unsafe.

She shook the feeling off and hung the garments she had washed on the towel rail; though the rail was warm, it would probably be this evening before they were dry. She rinsed out the handbasin, which was plastic and all of a piece with the matching shelf around it. Kate had not expected to find her hotel bathroom no different from those in the West. The guide book she had bought in London had advised taking a plug for the bath; a toilet roll, too, since the Russian variety was reputedly inferior. In this hotel neither was necessary. And to Kate's amazement there was a fridge in the bedroom. But it was possible that other tourists found themselves less fortunately accommodated, and would return home thinking that all Soviet hotels were as crummy as theirs.

People viewed things according to their personal experience, she reflected. And few Westerners were likely to experience any of this. If Kate hadn't met the Rosses, seen for herself what meeting them had led her to see – Well, you'd have got back on the plane, next Thursday, none the wiser about what the oppression of Soviet Jews really means for those it's happening to, wouldn't you, Kate?

She left the bathroom with a grim expression on her face. It softened when she saw Calvin seated in his room, with Yuli cradled on his lap. Calvin had wrapped him in the faded patchwork quilt, and was humming a tune to him.

Kate provided the words. "The Teddy Bears' Picnic" had been a favourite song at bedtime when Emily and Jason were small. Was there a Russian version? Probably not. Yuli seemed to be enjoying it nevertheless. Though he was eyeing them somewhat warily, there was again the hint of a smile about his lips. What would it take to get this child's trust? If we could talk to him in his own language, tell him we care about him . . . If, if, if!

These were Kate's poignant thoughts while she went on brightly singing, and Calvin's humming, to which he added an occasional 'pom-pom', sounded as falsely cheerful as she felt. There was nothing to be cheerful about. But they were putting on a show for the child. What was he thinking? Confusion had to be uppermost.

When the improvised concert was over, Yuli got down from Calvin's lap and went to gaze through the window, trailing the quilt, like a voluminous cloak, around him.

The picture he made, the lost look there was about him, caused Kate's eyes to sting with tears. But anger was present in her, too. She felt like throttling those who had brought Yuli's situation about. Nor had she yet recovered from the unhelpful intervention of the embassy men. Unhelpful was an understatement. Cold and clinical was the only way to describe their attitude.

'What went on with your bloke and mine was a terrible shock to me,' she said to Calvin.

'And I have to say that how you handled it was something of a shock to me,' he replied.

'What d'you mean, how I handled it? They got my back up, didn't they? Yours, too, I would've thought.'

Calvin got up and tidied his dressing-table, though it did not need tidying. Kate watched him move his hairbrush an inch to the left, and his comb an inch to the right, with the preciseness she had begun to notice characterised everything he did. In anyone else, she would have thought it meant they had the makings of a pernickety person, but she didn't want to think that about Cal.

'Sure they got my back up,' he answered eventually.

Another of his habits that Kate recalled from the cruise was his pausing to consider a reply, sometimes for so long that you thought you weren't going to get one. Not like Kate, who was inclined to deliver the first answer that came into her head.

He paused again, before saying, 'But I wouldn't call it politic to have let them have it as strongly as you did.'

Kate glanced at Yuli and managed to keep her tone even. 'Politic? But that's exactly what *they* are being, isn't it? And, at the moment, it's also what the you-know-who are being. The mistake I made was expecting the visitors we had this morning to be automatically on our side, and the heck with being politic!'

'Calm down, Kate.'

'I am perfectly calm.'

But Calvin read in her eyes that she was still inwardly seething, and he was aware that only the presence of Yuli and the bug were restricting her from expressing her wrath more fully.

'Why don't you put on your coat and go take a walk?' he suggested when she began restlessly pacing.

'Who would that help, apart from me?'

It was then that Calvin really became aware of the responsibility they had jointly undertaken. Compassion had led them to whisk Yuli from where they had found him – who wouldn't have? Weighing up the pros and cons hadn't come into it, and now he'd had time to consider, Calvin would do the same again. But where did they go from here?

'In a way, this reminds me of when I tried to help an old lady,' Kate muttered.

She was standing with her hands on Yuli's shoulders, gazing over his head at the view from the window, noting the abundance of trees, and the towering blocks of flats, as she had last night. There were plenty of people around, bundled in thick, shapeless coats, hats pulled down on their heads. Didn't the Russian stores stock women's coats in colours other than black, brown, or grey? The same went for hats. Did the drabness Kate was looking down on epitomise their lives? She would hate to think so. But from here, the Russian families she could see to-ing and fro-ing at a solitary block of shops – well, it was like watching ants moving back and forth. There wasn't the air of dalliance, or, alternatively, of purposefulness with which people went about on Saturdays at home.

'You're really the one for causes, aren't you?' Calvin prodded her.

'What? I can't say I've ever thought of myself that way.' But maybe she was? She stroked Yuli's hair, and was surprised that he let her, since he seemed to prefer Cal. Then the little boy allowed himself to rest against her, and she put her arms around him, enjoying his nestling close as Emily and Jason once had. You're a maternal woman, aren't you, Kate? – or you might've been earning what Audrey does, by now, with the sense of achievement that goes with it for women who make it to the top in a man's world.

She switched her thoughts back to what Calvin had just said. 'What I do know about myself is I can't stand injustice. Or bureaucratic indifference to human realities!' she flashed. 'My mum had a daily-help when I was growing up, more like a family friend, really, and after she retired Mum stayed in touch with her. We found out that the council had rehoused her at the top of a tower block. It was part of what used to be called a slum-clearance programme – they don't call it that any more, for psychological reasons, I suppose. Anyway, there old Rosie was, and when the lifts broke down or were vandalised out of action, there she had to stay. Added to that, she'd suffered all her life from a fear of heights, but when she told them they obviously thought it an excuse to get put on the ground floor. They didn't want to know.'

'What you're talking about is officialdom, Kate.'

'And we saw another example of it this morning. Of how cold it can be, I mean. Maybe those two blokes do have to stick to rules laid down from above – but it wouldn't have hurt them to've given this kid a smile.'

'I kind of got the impression that Yuli's presence embarrassed them. And I have to ask myself why.'

'Perhaps because they're not going to help him,' Kate said tersely.

'Or because it isn't in their power to,' Calvin replied. 'Did you really think it would be, Kate? They're a couple of junior aides, and even at ambassadorial level, I doubt that much could be done.'

'All I was hoping for, Cal, was that they would try.' She turned from the window to face him. 'I mean – well, everyone said I'd never get old Rosie moved from the top floor. After badgering every official there was to badger, I eventually got her seen by a consultant psychiatrist, who certified that her fear of heights was not only genuine, but exacerbated by the insecurities of old age. My dad, bless his heart, footed the bill. A week after I threatened to publish the whole story in my column, Rosie got a letter telling her that a ground-floor flat on a different estate had been found for her. And it made me think of all the people who have nobody to fight for them.'

Calvin smiled. 'Yuli is lucky he has *you*.'

'But I don't need telling that this fight is a very different cup of tea. Only the issue itself is clear-cut.'

Calvin was relieved that she was now functioning on a cerebral level as well as an emotional one, but held his tongue, allowing her thoughts to proceed.

'Without a practical alternative to handing Yuli over, we're on a negative track,' she went on, momentarily forgetting the room was bugged. 'But how are we to get one, Cal? If Howard and Barbara were here they'd know who to contact, what to do. But me – well, it's no wonder that I feel as if I'm floundering. I've never been patient in situations where my hands seem to be tied, but that doesn't mean I'm going to give up.'

Calvin put his increasing admiration for her into one brief sentence. 'It wouldn't be you if you did.' He glanced at his watch and saw that the morning had sped away. 'Since they don't have room service here, what do we do about lunch for the little guy? We can't take him to the restaurant without pants, I guess.'

'I'll go down and fetch us something from our table.'

But Kate found that easier said than done. Daphne and her mother were not yet at the table. She sat in her usual place and made some sandwiches. Would Yuli prefer smoked fish, or cold sausage? She made him a dainty sandwich of each, trimming off the bulky crusts, plonked them atop the heftier versions she had put together for herself and Calvin, and was carrying the plate toward the door when the head waiter barred her way.

'Excuse me, please.'

'Yes?' Kate replied.

'It is to take meals from the restaurant irregular.'

Though the man was smiling apologetically, Kate bristled. 'Are you telling me it isn't permitted?'

'If you wish for a packed meal, I will for you arrange.'

'How long would that take?'

'Now is very busy time in the kitchen. It is usual to tell to the guide, who passes to me that you so require.'

'But I didn't, did I?' Kate felt sorry for him – like the others she had encountered, rules and regulations were the norm for him. But not for her. People had begun trickling into the dining-room and were eyeing her curiously – and not for the first time since she and Cal brought Yuli to the hotel. She would doubtless feature in their memories of Moscow as some kind of crackpot. So what? All the same, when she spotted Connie entering with her husband it was good to see a friendly face.

Connie asked, with a grin that enhanced her gamine appearance, 'Where are you off to with that loaded plate?'

'My intention was to take it upstairs, or we shan't get any lunch today.'

'Is the Russian kid sick in bed?' Brad inquired. 'He sure doesn't look too robust.'

'And he certainly isn't. But the bedroom picnic is because Yuli has wet his only pair of pants – we didn't pause to pack a bag for him! – and if you two would like to know in what circumstances, join us upstairs after you've eaten and we'll fill you in.'

She told them her room number and watched them make their way to their table. Would Brad now reiterate his insistence that Connie stay out of it? Meanwhile, the head waiter was still hovering beside her, stroking a lapel of the tailored jacket that singled him out from his staff, whom he must be as aware of as Kate was. The restaurant drill was that while the guests were eating – and few came late to disrupt the timing – the waiters stood in a posse, watching for the moment to simultaneously clear the plates from each course. The posse was now watching surreptitiously to see the outcome of the incident Kate had created. Where, except in a country where rules applied to absolutely everything and weren't bendable, could there be such an incident? If she sailed out of here with the plate, the head waiter's authority would probably be dented, but sorry, mate! I've got a hungry kid upstairs.

'This has never happened before,' he said as she stepped past him.

'If Mr Kropotnikov finds out, you may tell him that the culprit was Mrs Starling. He won't be surprised,' Kate replied.

After the sandwiches were eaten, Calvin went down to the hotel *beryozka* to buy some soft drinks, and Yuli turned out to be the only child they had encountered who didn't like Coke. Instead he reached for an open bottle of lemonade, tipped it back to drink from it as his elders were doing, and ended up with a soaking wet shirt.

'Now we have something else to wash and dry,' Kate said. Then laughter took over. But Calvin was laughing too. The funny side was visible again and thank goodness it was.

Yuli was eyeing them uncertainly, as if he wasn't accustomed to seeing people laugh. But when had there last been any reason for merriment in his family life? And when would there be? The thought quelled Kate's momentary lightheartedness. How could she relax for a *minute*, until she'd sorted out the mess this kid was in?

Connie and Brad's arrival cut short her cogitation. Brad had brought along some cans of beer, and Connie had a package in her hand.

'We gathered you folks are cooped up in here for the day,' Brad said, 'and I guess the beer'll be as welcome as the company.' He sat down on the bed, opening a can for himself, his gaze taking in the two-room suite.

'We started out on different floors, but, for one reason and another – well, this is how we've ended up,' Kate felt constrained to say.

Connie sensed her embarrassment. 'Look, you don't have to explain anything to us.'

'Why I'm here is, first and foremost, to say what Connie already has,' Brad put in. 'If there's any little thing we can do in the way of back-up, you only have to ask.'

'I gave him a talking-to,' Connie said.

'Okay, so I needed one. But I'm here now, aren't I? And back-up is what Connie and I know a thing or two about, isn't it, babe?'

'In other words, you're looking at a pair of NYPD off-duty cops, and one of them's a detective-sergeant,' said Connie.

'It isn't me,' her husband ruefully added, while Calvin was recovering from his surprise. Kate's reaction was astonishment. So much for her assessment, on face values, that Connie and Brad were the New York equivalent of the yuppies she saw carrying document cases in London. As the Baptist preacher had said – was it only yesterday? – nowadays the Bible was the only book you could judge by its cover.

It did not take Connie, who seemed the brighter of the two, long to grasp the nettle Kate had finally had to grasp. She paused only briefly after being told the gist of Kate and Calvin's meeting with the embassy men, before saying, 'If you don't have an alternative solution to letting them have him, you don't have a case.'

'We're hoping to come up with one,' said Kate.

'But the way things're looking as of now, we'd better all keep everything crossed except our eyes,' Connie replied.

Calvin agreed, but again held his tongue.

'You didn't give Yuli his present yet,' Brad reminded Connie.

She held the package out to the child, but he backed away from her, burying his face against Kate's skirt as he had against his mother's.

'Don't take it personally,' Kate said. 'He doesn't trust strangers – and why should he, when people he didn't know carted his parents away?'

She took the package and opened it. 'Look, Yuli. Connie and Brad have given you a toy bus! Isn't that lovely of them?'

It was the first of many such toys Yuli was to receive from tourists staying at the hotel. But Calvin and Brad had to get down on their knees and whiz it back and forth to each other in order to coax him to join them and play with it. In a little while he was contentedly playing with it on his own while the adults chatted of this and that. But Kate's gaze rarely left him.

'If you don't want a broken heart, I strongly advise you stop what you're doing,' Connie warned her. 'Emotional

175

Chapter Seven

It was strange to be where no church bells rang out on a Sunday. The more so, thought Kate, in a city whose skyline was graced by the majesty of gleaming cathedral domes. Incongruous, too, that these one-time places of worship were sited in the heart of the Kremlin, where doctrines now held sway which had replaced the teachings of the Bible.

Though Kate was not a regular church-goer there had been times in her life when she had found herself silently praying for God's help, and it was good to know she lived in a country where religious observance was not made difficult for the devout. But that was the essential difference between home and here, she reflected when she and Calvin finally ventured forth with Yuli on their delayed shopping expedition. Freedom of choice.

They had left the hotel after breakfast, their destination Red Square where GUM was open on Sundays, though the jovial Russian on the train had advised them that the store would be packed with people. Fitting up Yuli with a change of clothes could not be put off, and for Kate it was a relief to have something definite to do. Mundane though the purpose of the outing was, it served as a small goal amid the surrounding uncertainties.

The mundanity ended when she and Calvin descended the hotel steps, each of them holding Yuli by a hand. The man who had followed them from the Smolenskys' flat was there on the forecourt, still picking his teeth.

Kate controlled a shiver.

'You look surprised,' Calvin said.

'Of course I'm not.' It was to be expected that they would be watched wherever they went, but how much more chilling was the actuality.

She turned up her coat collar against the physical chill of the April day, more noticeable after being confined within an overheated atmosphere, using her free hand – not for anything would she leave go of Yuli's!

'Okay. We're on our way,' Calvin said briskly and they set off down the incline toward the main road. 'Which is it to be, Kate, the metro or a cab?'

'I've had my fill of the metro escalators,' she said fervently, 'but a *parked* cab around here could be risky.'

They looked down at the small figure between them, who must surely be wondering where they were taking him. Their total ignorance of his language was an insurmountable handicap in their efforts to reassure and comfort him, and his silence indicative of the anxiety stilling his tongue. This morning he had suddenly said 'Mama', fisting his eyes as if about to burst into tears, but again none had come.

'When my gran died, I couldn't cry. The grief wanted to pour out of me, but it just didn't,' Kate recollected aloud, as they managed with difficulty to stay three abreast on the narrow pavement beside a constant stream of cars and Intourist buses. 'How much worse must it be for a small child. And after what he's been through, this one is going to need expert treatment, so he won't be scarred for life,' she added with feeling. 'Or, at the very least, a stable family environment until he gets his mum and dad back.'

'Is that what you're hoping to fix up for him, with only three days to do it in?'

'Yes, as a matter of fact.'

'Would you mind telling me how?'

'Since I don't know myself, that's a damn stupid question. I said "hoping", didn't I?'

'But hope without action rarely gets anyone anyplace. And, right now, all the action there is is the guy on our tail.'

They could hear him plodding behind them, his presence and its significance impossible to ignore. Though Calvin would not have admitted it to Kate, it was giving him the creeps and making him feel like the criminal he knew he wasn't. Kate was thinking there wasn't going to be a

178

mundane minute until she was safely back aboard the plane home – and even then she wouldn't breathe a sigh of relief until they were out of Soviet airspace.

Safeness aside – illogical though it was, she could not shake off the personal dread that had dogged her since her meeting with Irina's family; the necessity to watch what she said in her hotel room, or in the restaurant, was not only innately repugnant, but a strain for one unaccustomed to a totalitarian society. Yet the Russians, who had no option, took it all in their stride.

They were crossing Mira Prospekt, the wide avenue that led to the city centre. A seemingly endless horde of people was pouring out of the metro station, reminding her of the Piccadilly Circus Underground. But in London – if you had time to notice them – the throng was an interesting assortment of people, like you would expect to find in a city which was pulsing with life. In Moscow, despite its huge population, and the cultural and historic splendours for which it was renowned, the throb of life seemed missing, though there was no lack of bustle in the scene Kate was viewing now. And the people, especially those no longer young, had a uniformly stolid look about them.

Kate felt conspicuous in her camel coat and tammy hat, aware of stares from the crowd at a taxi-rank, the women in particular, and wished she had not left her grey, fur-collared raincoat at home. It was the sort of thing many of the Russian women of her age were wearing and would have helped her dissolve into the crowd. Though Calvin's overcoat was well cut, it was a dark blue cloth, and he could probably pass as a Russian with that fur hat on his head.

But why should we have to pass for Russians? The heck with dissolving into the crowd! It's those who are making me feel like this who are the wrongdoers. What Cal and I are trying to do for Yuli is what's right.

A tram halted to disgorge its passengers, among them a group of young children in neat grey and red uniforms.

'Look, Yuli, don't they look nice?'

He glanced briefly to where she was pointing her finger and gave her a fleeting smile.

179

'Those kids must be going to the Exhibition of Economic Achievement,' Calvin remarked as the children formed themselves into pairs and followed a young woman. 'They seem a happy lot.'

'Healthy, too,' Kate agreed. And what a contrast between their demeanour and Yuli's. What had this poor kid done to deserve what was being meted out to him? 'I told my son I'd try to take some snaps of the spacecraft section of the Exhibition for him,' she said ruefully.

Calvin hailed a taxi, but his raised arm was ignored. 'There's no reason why you shouldn't, Kate.'

'I doubt I'll have time.' She touched the pom-pom atop Yuli's knitted hat. 'Even if I had the heart to.'

They fell silent, then Calvin said, 'I guess the same goes for me taking in the museums. Not too many American art dealers get to see Ivan the Terrible's throne, or the icons in Pokrovsky Cathedral, and here am I passing up the chance! Sandy isn't going to believe it.'

'*Everyone* must be going to the Exhibition,' Kate said, as a family group, the man carrying a chubby toddler, and the woman ushering along three older children, brushed past her. In the few minutes they had been standing there, the crowd had built up; everyone was heading towards the curved obelisk in the vast, ornamental park with its numerous pavilions.

The child clutching her hand had been no older than the toddler who had just passed by, when his parents applied for an exit visa. Since then, the consequences had dominated the Smolenskys' lives. Carefree outings like the weekend excursion that young Russian family were enjoying had long been impossible for Yuli and *his* family.

'If we don't pick up a cab soon, it'll have to be the metro,' said Calvin, and Kate was steeling herself for some more escalator-vertigo when he managed to hail one.

The toothpicker, they noted, strode immediately to the edge of the pavement, flashed an identification card at a man who was just getting into another taxi, and elbowed him out of the way.

'What would he have done if that cab hadn't been there?'

180

Kate said when they had set Yuli on the seat between them and their driver began nosing his way into the stream of traffic on Mira Prospekt.

'He'd have stopped a passing motorist, I expect.'

'And there was I, thinking we were in luck, that we'd shaken him off. I even envisaged him getting clapped in irons for losing us,' Kate said with a grim smile.

Calvin paused to study her expression. 'Would you really wish that on the guy?'

She gazed through the window while she thought about it, absently taking in the small cars crawling like chunky beetles alongside the taxi.

'I wouldn't wish it on anyone, Cal,' she eventually replied. 'But since we walked in on what we did, on Friday night – well, there've been moments when I don't recognise myself. I have never been a vengeful person. Alun is the one in our house who's given to saying he'd like to pay someone back for this or that. But when I saw this kid cowering in the kitchen something inside me boiled over. If I'd had a knife in my hand, and the people who caused it had been present, I would probably have used it on them.'

'It might help you to know,' said Calvin, 'that the very least I would doubtless have done was knock them cold – and a habitual pugilist I'm not.'

Since the taxi driver spoke no English, having shrugged and grunted something in Russian when Kate inquired if he did, they made no attempt to talk to him. Their conversation would presumably be taped and delivered to the KGB along with those of other Westerners who travelled by cab – Kate was again sickened by the thought, but did not mind those who had wrecked the Smolenskys' family life learning how *these* two Westerners felt about them and their methods.

She stroked Yuli's hand, and received another fleeting smile. 'We're going to get you some lovely new clothes, sweetheart.' The little boy rested his head against her. 'He's beginning to put his trust in us. It's making me feel worse, Cal.'

Kate had no time to analyse why she felt that way. The

cab was approaching the Kremlin and a moment later they were deposited at the car park beyond which only official vehicles were permitted to enter Red Square.

They stood for a moment on the edge of the cobblestones, transfixed by the splendour at close quarters of the gold domes, affected by the vastness of the Square itself, and, too, by their own proximity to the place where decisions that could influence the future of mankind were made, for better or worse. Was the man in whom many Westerners – Kate among them – had put their hopes for lasting peace seated at his desk behind those towering red-brick walls, right now? And would he put into practice attitudes, more humane than those of his predecessors? If Mr Gorbachev was sincere – and even with Yuli by her side, Kate still wanted to think that he was – he would have to overcome the opposition of the old breed, steeped in their totalitarian methods of government, which included the strong arm of the KGB. Was he in with a chance? The only certainty was that he still had a long way to go, or, given that he *was* sincere, people like Irina and Lev Smolensky wouldn't be in prison, nor the labour camps in Siberia full of dissidents.

Outside Lenin's tomb, people were queuing the full length of the Square waiting patiently to pay homage, another party of children in uniform at the tail-end, bunches of flowers in their hands.

'We're here to go shopping, aren't we?' Kate reminded Calvin and herself. 'And that building on this side of the Square must be GUM. I don't see the toothpicker, do you?'

'He's talking to one of the guards – or is that guy a policeman?'

There were so many uniforms milling around that Kate had difficulty in picking out one from another; and could not see the man following them. Calvin had now lost sight of him, and said, 'If shaking him off would make you feel good, Kate, now's our chance.'

They hurried across the cobblestones, pulling Yuli with them, and fought their way into the store.

While they had been waiting to hail a taxi, Kate had

thought that everyone in Moscow must be heading for the Exhibition; it now seemed to her that every Muscovite and his wife and children were packed inside GUM. She had expected something along the lines of Selfridges, and found herself instead in an arcade, its glass roof towering to a great height, and its upper level bridged at intervals.

'You'd better pick Yuli up,' she said, 'or he's likely to get trampled underfoot. This is what it must be like for a tinned sardine!'

'Well it sure beats the spring sales back home.'

'What makes you think there's a sale on? I mean, why would they have to mark down the prices when, from what I've heard, there aren't enough goods to go round.'

Kate balked when she saw the prices. The arcade was lined with small shops, but none on the ground floor seemed to sell children's clothing, and they made their way to the upper level, where Kate was jabbed in the ribs by someone trying to precede her to where a meagre selection of jeans was on display. Beside them, she espied a small red pullover. But thirty-odd pounds for *that*! Given that the average wage in the Soviet Union was two hundred roubles a month, and a rouble was approximately one pound, if Kate had to clothe her kids here, they would have to go naked.

'Let's insure against accidents, get Yuli two of everything he needs,' said Calvin, who had cashed some travellers' cheques at the hotel.

Inside the shop a solitary assistant was doing her best to deal with a mob of customers trying on shoes, the piled boxes on the floor indicating that a consignment had just been delivered – and, at this rate, they'll be sold in no time, thought Kate, observing the frantic activity around her; there were no chairs, and men and women were slipping their feet in and out of the shoes and boots standing up.

On the counter was some children's underwear and a few shirts, none of which was Yuli's size. Kate scanned the wall behind it, where an assortment of garments were displayed on hangers, and spotted a child's anorak – but it would be miles too big for him.

She tried to engage the assistant's attention and failed. 'This is hopeless, Cal!'

'I thought all we'd have to do was use sign language.'

'But to whom?' Kate said exasperatedly.

Someone behind them said, 'I am willing to assist you.'

They turned around gratefully and found themselves face to face with the toothpicker. Calvin tightened his hold on Yuli, while Kate told herself not to be daft; the back of her neck was prickling again.

'What is it you are wishing to purchase?' he inquired.

They exchanged a glance. What a nerve! But why not make use of him? thought Kate. Calvin, who had expected her to tell the man where to go, saw her force a smile.

'We're trying to fix Yuli up with some new clothes,' she replied, 'but it isn't easy.'

It presented no difficulty to the KGB man. All he had to do was flash his identification and click his fingers. A momentary hush was discernible in the shop, and a brief ceasing of activity. Then the trying-on of shoes and the examining of garments was resumed, as if the incident was an everyday fact of life.

But for those to whom it wasn't . . . Kate and Calvin exchanged another glance, while the toothpicker lounged against the counter watching the assistant, who was old enough to be his mother, accord him the respect he ought to be giving her. She looked flushed and flustered, and her pouter-pigeon bosom was heaving beneath her white nylon blouse.

Did the young man enjoy his power? Or simply take it for granted? Kate restricted her conversation with him to the bare essentials. Not only was what he represented odious to her, but his breath reeked, and his lank hair looked as if it needed washing. His black leather jacket and blue jeans looked brand-new, and must have cost the earth here, but neither the price nor the shortage of goods was likely to be a problem, Kate surmised. Even the lower echelons of the organisation he represented would have ways and means of getting anything they wanted. She glanced at the placid Slavic faces of the customers, people who had accepted their lot and grown used to it. No, Kate; they've never known anything else. Could things change for the better for them, as well as for the dissidents and refuseniks? Again Kate prayed that the new man in the Kremlin was genuine.

By now Yuli's new wardrobe had accumulated on the counter.

'You see? To buy in the Soviet Union whatever you wish is a simple matter,' the toothpicker said, while the assistant was packing the small garments.

For you it is, Kate silently echoed her surmisal. 'Why don't we let Yuli wear the anorak, and dump the one he has on?' she said to Calvin.

'Would you put it on him, Kate, while I pay the bill?'

'Got enough roubles?'

'Only just!'

They were leaving the shop, with Yuli resplendent in bright blue, when Kate realised they had forgotten to get him some shoes.

The KGB man led them to the bridge. 'Over there we shall find for him boots of leather.'

And what a cosy shopping party we are, thought Kate, suppressing a giggle at the incongruity of their following him, instead of the other way round. She paused on the bridge to gaze down upon the milling crowd below, the atmosphere more reminiscent of an indoor market, than of a store. The aromas of cheese, and garlic, and fresh baked bread, drifted upwards. She'd love to have a look at the food shops and watch the Russian housewives shopping – several, she could see, had loaves protruding from the oilcloth holdalls they were carrying. And what was that man clutching to his breast? It looked like a rolled-up blanket, and they too must be hard to get from the way he was nursing it. Kate could have stayed there all day, drinking in the sights and the sounds.

'Come on!' Calvin called to her. Though he too saw the irony of the situation, he longed to rid himself of the KGB guy. Having him close and chummy was somehow more unnerving than hearing his footsteps behind you. And hadn't Kate noticed how Yuli had cringed when the creep joined them?

They followed the Russian into a shop that didn't have windows, just a raised shutter like a fishmongery. While their interpreter gave a repeat performance of establishing his authority, Kate averted her gaze to an embroidered tablecloth pinned to a wall. Only for Yuli would she lend herself to the loathsome influence being exerted on her behalf! As for the motley assortment of clothing and linens, none of which Kate would have bought at any price, well, she was sorry for the ordinary Russians.

'I don't see any shoes on offer,' she said crisply to the KGB man.

Then a small box was produced from under the counter, and a slightly larger one when the contents of the first proved not to be Yuli's size. Though the second pair of boots were long enough, they were too wide, and even when laced looked like boats on the child's feet. But they would have to do, and he left the shop wearing them, with Kate wishing she could have taken him to a children's shoe department at home where they would have carefully measured his feet.

Calvin divined her thoughts. 'What he wears on his feet is the least of his present problems, Kate. Want to go back to the hotel for lunch or shall we try to find something here? The little guy must be hungry.'

The KGB man overheard and invited them to join him at a snack bar on the ground floor.

Nerve wasn't in it! 'Thank you, but we can find our way there,' Kate replied!

He entered the snack bar behind them, gave them a matey smile and ushered Kate toward the one vacant stool. Fortunately for him the ushering was by gesture not touch, or Kate's elbow would have effected his departure from her side.

Since only a platter of cheese sandwiches was on offer, Calvin was able to order their lunch by pointing to it and holding up three fingers, and their bottled drinks by the same method. Watching him unzip the little boy's new

anorak before letting him drink, Kate thought again what a
super dad Cal must have been to his son. Everything she had
seen him do for Yuli had been done with patience and
tenderness, she was reflecting when the fourth member of the
luncheon party, whom she was still trying to ignore,
demanded her attention.

'Why is it, please, that you are making it your business
what you do not understand? I would not come to your
country and poke in my nose.'

Before Calvin had time to think of a suitable reply, Kate
had delivered hers.

'Let me tell you that in my country cruelty to children is a
punishable offence.'

'And the same goes for mine,' said Calvin.

'That is equally so in the Soviet Union.'

'Then why aren't the people who left this child to stew,
now in jail?' Kate inquired. 'If we hadn't by good luck
found him, he might have ended up dead, like his grandmother.'

The KGB man replied through a mouthful of bread and
cheese, 'For that the child's parents would be responsible. It
is this that the Jews who come from the West to interfere do
not understand.'

'We're not Jews,' Calvin told him.

The man put down his bottle of Pepsi and looked puzzled.
As if it was only those of your own religion whose victimisa-
tion could arouse your compassion, Kate thought.

'You are the members of Amnesty perhaps?' he asked,
and seemed even more mystified when they shook their
heads.

'Just common-or-garden members of the human race,'
Kate said, 'who are lucky enough to live where people are
more important than politics.' In some respects that last
bit wasn't entirely true, but compared with what went on
here –

She fed Yuli some of his sandwich and handed the rest to
Calvin, who had finished his.

'You've hardly touched yours, Kate.'

'I'm not hungry.' Indeed, the little she had swallowed had

felt as if it would stick in her throat. 'I'm ready to go if you are.'

Calvin took Yuli from her, hooked the huge bag of clothing over his arm, and they rejoined the shopping Muscovites, the KGB man, his toothpick again in action, just a few paces behind them.

It was raining when they emerged into Red Square, bitingly cold, too. But the queue outside the Lenin Mausoleum had lengthened, and people were still flooding into the Square; making their way across the now slippery cobblestones; pausing to gaze up at the domes.

When they eventually managed to get a taxi, Calvin asked Kate if she would mind if he asked the driver to show them a few sights before they returned to the hotel.

How can he be interested in sight-seeing, she thought, when all I feel right now is depressed. Then she recalled how she had wished she could see all she would have liked to at GUM, and agreed to Calvin's request. Though Yuli's plight was casting a gloom over their trip to Moscow, when the opportunity presented itself they'd be daft not to see what tourists came for.

Driving around Dzerzhinsky Square the driver, whose English was quite sufficient, made no move to identify the building outside which a number of limousines were parked, their rear windows curtained. Kate knew it must be the KGB headquarters and could not control a shudder. If we don't do what the chaps in that place want us to, with a good grace, it could soon be off with the kid gloves. The driver pointed out the huge granite statue of Karl Marx in Revolution Square, opposite the Bolshoi Theatre, its monumental colonnade topped by a quadriga of bronze horses. But the rest of the sight-seeing was for Kate a blur. What were monuments and architecture, compared with the fate of the child on her lap? She could feel his warmth against her breast, and he had just put his hand in hers.

Calvin asked to be shown the Music Conservatoire, and said as they approached it, 'Did you know that Vladimir Horowitz is due to play here next weekend, Kate?'

She shook her head.

'I read about it in the papers back home, and was amazed that the Soviets are welcoming him back – '

'Why would we not?' the driver cut in. 'Here is his motherland, and of the maestro who would not be proud? My wife, she is standing in line now, to get for us the tickets for this great event.'

Yuli had fallen asleep, and Kate was looking exhausted. Shopping expeditions wherever were fatiguing, at any time but it was stress that had drained the life from Kate's face.

Calvin told the driver to take them to the hotel. Kate wouldn't enjoy anything till they'd done all they could for Yuli, and nor would he. As for her autocratic requests to the embassy guys, well, she'd be lucky! Did she really imagine a Jewish funeral would be arranged for Yuli's grandmother just because an Englishwoman had asked for it – and in a country where religious expression was viewed as a threat to the régime?

Calvin hadn't bothered telling Kate that Yuli couldn't attend the funeral because Jewish kids never did, however close the relative. What was the point of mentioning it, when what she'd asked for wasn't going to happen?

That evening, Daphne, whose room was next to Kate's, knocked on Kate's door, her embarrassment plain when it was opened by Calvin.

She was dressed for dinner and stood nervously fingering her pearls after Calvin invited her in. 'I could've picked a more convenient time, couldn't I?'

Here's someone else, as well as Connie and Brad, who imagines we're doing what we're not, thought Kate. She and Calvin were wearing dressing-gowns, and the door between their rooms was wide open as usual.

'Where's the little boy?' Daphne asked, glancing around. 'Is everything all right?'

Kate was touched by her concern. 'If you mean is he still with us, yes,' she replied.

'What we don't know is for how long,' Calvin added.

'Right now, he's in the bath, along with that toy duck you gave him yesterday, Daphne. Is it okay if I call you Daphne?'

'Oh, I'd be more than delighted if you both did,' she replied with a smile that lit up her sallow face. 'And I'm so pleased that little Yuli likes the duck. Mother wanted me to get him a stuffed bunny, but I thought a toy for the bath would be rather nice. I had one myself, and I still remember it.'

Her beaming pleasure again aroused Kate's sympathy and she surmised that there were perhaps not too many pleasures in Daphne's life.

'We were just going to get Yuli out of the bath and dry him, when you knocked, Daphne – '

'Would you like me to do that for you? I'd absolutely love to. It's the bit I enjoy most when I baby-sit for my brother and sister-in-law.'

'And we'd sure take you up on it if we thought Yuli would let you,' Calvin replied.

'What Cal means – ' said Kate.

'Oh, there's no need to explain,' Daphne cut in. 'It was silly of me to suggest it, when the poor mite has only just got used to being looked after by you two, instead of his mummy and daddy. As for his circumstances – well, learning what had happened to Yuli upset me dreadfully. Even Mother was affected by it. But I'd rather she didn't know what I came to suggest – my getting involved would worry her.

'I could tiptoe in tonight, after Yuli is tucked up and asleep, and you could go out for a walk, or have a drink in the bar,' she offered.

'That's a kind thought,' said Calvin.

'But Cal won't let *me* guard Yuli on my own, and he's right,' Kate added. 'Nor, speaking for myself, am I in the mood to go out.'

'Me, neither,' said Calvin, 'but thanks anyway, Daphne.'

'Isn't there *anything* I could do to help?'

'There is if you like sewing,' Kate answered with a smile, 'which I don't, though I quite enjoy knitting.'

She showed Daphne the clothes they had bought at GUM.

'Look at these shirts – the buttons are barely sewn on, they'll be off in no time. And the side seams are coming undone.'

Daphne examined a vest. 'The seams need strengthening on this, too.'

Calvin left them to it and went to get Yuli out of the bath, his expression wry. Whatever he'd expected his trip to Moscow to encompass, it sure hadn't included any of this.

CHAPTER EIGHT

THE ALACRITY with which Kate's parting shot – for such it
had seemed to them – was facilitated astonished the embassy
men. Never had red tape been cut through so swiftly but
neither Farringdale nor Arbington deluded himself that this
was a good sign. Since the Russians were not known for their
amenability, it indicated that there was more at stake than
was apparent.

Be that as it may, she's won this round, thought Farringdale,
noting Kate's rigid stance, at the old lady's graveside. And
it's one up for *us*. Arbington, no doubt, had conveniently
forgotten whom he had labelled the ringleader, and was
thinking it one up for the USA.

What Arbington was actually thinking was that Kate
Starling had magnificent legs. Was Fenner bedding her? He
was a fool if he wasn't. But those two wouldn't take their
watchful eyes off the kid for as long as it took, though they'd
had to leave him in someone's care while they came to this
funeral.

When Calvin told Kate that Jewish children did not attend
burials, she was torn between reluctance to leave Yuli at the
hotel, and the compulsion to see Irina's mother laid to rest.
Calvin's suggestion that she go without him had been out of
the question. Sad though this occasion is in one way, in
another it's a victory and Cal's entitled to share it with me,
she thought, glancing up at him; as he's shared the whole
harrowing experience I got him into.

The burial service had not yet begun. Overhead, the sky
was grey as the sea of gravestones stretching on either side of
Kate and ahead, where the stark outline of some distant trees
enhanced the air of desolation. All about her, too, was the
stillness peculiar to cemeteries, and in her nostrils the dank

smell of the newly-dug grave. Several minutes had passed since the simple coffin was trundled toward it. The rabbi, his black hat and cassock emphasising the paleness of his bearded face, stood clutching a prayer book and quietly conversing with Caspar and Boris – a reminder that Irina's dead mother was being used as a pawn. Kate needed no telling that the agreement to her request was an attempt to soften her up. As for its speediness – were they losing patience?

Calvin saw her shiver, and linked her arm. 'How many berets do you have with you?' Yesterday she had worn a yellow one.

'Berets are my one extravagance, and fortunately they don't cost much,' she replied. 'So I have an assortment of cheerful colours.'

But today's was black; a symbol of the mourning she was doing on behalf of Irina, with whom she seemed to have become emotionally embroiled though they had met but once.

'I wonder what's causing the hold-up, Cal.'

'I guess they must be waiting for the necessary quorum,' Calvin answered. 'Of Jewish men, I mean. I'm not sure what the number required is, but it seems they're not allowed to hold a service without it.'

The only Jew present, apart from those beneath the gravestones, was the rabbi. Would the funeral have to be called off? Kate thought with dismay.

Calvin noted her expression. 'They haven't gone to all this trouble for nothing, Kate.'

'But where are they going to get the quorum from?'

'I can't answer that. But I was once at a Jewish friend's home when someone called up, and he dashed off: he said he had to go make up a *minyan*; that no Jew would refuse to do that duty even for a total stranger.'

'But we're not in America, are we?'

'I'd venture to say that Jewish tradition is universal, Kate.'

They were talking in an undertone, aware of Caspar and Boris now impatiently pacing back and forth on the other side of the open grave, a cigarette drooping from between Boris's lips even on this hallowed ground. But it wasn't hallowed to him, and in daylight his hooded eyes seemed even more snakelike than they had when Kate saw him seated in the car. Like his partner, he was dressed in a bulky dark coat and a brimmed black hat, and both wore plaid scarves which Kate found incongruous with their overall appearance. When Boris glanced at her, the now familiar prickling at the back of her neck was there again.

Would the tradition Calvin had mentioned apply to making up a *minyan* for the funeral of a refusenik? She saw the minister look nervously at his wristwatch, and whispered to Calvin, 'If supplying the number required was part of the deal, and the men don't turn up, it could be heaven help the rabbi.'

'If that was a pun, Kate, I'll let it pass. But it had occurred to me. And the way you got what you demanded so fast has me thinking, by the way, that wheels-within-wheels doesn't just apply to the Russians.'

Calvin glanced at the KGB men whose pacing was making him as edgy as Kate. 'I have my doubts that your mentioning a Jewish undertaker to those two on Friday night would have got you anywhere without the intervention of the embassy guys.'

'And what does that lead you to suppose?'

'What I just said. About wheels-within-wheels. But I guess they're part of what diplomacy is, whatever the flag it's flying.'

'What it leads *me* to suppose,' said Kate, 'is that the embassy blokes, too, are trying to soften me up. I've got what I wanted for Irina's mother, but the reason she's getting what she's entitled to is enough to send me home a hardened cynic.' Until the coffin was in the ground, she wouldn't trust the KGB not to change their minds. Don't be daft, Kate. Their strategy is to convince you you're wrong about them. That they're really good chaps, so you'll let them take Yuli without a fuss.

'Farringdale's call about the funeral had me so rushed, I

hope I explained to Connie and Brad about the lemon and honey for Yuli's cough, and his vitamin pills.'

'Don't worry, I did,' Calvin reassured her. 'And I guess it's handy Connie and Brad turned out to be what they are. Who better to protect him in our absence?'

Time was ticking by. The KGB men had stopped pacing and were again talking to the rabbi. And Kate could think of more cheerful places to stand and chat to Calvin than beside an open grave.

'If you're worrying about how they'll cope with Yuli, I don't think you need to, Kate.'

'It's him I'm worried about, not them. Did you see him watching us put our coats on?'

'But he knows we've left him with friends. He hasn't forgotten that they gave him his toy bus.'

'You sound just like Alun used to, when I ruined his night out by worrying about leaving Emily and Jason with a new baby-sitter. And Yuli's expression reminded me of theirs when I did. But Yuli has a lot more to be anxious about than they had. I wouldn't give that kid an extra ounce of stress if I could help it, Cal. And what's the betting he's now wondering if the people he thought he could trust will come back?'

Kate switched her gaze from the coffin to the distant trees, recalling the scene in her room, before she and Calvin left. The floor heaped with the toys Yuli had been given in the restaurant last night, among them a bus from the Aussie-with-the-motto. Yuli seeming bemused, and Brad pulling funny faces to distract him from Kate and Calvin's departure. Connie unwrapping a Hershey bar and putting it into Yuli's hand. And good old Daphne hovering by and, as usual, fidgeting with her pearls. The object of their attention had not looked happy – and when would he? she was reflecting, when the rain that had threatened all day began to fall. Kate couldn't remember ever attending a funeral when it hadn't rained.

Farringdale came to offer her the shelter of his umbrella.

'No, thank you, Mr Farringdale.'

'Your independence,' said Calvin, when the embassy man

had returned to his place on a grassy slope behind them, 'is liable to get you drowned.'

'I don't want him beside me by the grave. The funeral is nothing more than a diplomatic manoeuvre to him and your bloke. I would much rather they hadn't come.'

'Here comes the *minyan*, Kate – '

They watched the arrivals quietly group themselves around the rabbi. All were elderly, and soberly clad in dark overcoats and trilby hats. The kind Kate had seen seated on park benches at home, whiling the hours away; or on seats provided near some suburban bus stops, where pensioners could be seen reading newspapers, or gazing at the passing traffic.

'They look as if they might have been collected and delivered in a minibus,' Calvin said, 'as if they were being taken for a treat.'

But this was no treat. A duty no Jew would refuse, not even for a total stranger, Calvin's friend had said – but on this occasion there was an added element. Few Russians, Jew or gentile, would risk displeasing the KGB. The refuseniks had dared to, and these old gentlemen had seen where it had got them. Kate had never encountered a nervier-looking lot, and had to avert her eyes from the one who kept twitching his neck. The presence of two watchful figures directly behind them must account for it.

The rabbi opened his prayer book and cleared his throat, as ministers tend to do the world over, and the service finally began.

What sort of life had the old lady's been? Was she happy with her husband while Irina was growing up? Kate tried to visualise the face that she had seen but twice, looking young, and found it impossible to strip it not just of age, but of the weariness put there by sickness and oppression. Kate could remember her grandmother once saying that every line on her own face could tell a story. But all I'm ever going to know of this woman's story is the last chapter. For Irina's mother there had been no death-bed scene with those she loved gathered around her saying their farewells, and only strangers were beside her grave as the small coffin was lowered to its resting place.

Few could fail to be moved by the solemn recitation of the *Kaddish* prayer, and given the circumstances under which he stood listening to it, Calvin had to be prodded from his thoughts by Kate, when the minister addressed him.

'In the absence of relatives, the task to put into the grave the first spadeful of earth is yours, sir.'

Calvin did as he was bid. But how truly bizarre this was. Me being deferred to as the chief mourner, when I never even met the departed. Would the wheeler-dealers of three nations who'd contrived the funeral have the *chutzpah* – only that Jewish word fitted – to take their turn at shovelling in the earth? Calvin was not surprised when they did.

The rabbi gave Kate a warm smile. Was he a Judas disguised as a man of God? For all she knew, he could be an actor engaged by the KGB for a morning's work. She wouldn't put anything past them. But all that mattered was that the funeral rites were as Irina and her mother would have wished. Though what lay behind this man's smile was open to doubt, the way the *minyan* had participated in the rite, as if every word of it was familiar to them assured Kate that the service was the real thing.

Nevertheless, she was again daunted by this being a country in which all whom she encountered were not necessarily what they appeared to be; where even the old women selling flowers in the street could be a front for the KGB. Where a friendly gesture had to be carefully considered, lest its purpose be quite the opposite.

How do ordinary people live with it? she was asking herself when the rabbi came to shake her hand and Calvin's, his cassock flapping in the wind.

'Mrs Starling and Mr Fenner. My heart is warmed by the trouble you have taken for an old Jewish woman.'

'Did you never hear of Christian charity?' Kate answered.

'Of course, of course. But I have never before seen it so well illustrated.'

'Your English is excellent,' Calvin said, to bridge the silence generated by the piercing look Kate was giving the guy.

'I have made it a point that it should be. Without

language, how shall the barriers between nations be broken down?'

'Your country,' said Kate, 'could make a start by letting its citizens out, instead of just letting some of *us* in.'

He spread his hands eloquently. 'I am but a minister of religion, Mrs Starling.'

Give or take the occupation of the speaker, that excuse was becoming too familiar. And Kate had not failed to note the rabbi's sidelong glance at Caspar and Boris, who had placed themselves one on either side of a nearby gravestone. Boris had just struck a match on it, to light one of his foul-smelling cigarettes – with as much respect for the dead as he would show for the sole of his shoe, probably less. Kate saw one of the *minyan* open his mouth as if to rebuke him, then think better of it. Had the KGB man done it without so much as a thought? Or deliberately, for the *minyan*'s benefit, since whoever lay beneath the gravestone was Jewish.

Stop trying to figure out how minds like Boris's and Caspar's work. The mental machinations that equip them for their job would doubtless have won the approval of Machiavelli.

'I understand there is a problem about who shall now take care of the Smolensky child,' said the rabbi, 'and perhaps I can help?'

Kate eyed him warily. 'How? Jews who haven't applied for exit visas could get into trouble for helping those who have.'

'And there are those who would not find blameworthy an unwillingness to endanger oneself.' The rabbi hesitated, cast another glance at the KGB men, and lowered his voice. 'What would be your summation, Mrs Starling, of a person who set forth to cross the street with his eyes shut, closing his ears also to the warnings of his brothers and sisters that he may not reach the other side?'

'But there are some who do, aren't there?' Why didn't he just say what he meant: that the rest of the Jewish community considered the refuseniks foolhardy? And he might be right about people like the Smolenskys turning a deaf ear to warnings, but their eyes had been wide open to the consequences. Staying with the crossing-the-street analogy, what Irina and Lev saw there was Yuli with a prayer book, beside the Western Wall in Jerusalem. Would it prove to be only a mirage?

'And a great many who do not,' the rabbi replied, as if telepathically. 'For which they are paying the price,' he added with a sigh. 'In a lifetime one is called upon to make many compromises.'

Since his final words were patently on his own behalf, Kate didn't envy him his conscience if he had made the one she suspected.

Calvin felt like saying, 'Cut the sermon,' but said instead, 'May we return to your initial subject?'

'Despite what I have been saying to you, it is possible that a family could be found who would take the child.'

To Kate the rabbi's offer smelled – and the only thing she had left to trust was her nose. 'No, thanks.'

The short encounter, like others Calvin had shared with Kate, was decisively over before he had time to utter – and how did Alun Starling live with that? Always coming over as the passive partner to a forceful female?

It happened again when the embassy men, who had stood by while they talked to the rabbi, joined them on the walk to the cemetery entrance.

'I hope all went to your satisfaction, Mrs Starling,' said Farringdale pleasantly.

'Since it's the first Jewish funeral I've attended, I must presume that this one was no different from usual. Excluding some of the onlookers, that is.'

'May we give you a lift to your hotel?'

'No, thanks.' Kate ducked away from his umbrella, with which he was attempting to shelter her. 'We got here by taxi and we'll get back the same way.'

Arbington was wondering how Farringdale could think that likening Kate Starling to his mother was a compliment to the woman who had borne him.

'There are one or two matters we'd like to discuss with you and Mr Fenner,' said Farringdale.

'It will have to wait. This is neither the time nor the place for your kind of discussions.'

Kate stalked off down the path, with Calvin – as usual – hard on her heels.

Arbington shook the rainwater off his trilby, and clamped it back on his head, as he and Farringdale followed at the leisurely pace that characterised their profession. 'That woman has got to be a tiger in bed.'

Farringdale, whose wife was anything but, nor would he have wished her to be, squirmed visibly. 'Really, Harland – '

'Really, Harland what?'

'Comments of the kind you just made are out of court.'

'Are you protecting your client? Or just plain embarrassed, Charles? I'm intrigued by the relationship between those two, is all.'

'We are not assigned to be intrigued, but to unravel existing intrigue, or enter into it when necessary.'

'And where would you predict today's exercise in that respect will get us?'

'My candid opinion is precisely nowhere.'

For Calvin, the stalemate was intensifying with each passing day – and it was now Day 3. If Kate was as strung up as she had just graphically displayed, how would she be as time dragged on without Yuli's future yet settled? – if the KGB allowed it to, when their softening-up tactic proved not to have worked, he thought when they were side by side on the lumpy back seat of a taxi. In an atmosphere that felt to Kate like a gathering storm.

'If you feel like smoking a cigar, I don't mind,' she said, to lighten it.

'If I did, I'd have asked your permission to.'

'Since you haven't smoked at all because of Yuli's cough, I just thought you might like one while he isn't with us.' Why were they having this stilted conversation about cigars? You started it, Kate. And why did Cal look so tight-lipped? 'Did the minister get to you? Or was it the embassy blokes?' she asked.

'Neither. You did.'

What had she done? She was about to find out.

'And I have to add that the rabbi addressed his remarks to the person who took over the conversation,' Calvin went on. 'Does it never occur to you, Kate, that I too might wish to express an opinion?'

A short silence followed.

Then Kate said, 'You think I'm bossy, don't you?'

'I wouldn't put it quite that way, though I could be forgiven if I were coming around to thinking it.'

'Then how would you put it?'

'I already have. But if you'd like it in different words, and at greater length, the way you sometimes rush off at a verbal tangent, speaking solely on your own behalf, is liable to send me hopping mad if you go on doing it.'

'I'll try not to. But have I said anything to anyone, yet, that you didn't agree with?'

'No, but it's the way you say it. Can't you stop rubbing everyone up the wrong way?'

'You're saying I've elected myself the spokeswoman, and I didn't mean to.'

She was never going to see the point. 'Forget it.'

'But will *you*?'

She had turned to look at him, and Calvin saw that there were tears in her eyes. Because he'd upset her? Or had the hopelessness of what they'd taken on chosen this moment to hit her? He had not expected ever to see Kate Starling looking vulnerable, and wanted to comfort her in his arms, as a man did a woman.

Instead, he linked his fingers through hers, and said with respect for the special woman she was, 'You're a helluva person, Kate, and I guess I wouldn't change a thing about you – even though you do, at times, get my goat.'

Kate stopped herself from resting her head on his shoulder. Getting more involved with each other than they already were would bring headaches and heartaches they could both do without. How could they continue a love affair begun in Russia once the Atlantic was again between them?

An affair was all it could be if several lives, including her children's, were not to be disrupted. The idea of Emily and

Jason shuttling back and forth from England to America was sufficient in itself to put a brake on the wild thoughts racing through Kate's brain.

The pressure of Calvin's fingers on hers was responsible for those thoughts – and given the feeling now coursing through her, she was surprised at her ability to apply her common sense. Since the word 'brake' had entered her mind, she told herself firmly that the mileage for herself and Cal was nil.

And what made her think he would leave Sandy for her? Or that if they slept together – behind Yuli's back! – it would be for him the same commitment it would for her? The answer was that though Kate was discovering that there were many senses in which she and Calvin were *not* two of a kind, she was sure that in that way they were. Her tendency to rush in where angels feared to tread had never included leaping into bed with someone she fancied. She had to be in love, and to know it was reciprocated. If what she and Cal felt for each other *was* love, they had best keep it bottled up, lest its consummation be something they found impossible to forget.

'Why wouldn't you let the embassy guys drive us back?' he asked.

Was it the sight of the Kremlin domes, now distantly visible, that had returned him to a less personal plane? Kate had no doubt that the thoughts he had just switched from had closely resembled her own – including the brake.

'Tweedledee and Tweedledum, you mean?'

Calvin had to laugh. 'Is there anyone you don't have a nickname for?'

'Well, their names are rather a mouthful, aren't they? Especially when said together. And when one thinks of the bumbling picture of ineffectuality they present, on behalf of my country and yours – '

'You're ignoring Mr Peabody's advice about snap judgements again.'

'I didn't say they *are* ineffectual, only that it's what they appear to be. And why it's necessary to put on the silly show they do . . .'

Kate lapsed into silence, mindful of the tape recorder secreted in the vehicle's dashboard. Did the cab drivers have to hand them in to a special office in Dzerzhinsky Square, on their way home from work? But that didn't make them bad guys; since the State was their employer, they had no choice but to. Of course they had a choice, they could opt not to drive a cab, be a bus driver instead, or whatever, like the Smolenskys' neighbour. But taxi drivers received tips, didn't they? It was as simple as that. People swallowed their scruples, for money, the world over. Well, some did. And Cal and I are still holding hands.

Kate turned from watching the stream of austere little cars heading toward the city centre. 'The reason I didn't take the offer of a lift,' she finally answered his question, 'well, one of them, was that I felt like being on my own with you.'

'We weren't a twosome for long, were we?' he said with a rueful smile.

'Don't you think it's perhaps as well?'

It was out in the open now, that she was as drawn to him as he'd implied on their first evening together, he was to her.

Calvin's 'Probably', got lost in what immediately followed. Kate could not be sure which of them moved first, or if it was a simultaneous coming together. Whichever, their first kiss was for both of them a sensually explosive experience into which tenderness somehow managed to find its way.

When they emerged from their dazed aftermath, the driver was grinning through his mirror, and telling them, 'You pay double, I take to hotel more quick.'

While Kate tried not to blush, Calvin sheepishly wiped some lipstick off his chin. Like a couple of kids, caught doing what we know we shouldn't, thought Kate.

Calvin was reminded by the driver's joke, if it was one, that privacy was no longer available to them. Not only did they have a child with them, night and day, but the supporters of his cause were liable to come knocking on the door for this reason, or that. Not that Connie and Brad were the prissy kind, but Calvin didn't want a hole-in-the-corner flavour to permeate what he felt for Kate. As for when they got back to the hotel, it would be churlish not to invite Yuli's stand-in guardians to have a drink. And while this conviviality was taking place, what was the betting the phone would ring, summoning him and Kate to another meeting with Tweedledum and Tweedledee. One of the limousines in the special traffic lane probably had Caspar and Boris in it, and the toothpicker was no doubt still stationed outside the hotel.

'Our trip to Moscow is turning into a three-ring circus without the fun, Kate!'

'Does that remark have any relevance to what just happened between us?' she said stiffly.

'It sure does.'

'Be that as it may – '

'You sound like Tweedledum, and he is definitely the one with the umbrella!'

Kate ignored the interruption. 'I hadn't envisaged what you term fun being a feature of our trip, though you apparently had. Nor is it too late for you to opt out from what you distastefully call a circus.'

'If you'll allow me to explain, Kate – '

She gave him a withering look. 'There is nothing to explain. I have erred in my judgement again.'

The taxi pulled up, and Kate leapt out and marched into the hotel.

As only she could, thought Calvin, eyeing her ramrod back. Daphne's mother could have taken lessons from Kate! The necessity of paying the driver prevented Calvin from rushing after her, and he felt like socking the smirking little guy on the jaw, for making the snide remark that had led to this. His feelings were not improved by the toothpicker giving him a commiserating glance. The ups and downs of our relationship are being observed along with the rest, he thought, which probably provides the observers with some light relief.

By the time he was riding upwards in the lift, he was seeing the episode as more of the black comedy they had laughed about on the metro platform, though this was closer to farce. Crossed wires wasn't in it! But how was he to get Kate to see it that way?

Dinner that evening reminded Kate of a long-ago family holiday mealtime when 'Tell your daddy . . .' and 'Tell your mummy . . .' was how she and Alun had avoided addressing each other directly, after a quarrel. If she and Calvin were a married couple, and Yuli their child, they would probably be doing that now.

While they awaited the second course, Calvin sat crumbling some bread, and Kate gave her attention to the symbolic pepper-pot. Was it really only four days since she ate with the Rosses, unaware of what it would lead to? What a short time in which to have one's eyes opened in so many different ways. To see the meaning of persecution in all its grim reality. That those who fronted for the "goodies" were not averse to dealing with the "baddies" if it suited them to do so. And that what the dealing was all about, a tiny scrap of humanity whose life stretched precariously before him, was of less concern to *any* of the dealers than coming off best. If that's an injustice to Tweedledum and Tweedledee, they've yet to prove it to me, she thought, aware that Yuli's expression, as he did his usual glancing back and forth to herself and Calvin, was tonight, like this morning, one she'd seen on her own kids' faces.

God knows, this child has enough to cope with, without us shaking the bit of temporary security we've given him, she wanted to say to Calvin, but could not bring herself to reopen the door she had slammed on her own foolishness. Nor did four days seem long enough for Kate's wayward feelings to have boiled up and over, the way they had in the taxi. And what an ignominious position it had put her in.

She had slammed shut the door between their rooms, too – but that couldn't undo that kiss, and what it must have implied to Calvin: that she was the easy lay he'd reckoned on her being. Face up to it, Kate. Stimulating companion

205

though he might find you on a cerebral level, that wasn't what he'd come to Moscow for.

Calvin was wondering why Kate was now glaring at him with renewed animosity. His attempts to explain to her that she'd got him wrong had fallen on stony ground. As if he had hurt her so deeply, she had locked herself away from him – which her slamming the connecting door emphasised.

When the soup was brought to the table, Yuli handed his spoon to Kate, though when he felt like being spoonfed it was usually Calvin to whom he handed it.

He's got me sized up as the guilty party, Calvin reflected, and I inadvertently am. 'Isn't your refusing to speak to me a bit absurd?' he ventured to Kate.

She broke her silence only to tell him, 'The truth of the matter, Calvin, is I've *stopped* behaving absurdly, and am thankful I was brought up short before I made a *real* fool of myself.'

'In that case, so am I,' he said abruptly.

Then they saw a tear run down Yuli's cheek, and wanted to throttle themselves and each other for upsetting this sensitive kid.

Kate managed to distract Yuli with a toy someone had brought to the table for him.

'He already has two buses like that,' Calvin remarked, 'and if people go on giving him toys, we shall soon have to move out of our rooms to make space for them.'

'All I'm concerned with, Calvin, is that *you* stay out of mine.'

'You've already made that clear. And isn't it time you told me who called you? Unless, when I heard your phone ring, it was a personal call, of course – '

'How could it have been? When nobody, not even my husband, knows where I'm staying.' Had she mentioned Alun to remind Calvin forcibly that she had a man waiting for her at home? But she needed reminding of that herself! 'It was Tweedledum,' she told him.

Like it or not, there were going to be things she had to speak about to Calvin. One thing hadn't changed. They still had a common purpose, and mustn't let anything get in the way of it.

'And what did Tweedledum have to say?'

'Something along the lines that in the end I was going to have to be reasonable. Your phone rang too.'

'Needless to say, it was Tweedledee. The only difference between what he said to me, and what your guy said to you, was "sensible" was substituted for "reasonable". Yuli has soup dripping from his chin, Kate – '

Kate brushed aside a vision of Farringdale and Arbington, side by side and each with a telephone receiver in his hand, and dealt with the homely matter requiring her attention. What the heck did those two care about the small everyday needs of a child? Or, indeed, for Yuli's welfare in any respect but how it suited them to view it from their remote, political standpoint.

'His chin needs mopping again,' Calvin said to her.

'I don't believe in doing it after every spoonful.'

'You wouldn't have jelled with Lori.'

'Any more than I do with her ex-husband. What did you reply to Tweedledee?'

'I told him to go take a running jump.'

'I didn't put it that strongly to my bloke – we might find we need them, before this is over – though the way I feel about them right now, they can *both* take a running jump into the River Moskva! Tweedledum would probably do it with his umbrella up.'

'I agree.'

Yuli saw them smile as they imagined it, and his own face lit up.

'Looking a bit livelier, isn't he?' said Kate. 'And not quite so pale as when I saw him for the first time. The vitamins must have started doing their work.'

'But when is he going to speak to us?'

'If he heard us talking his language, I expect he would have already.'

But the difference they had sensed in Yuli, after just a few days in their care, could be undone even more quickly. All it would take to rock the ground from under him again was a ride in one of those limousines. And when he got to the place where they would surely put him – that he'd be well looked after physically was the best that could be said. Kate thought of Irina and her hopes, and lifted the little boy onto her lap to hold him close.

'He's smearing soup on your dress, Kate – '

'I don't care.'

We can't let Yuli be put in one of their Children's Homes, she wanted to add fiercely. But what could she do to stop it from happening? Oh, the protectiveness this child had stirred in her.

Calvin had put down his own soup-spoon, affected by Kate's emotional reply, and by the picture the two made, Kate with her arms wrapped tightly around the child, who was gazing up at her.

'Put him back in his chair, Kate.'

'I don't want to.'

'Is Yuli not feeling well?' Daphne put in from the other end of the table.

'He's fine. We're just having a cuddle, aren't we, Yuli?'

'In the middle of dinner?' said Mrs Caldwell, sounding shocked. 'Daphne and her brother were shown their fair share of affection, but never at the table.'

'We got it after nursery tea, actually,' said Daphne. 'Nanny used to wipe the jam off our faces before you came in to say goodnight to us. But affection should be spontaneous – in my opinion, that is,' she added with more spirit than she had displayed when Kate and Calvin first observed her attitude towards her mother, whose reply was becoming increasingly familiar: 'Why did I let you talk me into coming to Moscow, Daphne?'

'If Daphne stays a rebel when she gets home, I get the feeling you and I will be blamed for it,' Calvin said in an undertone to Kate while she was putting Yuli back in his chair.

'And I'd consider it an achievement, wouldn't you? Daphne has a lot to give if she can manage to get the chance to. Want to know why I took Yuli on my lap? I just can't bear to think of him growing up to be another Mr Kropotnikov. Do I need to explain what I mean?'

'No, Kate.'

The rapport between them hadn't been banished along with Kate's foolishness. Maybe it couldn't be, she briefly reflected.

Calvin served them all with some meat from the platter of cold cuts set before them, and joked, because Kate's expression was so intense, 'And I sure hope Yuli isn't going to grow up that fat!'

'Would you mind being serious?'

'What makes you think Mr K. was raised in a Home?'

'He like as not wasn't, but he's an example of what Yuli would be turned into. Why must you always split hairs?'

'I'm a more factual person than you are. I also know when I'm swimming against the tide, Kate, and you don't.'

Kate stopped cutting up Yuli's pressed veal. 'What sort of defeatist statement is that?' She gave the child a slice of cucumber and put down her knife and fork. 'We won round one, didn't we, Calvin?'

'Only because it suited the other side to let us. I think it was Henry Kissinger who said the secret of success in international negotiations is to begin by making some small concessions.'

'That's just another way of describing the softening-up tactic.' Kate pitched her voice even lower than it already was, and transferred some bits of veal to Yuli's mouth. 'Why don't we give them a run for their money, Cal? Play their tactics against them? If they'd let me see that friend of mine, she might have a suggestion about – '

'You were told by Tweedledum – or was it Tweedledee? – to forget it,' Calvin cut in. 'And I doubt that they could fix that one up for you.'

They were careful not to mention Irina's name in Yuli's presence, lest hearing it distressed him.

'Not even if you slipped it to *your* bloke that you think I might play ball once I'd seen her?'

'You wouldn't, of course.'

'That's what would make it winning round two – and where *our* tactics come in.'

'What a shrewd cookie you are, Kate.'

But not shrewd enough to have tumbled to you. And if you think the seemingly friendly chat we've just had means I'm again open to your advances, forget it, mate!

Calvin felt the chill breeze suddenly drifting his way from across the table. Was Kate going to be cool with him for the rest of the trip? The after-dinner hours, watching over Yuli while he slept, were going to be hell if she was. And he never wanted to see a communicating door again. Theirs would have to be reopened overnight, but the communicating that in the cab had seemed inevitable had, for some reason, sent Kate heading away from him. Off on another of her tangents, which were not always the verbal kind.

He escaped hell that evening by gratefully accepting Brad's invitation to join him for a drink while Connie, who said she was in the mood for some "girl talk", kept Kate company.

'Which of the bars have you taken a shine to, Cal?' Brad asked as they crossed the lobby.

'You're not going to believe this, but Kate and I haven't yet set foot in any of them, Brad.'

'Then why don't we go find ourselves a table in the one with the live music? It's the only spot in this whole goddamn hotel that lets me believe I'm vacationing in Russia – and I have to tell you I'm already wishing myself back home.'

Brad led the way to a bar in which some men in gold-braided red outfits were seated on a small stage, making a noise with a violin, a piano, and what Calvin took to be a balalaika. All three of them were middle-aged, and before them stood a plump lady garbed in a black dirndl skirt and a peasant blouse, clutching a microphone and belting out the words of a song in a trembling soprano voice.

'I didn't say I enjoyed the music,' Brad said, noting Calvin's expression. 'But it's all that's on offer,' he added, smoothing back his sleek dark hair and giving his tie a twitch, while they looked around for a place to sit, 'and I guess I thought you'd get a laugh out of the band. You sure as hell need one, pal.'

'I'd be lying if I said I hadn't had a depressing day,' Calvin replied, as they made their way to an empty table, unoccupied because nobody would want to put themselves right next to that band. All the others had parties of tourists crowded around them, laughing and joking. Taking a night off from being culture vultures – and Moscow was the place to be one.

'Have you and Connie been out on the town on your own, here?' he asked Brad.

'Where is there to go? Ballet dancers and opera singers have never been my style. They say the Russian movie industry has livened up a little since the new guy got into the Kremlin, took vodka off the bar menus, and is still trying to find a way of keeping the people what passes for happy here, without it. But I don't see the new-style movies being what we get to see back home.'

Calvin smiled. 'Decadent, you mean?'

'What I mean is the whole spiel, like if a director has something he wants to tell the world on the screen, nobody is going to stop him from doing it. Anyroads, Connie and me, we don't speak the lingo, so going to a movie here is out. We heard there were some jazz clubs, but I guess they're keeping them hidden. The lady at the entertainments desk said she thought there might be one, or two, but she had no idea where. And like I said to Connie, a dime to a dollar she goes to one every Saturday night, wearing dark glasses.'

That wouldn't surprise Calvin. A society as stifling as this one was ripe for the minor personal rebellions Brad had just suggested. And the signs were that the new leader considered them a safety valve and was not doing too much to put the clamp on. Conversely, the small beginnings of the drugs problem that had recently emerged here would not be allowed to burgeon as it had in the West.

'Okay, so Connie and me, we didn't go out on the town,' Brad said as their drinks were brought to them.

'What did you do, Brad, order these in advance?'

'Sure, like I do back home. My regular bartender always has a beer lined up for me when I get there.'

'How did you know I'd want beer? Or that I'd accept your invitation to join you?'

'To the former, you look like a beer guy – you didn't

exactly knock back the bourbon we had in your room. To the latter, I didn't intend taking no for an answer.'

It was hard for Calvin to relate Brad's off-duty appearance to a uniformed cop tangling with a hoodlum in the Bronx, where he had said his police precinct was. And even harder to imagine Connie in that context.

'How did that dainty dish you're married to get to be what you and she are?' he asked with a smile.

'My baby doll is tougher than she looks, and could take apart that hefty lady singer, or toss her out the door, as easy as pie.'

'Then why don't we send for her and get her to do it?' said Calvin as the soprano teetered on a top note.

'The alternative is we go to a different bar for our next drink.' Brad drank some of his beer and set down the glass, before adding, 'But I'd like you to know that in our apartment, well, I guess she knows which of us is boss. Though I may as well tell you before she does that she made the sergeants' exam, but I'm still getting there.'

'Does that bother you?'

'Wouldn't it bother you? Brains is what it takes to pass those exams, not just boning-up, and how does it look for her to pass and me not to? When we hit New York again I won't find it easy to call my wife "sarge" in the course of duty.'

'A friend of mine in Boston works for a company where his wife has risen to vice-president,' Calvin recalled.

'I'm surprised the marriage has lasted. But me, I'm reckoning on Connie having a kid and staying home, sooner or later.'

'It doesn't always happen that way.'

'With my wife, it sure as hell had better. How's it going with you and Kate?'

'We've planned our next move.' But the truth was that Kate had. And Cal could well imagine the feelings of a guy whose wife was always a step ahead of him. 'And the hell with moving to a different bar, Brad. Let's drink up and order another.'

'That's one way of drowning out the music.' Brad waited until their second glasses of beer were before them, before saying, 'Which front did you plan the move on? The one concerning what you and she are into, or the personal one?'

'Which personal one?'

'The one that struck Connie'n me, when we all shared your bourbon before dinner, as being a skating rink – and the ice sure seemed to be getting thin on it this evening. What's with you and that English lady, if you don't mind another Yank asking? You can cry into your beer while you tell me.'

'Kate and I are nothing more than friends.'

'If you want to put me on, go right ahead. A guy who has to kid himself has to kid himself, but that makes no difference in the end. Why d'you suppose I asked you to come have a drink? And Connie doesn't need the girl-talk, she thinks Kate does.'

But Calvin doubted that Kate would reveal much, if anything, to Connie. Even if she felt like doing so, their personal situation was too complicated for her – or him – to fully understand. And the part of their story being written in Moscow was but a sequel to an earlier one. What was between them now had begun on the Black Sea cruise.

'I appreciate your concern, Brad,' he replied. 'I guess the responsibility of trying to sort things out for Yuli, and not knowing how it'll turn out, *has* made Kate and me a bit edgy with each other.'

'If that's the answer you prefer to give me, okay, Cal. And if you'd like Connie and me to pretend we're blind, deaf, and dumb, we'll go along with it. But that needn't stop us from getting a load on tonight.'

'I'll drink to that.'

Yuli's awareness that all was not well between Kate and Calvin was illustrated by his clinging to Kate after Calvin had left the room with Brad. It had taken her some time to soothe his fears, and get him to relax with his toys. This left her in no doubt that the little boy had indeed begun seeing herself and Calvin as surrogate parents, from whom he might be made to part. How would he not fear it – given what had happened to Irina and Lev?

It had not taken much to shake his fragile security, and, come what may, that second parting would be inevitable. Kate could hardly bear to look at him, such was the compassion he aroused in her.

'You sure have the right touch with kids,' Connie remarked, after Kate had rocked him to sleep in her arms, and tucked him into bed.

'I have two of my own.'

'Something had to account for it. Brad thinks we're trying to get pregnant. What he doesn't know is I'm still on the pill.'

'Isn't that rather a serious thing to fib to him about?'

Connie, who had brought along a bottle of vodka, poured some into a couple of glasses. 'I'd say it was less of a fib than the one you must've had to tell your husband. Does he know about you and Cal?'

'There's nothing to know. And how do you know I'm not divorced, or separated?'

'I'm not a detective sergeant for nothing. And while we had drinks before dinner, you told me a little about your life in London – but you didn't say "I". You said "we".'

'I could be living with someone, couldn't I?'

'Sure you could. But I guess you're not.'

'All right. I'm not.'

'So how come you're here with Cal, instead of with the other half of your "we" – if there's nothing to know, like you said?'

'Is this how you conduct your investigations!'

'That depends on who I'm investigating. With some, they have to feel you're not interested in what got them in the fix they're in, and they'll then feel the need to spill all. With your kind, I guess it's the opposite way round. I'm dying to know, and you're not going to tell me.'

Though Kate had made the quip about investigation, the atmosphere now was more reminiscent of her teenage schooldays, when she and her closest friend right through from their kindergarten days had sometimes stayed the night at each other's homes. Oh how bright the future looked to us then. Me, always top of the class for English, and not a doubt in my mind that when I left school it would be full-steam-ahead for Fleet Street. And Sally wanting nothing more than a roses-round-the-door marriage, and lots of kids. Not that the present always seemed bright to us! Kate saw them again, in her mind's eye, sitting glumly on her bed or Sally's, on nights when some trivial happening had briefly sent life awry for one or the other, she with her fair ponytail, escaping from the slide as usual, and Sally's neat, dark bob framing a face dominated by soulful brown eyes. Sally had got what she wanted, but it hadn't lasted. All she had left was the kids. Audrey's marriage, too, had ended on the rocks, but that was Audrey's fault; it was she who had gone astray, not her husband. Sally and Audrey were two very different women, who'd started out wanting very different things from life. Neither now had *all* they'd wanted, though Audrey gave the impression that she had. Who has, Kate? And in some respects you still don't know what you want. The cut-and-dried ambitions of youth were liable to be side-tracked by the unexpected. Like me meeting Alun. Or to rot when they reached fruition as Sally's had, if domesticity was your all and you found yourself married to a Don Juan. We couldn't even have visualised all that's gone on in our lives since the night we were closeted together in my bedroom, mourning the loss of Sally's current crush to another girl in our class.

'Why the wry smile?' Connie asked. 'Not that I'm not pleased to see you smile.'

'I was recalling how I and a chum of mine used to drown our sorrows in Coca-Cola as if it were gin, when we were growing up.'

Connie set down a glass beside Kate. 'But seeing as we're where vodka's the national sorrow-drowner, here goes!'

'Would you mind if I asked why you and Brad decided to take a holiday here?'

'If you'll promise not to laugh when I tell you. And Brad sure isn't laughing now we're here. I saw this travel agency ad. offering a special deal. The special part was you got to fly clipper class, without the vacation costing you more. I guess it was a carrot to sucker people into filling places on a vacation they might not otherwise have opted for, and the

215

agency thought it worthwhile to stand the price difference for the flight. It sure worked with me. How else would I ever get to travel any way but cabin class?'

Though Kate's present mood of dejection felt like a dark cloud hovering over her, she could not but find amusing the idea of the mode of travel seeming more important than the destination. Two more unlikely tourists, for what Moscow had to offer, would be hard to find.

'Brad is never going to let me hear the end of it,' Connie said. 'All the excursions we've been on have entailed a lot of foot-slogging, and what he likes to do on vacation is rest his feet.'

Kate paused. 'Getting involved with us has made it something of a busman's holiday, but we're more than grateful to you.'

Connie looked at the sleeping child. 'I just hope some good will come from the stand you and Cal are taking.'

'That's still in the lap of the gods, Connie.'

'Which isn't what *I'd* call the guys in the Kremlin, though the citizens here seem to think that's what they are.'

Kate recalled the student who had stopped her in the street in Odessa, and the views he'd expressed to her about the régime that deprived young people like himself of the reading matter they craved. 'There are lots who don't, Connie.'

'But instead of getting political, why not let your hair down about you and Cal?'

'I don't find it as easy to open up now as I did when I was a schoolgirl,' Kate replied frankly, and doubted that she could bring herself to tell even Sally or Audrey that she had almost let a man lead her by the nose to bed.

'Let's just say I thought I was faced with two problems, and now there's only one,' she said finally.

'And Yuli is *still* one, which leaves me in no doubt what the other one was. Something's happened to stop you having to choose between your husband and Cal.'

'You're too good a detective by far.'

Connie eyed her reflection in the dressing-table mirror, ran a hand through her curly chestnut hair, and accepted the compliment without modesty. 'Also one who's seen enough situations change overnight to know this one could.'

She sat down on the stool and toyed with the emerald green scarf she was wearing tonight with her black dress.

'I once got a call at the precinct from a woman who asked for her boyfriend to be put where he couldn't take an axe to her. Since he was threatening her with it when we got there, we hauled him off to the slammer, like she'd requested. Next morning, she called up to tell us it was just a love tiff, and she wasn't going to prefer charges. She wanted him back.'

'What exactly are you trying to tell me, Connie?'

'I guess that when the motivation is love – and whoever said love and hate are twin emotions sure had a point – about-turns are not uncommon, Kate. Which isn't to say the axe didn't get used on her a few weeks later.'

Her matter-of-fact tone made Kate shiver, though to Connie it was probably all in the line of duty. And it could be that the real moral of the story was contained in the endpiece.

'Anyway, Kate, forget the busman's-holiday crap. If you need back-up, you know to whom you can come. Any time. But how I'd play it, if you don't mind a spot of advice, is real cool and one step at a time – '

Kate put a cautioning finger to her lips.

'If that means what I think it does,' Connie said with a grin, 'Brad is going to have to rethink his pillow-talk.'

Kate said, for the benefit of whoever was secretly listening, 'Since this is Monday, and I'm due to leave Moscow on Thursday, all there's time for, Connie, is for those who want me to hand Yuli over to them to convince me, somehow or other, that their hearts are not entirely made of stone.'

CHAPTER NINE

KATE COULD not have foreseen the flurry of behind-the-scenes activity the performance she had put on for an unseen listener would set in motion. But it was Calvin's afterwards carrying through the tactic she had suggested which dictated the form the KGB's next attempt to soften up Kate would take.

On their personal front, it seemed to Calvin that Kate had *hardened* her attitude. His return from the drinking session with Brad was greeted by Connie opening Kate's door when he knocked, and closing it again after stepping into the corridor to join her husband.

The 'thumbs down' signal he received from Connie, and Brad's commiserating smile, caused Calvin to begin viewing his own position as ignominiously as Kate was seeing hers, and where there is ignominy, anger is not an unknown follow-up. The hell with her! he was thinking by the time he flopped into bed and pulled the covers over his head.

He could not have known that she lay awake for half the night, as he did, despising herself for thinking that if Yuli cried out, it would bring Calvin rushing to her side. The connecting door being only slightly ajar was the opposite of the rift that now yawned between them. Part of her longed for him, and the rest of her hated him – which caused her to reflect upon Connie's words in that respect. Which of those equally powerful emotions would she allow to win? Remember the tailpiece to Connie's story, Kate. But no battle was harder to fight than the ones you have with yourself.

Later, her fitful slumber was accompanied by a vivid dream in which Superman landed a helicopter in Red Square, snatched Kate and Yuli from under the gaze of the toothpicker, and bore them triumphantly away to England.

Then England turned into America, and Superman's face became Calvin's.

Before sleep put Calvin from his misery, he told himself, over and again, that he was lucky to have discovered Kate's unreasonable streak before he'd got in deeper. But an inner voice kept saying, 'How much deeper than contemplating another hetero relationship could you have got?' He thought, too, of Alun Starling, and decided to put away the envy and definitely pity him. It was not until he awoke to the greyness of another early spring day in Moscow that he reflected guiltily that since he and Kate shared that kiss in the cab, he had not thought of Sandy at all.

They emerged from their respective bathrooms to find the communicating door wide open, and Yuli whizzing one of his toy buses back and forth from Kate's room to Calvin's. To the child, there was no reason to behave any differently today than yesterday, and they managed to put on a show of friendliness, as parents might when a quarrel lingered on and their children had shown signs of distress on that account.

Before breakfast, Calvin called Arbington to arrange a meeting, and was instructed to find his way to Alexandrovsky Gardens.

'Think I should go by metro, and try to give our friend with the dental fetish the brush-off?' he said to Kate.

'Since Tweedledee wasn't the only one on the line, and he knew it when he fixed the venue, it would serve no purpose,' she replied.

A step ahead of me, as usual, thought Calvin. They were heading along their corridor toward the lift, and passed Babushka talking to one of the chambermaids, beside a linen trolley. 'It would serve a purpose for me,' he said vehemently, 'to have the satisfaction of going someplace, just one time, without feeling the hot breath of intrigue on the back of my neck!'

Kate's cool answer was, 'In the case of the toothpicker, I suggest you substitute halitosis for the imagery you chose.

Did you notice his breath when he got close to us at GUM? It almost knocked me over. And don't be surprised to find the limousine parked near where you're meeting Tweedledee.'

Her perfunctory tone served not just to emphasise their rift, but to make Calvin feel he was her lieutenant. Well, aren't you? he thought later, seated in yet another cab, approaching yet another milestone on the road to nowhere, though the milestone the funeral had represented would be something comforting for Kate to tell Irina if today's tactic worked. There would be no way of comforting Kate, when she finally had to accept what Calvin had seen from the first as the inevitable.

When he left the hotel, the toothpicker had stayed put beside the entrance, and Calvin had realised that Yuli was the guy's assignment; where the child went, he went – but that didn't mean that others, whom they had no way of recognising, were not among those hanging around, for one reason or another, outside the hotel. The scene while he'd stood on the steps putting his coat collar up and pulling on his gloves had not, apart from the toothpicker, included anyone or anything out of the ordinary. A group of women boarding a tour bus, over at the car-park. Some guys standing together and casting impatient glances toward the revolving door, as if perhaps their wives were still inside and holding them up, like you saw outside hotels wherever. And a few people standing alone, stamping their feet against the cold, he recalled. Had any of them looked Russian? He'd only got a back view of them, and absently at that; he'd been interested only in the creep with the toothpick, but remembered noticing a fur hat like his own on a guy in a bulky overcoat. But you're not the only tourist you've seen wearing one, are you? And getting as paranoid as Kate! Nevertheless, it is possible that a KGB operative was assigned to cover any lone venturing forth we might do. Calvin found himself prey to a shiver, affected, as he knew she was, by the faceless quality of their real adversary – and was none too happy when the taxi pulled up beside the walls of the Kremlin.

'Why have you stopped here?'

'Alexandrovsky Gardens it was that you told to me?'

'Correct.'

The driver pointed a stubby finger to some iron railings, behind which trees and bushes were visible.

Calvin swallowed hard. 'I – er – wasn't expecting it to be here – '

'Our famous Alexandrovsky Gardens, it is where you may take a walk beside many great monuments,' the bearded Russian began a familiar display of national pride. 'Here is not the main entrance, near where is the memorial to the revolutionaries.'

'Then why are you dropping me here?'

'It is the main gate you wish? You are meeting someone, perhaps? But to enter there, you must – '

'No,' Calvin said more loudly than he had intended, and got out of the cab. 'You guys sure know your country's history,' he heard himself jabber while paying the man, reminding himself of Kate's inane chatter when they got off the train with Yuli as if the toothpicker weren't there.

'If you wish perhaps to engage me for the day – '

What opportunists the cab drivers here were, but who could blame them? 'Thanks, but I'd prefer a quiet stroll in the Gardens. Allow me to compliment you on your English.'

Calvin took a cigar from the pack in his pocket, and while he lit it watched the cab move off and join a stream of traffic. There was no shortage of official cars in the special lane, but in this vicinity that was to be expected. No sign of Caspar and Boris in a parked one, though – Kate was wrong about that, and why did it give him a glow of strictly personal satisfaction?

He cast introspection aside and with some trepidation entered the paved gardens he had not known were adjacent to the seat of power. Nor was it easy to relate flower beds and park benches to what the Kremlin represented to the West. Though no flowers were yet blooming in Alexandrovsky Gardens, only the hum of traffic disturbed the ambience of a peaceful green haven. But a Russian would probably find

221

the peaceful, White House gardens equally at odds with the threat the Oval Office and its occupant must seem to him. It's all in the mind, Cal – but not without reason for the man in the street, Russian or Yank. Pretend you're really just having the quiet stroll you lied to the driver about. But Calvin couldn't keep his eyes from the wall, or his mind from its symbolic significance in his and Kate's situation. It was the wall they'd joked about ending up like swatted flies on – some joke! Why in the hell did Arbington suggest this venue, instead of Gorky or one of the other parks? And why wasn't he here? He'd said a cab driver would drop Calvin by the pedestrian way in, so this had to be the right end of the Gardens which stretched ahead behind the wall to where a grey obelisk loomed.

Calvin glanced at his watch, sat down on a bench and got up again, thankful there was nobody around to witness his jumpiness. A good thing this assignation had fallen to him rather than Kate, whose state of tension was increasing day by day, though she was trying not to show it. Those we're playing games with – which now includes our own embassy aides – are a lot more adept at it than we are. He walked as far as the next bench, put his foot on it, undid his shoelace and retied it, feeling like a character in one of those novels about the CIA where the contact fails to show up. And still no sign of his after he had done a job on his other shoelace. What the hell are you so jumpy about, Cal? All you're doing is meeting a guy for a chat. Then why did it feel like participating in a war of nerves?

He emerged from his conjecture and saw Arbington heading toward him, hands in his trench-coat pockets, and an apologetic grin on his face.

'I got held up by a phone call. Sorry to've kept you hanging around, Fenner.'

But Calvin had the feeling that this was a timed late entrance. Leaving him to stew in his nervous juice at a venue calculated to bring home to him that American tourists, if they knew what was good for them, didn't try to get the better of the Soviets. Hadn't Arbington's British counterpart said something of the kind to Kate on Day 1? That she was either some kind of nut, or a lady too intrepid for her own good. It hadn't stopped her in her tracks so they were now trying to put the brake on via Cal, and he wouldn't put it past this guy with the nice, open expression to have peered through the railings near the entrance to get a glimpse of his treatment doing its stuff.

Calvin felt like wiping the smile off Arbington's face, but managed instead to put one on his own. As Kate had said, though in other words, you didn't aim a left hook, verbal *or* physical, at someone you still needed.

'Is it because I'm meeting with you that I don't seem to have been tailed this morning?' he said as they began walking. Snide remarks were allowable!

'I guess it has to be because the child isn't with you,' Arbington confirmed his supposition.

'Nobody had better try grabbing him in my absence. He and Kate are with the folk who cared for him while we attended the funeral. They happen to be a couple of New York's finest.'

Arbington froze in his tracks. 'They're what?'

Calvin said with immense satisfaction, 'Is there actually something you guys didn't know?'

Arbington evaded the implication. 'Do you realise how this is going to look to the Brits, Fenner?'

'I thought it was the Russians we had to worry about.'

'And, in that respect, all I needed was for the NYPD to enter the game.'

'Which particular game is that?'

Arbington ignored the sarcasm – or were there so many backroom games, in addition to the waiting one, that it had gone over his head?

'Or should I have said the scenario,' he went on. 'Given what cops stand for here, that aspect isn't going to look good to our hosts.'

'Since they don't have on uniforms, or badges, how would the Russians know they're cops?'

'The same way they know Mrs Starling is a journalist. And that you own an art gallery. Did you forget you had to state that when you applied for a visa to come here? And how

223

you and the visa they gave you, also your passport, were scrutinised at airport immigration?'

Calvin had momentarily forgotten. But how come *Arbington* knew his and Kate's occupations? Had the KGB sent them an urgent memo about their troublesome nationals, including such possibly helpful details as those?

'And Farringdale, of course,' the embassy aide continued, 'is going to think I knew about your back-up and didn't let him in on it, which will lead him to wonder why. This isn't going to further the alliance, Fenner.'

It was now Calvin's turn to stop dead. 'For Christ's sake, man! We are not discussing a joint US-British naval exercise, or some delicate negotiations to avert a nuclear war. All Kate and I are trying to avert is misery for one small human being. It's time you and your British opposite number began seeing it in that light.'

Arbington sat down on a bench, leaving Calvin no option but to join him. Since it was a bitingly cold day, and a high wind doing battle with the branches of the trees, none but themselves and a stray mongrel dog had chosen to visit the gardens that morning.

'What's your real angle, Fenner?'

'If you don't know, it has to be because you've forgotten how to function on a human level. And if you tell me you have kids of your own, I am going to throw up.'

Arbington's response to the jibe was, 'Mrs Starling has sure got to you. You strike me as a guy whose common sense must have told him from the off that playing footsie with who you and she are playing it with isn't going to change the outcome.'

'Can't you people see anything except in terms of games!' Calvin wasn't going to defend his own intelligence at Kate's expense. Nor would it be helpful, at this stage, for Arbington to know Cal didn't share her hope.

He received another of Arbington's too-frank smiles. 'The alternative, Fenner, would, I have to tell you, be a good deal less pleasant for all concerned, including the child. And the other side want this particular game played low-key as much as we do.'

'They're afraid of how we found Yuli hitting the headlines back home, aren't they?' As Kate and Calvin had divined, and it was the only weapon they had.

'Shall we just say, Fenner, that Mrs Starling's intervention in the Smolensky case, given her profession, and at this point in time, isn't what they're looking for to enhance their reputation in the West. Farringdale's and my summation of the current climate is that the winds of change have begun blowing – '

'I hope you're right, who doesn't?' Calvin cut in. 'But it'd take a stronger wind than is yet evident to blow down the labour camps and prisons and let people like Yuli's parents go free. And, since we're talking imagery, to fling back the gates standing between the refuseniks and where they want to go to. If that were any place but Israel, d'you think the Soviets would let them go, Arbington?'

'Given the example they're setting of a minority group who won't succumb to pressure, and the sticky situation in the Mid-East, that would have to be my reading. But let's not get into the Soviet-Arab relationship. What we're concerned with at *this* particular moment in time is the tricky situation you and Mrs Starling have created for your embassies here.'

Calvin stopped himself from saying forcefully that that wasn't what he was concerned with, and sat listening to the wind, that unlike Mr Gorbachev's wind of change had nothing to restrict it, do battle with the branches of the trees. A tricky situation was how Arbington and Farringdale viewed Yuli's piteous plight, and trickily was how their end of it was being handled, as it was by the other side. For both, the outcome had to be that the *status quo* remained unchanged. With nobody losing face. It seemed that what the *Ocean Queen*'s purser had said in that respect didn't apply only to the Soviets. But Calvin would not have envisaged the practice being taken to the lengths he and Kate were now experiencing. Or that he would be called upon to resort to their kind of chicanery to achieve his own end.

He plunged in with the crafty move that Kate had plotted,

hoping he was a better actor than he felt. Arbington sat silently stroking his chin.

'Thanks for confiding in me, Fenner. And you can trust me not to let Mrs Starling know this suggestion came from you. Believe me, I'll make double sure that Farringdale is well briefed on this one. It's good to know you feel you *can* trust me. I was getting the impression you didn't.'

Calvin let that pass.

'Just to recap,' Arbington said briskly. 'It's your considered opinion that Mrs Starling being allowed to see the child's mother could achieve the low-key outcome we're looking for.'

'I would certainly call it a step in the right direction,' Calvin went on playing his part.

'Are we talking on the principle that every little helps?'

'At this juncture, and from where I'm sitting, I would double-definitely have to say that I couldn't have put it better myself.'

'In that case it must be taken with the seriousness it merits. Mind if we stretch our legs?'

Like the sarcasm Calvin had been unable to resist a few minutes ago, his mockery of the circumlocutory jargon had made no mark on Arbington, whose idea of stretching his legs proved to be a few paces in one direction, then a U-turn to retrace them, with Calvin and the mongrel dog following suit. What a sorry-looking wretch the animal was – if Kate were here, she'd want to take it home and feed it.

Arbington came to an abrupt halt. 'I make you no promises, Fenner. But with just two days till deadline – and neither we nor the other side are looking to the child having to be taken forcibly – if Farringdale agrees we'll go with your suggestion and see how it pans out.'

While he and Arbington continued strolling the path, as if they were old buddies who'd met for a private chat about this and that, it struck Calvin that, on a smaller scale, the hanky-panky going on about Yuli had parallels with that surrounding Shcharansky's release to the West. Shcharansky was not a spy and everyone knew it, and by the time they let him go, the international furore about his case was such that the Russians must have been glad to see the back of him. But they had insisted upon that final tactic of releasing him as part of a spy-exchange, and the US had accepted it, albeit tongue-in-cheek.

'Would you happen to know what Mrs Starling had in mind, when she first refused to hand over the child?' Arbington inquired.

Calvin's reply was acerbic. 'Believe it or not, Arbington, there are some folk whose reaction to finding a small boy alone in a flat with a dead body wouldn't be a considered one, and it's not surprising that after learning the circumstances, they'd be unwilling to entrust him to those who created them. What are the chances of Yuli's parents being freed?'

Arbington said hastily, 'Don't let's get into that one. Farringdale and I have enough on our plates dealing with what you and your girlfriend have already landed us with.'

'Mrs Starling isn't my girlfriend.'

'I don't give a shit if she is or not, Fenner. Forget what you just asked me about the child's parents. Enough toes have been stepped on already. Heads are being scratched at a high level about who sent you two to throw a spanner in the works. Your arrival on the same day from opposite sides of the Atlantic doesn't help.'

'Believe it or not, we're just a couple of tourists.'

'But the Soviets are never going to. And I have it that they're particularly foxed by neither of you being Jews, nor members of Amnesty.'

Calvin no longer found it remarkable that information gleaned from him and Kate by a KGB operative in a GUM snack bar on Sunday had by Tuesday reached the ears of the US embassy, and could not resist replying, 'But we did have a meeting with a visiting Baptist.'

'Oh, my God, you're not into that one, too? I shall have to put a Scotch into Farringdale's hand before I report back to him. But getting back to the child, Fenner – well, I guess it's just his misfortune he was born a Russian Jew.'

Calvin's response was biting. 'Weren't those the sentiments expressed in the Thirties about the Jews in Hitler's
Germany?'

Calvin had returned from his meeting with Arbington with
the instruction to stay in the hotel until they heard from him.

They were in the restaurant, and lunch almost over, when
a message was delivered to them by Mr Kropotnikov in
person. If Mrs Starling would please be ready in fifteen
minutes' time, Mr Farringdale would be in the lobby to
escort her on the visit she had expressed the wish to make.

When the assistant manager had departed, Kate touched
the pepper-pot for luck, and said to Calvin so warmly that he
thought she had forgotten their estrangement, 'You did it,
Cal! We've won round two!'

'Does that friendly smile mean what I'm hoping it means?'

'All it means, Calvin, is we are still partners in this, and I
would never be so churlish as to refrain from congratulating
you on what you pulled off. It couldn't have been easy, given
the mulish impression Arbington must have of me.'

Nor is he the only one, Calvin silently replied on his own
behalf.

'I'll leave you to supervise the rest of the little one's meal,
while I nip upstairs and get my coat. And don't let him have
any ice cream, Cal, while I'm not here to see. I wish they'd
stop plonking it down in front of him; it could set his cough
back.'

A distant memory returned to Calvin. Himself and Lori
beside the bed in Gary's nursery, exchanging anxious
glances because their child was running a fever. A teddy-bear
bigger than he was propped up in the blue basket-chair.
Gary's stars-and-stripes patterned pyjamas. A glass of milk
they couldn't get him to drink, on the bedtable. And the
window drapes drawn to shut out the daylight. It must have
been when he had German measles.

'When Gary got wheezy once, I recall the doc recom-
mending we *feed* him ice cream – or was it when he got
tonsillitis . . .'

'Whichever,' said Kate, 'I'm sticking with my gran's remedy, it's doing him good.'

She rose and hugged Yuli, her expression fleetingly poignant, and Calvin knew she was wishing she could take him with her to see his mother. But what was that look in her eye, now?

'One round has to lead to the next until the fight is over,' she said enigmatically, and was gone before Calvin could collect his thoughts.

What could she have meant? Not only was she a live wire, her mind was like quicksilver, and her thoughts were put into action while Cal was still getting his breath back. How did Alun cope with her? Meanwhile, Calvin was left to cope with his own uneasiness on her behalf, to peel an apple for the little boy gazing questioningly at him, while contemplating Kate's possibly saying or doing, while he wasn't along to intercede, something that might lawfully entitle the KGB to take stronger action than mere deportation. The unaccustomed velvet gloves with which they were still handling her must be making their hands itch already. And if what I'm going through is a sample of Alun Starling's wedded bliss, give me my placid home life with Sandy!

He made himself calm down, and sliced the apple into quarters for the innocent cause of the back-room wire-pulling he had set in motion this morning.

'*Nyet*,' Yuli said, shaking his head. '*Ya khachu peets vadoo* –'

'Oh! Yuli's begun to talk, isn't that marvellous, Mother?' Daphne said from the far end of the table.

'Well, he had to come out of his shell sooner or later, Daphne dear.'

But even Mrs Caldwell seemed moved by the event and said in a kinder tone than Calvin had yet heard her employ, 'I should get on and pour him some water, if I were you.'

Since Yuli had pointed to the jug while speaking, Calvin emerged from his private joy and gave the child what he had asked for.

'*Nyet*,' was Yuli's response.

'Oh dear,' said Mrs Caldwell, back in character, 'he's

being naughty, Mr Fenner. If my children had behaved like that they would have received a slap on the back of the hand.'

And Calvin would lay odds that the back of Daphne's hand had suffered much when she was little. *But why is Yuli playing me up? And why has he suddenly begun talking?* All they'd yet heard from him was an occasional "Mama", as if what he was bottling up was epitomised by that word and he sometimes allowed himself the relief of uttering it.

He offered Yuli a chunk of apple. The little boy took it from him and threw it onto the table.

'Oh, dear, dear me,' said Mrs Caldwell.

'He's getting his spirit back, Mother.'

Which any fool could see – and thank the Lord for that!

'*Ya khachu* Kate!' Yuli said, and a torrent of Russian followed. Then he turned to look at the doorway. '*Gdye* Kate? *Ya khachu* Kate!'

Calvin lifted him from the chair. 'Okay, let's go see if we can catch her before she leaves.' *You didn't need to understand Russian to realise Yuli had been asking where Kate was. Or be a child-psychiatrist to divine that her rushing out of the restaurant without him had triggered off what followed. Who could know what went on in a kid's mind – and in this kid's especially,* Calvin thought, striding with Yuli in his arms to the foyer.

Then Yuli said, as though he was practising saying the two names their addressing each other had made familiar to him, 'Kate, Kate, Kate. Cal, Cal, Cal.'

He went on reciting them until they reached the lift, and, when Kate stepped out of it, held out his arms and greeted her delightedly.

'Kate! *Ya khachu* Kate! Cal, *ya khachu* Kate!'

'I think he's telling me it's you he wants. And now he's started, there seems to be no stopping him,' Calvin said with a smile as she took the wriggling child from him.

'Nor shall there be, if I can help it.' Kate pulled down Yuli's rumpled red sweater as they walked toward the hotel entrance, where she could see Farringdale waiting for her, both hands clasped on the handle of his umbrella. She set

Yuli down and straightened his hair maternally. 'It isn't just his cough that could be set back, and the doing of it wouldn't be as pleasant as ice cream.'

They had halted in the centre of the foyer, amid the usual bustle of activity, and the to-ings and fro-ings of those using the curving stairway, Kate fondling Yuli's cheek and Calvin smiling down at him.

'Kate, Kate, Kate! Cal, Cal, Cal!'

'But Kate has to go now, Yuli. She'll be back before you know it, little guy, and Cal will be here all the while with you.'

Yuli looked from Kate in her coat and hat, to Calvin's indoor clothes.

'Okay, little guy?' Calvin said reassuringly.

The child nodded and they shared a glance that said: We've brought him this far and all we've gone through on his account was worth it.

Whatever comes or goes between us, this is something Kate and I will always share, thought Calvin.

Kate's mind had already switched to matters more practical. 'Don't let Yuli follow me to the door, Cal – '

'I wouldn't think of it.'

Neither had much doubt about what Kate's conveyance was likely to be, and it would do Yuli no good to see her getting into the kind of vehicle in which his parents had been driven away. Before coming to Moscow, Kate had associated gleaming black limousines with weddings, but would she ever again see one without it conjuring up deportations and worse?

'Thank you for being so prompt,' said Farringdale.

'Thank you for making the arrangements,' Kate answered in the same artificially polite tone.

He paused outside the hotel entrance to hand her a gift-wrapped parcel. 'It occurred to me you might like to take along a little gift, since we British never like to arrive empty-handed.'

One would think they were off to a dinner-party! 'That was a kind thought, Mr Farringdale. But shall I be allowed to give it to her?'

'Since this excursion is, to say the least, something of a precedent, we shall have to wait and see.'

Was it him, or his calling, which made everything he said sound like a formal statement? Kate was bucked by the implication, but how far would the KGB be prepared to go with their special favours, in order to avoid a confrontation that could damage Mr Gorbachev's image?

'Before we get into the car, let me caution you to say nothing to complicate this already complicated situation, Mrs Starling.'

'I'm not *that* foolhardy, Mr Farringdale.'

Boris was holding open the car door for her, and Caspar, behind the wheel, gave her a nod so pleasant it must mean that they'd been instructed to treat her like a VIP. She could have been forgiven for feeling power-drunk again, but Kate Starling had in a few short days learned to recognise a tactic when she saw one. A car rug for her legs was included in the treatment. Was Boris going to try to tuck her up in it? – foolhardy or not, he'd get a clout for his trouble.

'No, thank you,' she said, handing it back to him. And what was all this for but to convince her that she'd got them wrong, that what she'd seen with her own eyes was just a little slip someone had made, and that Yuli would be safe with nice chaps like them.

Meanwhile the car was heading down the incline towards the main street. And Farringdale was talking inconsequentially about his wife's interest in horses. By the time they turned into Mira Prospekt, Kate was getting a picture of a sturdy girl in riding breeches who had somehow managed to make an austere Moscow apartment look and seem like a bit of old England.

'Val kept it as a surprise that she'd asked Mother to send her the chintz curtains and cushion covers, and when I arrived home from the office and saw the drawing-room – well, it warmed my heart. By the way, it was she who made it possible for you to take along the little gift,' he added, glancing at the beribboned parcel lying on the seat between them.

How could anything warm his heart when he hasn't got

one? Kate was thinking. 'It's beautifully wrapped,' she contributed to the conversation that was far, and absurdly, removed from the purpose of this journey. But it was a safe subject. What on earth would she and Tweedledum find to talk about next?

But he had not yet exhausted this boring topic. 'As I was saying, Mrs Starling, I can take no credit for any of it. Val was given the box of chocolates – they're Swiss – by a friend of hers who came to stay, and she presented me with them to bring to you, before I left this morning.'

Kate was registering that it seemed his wife had a heart, when he added casually, 'They were meant for *you* of course, and it's kind of you to have decided to give them to the lady you are on your way to visit.'

Kate was momentarily bemused. Was all this bumbling on about his wife and the chocolates an oblique way of making it plain to the KGB men that it wasn't a British embassy man who was making a direct gesture of kindness to an imprisoned Soviet citizen? Of course it damn-well was! Why hadn't he just said, when he handed them to her outside the hotel, 'Look, I got these for Irina Smolensky, but I'd prefer that only you know it.'? Or, 'My wife would like her to have them.' Because it wasn't politic to allow even Kate to think her embassy, whose representative he was, would make the gesture. Had the man stopped seeing himself as a person? Or was diplomacy so tricky it spilled over into your personal life?

Still, the gesture proved Tweedledum not quite the cold fish she had assumed, and she had to concede that it wasn't impossible that those in her embassy, and Cal's, unofficially – that word again! – did what little they could for the refuseniks. I shall never know if they do, or not, she realised, but it was warming to let herself think so amid the cold realities she'd encountered, left, right, and centre.

'What I should have liked to do,' she said to Farringdale, 'was to take along some flowers. But the arrangement was made too suddenly for me to get any.' Flowers, with their living beauty, would have helped Irina remember there was a world waiting for her outside her prison.

A minute or two later, Caspar was halting the car beside a flower stall.

This pandering to Kate's every whim was enough to make her head whirl – but what was behind it was more than enough to keep her feet on the ground. She got out of the car to buy some of the undersized daffodils on offer, and managed to smile while the old woman in charge of the stall, whose complexion had the texture of a walnut, wrapped the several bunches she had selected. It wasn't until they were handed to her that she realised the only Soviet currency she had was a few kopeks Calvin had given her for the metro slot machines on the night they had to keep riding up and down escalators to find their way to where the Smolenskys lived. Exaggeration though that was – there had been only two, or was it three? turnstiles involved, though the same could not be said of the escalators – looking back on it was like viewing the traumatic beginning of a story not yet over. One in which Kate Starling was keeping the KGB and a British Embassy man waiting while she bought flowers. Unreality assailed her again. Then she called to Farringdale, 'You're going to have to lend me some roubles, I'm afraid. I didn't get around to cashing any travellers cheques. With one thing and another!'

She had let Calvin foot all their expenses, and mustn't forget to settle up for her half of them, including Yuli's new clothes, before they left Moscow. Meanwhile, Caspar had got out of the car and was hastening to her side to complete her transaction with the flower-woman. It was over and done with while Farringdale was still sliding along the seat towards the car door, and even from this distance she saw him give her a warning glance, and returned with Caspar to the limousine. What had Farringdale thought she might be going to say or do? Oh, the impression everyone, including Cal, seemed to be getting of her. If they saw me at home – trundling a shopping trolley around the supermarket with all the other housewives; serving my family their dinner; dealing with the week's laundry on Monday mornings – and, give or take the odd exception, never saying boo to a goose, they'd know the sort of woman I really am. That I'm not the sort to throw my weight around at the drop of a hat. But Yuli's situation, a little boy put through the mill along with his parents for political reasons, was a good deal more than the drop of a hat to Kate if not to the men in the car with her.

'There is not the necessity for you to repay me the roubles, Mrs Starling,' Caspar said when the journey was resumed. 'I shall charge to my expenses.'

This was all Kate needed to hear. The KGB buying flowers for Irina? Much that had happened since Kate and Cal got into this could be termed bizarre, but this one took the biscuit! She said deliberately, 'My embassy representative will reimburse you, and I shall reimburse him.'

'Whatever you wish, Mrs Starling. And if you would prefer that my colleague should not smoke in the car, I shall oblige by telling he should put out the cigarette.'

Kate wanted to say that if she looked as if she was choking it wasn't from the smoke, though there was an ongoing blue fug issuing from the front passenger seat, but the effect of such close proximity to calculated hypocrisy.

Farringdale noted Kate's clenched fists, and said, 'You really should meet my mother.'

She was treated to yet more of his small-talk, this time about the lady who, among other accomplishments, it seemed was a dab hand at making lemon curd.

Rather than let a tense silence gather – he knew when not to, as well as when to use one to his advantage – in the presence of those doing Britain, in the person of Kate, a favour, he was keeping a light conversational ball rolling. All Kate need do was put in the occasional, 'Really?', as though he were the batsman and she the fielder.

Where had she been all her life, that she'd thought men like those with whom she was now dealing, on both sides, were any different in the flesh from how they were presented in fiction? Though the KGB's methods were no secret to the West, you had to tangle with them yourself, as Cal would put it, to know what it could do to a person, and the tangling didn't have to be physical. As for Farringdale, what gave him the right to barter and bargain away the welfare of a child in the name of a country whose citizens would surely be outraged if they knew? And the same went for Cal's bloke and the American people.

'Last year, Mother won the prize-cabbage rosette at the village flower-show,' Farringdale informed her.

And a prize cabbage was what his mother sounded like. 'Is that so?' she varied her response, while allowing herself a vision of all the mothers of Britain and America rising, as one, to storm the Soviet embassies in London and Washington, on Yuli's behalf.

The vision faded. Only chance had brought Kate to Yuli's aid, and led her to discover what she was now aware of. That what the ordinary citizens of democracies *didn't* know about what went on in high places, in their name, was frightening. Kate and Cal were witnessing diplomacy in action, the bargaining and bartering in which human costs seemed of little account.

While Farringdale described the succulence of his mother's 1985 raspberry crop, she noted that they had left the city perimeters behind, and were now travelling through countryside.

'Is the prison outside Moscow?' she asked, when he paused for breath.

Caspar chipped in, with a throaty chuckle. 'What is this prison Mrs Starling has mentioned?'

'Please tell him I'm not in the mood for joking, Mr Farringdale.'

Farringdale put a hand on her knee and exerted a modicum of pressure.

Since this was hardly the time for him to make a pass at her, it must mean he wanted her to shut up.

'If I were you, Mrs Starling, I would sit back and enjoy our mystery tour.'

Translated from diplomat lingo, that meant it was a mystery to him, too. But he showed no surprise when, after speeding for a further fifteen minutes along a winding road past what looked to Kate like apple orchards, Caspar turned the car into a narrow lane at the end of which stood a large house.

They had reached their destination, and Caspar hadn't

236

been joking. In his job, he'd probably forgotten how to; as Farringdale, in his, had doubtless lost the capacity to be surprised.

Caspar parked the car on the crescent-shaped drive, which was bordered by tall bushes. The house had a mellow appearance, its stucco façade had been painted cream, and its windows were glittering in the first rays of sunlight Kate had seen since she arrived in Moscow. As if the KGB had coerced the sun to emerge from behind the clouds and help them put her in a good mood, she thought as she got out of the car, her shoes crunching on gravel as she and Farringdale followed Caspar to a door with a brass knocker on it.

'What is this place?' she asked Caspar.

'It is what it appears to be, Mrs Starling,' he replied while wielding the door-knocker.

Kate had yet to find that applicable to anything or anyone she had encountered so far – other than the victims at the heart of the matter.

The door was opened by a white-haired woman whose pleasant appearance confirmed Kate's impression that she was being subjected to a hard-sell; right down to the woman's cosy carpet slippers and her homely flower-patterned overall. Since they couldn't expect anyone from the West to believe that this was the ambience in which they held those whom they arrested – Lefortovo prison, where Lev was, was notorious for its conditions and cruelties, and that was but one of the many that human rights activists were campaigning about – they evidently wished Kate to think that Irina was in some sort of rest-home for wayward refuseniks. No, the truth is probably that they just don't want me to see the environment they're holding her in, and they're putting on this show for good measure.

Kate got a fleeting glimpse of polished wood, and a painting on the wall, as she left Farringdale seated in the hall and followed the woman upstairs to a square landing, where a vase of hothouse blooms greeted her from a corner pedestal. Given the outrageous price of the wilting daffs she was clutching, no expense, nor trouble, had been spared to impress her. But don't let it go to your head, Kate. You don't matter a fig in all this; they'd just as soon, and much more gladly, grind you underfoot if they could achieve their end that way.

'You are in time for tea,' the woman paused to say to her. 'And I have even remembered that the English, they prefer to take it with milk.'

Kate could imagine Farringdale saying, if he, too, were brought tea with milk, 'By Jove! A real home from home.' A ham actor saying the right lines to a ham actress was a feature of how he and this "motherly" KGB woman played their parts.

The comic side of what she was experiencing was there; but this afternoon laughter would have died in Kate's throat, stifled by the sinister overtones which had hovered in the air from the moment she got into the limousine, and by the reason she was here. Nor would *she* play this bit of the exercise their way.

'I didn't come for tea,' she said coldly, as the woman opened a door for her to enter.

'I have already prepared it for you, and shall bring in the tray for you to enjoy it.'

She would be lucky if Kate didn't throw the teapot in her face!

Then the door was closed, and Kate loosened her fists and found herself in a spacious room that even Farringdale's wife would have considered a drawing-room. Whose country retreat was this? The walls were covered with a blue patterned fabric, and a crackling log fire, with a sofa placed before it, enhanced the bogus cheer.

Only Irina, standing with her back to the window, looked out of key with the setting, though attempts had evidently been made to ensure that she looked presentable, thought Kate, in the silence that followed her own entrance.

Irina had on a starched, printed smock that hung from her bony shoulders like a tent, and a red polka-dot kerchief was tied gypsy-style around her head. Her hands were resting on her swollen belly, and Kate would not easily forget the pathos of her stance, or the grey sky behind her silhouette, which

238

seemed at that moment like a chilling omen after the fleeting sunlight that had just shone upon Kate.

Which sums up the difference between my lot and hers. Kate was too moved to speak, and it was Irina who ended the silence.

'They cut off my hair.'

Kate dumped the daffodils on the table by the door and went to embrace her.

'And I smiled while they did it,' Irina went on, 'for by doing so they have made of me a more religious woman, when their purpose is for me to stop being a true Jewess. The ultra-orthodox of my religion decree that a married woman shall do what has been done to me, and to cover her head afterwards, until the day she dies, with a wig if she so chooses, or with a covering like I am now wearing. But that orthodox, I never was.'

'My grandmother used to say that God's ways are weird and wonderful,' was all that Kate could think of to say.

'It is what I, too, have been thinking. And I shall never, from vanity, defy His laws again. It is a lesson He has taught me.'

But would God go to such lengths? Kate cast theology aside, since she was certainly no expert on the subject. 'I'm so pleased to have this chance to see you again, Irina.'

'I, too, to see you, Kate. Though it was Barbara whom I thought to see.'

'They didn't tell you it was me?'

'Only that it was an English woman.'

'How are you, Irina?' What a stupid question! But the atmosphere was so charged, it was difficult to find the right words.

'My unborn child is still kicking to let me know she is alive, I am thankful to say.'

'You are hoping for a girl, are you?'

'Since I have already a boy, of course. What more can a woman ask than a son and a daughter to care for her in her old age?'

How simple Irina's wants were. Possibly they hadn't

always been. But what life had imposed upon her would surely equip anyone with a true sense of values.

'Also to be allowed to dwell in peace,' Irina added. She managed to give Kate a smile. 'You are a good friend. And perhaps you bring news of my mother and Yuli? Of how they are managing without me, I am so anxious. *Matushka*, she will do her best to care for him, and she has not the strength.'

Kate led Irina to the sofa before the fire. Then the woman entered carrying a tray, put it down on the low table in front of them, and left.

On the tray, an afternoon-tea had been set, complete with a pewter teapot, china crockery, some bread and butter, and a dish of jam. As if they'd had it flown in from the Ritz. Well, not quite. But hang on to your sanity, Kate!

While she poured the tea, she sought for a way of softening the blow she was about to deal Irina, whose anxious gaze was riveted to her face.

'First, let me tell you that Yuli is fine, though he misses you.'

'And my mother?'

'Your mother is dead, Irina.' There *was* no way of softening such a blow. 'And Yuli is at present in my care. Right now, a trusted friend of mine is watching over him. Please believe me that your little boy is fine.'

Irina was trying to take in the bitter-sweet information she had just received. Though tears eluded her, she briefly covered her face with her hands, and Kate knew she was weeping inwardly for her mother.

'Drink some tea, Irina. In England, we think there's nothing like it for helping a person hold themselves together.'

'I am not coming apart, Kate.'

'I'm very pleased to hear that.'

'If I were the kind who does, I would have already been in pieces when you met me.'

She sipped some tea, nevertheless, and gazed pensively into the fire.

'When I was a small girl, I had a story-book in which was a picture of children seated beside a hearth where flames were dancing as are those in this hearth. It became for me my childish ambition to one day sit by a fireside, to be warmed within and without by the glow. Apartments here, they do not have them. When I grew older, I asked one day of my father why the children in Soviet cities were allowed the books to make them wish for what they could not have.'

Irina's expression, as she stared absently at the burning logs, told Kate that she was re-living the conversation with her father.

' "What do you mean, Irina?" he said to me.

' "Since we are city-dwellers, I cannot sit by a fire, and I should like to."

' "To wish to sit by a fire will not corrupt you," ' he replied. ' "But it was clever for one so young to see what you have seen."

' "What is it I have seen?"

' "Did you not use the word 'allowed'?" '

Irina emerged from the memory and drank some more tea. 'It was of course beyond the understanding of a girl of twelve. But as the years passed by, I have many times had reason to recall that talk with my father.'

Was Irina deliberately blocking out her mother's death, by turning her mind to the past?

But what she said when she had put down the teacup showed how closely related to the present her seeming digression was.

'And when, today, I was brought into this room, and saw the hearth, Kate – Who would have thought the KGB would make for me the dream come true?'

She took a piece of bread and buttered it. 'I had better not to waste this nourishment, for the sake of Yuli's baby sister.'

Kate mustered a smile. 'If it turns out to be a boy, he's going to look funny with a bow of ribbon in his hair.'

'In Israel, a *yarmulke* will adorn his head. And Yuli's Bar Mitzvah shall be celebrated beside the Western Wall.'

The possible mirage Kate had tacked on to the rabbi's analogy about those who heeded no warnings about crossing the street. And given the existing situation, substitute "probable" for "possible".

Kate was loth to bring Irina down to earth, but it had to be done. Nor have I yet told her something it will be comforting to hear. 'Your mother had a Jewish burial, Irina. My friend and I were able to arrange it, and attended the funeral. But in two days' time our visas will have run out, and we shall have to leave Moscow. To whom are we to entrust Yuli?'

Irina stopped eating, and returned her gaze to the fire. 'Much though I love my husband, that there is no one now to turn to is Lev's doing.' She raised her head to look at Kate. 'Always, he has been a man who despises in others the need for friends. Such a terrible independence, he has – '

That certainly fitted what Kate and Cal had gathered from the Smolenskys' neighbour. 'There is a saying, that no man is an island,' she said.

'How many times,' said Irina, 'did I try to make Lev to realise it? If it were not so, would you be now here with me? Since they have taken me, like an island of sorrow is how I have felt. The sorrow, it is still with me, how could it not be? But alone I no longer feel.'

Irina went on eating, as though doing so were a task which must be completed. 'When first we applied for the exit visas, many who also had done so came to welcome us to the refusenik community. Most did not know us, but they came all the same.'

She absently licked her finger. 'I had forgotten what butter it tastes like.'

'Yuli's been plastering it on his bread every mealtime, at my hotel.'

'Did the rich food not make him sick?'

'Cal made him go easy at first.'

'Cal is the name of your friend?'

'It's short for Calvin.'

'Please say from me to him thank-you. He sounds to be a nice man.'

Had Kate been too hasty in deciding otherwise, so far as he and she were concerned? She hadn't let him explain why he suddenly came out with what he did in the cab, had she?

But this wasn't the time to review *that* situation. She watched Irina stoically munching.

'Yuli's little sister, she will have the indigestion tonight, Kate.'

'Why not give her some of the jam, too?'

'It would be bad for the teeth she has not yet got.'

When the bantering was over – and how brave it was on Irina's part – Irina went on with what she had been telling Kate about Lev.

In essence, it was more of the same, but if talking about it helped her, Kate was willing to listen. And what it boiled down to in a word was isolation.

'But I shall not forget my visitors from England,' she said finally, 'and how one of them has told me in my time of sorrow the words I shall keep telling myself, when I am back in the place they brought me here from.'

'If you get to Israel, Irina, I'll come and visit you, and bring you a volume of the poetry that line is from,' Kate said impulsively.

'It is poetry? And not "if", Kate "when".'

'But that line is considered a bit hackneyed, it gets quoted so often.' Don't waste time discussing poetry, Kate, as if you were hobnobbing at a literary cocktail party. Get down to brass tacks. 'Can you think of anyone at all, Irina, who would take care of Yuli until you're released?'

'How can I now ask those whom my husband by his behaviour has offended to do this for him and for me? *Mitzvah* though their doing it would be.'

'What does that word mean?'

'It is to perform a charitable act, and in my religion is considered an honour. I wish for the blessing to come upon you, Kate, that is said to result from such a deed. For all that you, who are not a Jewish woman, have done for me.'

Irina lay back and closed her eyes. 'Excuse me if you please. I am feeling a little malaise. But it seems that when I need the special strength, somehow I find it. And it has to be God who provides it.'

'Would you mind Yuli living with a Jewish family who aren't refuseniks?'

'So he would accuse his parents of a foolishness that parted him from us, when next he sees us? Who can know how many years from now that may be?'

And the same applied – only worse – if Yuli were to be raised in a Soviet Children's Home. The fate of the baby Irina was now carrying was something Kate daren't let herself think about.

'I asked you because of an offer made by the rabbi I met at your mother's funeral,' she told Irina. 'Something made me say, "No, thanks" to him.'

'It could be that you have good instincts, Kate.'

'But that doesn't solve our problem, does it?'

'We must leave that to God to do for us how He thinks best.'

And God might be listening in, but so were the KGB or the cosy wardress would not have left them alone together.

'There is still a little time left before you must return to your own life,' Irina went on. 'And I have for a long while been living mine day by day, and putting my trust in Him. Thank you for bringing to me the flowers, Kate.'

Kate thought of all the children God had let go to the Nazi gas chambers. And of how the mothers of Argentina's "disappeared ones" had finally risen from their prayers, and their private heartbreak and public demonstrations to rout out the men responsible, though by then, it was too late for their own sons and daughters – and where was God when *they* were taken? The best that could be said was that when it came to salvation, He required a lot more assistance from the ordinary people of His universe than He was getting. Only the intervention of a pop singer had saved a generation of Ethiopian children from death by starvation; but Bob Geldof was the number-one exponent of the 'no man is an island' theme, which too few people and nations embraced on a scale forceful enough to evoke change.

When the door was opened to signal that it was time for Kate to leave, she kissed Irina's pale cheek and said quietly, 'I envy you your faith.'

Irina's voice, saying, 'before you must return to your own life,' echoed in Kate's ears on the drive back to Moscow. But putting the Soviet Union behind me – and that time can't come soon enough – isn't going to include turning my back on Irina. The immediacy of Yuli's plight had, of necessity, loomed largest, but when Kate got home it wouldn't be enough just to ask the Rosses to add Irina's name to the list of incarcerated refuseniks for whom their organisation was campaigning. Getting freedom for the girl whose child she was still fostering would be a task Kate would never give up on. And not just freed from prison, but to where the Western Wall was. 'Not if, Kate, when,' she had said. Irina's spirit was worthy of more than mere admiration.

A vision of Irina being hustled back to her prison cell, now the elaborate charade was over, made it no easier for Kate to sit listening to some more of Farringdale's inconsequential blathering – as if his life depended upon it. His job probably did. As for the two in the front of the vehicle, who had maintained their phoney pleasantness when she got into it – she felt like yelling, 'Stop the car and let me out!' The sole reason she didn't was she was still playing a game with them, as they were with her. Only the extra card she'd hoped to get up her sleeve, the name of someone Irina would trust to foster Yuli, hadn't been forthcoming.

Since the KGB were evidently desperate to achieve what Arbington had this morning called a low-key finale, they might have accepted the suggestion. But there was now nothing left for Kate and Cal to bargain for.

Later, when Farringdale had escorted her to the hotel entrance, she asked him where Irina was being held. 'And if you say where is who being held, Mr Farringdale, as if you've never heard of her, and she isn't, I shall scream so loudly you'll wish you hadn't said it.' Right now, Kate didn't give a tinker's who might be within earshot, and she'd had enough duplicity – no, multiplicity – for one afternoon!

'My mother would absolutely adore you.'

Was this some more of his stalling? Or had he got a mother-complex? The inner workings of the outwardly smooth Tweedledum and Tweedledee were beyond Kate. Nor had she the time to dwell on it now. 'Would you mind answering my question?'

When he had done so, he added – which didn't surprise her – 'But you didn't get it from me.'

Calvin watched Kate take off her coat, and the yellow beret she had probably put on to match the more cheerful mood in which she had set off to visit Irina.

'I'm glad to see you back, Kate.'

'It's a relief to *be* back, Cal.'

'Kate, Kate, Kate! Cal, Cal, Cal!'

They glanced at Yuli, who was shooting toy buses, two at a time, between the rooms, his little legs running apace with them.

'He's been jabbering away in Russian, the whole afternoon,' Calvin told Kate.

'And since that's how we want to keep it, let's be even more careful than usual not to mention names. Little piggies have big ears, and we don't want to set him back now. The big bad wolf has big ears, too.'

'Bearing both those facts in mind, can you tell me anything at all, right now?'

'After you've given me a drink. Is there any of that bourbon of yours left?'

Calvin fetched the bottle and poured some for her. 'As bad as that, was it?'

'But not in the way I'd expected it to be. On the surface, it was like one of the cosy têtes-à-têtes I sometimes have with my chums.'

'The visit was in one of the prison offices, you mean?'

'What prison?' said Kate, pointedly. A toy bus halted beside her, and she sent it whizzing back. To the child who was not here!

'I've been to a nice tea party, Cal, in a pleasant country house.'

Calvin got the message. 'I see.'

'And when I get home, I'll be able to write an article about it, won't I? Tell my women readers how impressed I was by the treatment those in my friend's position receive. That she'd been given a pretty smock to wear, and enjoyed her tea.'

Kate cradled her glass. 'The most uplifting aspect of my outing was her remarkable and sustained faith in God,' she told Calvin and the bug. 'Considering what she's gone through I don't know how she does it. And if I may share a sacrilegious thought with you, God's non-interventionist policy is beginning to get up my nose.'

'There's another way of looking at it, Kate.'

'Try to convince me.'

'Could be He's washed His hands of the human race. Look what we've done to the world He created.'

'I'm a conservationist, too, but I wouldn't stand by, like He is doing, and see my children do terrible things to each other, just because they'd polluted my garden fish-pond with a bottle of ink. And God could have avoided the evils of the world by refraining from creating the serpent.'

'Since you've leapt to the biblical, may I mention the apple?' said Calvin. 'Which you seemed on the point of offering me, but changed your mind.'

'You changed it for me.'

'But I still don't know how, do I?'

'Nor was what you just said an accurate description of what happened in the cab.'

'Okay. I'll withdraw it. What I'd like for us to do is start afresh, Kate – '

The shrilling of the telephone on Kate's bedside table intervened, but they let it go on ringing, prey to their private thoughts. Starting afresh meant cleaning the slate, but it couldn't be done, and both knew it. Their relationship had reached a point of no return when they shared that kiss.

Kate had allowed what followed to influence her judgement of Calvin, and the conclusion she had leapt to didn't make sense with what she knew of him. But it had given her a let-out from taking what would be for her a major step, and possibly she'd clutched at it for that reason.

The way he was looking at her now was with affection, not lust.

They became aware that the phone had stopped ringing.

'Yuli's answered it for us, Kate.'

'Well, not quite – '

'But he's sure come on a ton, hasn't he?'

The little boy, though he had not spoken into it, was holding out the receiver to them, and they exchanged an amused smile when he put it down on the bedtable with a shrug and resumed playing with his buses.

'Think whoever called you is still holding on?'

'Unless it was Connie, or Brad, or Daphne, I couldn't care less. Let's find out.'

How worn out she looks, Calvin observed as she picked up the receiver. He saw her eyes narrow. What now? Their moment of pleasure hadn't lasted long!

'Haven't you gone home from work yet, Mr Farringdale?'

'Alas, no. My working day doesn't end at 3.45. I wish it did.'

Kate glanced at her wristwatch. He'd picked her up at half past one, and she'd been back, talking to Cal, for about twenty minutes. Her outing – for want of a better word – had taken less time than its exhausting effects had led her to suppose, and the gathering dark she could see through the window had impelled her to make that crack to Farringdale, though jibing at people was no more her style than the rest of how she was behaving here.

'I have in front of me the box of chocolates my wife sent for you, Mrs Starling.'

Kate recalled his carrying the fancy parcel into the house for her, but she had not given it a further thought. What an empty social gesture presenting it to Irina would have seemed.

'It was kind of your wife, Mr Farringdale. But, as my forgetfulness indicates, I have other things on my mind.'

'Could you be ready fairly shortly?'

'Ready for what?'

'Oh, didn't I mention it? Our Soviet friends would like you to see one of their Children's Homes.'

Kate's expression hardened.

'What's wrong?' Calvin asked.

She covered the mouthpiece and told him, while Farringdale was waffling on about getting her back to the hotel in time for dinner.

A silence followed her replacing the receiver.

Calvin picked up the notepad and ball-point pen beside the telephone and scribbled: Either they want your approval for where he'll be put if you hand him over, or they took literally what you said to me about writing a feature when you get home.

Kate took the pen and wrote furiously: Why not both!!

The exclamation marks revealed the mood she was in, which her expression confirmed. When Calvin got her coat and held it out for her to put it on, she shook her head mutinously.

He wrote on the pad: What can we lose by playing along?

She grabbed the pen that seemed the only safe way of privately communicating indoors, her feelings exacerbated by having to stop the words from pouring off her tongue: Only our minds!

Yuli came to join in the pen-and-paper fun, as any child might. But this was not any child, and it was poignant for both to see a little boy, unaware of what might shortly befall him, seat himself cross-legged on the floor, the pad balanced carefully on one thigh, while he made a spidery drawing of what was unmistakably a house.

'*Mama, i Papa, i Babushka, i Yuli,*' he said, pointing to it.

'And I guess it isn't *our* Babushka he's referring to,' Calvin said.

'*Ya khachu eedtee damoy,*' Yuli said, while adding a tree to his work of art.

'Could he be telling us he wants to go home, Kate? Though I don't recall seeing trees close by – '

'It must've been what he was thinking when he drew the picture, but he's probably thinking it all the time, isn't he? Only an idiot would assume that the way he's responded to kindly treatment means he isn't pining for his mum!'

'Why are you letting me have it?'

Kate borrowed the pad and pen from Yuli, who did not look too pleased about it, and thrust her written reply under Calvin's nose: We can't make things right for him, can we? And I can't bear it.

She gave the pen and pad back to the child and put on her coat. Calvin was right, of course. Nothing would be lost by their playing along, and some more time would be bought, while they hung on to Yuli. Though restoring his family life was beyond them, they might still find a way of keeping him out of an institution. Like to tell yourself how, Kate?

'Which of your berets shall you wear for *this* little excursion?' Calvin asked more lightly than he felt.

'Why not the colour I associate with hope?'

Calvin watched her pull on her white one, without bothering to look in the mirror as most women would have, and resolve was in the way she did it. Nor would it have faltered during her mutinous moment. Kate was not going to give up until the final bell. And she hadn't yet explained the enigmatic parting remark she'd made in the restaurant, that had worried him stiff.

He fetched the pad and pen from his own bedtable and scrawled: What was all that about one round always leading to the next?

Kate took the pen: But it didn't come off, or I'd be visiting possible foster parents now. Irina couldn't suggest anyone.

Calvin owed her an apology, since he'd envisaged her doing something hazardous and without having consulted him. Like what? Whatever, with Kate Starling a guy got the feeling she might.

'I thought you knew what I had in mind, Cal.' And let those at the other end of the bug make what they would of that! she thought, buttoning her coat. The prospect of another car ride with two of their kind was enough to make her ask Calvin to pour her some more bourbon.

Calvin's reply was, 'You have so many things in mind, Kate, it's hard to keep up.'

'I wish you could come with me. We could've asked our friends to stand in again.'

'Sure. If I'd been invited along. But I'm getting used to the role reversal.'

'What role reversal?'

'You getting all the action, and me staying home.'

Yuli came to show them some more of his spidery drawings. Though a house was in each of them, some shapes recognisable as animals were there, too.

'Think he'll be an artist when he grows up, Kate?'

'A Picasso, I'd say, if that cat with an eye where it shouldn't have one is anything to go by.'

'How do you know it isn't a dog?'

'It's got whiskers – look – '

Yuli was gazing up at them, awaiting their approval. Kate gave him a kiss, and Calvin said, 'We ought to've got you a set of crayons, little guy.'

One of the piping torrents of Russian they were getting used to, followed before Yuli resumed his drawing.

'Wouldn't it be lovely if we knew what he was saying to us, Cal? And the other way round.'

Nevertheless they had somehow managed to reach him, and he knew he was safe with them; little by little, the tensions to which no child should be prey were loosening their grip.

Homesick though he must be, thought Calvin, home was a place where he saw terrible things happen and lived in fear of them happening again. It wasn't surprising that the animated kid he'd shown himself capable of being, today, had hidden himself inside his shell – though it was his way of coming out of it that Daphne's martinet of a mother had disapproved of. While Kate was out, this afternoon, he'd crept back into it and sat staring into space a few times, as was to be expected. The few days he's spent here with us is just the beginning of the rehabilitation Yuli needs, but what was the chance of him getting it?

Kate was thinking that Irina would perhaps find it hurtful to see Yuli as he was now despite his separation from her – what mother wouldn't? But only a selfish one, which Irina wasn't, would choose to have it any other way.

Before leaving, she ripped from both pads the notes she and Calvin had written, tore them to shreds, handed them to him, and pointed to the bathroom.

Since at this stage most of their conversations were likely to be on paper, the flush on the john was sure going to be kept busy! he thought when she was gone, and derived some sardonic amusement from performing his lowly task.

Yuli came to investigate the repeated flushings, and stood in the bathroom doorway watching Calvin wield the handle.

'Wondering what's going on, little guy? Well, it's like this, you see. The chief told me what to do and I'm doing it.' But what makes Kate think I needed telling? What a woman!

While she and Farringdale were being driven to the place the KGB wanted her to see, Kate asked herself a difficult question. In Irina's position, would she have agreed that the rabbi's offer should be turned down?

The answer was that for Irina, as for Kate, the well-being of a child could not be ensured by providing three meals a day and a roof over its head. Or I wouldn't be so dead against Yuli's being put into a Soviet Children's Home. There was the future to bear in mind. The five-year-old who entered the Home would, as Kate had pointed out to Calvin, if he remained long enough emerge the person whom life within its walls had moulded.

The same applied if Yuli were to be placed for an equal length of time with a non-refusenik Jewish family, though the moulding might not be deliberate; children absorbed the attitudes of those who raised them. Emily had a schoolfriend whose parents Kate and Alun considered racist, and at her daughter's last birthday party, Kate had noted the girl's reluctance to sit between two black girls at the table, and the look which had said, 'Why did you have to put me here?'

Farringdale had fallen briefly silent, and was gazing through his window at the lit-up city, as Kate was. Boris, like an ongoing chimney, was again belching out his acrid smoke, and Caspar had begun quietly humming a tune; as a man might when he has in sight the end of a difficult job of work.

It wasn't just time that was on their side, Kate registered. It was everything. This was their terrain and it was like none Kate had ever before trodden. Nor had she imagined herself a match for them. How could someone with normal standards of human behaviour hope to come off best with these unscrupulous men? Yuli was but a pawn to them, as his dead grandmother had been, or she wouldn't have had the religious burial that was her right.

When she stood on the pavement outside the Children's Home, surveying for the second time that day a building the KGB considered it suitable for their own ends for her to enter, unreality enveloped her again. She shook it off, and thought, as Caspar and Farringdale escorted her along a broad path toward a red-painted door, that it probably hadn't occurred to Irina that Yuli might end up in an institution. Irina wouldn't have *let* that thought cross her mind, any more than she would the idea of her son being raised by non-refuseniks. God was there to make all come right for her, wasn't He? And making things come right couldn't include what God, like Irina, knew was the opposite of right for her child. Leaving everything to God, as Irina was, had to involve that kind of reasoning – if reasoning entered into it at all.

A woman whose appearance reminded Kate of the cosy wardress opened the door – but there was something about her that gave Kate the feeling she was the real thing, that motherly and warm she really was.

'Here are our important British visitors, Sofia Ivanovich,' said Caspar heartily. 'They may stay for as long as they so wish. I shall await them in the car.'

'Please to come inside, Mrs Starling.'

And that takes care of which of us is the VIP to be impressed. The phones had been busy setting in motion another charade, though Sofia Ivanovich seemed out of key with KGB trickery. Was there in Moscow, by now, anyone on their pay-roll who didn't know Kate's name?

'I am here the matron. And these beautiful paintings you see now, they are the work of some of our children,' Sofia said, indicating the framed pictures on the walls of the pleasantly furnished hall.

'I say!' was Farringdale's suitably admiring response.

'Under this roof is much – how do you say? – talent,' said Sofia with a beaming smile.

Her pride was like that of a fond granny showing off photographs of her brood, and Kate felt obliged to view the paintings one by one, with an enthusiastic Farringdale by her side.

Sofia remained at the foot of the stairs, and though her mood was the opposite of humorous, Kate couldn't resist the opportunity to quietly give Farringdale a dig. 'You're officially here on this one, are you?'

'As I was on our mystery tour.'

'But not to the extent of participating in the visit.'

He let that pass. 'This Home is quite a showplace, Mrs Starling, though I haven't had the pleasure of visiting it myself until now.'

'I bet it is,' Kate replied. 'Nor would I doubt that all Soviet Children's Homes are of equal standard,' she was saying when they rejoined the matron.

'That of course is correct,' Sofia said. 'In our great country our children are the pride and the joy. Where else is the future of a nation but in its young ones?'

Kate believed her. But for the men in the Kremlin, her second pronouncement would have priority. Nevertheless, she noted as the tour progressed, this place lacked nothing in the way of amenities for a happy childhood – except the parents these kids presumably didn't have.

'Are *all* these children orphans?' she asked Sofia as they passed a bunch of healthy-looking little lads on the broad staircase.

'Those boys, they are going now to watch a game of chess which is between two of the older ones. It is what they like after their supper the best to do.'

'Would you mind answering my question?'

'Technically, in every case that does not apply,' was the careful reply.

But the matron of a showplace Home in Moscow would need to be not only motherly, but an expert in verbal fencing, since visiting politicians from the West would surely be brought here on the special tours laid on for them. Did any of them ever get to see the grim realities Kate and Cal had?

'Tell me about the children it doesn't technically apply to, please,' Kate persisted. And the heck with Tweedledum coughing behind his hand and shooting her a cautioning glance. Since it was odds on, now, that Yuli could end up one of them, she wanted to know the backgrounds of the others. 'Why are they here if they're not orphans?' she asked bluntly.

'Do you not have in your country children whose parents are unable to take care of them?'

'Certainly. But I'd be interested in the reasons for it in yours.'

'My function, it is solely to conduct you around,' said Sofia, ushering them into a dormitory. 'Here is where some of our girls, they sleep.'

The room was unoccupied, but there was about it a too-tidy look. Not a garment in sight, nor a book, or magazine left lying on a bed. On the walls were some of the bright coloured posters whose larger editions were to be seen on hoardings and walls wherever one went in Moscow, the figures they depicted exuding solidarity and strength. Kate contrasted them with the pictures of pop groups and rock stars her kids had stuck on their bedroom walls, expressions of their own interests; not those of the parents who knew, on a wider level, what was best for them, but were allowing them to feel their way and find out for themselves. Irina had, when recalling her long-ago talk with her father, revealed that she had learned the significance of the word 'allow' at an early age. Kate thought of the young people she had noted in the metro train; how their Russian version of the outfits worn by their counterparts in the West had struck her as a brief rebellion against all that that word meant in the Soviet Union. Though it would get them nowhere, a breath of free air had got to them, and that was better than never having experienced the mind-stretching it was. But the kids who were raised in a place like this . . .

'You will see, Mrs Starling, that each girl has on her bed a beautiful doll.'

And the doll on each bed was sitting in the identical position to all its little friends. Stop trying to find fault, Kate!

Farringdale's reaction was the approving wonder he had

evidently seen fit to display since they arrived. 'Oh, my word!'

And never had the overly British utterances he kept making seemed more fatuous to Kate. 'Do the public send gifts for the children at Christmas?' she inquired. 'Like people do in England?'

The mention of Christmas caused Farringdale to again cough behind his hand, as if Kate had mouthed a dirty word in a convent.

Sofia gave her a proud smile. 'Soviet children, they do not require what is in the West called the charity. All children in our great country are well cared for and equal.'

The heck with this double-talk! 'Except the Jewish refuseniks.'

Sofia looked briefly uncomfortable, before countering, 'We have here a child of Jewish parentage, who is, of course, cared for as are all the other children. That is she whom you can hear is playing the piano. If you would please to come with me, I shall now take you to our music room.'

Kate had supposed the strains of Mozart drifting into the dormitory to be coming from a radio or record-player somewhere in the building, and received a glance of disapproval from Farringdale as the matron led them downstairs.

The music room was at the back of the house, and unoccupied except for the child seated at a grand piano, her eyes closed, and her fingers as if caressing the keys. Though Kate had been conscious of her heels clacking on the wood floor, the little girl was so lost in her music she had not heard them enter.

'It is when she may have the room to herself that Ida best likes to practise,' Sofia told them quietly.

'And she's a jolly good player,' said Farringdale, as though he were watching a hockey match.

It didn't sound like practising to Kate, more like a concert performance music-lovers paid to hear. 'How old is Ida?'

'She is soon to be eight.'

And looked like a miniature madonna, with that rapturous expression on her small, sculptured face, and her silky dark hair drawn back and held by a slide. If ever there were a child prodigy, thought Kate, I'm seeing her now. It wasn't just the music, but everything about her.

'How long has Ida been here?' she inquired.

'Ida has known no other home. Her father, he was sentenced for his anti-Soviet crimes, and is in Siberia. The child was born while her mother, who afterwards received also that sentence, was awaiting trial. The Soviet government does not punish little children and babies for the crimes of their parents, and took it upon themselves to raise Ida in a suitable environment for a Soviet child.'

Remembrance returned to Kate of how she and Calvin had found Yuli cowering in a pool of urine. Punishment could take many forms and be indirectly dealt. What she had just learned was like seeing the fate of Irina's unborn baby written on the wall. They would probably take it from her immediately it was born, and instruct one of their functionaries who happened to be a nursing mother to suckle it, so it would imbibe what they intended instilling in it with its first mouthful of milk!

Farringdale noted Kate's expression and coughed ostentatiously, thankful there was but one more day to go before this unprecedented affair reached its inevitable finale, though he doubted it *would* be a low-key one. A day and a half, he corrected himself, if the other side let it run on unto the eleventh hour. The woman who personified for him what his mother did, would not concede defeat until there was absolutely no alternative, and even then they would have to tear the child from her.

'You are enjoying the music, yes?' the matron interpreted Kate's silence. 'It is possible that the Soviet Union may one day be rewarded for our government's great kindness to Ida. Already, she has given her first recital to the public.'

'I say!'

The young prodigy was now playing a Chopin nocturne, and still oblivious to their presence.

'Ida, she is already being tutored at our famous Moscow Conservatoire, and perhaps will follow in the footsteps of our revered Vladimir Horowitz.'

257

A Jew who had shaken the dust of his native land off his feet as a young man, and given her conditioning Ida would not be following in his footsteps in that respect, nor would she be allowed to. And how paradoxical it was that the Russians claimed him as their own. But they were a music-loving nation, and art transcended politics, as the pen was mightier than the sword. How had those in the Kremlin, who stifled the pen and wouldn't hesitate to wield the sword, contrived to let the great pianist, now an American citizen, back into the Soviet Union without their losing face? It was a triumph for freedom in anyone's book, but Kate didn't doubt that they had found a way – even if it was just making much of Horowitz's wish to perform for Soviet audiences.

'I am told that you are a journalist, Mrs Starling,' Sofia Ivanovich said as they left the room. 'And we are hopeful that you have made here the good comparison with such places for children in your country. There is left now to see only where the chess match is being played – '

'That won't be necessary, thank you. I've seen enough.'

On the return journey to the hotel, through Moscow's seething rush hour, Farringdale made no attempt to engage Kate in conversation. He's letting the good impression he hopes I got of the Home quietly do its work, she thought, and on the surface there was nothing to fault. Kate hadn't really expected that there would be. She was glad that the children who lived there were happy and healthy. But lending herself to Yuli's joining them – ? Oh, no. Would you mind telling yourself what the alternative is to your lending yourself, Kate? Other than having him taken from you and put there, where he and little Ida can grow up side by side believing their parents are enemies of the State?

When again Farringdale stood with her for a parting word outside the hotel, she brushed aside her depression and gave him a chance to defend himself.

'Why are you and Mr Arbington helping the KGB achieve their ends in this matter?'

'Is that really how it appears to you?' He looked immensely shocked.

The shock seemed genuine, and possibly it was. Perhaps those whose job entailed the means being as important as the end lost the capacity to see things in perspective. 'How else *could* it appear to me?' she said tersely.

There were times when Farringdale wished himself in some other profession, and this was one of them; so that he could openly ally himself with what he knew to be just and let the intricacies of diplomacy go hang. Instead he must evade the issue. But how, when confronted by those blazing green eyes that all but reduced him to a small boy again, receiving a deserved ticking-off from the woman he had thought unique before he encountered Kate Starling?

It was beside the point that if his wife were of the same calibre he wouldn't have married her, he thought, while formulating a suitable reply.

'Let's forget how things appear,' Kate prodded him, 'and get down to what you are in effect doing.'

'Protecting our own nationals,' he parried.

'From what, exactly?'

He looked from where the toothpicker was still stationed to the limousine which was just leaving the forecourt. 'Would the word "unpleasantness" suffice?'

'It more than describes my impression of the KGB.'

'Some would call what you've experienced unprecedented pleasantness.'

'And if I hadn't known there's such a thing as unpleasant pleasantness, I should know it now, Mr Farringdale.'

'You have yet to experience what Arbington and I are trying to avoid on your behalf.'

'On *whose* behalf? What you two are trying to avoid is an incident that could make things difficult for your embassies, and never mind the poor kid who's at the centre of the matter. I would rather have had a head-on clash with the KGB top brass, than have been a party to what I have.'

'Then why did you acquiesce?'

'From a man who could give me lessons in the means justifying the end, that's some question! And the answer, in a nutshell, is that Mr Fenner and I were prepared to swallow our disgust, in what seemed to us the best interests of the little boy. Nor have we yet given up hope,' Kate added, though hope was flickering low.

'Do you have something specific in mind?'

'I'd be a fool to tell you if I had.'

'It would go no further than Arbington.'

They were briefly distracted by an Intourist bus disgorging a group of people laden with packages.

'They must've been on the organised tour to the big *beryozka*,' Kate remarked, 'which Mr Fenner and I wouldn't't've had time to visit even if it were in the city centre. I wonder why it isn't?' Was it because the Muscovites weren't allowed inside it, and the authorities hadn't thought it suitable for them to have amid their own stores one in which foreigners could buy the kind of luxury goods not available to them?

If Farringdale had an opinion he did not express it. 'We seem to have wandered from the subject,' he said with a smile. 'And I must ask you what your intention now is, with regard to the child.'

'My intention, Mr Farringdale, remains what it's always been. To try to make sure Yuli has a home with the sort of people his mother would think suitable on all counts. If I were able to find the right family, there'd be no reason to put him in an institution, would there?'

'Technically, no.'

They were back with the diplomatic double-talk, and just when Kate had thought she had come to grips with him. 'What the heck does that mean?'

'I was thinking aloud. Tossing the ball back and forth in my mind.'

He was never going to see this other than as a game. But hadn't both sides, between them, got Kate and Cal thinking that way?

A moment later, after transferring his umbrella from his right hand to his left, he was wordily presenting her with a possible final move. 'If you should manage such a solution in the short time left to you, it might, in my view, be acceptable to the other side provided they were able to construe it as an arrangement made by them.'

Briefly, Kate felt that Tweedledum was on *her* side. Then the feeling petered out and an upsurge of frustration replaced it. How was she to find suitable guardians for Yuli? And even if she did, it would all come to nothing if it couldn't be done with the condition Farringdale had attached to it.

'Would you and Mr Arbington be prepared unofficially, to help with the necessary conniving?' Not for the first time she saw the mask of diplomacy shroud the smile he had been giving her.

'My dear Mrs Starling, all this is pure hypothesis, and likely to remain so.'

He raised his hat and departed, leaving Kate to contemplate the two hypothetical problems he had firmly put into that category.

That evening, Kate and Calvin were presented with a situation they had not *allowed* themselves to hypothesise.

Kate returned to her room from her second traumatic excursion of the day to find Yuli already bathed and dressed and Calvin about to take his pre-dinner shower.

Calvin took one look at her exhausted appearance and decided that telling him all about it – which would have to be done on paper – could wait. 'What I suggest you do now, Kate, is lie down on your bed for a little while.'

'It would make us late for the meal.'

'So what? It wouldn't be the first time and Yuli's had a candy bar to keep him going.'

Yuli gave Kate a smile from amid the toy bricks with which he was building a tower, and the ache which just looking at him brought to her heart was still there when she had done as Calvin suggested and dropped off to sleep.

It seemed but a moment later when Calvin wakened her.

'Is Yuli in your bathroom, Kate?'

She forced her eyes open and saw Calvin, wrapped in a towel, stride past the foot of her bed on his way to find out. He returned with a stunned expression, matching Kate's feeling of being frozen into immobility. Then she leapt out of bed. 'How did they get him out of here without us hearing him scream?'

'Never heard of a hand being clamped over a mouth? It's way past dinner time, nobody's on the corridor, and Babushka's on duty to have noted that *we're* still in our rooms,' Calvin painted a picture to which Kate added Yuli wriggling and kicking as the KGB snatched him.

'Is that chloroform I can smell?' she said.

'No, it's my talc. You and your over-active imagination! Isn't the reality enough?'

'I wouldn't put it past them to have put him out with something, even if you would! And the bug is welcome to record my opinion of the KGB.'

'You've left them in no doubt of it already – '

Calvin's reply was made to the air. Kate had rushed from the room.

He chased her along the corridor. 'Where are you going?'

'I don't know.'

'And panicking will get you no-place!'

'Nor will your shouting at me.'

'All you'll get from Babushka is the usual non-reply.'

The floor-woman was watching them run toward her with no more interest than if they were a couple of joggers in a park.

'And all we need right now is Mrs Caldwell!' said Calvin.

Daphne's mother had just stepped out of the lift and briefly stopped in her tracks when she saw them. 'What are you people up to now?'

Her tone was sufficient to slow them down and halt them, and Kate made an involuntary movement to cover her cleavage. She had taken off her sweater and skirt before lying down and was wearing only her bra and half-slip. In an emergency, you didn't pause to put on your dressing-gown. And Cal's bath towel had come askew. Would Mrs Caldwell faint if it slipped to the floor?

'Would it not be letting the side down, Mrs Starling, I should feel it incumbent upon me to report this to the management,' Mrs Caldwell said when she reached them.

'As for your friend, his behaviour must be attributed to his being an American.'

Anyone else might have asked if our rooms had caught fire, thought Calvin, but all this woman is concerned with is respectability.

Kate, who had wondered why a woman as overtly maternal as Daphne was not married, got a vision of Daphne as a young girl bringing a boy home after a date and her mother waiting up to chaperone them. A boy who wouldn't bother dating her again. But these thoughts were in the midst of her misery about Yuli. The dash along the corridor was as futile as Cal had tried to make her see. Panic had set her running to she knew not where, like she'd leapt off the metro train on Friday night though she knew it wasn't the right station.

Its aftermath, this time, was despair. They had made no contingency plans for what had always been a possibility, preferring not to contemplate it.

Mrs Caldwell averted her eyes from Calvin's bare chest and edged past them to proceed along the corridor. 'If you will excuse me, I am on my way to fetch my daughter for dinner. I told her on the telephone to return the child to you and come directly to my room, but she has chosen not to.'

'Hold on a minute!' Calvin called to her receding back.

She stopped and turned around. 'I beg your pardon!'

'Are you telling us that Yuli is in Daphne's room?'

She gave them the insinuating sort of glance at which the sanctimonious excel. 'There is no need to dissemble with me. How convenient you must find it to have my daughter next door whenever you require privacy. That child would be better off in a Home, than in your care however temporarily.'

Mrs Caldwell did not stay to witness their shared glance of relief and they followed her down the corridor in what felt like the wake of a battleship.

'Such are the priorities of the narrow-minded,' said Calvin, 'whose minds are probably a lot more off-beat than yours and mine. It wouldn't surprise me if Mrs Caldwell put an invisible whip in my hand, when she saw me chasing you, both of us near-naked, and hell for leather.'

'If that last bit was a pun, I'll let it pass.'

'It wasn't. But I guess one has to feel sorry for people like her.'

They fell silent, as if, suddenly, neither could find anything to say to the other, conscious now of the near-nakedness Calvin had mentioned and aware of the sexual tension between them, which Kate's withdrawal since the kiss in the cab had exacerbated rather than eased. Kate was prey, too, to Mrs Caldwell's innuendoes tallying with the easy lay Calvin had apparently thought she was. If she hadn't been made to see that, would she have gone with the tide, and the heck with her marriage? A marriage where she'd let lethargy pass for contentment for some time, she was admitting when Daphne opened the door to her mother's thunderous knock and Yuli dashed past the dragon to be lifted by Calvin.

'Cal, Cal, Cal! Kate, Kate, Kate!' he reversed his usual order of reciting their names, and began gabbling in his own language while Mrs Caldwell gave Daphne a dressing-down.

Is it possible that our shared feeling for Yuli has intensified our feeling for each other? Kate thought. Something had to account for two people who hadn't seen each other for four years, who had lived their separate lives since then, becoming so emotionally entangled with each other in the space of a few days. It wasn't just sex. But Kate was not yet prepared to call it love.

'I'll be ready in a minute. Please don't make a fuss,' Daphne was saying to her mother.

'But you're still in your dressing-gown. And why are you keeping me standing in the corridor?'

'You're welcome to come in and wait; dressing never takes me long. Or I'll join you in the dining-room after I've had a word with my friends, Mother, which it's difficult to do with you standing in the doorway.'

'Why *did* I let you talk me into coming to Moscow!' Mrs Caldwell turned on her heel and left.

Daphne waited until she was out of earshot before saying, 'Poor Mother. And you must be tired of hearing the parting remark she made.'

Which, on this occasion, had doubtless referred to the company her daughter was keeping, thought Kate. 'You'll excuse our deshabille, won't you, Daphne? We just tore off looking for Yuli when we found he was missing.'

Calvin forgave her for including him in the panic.

'I assumed you knew he'd slipped out to visit me, and it was lovely to have him. I'm sorry you had the unnecessary anxiety – and about the chocolate on his sweater; I was just going to sponge it off when Mother knocked.'

'We'll deal with the scallywag, don't worry,' Calvin replied, 'and we'd better all of us get downstairs real fast. Come on, Kate!'

A hectic ten minutes followed while they got themselves and Yuli ready to go down for dinner, and a memory returned to Kate of herself and Alun and the children on a morning, years ago, when they had to drive to Gatwick, and had almost missed the plane because the alarm clock hadn't rung. Clothes being thrown on and hair being tugged by combs wasn't in it! She'd dealt with Emily and Alun with Jason. But despite the need for haste right now, Calvin maintained his gentleness when he changed Yuli's sweater.

'You're going to miss him, aren't you, Cal? Me, too.'

'But you have your own children to go back to.'

There was nothing Kate could say to that.

'My stint as a foster dad is almost over – '

Kate was impelled by his expression to cut in with, 'There's still tonight, the whole of tomorrow, and Thursday morning – and I'll let you do all the ministering, while I take it easy, if you like.'

'Forget Thursday morning, Kate.'

'Our flights don't leave until the afternoon.'

'I'm well aware of that. But use your head.'

'Is this your roundabout way of reminding me there's only one day left to put to practical use?'

'Why would I bother taking roundabout routes with you?'

he said abruptly. 'I haven't noticed your reluctance to ride roughshod over me. Now let's go gobble down all those courses waiting for us on the table.'

But Kate was not prepared to let it go at that and the discussion continued on their way to the lift, each of them holding Yuli by the hand, and over his head.

'Were you saying I'm the domineering type, Cal? Like Mrs Caldwell?'

'No, Kate. But you sure are a dominant personality.'

'I don't think of myself that way.'

'That's what stops you from being impossible.' Calvin smiled quizzically. 'Just when a guy is thinking the hell with you, he's disarmed by the vulnerable bit of you emerging. Like when you panic and need reassuring.'

'Is that what you call the way you shouted at me on the two occasions I did?'

'How did we get started on this?'

No more was said until they were in the lift, which they had to themselves, by which time Yuli, so sensitive to the atmosphere engendered by the adults around him, was looking questioningly from one to the other of them.

Calvin rumpled the little boy's hair and said quietly, 'I guess this kid we've both come to care so much for has set me going backward in time, Kate, to where I once was, and what I once had. But in another way I've been propelled forward,' he went on, 'out of the comfortable niche I truly believed would be where I'd stay for the rest of my days. And it now seems to me as if I've been marking time until now. Since you have to know why I'm saying this to you, let me also say I know I have no right to — '

'Nor I to let you.' Though marking time matched the lethargy she herself had mistaken for contentment – and the way they were looking at each other . . . In a minute they'd be kissing as they had in the cab, with Yuli looking on approvingly. 'Don't!' she said when Calvin took a step toward her.

Then the lift stopped at the second floor and they had company for the remainder of their descent to ground level.

Connie and Brad, who had finished dinner by the time they finally arrived, came to sit with them while they ate. While Kate listened to them tell of their afternoon at the Exhibition of Economic Achievement, she was aware of Mrs Caldwell eating in stony silence at the other end of the table, that Daphne seemed unperturbed by it, and that her own relationship with Calvin had in the lift been taken a stage further. While she watched Yuli eat his cold meat and salad, thankful that the main course this evening was not fish and chips, which by now would have been cold and soggy, she tried to analyse her own behaviour after Calvin made the remark in the taxi. It had caused her to lose respect not just for herself, but for him, too, and she hadn't given him the chance to explain what he meant but had preferred to go on interpreting it as it suited her. Like someone clutching at a reed when they were drowning. If he had taken at their face value some of the remarks *she*'d made off the top of her head he wouldn't still be giving her smiles across the table, as he was now; or showing his concern for her, as he had when she arrived back exhausted from her second outing. He would long since have told her to go to hell. You're going to have to stop clutching at that reed, Kate, and face up to what you haven't wanted to. What to do about Yuli isn't your only problem. There was what to do about Calvin, too. Also about yourself. And this evening to get through after Yuli is tucked up and asleep, and we two are left alone with our unfinished business. Unfinished it surely was. Kate had to keep trying not to meet Calvin's eyes, but they were drawing hers like a magnet, telling her how he felt about her, while Yuli prattled in Russian between each mouthful of potato salad, and Brad and Connie bickered in their lighthearted fashion about whether to repaint their living-room primrose, or change the decor to pale green. The introduction of this domestic topic stirred in Kate a nostalgia for home that was at odds with the thoughts and feelings she could no longer dismiss or deny. How could she be sitting here, acknowledging that Cal was very special to her, wanting his arms around her, while wishing she were by the hearth with Alun and the children and the cat? What you really wish, Kate, is that

267

you'd never been presented with the dilemma. There were times when she wished that about Yuli, too – who wouldn't, after all that had gone on? and it wasn't over yet – but Fate had put her there when Yuli needed her, and only a hard-hearted person would have turned their back on him. The admiration other tourists in the hotel had expressed for what Kate and Cal were doing, evinced whenever yet another toy for Yuli was brought to the table – even the Aussie-with-the-motto had managed a gruff, 'Good on you both!' – had, though demonstrations of support were more than welcome, caused Kate to say on one occasion to Calvin, 'Why do they think what we're doing is something admirable?' Kate didn't see herself in that light and she knew Cal didn't. But others seemed to regard them as some kind of hero and heroine, even Connie and Brad, and Daphne, whose involvement was by now deeper than merely giving Yuli a token of their sympathy for him.

'I couldn't put myself through the strain you folk are still undergoing,' Brad had just said, when his and Connie's lengthy debate about their living-room decor petered out. 'And I have to say I'm never going to forget meeting you both.'

Not just any hero and heroine: St George and Joan of Arc, from the look on Brad's face, thought Kate drily. But it's doubtful that if those two had met they'd have ended up in bed together, which can't be said of the possibilities for Cal and me.

'It was because there's only one day left for you to try to fix things for Yuli, and you both looked so blue, sitting at the table with him, that we came over to keep you company,' explained Connie. 'I guess it's the least we can do.'

'Want us to come by tonight with some candy and what's left of the vodka Connie bought?' Brad offered.

Kate was about to clutch at another reed – no, this one was only a straw – and say, 'Yes, please', but Calvin was already telling them that it was a kind thought, but he and Kate could both use an early night. Did he think it would be that easy to get her into bed? Don't kid yourself that it wouldn't be – but "mind over matter", Kate!

Later, while they were undressing Yuli, the little boy suddenly withdrew into a pensive silence again. Before he began talking, they had noticed that this was the time when his private thoughts brought a look of sheer misery to his eyes, and had surmised that he was missing his mother more at bedtime than at any other time of day.

'*Mama i papa*,' he said when Calvin was buttoning his pyjama jacket. Then a tear rolled down his cheek. '*Ya khachu shtorby preeshlee maya mama i moy papa.*'

Kate took him in her arms. 'We can't give you what you're asking for, sweetheart, and we know how dreadful all this is for you. All we can do is try to find a way of helping you – '

Calvin's emotion was such that he cut in with, 'Why don't we just sing him a song to distract him? Like I used to with Gary, when he grazed his knee, or whatever, to stop him from making a big deal of it.'

'My method with Emily and Jason was to stick an Elastoplast over the graze – but Yuli isn't making a big deal over something minor, and it's breaking my heart.'

Calvin's response was to begin pom-pomming 'The Teddy Bears' Picnic'.

'Is that the only children's song you know?'

Calvin paused only to say, 'Would you mind helping me along with it?' after which they put on a show of musical good cheer that sounded hollow to their own ears and did nothing to dispel the unhappiness of the child for whose benefit it was.

'I've never felt more inadequate in my life,' Kate said, when they tiptoed into Calvin's room after sitting with Yuli until he fell asleep, each of them stroking one of his hands.

The next few minutes were occupied by Kate telling Calvin, via pen and pad, the condition which Farringdale had attached to the KGB's consent to Yuli being placed with a suitable family.

Calvin's scrawled reply was brief and to the point: Since we're not going to find one, forget it, Kate.

She was seated in the armchair by the window and he stood looking down at her, while a silence gathered that said more than words. Giving Yuli their attention had been but a hiatus. The curtains were drawn and the double-glazing shut out the coming and going sounds of vehicles. Only the bedside lamp was on, and Kate could see her own shadow and Calvin's on the wall, as she had on the landing before they plucked up courage to enter the Smolenskys' flat. But the feeling she'd had then was one of foreboding. Coursing through her now – She provided a straw to clutch at, though she knew it would be only a diversion.

'We forgot to give Yuli his honey and lemon, Cal.'

'But I don't hear him coughing in his sleep, do you? Are you still holding against me what you wouldn't let me try to explain, Kate?'

'No, as a matter of fact.'

'It's occurred to me, since, that it gave you an excuse to follow your head, not your heart.'

'And I still need to be sure that it's our hearts we're talking about.'

'If what you mean is that for you sex is an aspect of love, I've always known you were that kind of woman.'

'But please don't fool yourself, any more than *I'm* fooling myself, that I'm incapable of mistaking an interesting relationship, that has in it the aspect you mentioned, for love. You know damn well how attracted to you I am, Cal, and you've left me in no doubt that it's a two-way thing. But what do we really know about each other?' There were still a lot of missing pieces in the picture Kate had put together from the few he had supplied.

'Would it help if I told you I know for sure, now, that what I am is a family man? That entails finding the right woman, and I guess I've found her. You and I are still young enough to have kids together, Kate.'

'And where do the two I already have, not to mention Alun and Sandy, fit into what you're saying?'

'Your children would make plenty of friends in Boston. Alun and Sandy wouldn't be the first guys to have to start afresh in their thirties, and Sandy'd be welcome to stay on at the gallery, though he might decide he wants a clean break. So it's over to you, Kate.'

It was the next best thing to a formal marriage proposal and Kate was unable to cope with it. If she stayed here another minute, the way Calvin was looking at her . . . 'What you told Connie and Brad about me being bushed was more than correct, Cal. And you've given me some thinking to do. Mind if I say goodnight, now?'

Thus it was that the crucial step she might have taken that night was averted, though for Calvin everything seemed cut and dried. While she undressed in her bathroom, she made herself confront the mechanics of committing herself to him. Her two closest friends were both divorced, and Sally had been glad to rid herself of a philandering husband by the time it came to it. Had Audrey felt as Kate was feeling when she contemplated leaving a man she now found dull – though she hadn't when she married him – for an exciting new colleague she had known for just a few months? Audrey never was one for considering the repercussions of her actions on others. Nor, apparently, was Cal. That didn't mean they weren't kind people; Kate couldn't have had better evidence of Calvin's kindness and compassion than she'd had this past few days. But there had to be a selfish streak in him – or was it ruthlessness? Only that sort of person could so easily have relegated Alun and Sandy to the painful position of having to start afresh, when both thought their present relationships secure.

Kate brushed her hair and asked herself if she was still looking for a let-out. A good solid reason to go no further than she already had. Could be. But she hoped she hadn't just found a significant piece of the puzzle he still was. And was it really Kate Starling he wanted, or a short cut to the ready-made family she and her children could be for him? Their still being young enough to have children was no guarantee that they would. Though, in her heart, Kate didn't believe that Cal could be that calculating, the way he seemed to have everything tied up, with not a loose end in sight, continued to disconcert her.

His bedside lamp was off when she got into bed and switched off hers, and she imagined him lying in the dark, the two of them having a sleepless night in their separate

CHAPTER TEN

THE FOLLOWING morning, they took Yuli window-shopping on Petrovka Street. As they had noticed on their taxi rides, there was no shortage of people queuing outside shops.

'I expected this street to be yards and yards of plate glass, with goods attractively displayed behind it, like in the West End in London,' Kate remarked.

'I guess it isn't my idea of a shopping street, either,' Calvin replied, 'but when we passed along here the day we did our lightning city-centre tour, I think I glimpsed a big store further along the street, opposite where the Bolshoi is.'

'Our *aborted* lightning tour, you mean. The mood I was in after lunching with our very own KGB man wasn't conducive to enjoying the sights! I'm sorry it stopped you from seeing a bit more of what tourists come to see – '

'Forget it,' Calvin cut in. 'I've had more important things to do. We both have.'

'But the most important one still isn't done.'

'I'd forget that, too, if I were you.' If Kate was still hoping for a miraculous solution to avoid Yuli being put in a Home, Calvin didn't believe in miracles.

They glanced down at the little boy, who, though he wasn't exactly talkative today, didn't look as unhappy as he had last night. Though their hearts weren't in it, they were doing what window-shoppers did, which, on Petrovka Street, was largely a matter of pausing to glance at inferior goods, drably displayed. The window they were scanning had in it a selection of dresses no Western woman would be seen dead in, thought Kate. Where was the evidence of the Soviet fashion industry she had read about in the *Guardian*, or was it the *Sunday Times*? On the backs of the

273

female élite? – since it was neither on display to tempt the ordinary Russian women passing by, nor on *their* backs.

'I've been on the lookout for women dressed like Mrs Gorbachev, Cal, but I've yet to see one.'

'That lady sure has good taste. And could be there's a better shopping street in Moscow than this one. Brad and Connie might know where it is, if you'd like to take a walk there.'

'No, thanks.'

Connie and Brad had offered themselves as back-up on the outing with Yuli. They – and the toothpicker – were trailing a few yards behind.

'You have that look on your face, Kate.'

'What look is that?'

'Your tight-lipped one.'

'I was feeling sorry for the Russians; thinking about the inequalities in this so-called equal society.'

A poster of Lenin wearing a proletarian peaked cap, on a hoarding across the street, compounded Kate's feeling that something had gone terribly wrong with what Marx and Lenin intended, and her mind returned fleetingly to the conversation she'd had with Alun about it, at the top of the Potemkin Steps. It wasn't a conversation, it was you delivering a monologue, Kate, and Alun with his mind on not being late back for the tour bus. An eventual Utopia was probably what the founder of the Soviet Union had dreamed of for the people. Instead a new dynasty, albeit uncrowned but employing the same methods, ruling by fear, had distorted the dream out of recognition. Weren't the men in the Kremlin autocracy under a different name? Mr Gorbachev had yet to prove himself otherwise in the matter of human rights. The signs that he had begun to hadn't yet extended far enough for Kate to believe them anything more than token gestures to placate the West. If he was really as humane as he wanted people to think, why hadn't he ordered the KGB to stop persecuting those who wanted to emigrate? The occasional release of a big-name prisoner of conscience, or letting a batch of refuseniks finally go to Israel, could not be viewed *other* than as token gestures by someone who had seen for themselves what oppression meant for those still on the receiving end.

Just one of its manifestations was the plight of the child trotting beside her. Yuli probably thought that the kind strangers taking care of him would go on doing so until he got his mum back, and this, for Kate, was too painful to bear. Even worse was that she knew his parting from her and Cal was nigh, and he didn't. Meanwhile, she wanted him to enjoy his last day in the family atmosphere they had created for him – or had it created itself? The few days Yuli had spent with them would slot into place in his memory, give him something warm and special to look back on.

Kate could remember every detail of the weekend when her parents had left her with the great-aunt who had raised her father, though she had no recollection of the reason for their doing so. She could not have been older than Yuli, and could still see herself, in a plaid kilt and a rabbit-wool jumper, a red slide in her hair, her little legs mounting the steep steps of the big house with difficulty, and Aunt Lizzie waiting in the doorway to welcome her. That patient lady, who had no children of her own, had shown Kate how to cut out a string of paper dolls, and had let her make free with a boxful of costume jewellery; and the most vivid memory was of being allowed to help ice the large cake Aunt Lizzie had baked for Sunday tea.

What would Yuli's be? And where would *he* be, when remembrance of this week returned to him in his manhood? Would he, by then, have celebrated his Bar Mitzvah beside Jerusalem's Western Wall? Or . . . ? Kate refused to let herself contemplate the possible alternatives. But wherever, with maturity the memory could not but be bittersweet for him.

As holding his little hand, like I'm now doing, and knowing I can't change things for him, is for me. Calvin, who had hold of Yuli's other hand, was no doubt affected as she was. And if one particular memory of Kate's trip to Moscow had to epitomise, in years to come, the overall experience, it would be of the three of them walking along together like this. It wasn't surprising that it had revived the self-stifled family man Cal was. Or that he had attached the newly released feeling to the woman whose presence had completed the image.

While they threaded their way through some people gathered around a hardware store window and blocking the narrow pavement, Kate reflected that Calvin would find it hard to pick up the threads of a life he now knew wasn't for him. Would he try to, if Kate said no to him? Or realise, as she had begun to, that what she represented for him was a female kindred spirit who would enable him to fulfil himself in every sense of the word, and that didn't have to be her.

They paused beside a shop that had towels and sheets in the window. Kate stared at the display without seeing it. Whatever the outcome for herself and Calvin, from now on nothing would be quite the same for either of them. There were some experiences that were turning points, though they weren't always recognisable at the time, but no mistaking that this was one for Kate and Calvin; whither it would lead them, and together or their separate ways, remained to be seen. All that Kate knew for sure was that she wasn't the same woman who had kissed her husband and kids goodbye before setting forth into the unknown: the unknown went for self-knowledge, too. From what Cal had said last night, it was the same for him. And what they had each learned about themselves could not but affect Alun and Sandy.

Yuli livened up and tugged them onward, and they exchanged a smile over his head, on which was Kate's red beret. Though it was too big for him, she had let him wear it when he took it from her collection and put it on.

'Going to let him keep it, Kate?'

'Why not? But I wish he hadn't chosen the red one, it makes it easier for the toothpicker to keep his eye on us.'

'You enjoy giving that guy a run for his money, don't you?'

'I wouldn't apply the word "enjoy" to any of this. Is he still behind us?'

Calvin didn't bother looking. 'Where else, today of all days? Deadline time fast approacheth, and his masters could be getting nervous we might attempt to lodge Yuli at one of our embassies.'

'A possibility that crossed my mind before Tweedledum and Tweedledee called on us and said their say. When I think of the disillusionment that interview was to me – '

'Kate, Kate, Kate! Cal, Cal, Cal!' Yuli had seen a window that was lit up and wanted to look at the display, which included some table lamps and a number of framed mirrors, in one of which he could see his reflection.

'Yuli!' he exclaimed delightedly. '*Zierkalo!*' he said, taking his hand from Kate's and pointing to the mirror.

'That's the word he kept saying this morning,' Calvin recalled, 'when he didn't want to let you take your hand-mirror from him.'

Kate had thought he might drop it and break it – broken mirrors were said to bring bad luck. But Yuli's luck could hardly get much worse than it already was. 'Let's go in and see if they have a small one he could keep, Cal. Since he's turned out to be vain,' she said managing to smile.

'You want to leave him with a souvenir, I guess.'

'Call it what you like,' she answered stemming her feelings. Petrovka Street was no place for Kate Starling to burst into tears. And strolling aimlessly along it was serving to emphasise that she'd been on the road to nowhere from the beginning. But today had to be got through, and this was better than sitting in the hotel biting their nails and waiting for something to happen, Kate thought as they entered the shop. If the toothpicker followed them inside to offer his help, she would surely break a mirror over his head!

The pleasant-faced woman behind the counter gave them a blank stare when they addressed her in English.

'What was the word Yuli kept saying, Cal?'

'We don't need to say it, all we need do is point to that one hung on the wall.'

'But that isn't the kind we want, what I had in mind was more along the lines of a tiny, handbag mirror. Yuli could have mine, but it's in a dressy bag I didn't bring.'

They tried sign language, which made the woman laugh. Then she shook her head and said, '*Nyet*', after which she went with them to the door and pointed to a shop on the other side of the street. '*Zierkalo*.' She smiled at Kate and gave a passable mime of putting on lipstick and powdering her cheeks.

'What a nice woman,' Kate said to Calvin, when they had thanked her and were heading towards what she had managed to tell them was a cosmetics shop.

'I guess they don't get too many foreigners in these stores – what is it, Kate?' She had halted suddenly. He followed her gaze.

A black car was parked further along the street. Were Caspar and Boris in it?

Kate tightened her grip on Yuli's hand, though she doubted the KGB would see fit to snatch him on a main street where tourists came to look, even if they didn't buy, and would witness the scene Kate would create. We just passed some Japanese, didn't we? she tried to reassure herself. And that couple waiting to cross the road had Pan Am flight bags slung from their shoulders.

Nevertheless, the heightened tension of this final day remained with her, and with it the depressing knowledge that what she was putting herself through was, in effect, only deferring the minute.

'Isn't that what you're looking for?' Calvin asked when they were scanning the window of the shop the woman had indicated.

Kate compared the meagre assortment of toiletries on offer with the abundance and variety of feminine beauty aids at home. Given the price of make-up here, it wasn't surprising that many of the women she had seen on the metro and passed on the street were not wearing cosmetics. Perhaps shortages had something to do with it, too. There were no lipsticks in the window, but, as Calvin had noted, there was a little hand mirror.

Kate did not see any lipsticks inside the shop either, but Yuli was able to choose himself a mirror from a box on the counter, and emerged with a red one which he had not allowed the assistant to wrap for him.

'Now, only one of us can hold his hand,' said Calvin.

'I think it had better be you. Did Connie and Brad cross the street when we did? All I can see is the toothpicker. Last night, I dreamt he was stalking me through a forest and woke in a cold sweat.'

'I heard you get up – '

'To get myself a glass of water.'

'At three o'clock precisely. And I felt like suggesting we comfort each other. Would you have agreed?'

'Probably. But the need for comfort can be misleading. Also the impulse to comfort someone. Not only misleading, but dangerous. Who was it who wrote *Beware Of Pity*? We had better be careful, Cal.'

'There's only one night left!'

'Exactly.'

'And pity doesn't figure in how I feel about you.'

'Ditto.'

'Was I, by any chance, among the matters that kept you tossing and turning for the rest of the night?'

The glance they were sharing aroused in both of them the feeling that overwhelmed them in the taxi and had threatened to do so again last night.

'How could you not have been?' Kate replied. 'Deadlines are part of my work routine,' she added, 'so I'm well used to them. But I never expected to be faced with two simultaneous ones – and of the kind that they are. You're damn right there's only one night left. Be that as it may, however –' she said as they resumed walking.

'You sound like Tweedledum.'

'It was just a preamble to reminding you that there's still the rest of today, before tonight comes, and I'm thankful we have a couple of professionals along.'

Kate had just seen Connie and Brad, in a doorway, near to where the shopping stretch gave way to a small market set back from the pavement.

'They must have decided to put themselves ahead of us, while we were in there buying the mirror,' Kate surmised.

And much use the whole lot of us would be if a KGB squad suddenly descended, thought Calvin. He had to stop himself from advising Kate to accept now what she eventually must. All he allowed himself to say was, 'If Yuli ends up where he might, think they'll let him keep his mirror?'

Kate recalled the clean and comfortable Home; the little lads whistling on their way downstairs; Ida, the child prodigy, her Jewish heritage gone from her along with her parents; the overall atmosphere of happy regimentation.

'They'd have a job getting it from him, and would be wiser to let him keep it until he's learned not to want anything the other children haven't got. Shall we go and have a look at the market, Yuli? The Russian who mentioned it to us on the train said it was mostly produce, didn't he, Cal – '

Ahead, where the market was situated, the pavement looked a good deal busier than it did here, and the throng seemed predominantly female. Women with headscarves keeping out the wind, or with shapeless felt hats plonked on as if how they looked was not important to them, some carrying empty baskets into the market and others emerging with laden ones.

'If you'd like to see what the Muscovite housewives are getting for the family meal tonight, that's fine with me,' said Calvin. 'But mind if we stop on the way, to look in that bric-à-brac store? I didn't get anything to take back to Sandy, yet, and I'd prefer it to be an old photo frame, or whatever, not one of those plaster busts of Lenin on sale in the hotel *beryozka*!'

How could he be so thoughtful about Sandy when he hadn't thought twice before deciding to ditch him? What a puzzle this man was, Kate was thinking as they cast their eyes over the selection of fusty-looking bits and pieces in the shop window, when someone standing next to her said, 'Please not to look at me.'

Kate briefly froze. If this had happened on Oxford Street she'd have thought she had encountered a weirdo. But it was Petrovka Street; and the stalker was halting whenever his quarry did. Had Calvin heard? No, he was listening to a request from Yuli which the little boy's upstretched arms made clear.

Kate managed a careful sideways glance without turning her head and saw a birdlike little woman, dressed from tip to toe in brown.

'I am old friend to Irina, and must not stay beside you

280

more than few moments. Please to continue admiration for antiquities in window while we speak.'

Kate did as she was bid, minus the admiration, and tugged Calvin's sleeve. 'Don't look round, Cal, but the lady on my right says she's a friend of Yuli's mum. Just put yourself casually where you can hear what she's saying – '

Calvin set Yuli down and obliged by putting an arm around Kate.

Trust him to take advantage of the situation! But at this stage of the game, Kate needed his wits as well as her own.

'It is my wish to take into my home the child,' the woman declared.

And damn right we need our wits about us! thought Kate.

'I was once neighbour to Irina,' this possible KGB operative went on. 'When she was expectant of Yuli – I, too, of my daughter who was stillborn.'

'Do you have other children?' Kate inquired as if she were interviewing her – and maybe she was.

'I regret no. And when it was told to me, only last evening, what has befallen my friend – it was not enough that her husband was taken!'

Was that genuine feeling? How could one know? And the compassion in this woman's eyes, when she risked glancing at Yuli, had to be questioned, too. If it was sham compassion, it *wasn't* a risky glance. And Kate was right back with the facelessness of what she was really up against. What you based your simple judgements on in the West had to be cast aside here, and the same applied to how you went about things. Kate would not have thought herself capable of the deviousness with which she had engineered the concessions she'd achieved this week. And the KGB allowing her them was but paving the way to her final defeat. Was this last-minute clandestine approach one that might help *avert* defeat? A kindly gesture from God to Irina, for maintaining her blind faith in Him? What was to be lost by hoping it was?

The woman she would like to believe was God's messenger was telling them she had followed them from their hotel – in the hesitant English which indicated she was not as easy with the language as Irina had seemed – and had finally found the courage to speak to Kate.

'It was that you might soon leave the street to visit the market, where we could not speak together with the lips unseen, that has given me the strength to do what is in my heart. I am not the brave person as is Irina, but cannot let be homeless a child punished thus for his parents' courage.'

'Does that mean you're not a refusenik?' said Calvin.

The woman shook her head. 'My husband, he would not think of taking that step, and has long ago begun making the best of things. But I have stayed beside you for too long, and shall now return immediately to my home, to await you.'

Kate found herself with a piece of folded paper in her hand, and the space on her right empty. When she and Calvin turned to face the street there was no sign of the person with whom they had had the short encounter.

'Did it really happen, Cal?'

Though they felt like rushing to where Connie and Brad were window-shopping, they made themselves saunter – if such were possible with Yuli tugging them along.

'The address on that bit of paper which is what it has to be, is evidence it did, Kate, or I might be thinking the two of us had shared a single hallucination.'

'Since we didn't, what's your gut reaction?'

'Gut reactions are too emotionally based for the tangle we still seem to be into.'

'You thought it was now just a matter of some more time ticking by towards an inevitable end, didn't you?'

'Since we were fresh out of moves, sure I did.'

'Kate having no option but to come quietly, you mean?'

'Quietly wasn't included.'

'But I hadn't quite given up hope of something unforeseen happening to save Yuli.'

'You and his mom!'

'So what gives?' Brad inquired briskly.

'Something has to account for the dazed look on their faces,' said Connie.

Kate and Calvin relayed the gist of their encounter.

'It seems heaven-sent,' Kate added.

'Too much so,' Calvin countered.

'I don't allow hope to dull my wits. I didn't say it wouldn't have to be checked out.'

'And just one of the things I'm asking myself,' said Connie, 'is how come this old friend'n neighbour just happens to've heard on the grapevine what's going down, in time for Yuli to get saved by the bell?'

'One thing we are definitely not going to do,' said Kate vehemently, 'is walk Yuli into a trap. They could be waiting to confront us in the privacy of a flat.'

'Why don't you guys go on taking Yuli for walkies, while Kate and I do the checking?' Connie suggested. 'Since we won't have him with us there'd be no need for a brawl.'

'And if it *is* genuine,' Kate added, 'women are better judges than men of what makes a good home.'

'Just so long as you don't turn down the offer solely on the grounds that the rugs haven't been swept,' Brad said.

Kate withered him with a glance. 'The flat Yuli lived in had no rugs, Brad, nor anything else that could be termed creature comforts. But I'd like to bet that Yuli was happy there, before his father was removed from the scene. If I hadn't had a true sense of values before, I would certainly have one now. Kids like my own, who think a catastrophe is the TV set going on the blink, don't know the meaning of the word. Nor are they ever likely to, in the sense that has devastated Yuli's life.'

'I was putting you on, Kate.'

'Possibly you were, but it still got my back up.'

'Does she get this way often, Cal?'

'At regular intervals, in my experience.'

'But your experience doesn't equip you to write me a reference, since the sum total of the time we've actually spent together doesn't yet add up to three weeks.'

'Is that a fact?' said Brad. 'Connie and I got the idea you two had a long-time thing going.'

In a way they were right, but a long-time thing Kate was still unable to classify.

'Back to business,' said Connie. 'Let's go get a cab, Kate. I wish the guy on our tail luck to split himself in half once we separate! You've only left Yuli's side three times, and each was to go where they'd arranged for you to go. Except for the funeral, they provided the transport. You suddenly taking off is going to leave him wondering.'

'It'll take the tail a minute or two to decide if we've maybe gone to a john, and think where the nearest one is,' Connie said to Kate when they and the men had parted company, 'and another couple wondering if he'd better call in to report.'

'How can you be sure of that?'

'I've been where he's at.'

'And it makes me feel stronger just to have you along, Connie.'

'What in the hell are you talking about? I never came across a stronger woman than you.'

'This is the first time I've ever really needed to be.'

'And you've come up to scratch, so you've made a discovery about yourself, haven't you?'

Nor was it the only one. Kate brushed her personal concerns aside, and kept her eye open for a passing taxi, quickening her pace to keep up with Connie, whose lack of height was belied by the length of her stride, as if she were all legs. Despite having to pick their way through the shoppers, they were past the market, and the Bolshoi Theatre, in no time at all, and approaching what Kate suspected was Dzerzhinsky Square. The sudden plethora of limousines in the area confirmed it.

'Don't let's go any further, Connie. I don't think it's wise to take a cab anywhere in sight of the windows of a certain building,' she rationalised her fears.

'You think your picture is posted in that building?' Connie ribbed her.

'Let's just say I'm recognisable by now to some of those who frequent it.'

'And I have to admit, Kate, that if I'd realised which square we were making for, I'd have headed in the opposite direction. Their police HQ wasn't mentioned when Brad and I did the city tour. But I don't imagine they want to give

284

the creeps to a busload of tourists whose money they're taking.'

'People pay to see the Tower of London, despite its gory past,' Kate said drily. It had done her good to hear Connie's admission.

'Past is the operative word. Here comes a cab.'

The approaching taxi was held up in the traffic, nor could they yet see if it was unoccupied, which gave Kate a minute to say to Connie, 'The saved-by-the-bell aspect smells to me, too. And even if we're proved wrong – and the KGB agree to it – well, there'd still be a problem. Irina doesn't want Yuli to live with a non-refusenik family.'

'She would have to be grateful the woman is Jewish, Kate. That poor girl is in no position to lay down conditions.'

'That's what my common sense tells me. But – '

Connie hailed the cab. 'But me no buts.'

'Let's be careful what we say in the taxi, Connie.'

'Think we don't have undercover agents driving cabs in the States?'

It's odds on we have them in England, too, thought Kate when they were on their way. But how would I know? It was only when the occasional Intelligence scandal hit the headlines that real life skulduggery briefly and remotely impinged upon ordinary people's lives. What the heck am I doing with a New York cop, who looks like a size-10 model, off to an address written on a bit of paper a complete stranger put in my hand in the street?

When she got home and told Alun, he wouldn't believe the chain of events her simple wish to protect a child had set in motion. Whether she would also have to make a shattering personal announcement to him was still open to question.

Was she opting out and leaving it to Fate, as Irina was leaving things to God? The difference was, Irina had no doubts, while Kate was prey to a multitude of them.

At eighteen, she'd been led entirely by her heart – who wasn't at that age? – or she wouldn't have married Alun. Nevertheless, and given that with maturity few would make the same choices they had in their youth, what an admission that was.

Ten years later, she'd met and felt herself drawn to Calvin. A time lapse had followed, but when they met again the attraction was still there. Was that something to be lightly discarded by a woman who had just faced up to what Kate had? Add to it Calvin's discovery that the life he was living was not the one he wanted, and . . .

In some respects, this trip's been a voyage of self-discovery for each of us, Kate reflected as the taxi crawled behind a huge truck, through a district of cheek-by-jowl blocks of flats depressing in their grey uniformity. But how Cal and I have had time to be so introspective, with Yuli's plight on our minds, day and night – It was as if the personal and the harrowing had been riding tandem, and still were. Nor was it impossible that the deadline aspect of the latter had increased the intensity of the former, or that the two were irretrievably entangled. People didn't live their every-day lives with all their emotions honed to a fine edge, as circumstances had imposed on Kate and Cal. For almost a week they'd been a team, in Yuli's interests. How would they be, together, in *normal* circumstances?

Though Kate's picture of Calvin was by now a good deal less vague, much of it was what she herself had built upon the few staple facts he had revealed. To believe that she now knew him would be pulling the wool over her own eyes. Nor did he really know her, and would probably be surprised to learn she was a good listener with those more forthcoming than he had yet been with her.

Connie stopped giving Kate an inventory of the bargains she had got at Bloomingdale's spring sale, and said to the driver, 'Would you please drop us here? I guess I'm feeling car-sick.'

'My daughter gets car-sick,' Kate remarked when they were on the pavement, and the taxi gone.

'Car-sick nothing, Kate. A couple of blocks back I saw one of those black cars edge into the traffic from a side street – and no awards for guessing who was in it.' She grabbed Kate's hand. 'Come on.'

'I didn't know you'd seen Caspar and Boris.'

'Brad and I saw you get into the car with that guy with the

rolled umbrella the day you went to see Irina. We were outside the hotel waiting to be picked up for the Lenin Museum tour. I nearly rushed over to ask where they were taking you to, but you didn't look too unhappy.'

'At that particular moment I wasn't, but I didn't come back with the information I'd hoped to get from Irina.' Instead, Kate was now pursuing a course of action Irina would deplore.

'Is that how you haul criminals away?' she said, when Connie stopped hustling her along and she found herself behind the half-open door of an apartment building entrance, with Connie squashed beside her. 'What's that perfume you're wearing?'

'"Opium" – and would you believe it, recommended by my girlfriend who's attached to the Narcotics department!'

They indulged in some girlish giggling, which helped relieve the tension; and did not detract from Connie's vigilance, Kate noted.

'Stay back behind the door, Kate. Let me do the watching out.'

They heard footsteps approaching. Kate gripped Connie's arm.

Connie gave her the kind of smile a professional gives an amateur. 'Relax, will you? That's only one person, and it isn't a guy.'

This might be all in the day's work for Connie, but it wasn't for Kate!

An elderly woman, her wispy hair escaping from beneath her hat, and puffing and blowing as if the two shopping bags she was carrying were weighing her down, entered and briefly rested the bags at the foot of the stairs. Kate could see a cabbage protruding from one of them. She held her breath. The woman hadn't noticed them yet – what would she do when she did? Let out a scream, as Kate might if she saw someone hiding behind a door – perhaps with the intention of mugging her? Instead they received no more than a curious glance, then the woman began lugging her burdens up the stairs.

'Her apartment has to be only one floor up,' Connie deduced, 'since she didn't bother taking the elevator.'

'And what's your estimate of how long it would've taken the limousine to reach and pass here?'

'Since you mention it, I guess it would be safe for us to resume our journey now.'

But Kate would not feel safe until she was aboard the British Airways plane. Would all that she had gone through on Yuli's account have been for nothing? There remained, now, a glimmer of hope, but it was clouded with reservations and were uppermost in her mind while she and Connie strode the length of a side street to where there was another main road. Connie considered it unwise to loiter on the highway from which they had fled, lest the limousine had doubled back.

'Imagine their faces, Kate, when they caught up with the cab we were in, and found the birds had flown?'

'I'd rather not, if you don't mind! And how, come to think of it, would they've known we were in it?'

'Why do you suppose they joined the traffic where they did? My reading is the toothpicker called in to report you'd split. His location was Petrovka Street, and – '

'Never mind, Connie. I'm getting dizzy from you whirling me deductions too technical for the likes of me.'

'And *I'm* getting hungry. It's lunchtime, and I need to eat.'

'How can you think of food, with Caspar and Boris on our tail, and if the woman in brown was a plant heaven knows what's waiting when we get where we're going?'

'If cops didn't eat for that kind of reason, Kate, you would now be walking alongside a bag of bones. What'd you say if I told you my partner and me, before I was made desk sergeant, have been known, on a stake-out, to have a hot-dog in one hand and our piece in the other.'

'Your what?'

'The item we're equipped with for self-protection.'

Kate glanced at the petite figure beside her, and found it difficult to visualise Connie toting a gun. 'Have you ever had to use it?'

Connie shook her head. 'Every cop's prayer is that they're never going to have to.' She glanced pensively at some trees relieving the drabness across the street. 'When someone does – well, how they feel afterwards rubs off on the entire precinct. Even though hesitating could have cost them their life.'

Though on the surface Britain was the same kind of society as America, it struck Kate now how fallacious that supposition was. There was no shortage of crime where she came from; but she still wouldn't want to see armed police patrolling the London streets, empowered with the authority to make the split-second decision Connie had just implied.

'And I still haven't got over how that old Russian lady took seeing you and me behind the door,' Connie harked back. 'If this were New York, she'd've asked us who we were and what we were doing there, and the rest of the residents would get hell from her for one of them leaving the entrance unlocked.'

'How do you know they won't?'

'Did she bother to fix the door herself? Though the apartment buildings we just walked by had their doors shut, I don't have the impression they bother about security here like back home. Could be that burglary and rape are not favourite pastimes in this country.'

'But breaking and entering for other reasons is,' Kate replied. 'Irina and Lev, before he was put away, were accustomed to returning home and finding the flat turned inside out by the KGB. My friends who were deported told me that's a popular harassment inflicted on refuseniks. And how else do people's homes get bugged here, if not while they're out?'

'Are we ever going to reach the end of this street, Kate! And my nose must be red by now, from the wind.'

'I was about to say, Connie, that much as I detest having to keep my house bolted against the side-effects of the lifestyle we have in the West, it must be easier to live with than having to keep what you *think* locked up.'

'I should tell that to the next person who comes to the

precinct to ask why we're not doing what we're paid to with the taxpayers' money. And while they're demanding to know, they're rubbing the lump that was left on their head when the silver their mother left them was taken. How did we get on this track?'

'I suppose because we're each, in our way, professional observers. I sometimes get back from interviewing someone for my column and find myself putting on paper details I hadn't consciously noticed while I was with them. If registering, and weighing things up, is part of your job, it gets to be second nature.'

'And I guess, between the two of us, sizing up the lady we're going to visit shouldn't be too difficult,' said Connie briskly, as they finally reached the main road, and stood scanning the traffic for a cab, wrinkling their noses as the petrol fumes hit them.

'If this weren't the Soviet Union,' Kate replied.

'But I'm coming down with her not being a plant, Kate. If she were, why would they need to tail us to find out where you're headed?'

Kate thought of the deviousness she had had no option but to emulate. 'The reason we're being tailed – and they haven't been too subtle about it – could equally well be that they want us to interpret it as you have. This whole exercise could be their double-crafty way of sending me home believing all's well that ends well. If they were capable of that charade with me visiting Irina in a house, a flat with a nice little woman in it, her heart breaking for Yuli, has to be seen as a possible set-up.'

'This is definitely going to be my one and only trip to Russia,' Connie summed up her feelings while they were getting into a taxi.

The driver paused only to start the engine, before saying, 'I would like, please, you should tell me why.'

'The climate doesn't suit me.'

'The climate?'

Connie's diplomacy wouldn't have disgraced Tweedledum and Tweedledee, thought Kate. But she had used a word open to more than one interpretation, and to a Russian who seemed in the mood to pick a row – maybe he'd got out of bed the wrong side, this morning!

'My friend was referring, of course, to the weather. And your English is very good,' she said, to divert him.

'I have made with myself conversant the language of corrupt capitalism,' he answered, 'necessary to buy from Western tourists goods I may sell. You have perhaps something for which you would take a good price?'

Kate and Connie exchanged a glance. This guy must have his device for recording passengers' conversation switched off. Or was he trying to trap them into committing an offence? For a tourist to dabble in the black market known to be thriving in Moscow could result in something worse than mere deportation. But Kate could not but be amused by the contradiction in terms she had just heard.

'You could get into trouble for asking us.' And he was eyeing her cameo brooch and Connie's gold earrings through his mirror.

He turned a corner with careless abandon, sending Connie slithering along the seat to collide with Kate.

'And would you mind keeping your eye on the road!'

'The trouble you mention, lady,' he said, 'I have so far avoided. And my brother, when once was taken from him a video, did not question what the official would afterwards do with it.

'But I am but the small potato,' he added. 'My brother also. It is those whose positions allow them to visit the West, the diplomats and the members of the trade missions, who can bring for sale the quality goods. The computer parts and the software,' he said longingly, 'the French perfume and the silks, the jewellery and the designer jeans – '

'Doesn't whoever buys them get asked where they got them from?' Kate cut in, before he worked himself up into a drooling frenzy about the things he wished he could get his hands on.

'How would that be my problem, lady? And I would be pleased you should give me American cigarettes, instead of a tip – oh, what a price do they bring. Did you visit, perhaps, the youth café on our famous Leninski Prospekt?'

'Speaking for myself, I'm past the age,' said Kate.

'But if you have with you some rock music tapes, I could make for you the big profit there. Where I am taking you to now is one of our small, residential districts. You have Russian friends?'

Why was he asking? Well, it is off the beaten track for tourists, isn't it? While Kate was telling herself not to be paranoid, Connie said glibly, 'Well, not exactly. I met this nice lady we're going to visit in a café, and she kindly invited me and my friend to come to her home and see how Russian people live.'

Kate had to hand it to her, though a likely tale it must seem to the driver! Even the women who had returned her smile on the metro had done so warily, and she'd think twice herself about asking a foreigner she'd got chatting to in a café to visit her home.

'What sort of people live in the district we're going to?' Connie went on casually.

'I do not understand the question.'

'Where I come from, people live in districts that fit their income. And my friend and I have been amusing ourselves guessing what this lady's husband does for a living. You know what we women are!' she added with a laugh.

Again, Kate silently applauded Connie's professionalism; she was arming them with some information to check against what the woman told them about herself and her husband – and every little helped in what they would have to decide: whether this possible foster-mum for Yuli was a KGB operative in a flat commandeered for the purpose. Kate hadn't needed telling by the others that this saved-by-the-bell solution had a bell that didn't ring true.

The driver had joined in Connie's laugh, and replied, 'How would a married man not know the ways of women? And one who lives at that address would not be a high ranking official. The apartments, though not so small as some, would not have too many rooms. If they owned a video, I would be surprised. A second-hand television set is possible. Also, among their neighbours could be Jews, with whom they would not, of course, mix.'

Kate felt her hackles rise; "of course" lent credence to what the Rosses had said about anti-Semitism being widespread in the Soviet Union. 'Why not?' she demanded.

'Who wants for friends those who are getting us a bad name in the West? As if our society is such that they wish to leave it. What they are after is to go where they can get rich with the rest of the Jews.'

Kate thought of Irina's reason for wanting to leave.

'Because it cannot be done here,' he pronounced, finally.

'But that isn't stopping *you* from trying to line your pockets, is it?' When was prejudice ever logical?

Since there was nothing he could say to that, having furnished the evidence of it, he switched on the radio, and they all listened to Brahms for the rest of the journey, their route circuitous, past buildings describable only as more of the same.

Their destination proved to be somewhat less bleak. The taxi halted near one of numerous large blocks of flats set behind a grassy area.

'You wish I should remain to drive you back?' the driver inquired while Kate was paying him.

'At your probably black-market price for doing so, no thanks. And take your beady eye off my brooch. If I wanted to sell it, it wouldn't be to a communist-capitalist who doesn't realise how ludicrous that combination is. Or that the régime he's so proud of is what's made him into one.'

'If not the brooch, perhaps the watch on your wrist?'

Connie burst out laughing. 'You wasted your breath, Kate! Business comes first.'

As if to prove it, he fished in his jacket pocket and handed Kate a card. 'Should you decide to sell, a message may be left for me at this number.'

'What I wouldn't mind letting him have, and for free, is some deodorant. I heard it's in short supply here,' said Connie, as they headed toward the flats. A small girl was playing with a skipping rope on the grass, her fair pigtails swinging as she jumped. 'That kid would be a playmate for Yuli, Kate.'

293

'But would her parents let her play with him, if she isn't Jewish? According to that odious man, the answer is no.'

'That could apply to a black kid living next door to a white one in the States, though it's less that way now than it once was. Don't let's add it to the problems we already have. Let's just stick with the basics,' Connie replied as they entered the building.

There was a notice pinned to the lift, and pressing the button raised no life.

'How am I gonna make it up three flights of stairs on an empty stomach?' Connie groaned while they toiled upwards. 'When I told you to stick with the basics, Kate, what I meant was this: Where you're at now, external conditions, and considerations, have to be set aside. Are you hearing me, Kate?'

'How could I not, when you're shouting it down my ear! Is this your sergeant-voice?'

'All I want is to get it into your head, since someone plainly has to. First there's Irina's objection to her child living with people who aren't refuseniks. Now you've come up with an advance objection of your own. Keep your eye on the number-one priority, Kate, which is getting Yuli fixed up with a good home.'

'It'd be less lonely for him if the woman had children – '

'You're still doing it!'

'Doing what?'

'Searching for the ideal set-up, and you're not going to find it with less than twenty-four hours to go,' Connie warned as they reached the top floor.

The apartment they were seeking was directly opposite the head of the stairs. As if I've completed the last lap of an uphill struggle, thought Kate. Did Yuli's salvation lie on the other side of that door? Physically, perhaps, and he would be raised as a Jew. Connie's advice was still echoing in her ears. But so were Irina's impassioned words. Was she to let expediency impel her to take into her hands what Yuli's mother had consigned to God's?

Throughout this traumatic week, Kate had used her wits in Yuli's interests. But this was a *moral* dilemma. If I've ever known a spiritual moment in my life, this is it, she was thinking when Connie said, 'Ready?', and knocked on the door.

Kate would never be ready to part with Yuli. No woman could foster a child so vulnerable, even for a brief while, without taking him to her heart. Long after this episode was over, however it might end, she would see his questioning dark eyes glancing from herself to Calvin, and hear him chanting their names. But tomorrow, one way or another, he would be gone from her, and she had better switch her mind to the present.

Was this nice little woman, welcoming them to her home, a fake?

The greeting could not have been warmer, and seemed to be laced with relief.

'I had begun to think – But I am so pleased that you have come.'

They followed her from the small vestibule into a pleasant living-room.

'What a cosy place you have,' Connie remarked.

Kate could not deny it. Why did she wish she could? Stop contrasting it with what Irina was reduced to, she admonished herself. There are those prepared to risk all, against the odds, and others who resign themselves to their invisible shackles. If this woman was genuine, she was one of the latter. It was as simple as that. But which of the two categories of Russian Jew would Kate, if she were in their position, now be in? Until you were faced with the choice, how could you know?

Nevertheless, it was difficult to swallow her partisan feeling, and nothing could detract from her respect for the Smolenskys. The courage of one's convictions was the hardest kind to follow through.

'Was it here that Irina was your neighbour?' she inquired.

The woman shook her head. 'It was a few months after . . . that I moved here to this apartment.'

'After what?'

'When my baby girl she was lost to me. Please to sit down.'

Kate and Connie placed themselves at either end of the

sofa. She sat down in one of the two armchairs. 'Here is where I sit to do my sewing. Would you mind, please, I should continue?'

Connie doubted that the KGB would have provided her with a pile of darning to enhance the homely picture. 'Go right ahead,' she said with a friendliness Kate was not displaying. 'If I'd known you'd be having a mending session, I'd've brought along one of my husband's socks, that sprung a hole yesterday!'

The woman opened a workbox that was on the small table beside her chair, and brought out a square of white fabric. 'Today, I am not mending, I am making. It is a handkerchief for my husband.'

While Connie went on talking inconsequentials, as if this were the social call all three of them knew it was not, Kate sat glancing around her.

'I can't get over you making your husband's handkerchiefs,' Connie was saying.

'I could not be so wasteful, to throw away the bed linen that is past repair.'

Was that an indication of personal thriftiness? Kate wondered. Or that her income required thrift? Whichever, though this room fell far short of luxury, and had in it only one of the modern amenities Westerners took for granted – the TV set which the cab driver had said was possible – nobody could deem it shabby, or lacking in homely touches.

The sofa was of the utilitarian design Kate had noted in a furniture-shop window. She had bumped her elbow on the high, wooden arm when she sat down. But hand-embroidered scatter cushions had been added to it, and the curtains looked crisp and fresh. This woman's favourite colour must be brown, since the carpet and curtains were a matching shade of it; and the dress she had on heightened Kate's remembered illusion of a little brown bird fleetingly appearing at her side on Petrovka Street.

Kate continued her silent survey, noting some framed photographs on top of the bookcase. But, as she'd lashed out to Brad when he seemed to think otherwise, what did the place itself matter? Am I hoping to judge this woman, including her integrity, by the kind of home she has? And given the territory and the circumstances, what do I base my judgements on? Instinct would have to do, and though the woman herself could turn out to be fake, the KGB hadn't set this scene and put her in it. This was definitely her home.

'My husband, he works in a library,' she was telling Connie.

'As the Smolenskys once did,' said Kate.

'And I am sorry to say he did not have the sympathy, for why it is that they no longer do. Also, he did not much like Lev Smolensky.'

It seemed that few did, but Kate nevertheless asked her why.

'He found him – how do you say?'

'A prickly person?'

'It was not only that.'

'Too . . . opinionated?'

'How did you know?'

Kate could think of no better word to sum up her pieced-together impression of the father of the child who had become so dear to her.

'Let's just say I guessed,' she replied. 'Did you find him that way, too?'

'I have not too many times spoken with him.'

'Does that mean you kept out of his way?'

'Why would Lev Smolensky have the time for someone like me? If I had not liked so much Irinshka I would not, more than once, have invited the Smolenskys into my home. From Lev, I had always the feeling that, for him, I was not there. But it was the contempt he himself received that my husband he did not like.'

'Yet he's prepared to give a home to Lev's son,' said Kate.

'There are many who would.'

Because it might in some way help them, if *they* helped the KGB? Don't be so damned cynical, Kate. But that possibility couldn't be dismissed.

The woman put down her sewing. 'Come. I shall show you where the child would sleep in my home.'

Kate and Connie followed her across the vestibule to a

small room, in which was a narrow bed covered by a patchwork quilt like the one Kate and Calvin had wrapped around Yuli – and seeing it was for Kate as if events had come full circle to where they began. Yuli was still homeless, and his welfare still in her hands.

But this quilt looked brand new, as did the red rug on the wood floor. The immaculate white walls had no pictures on them. A yellow felt rabbit was sitting on the bed.

'The toy I have made for my baby, and have kept.'

'It's a nice, bright room,' said Connie. 'Isn't it?' she prodded Kate.

'Yes.' But the woman had tiptoed into it. Was it a shrine to a stillborn child? Or one awaiting a replacement that might never come?

'I have not yet offered to you some tea,' she said when they had returned to the living-room.

'Please don't bother. Tea isn't what we're here for.' And it's time for some straight talking, loth though Kate was to pry into someone's private life. 'Were you unable to have any more children?'

'That is how it so seems. And my husband – he is not too much at home any more.'

The woman picked up her sewing and gave her attention to it. But the "any more" indicated that Kate had led her to difficult ground.

'I would have liked to meet your husband, as well as you,' Kate said carefully.

'Please to believe me, he is a kind man to children, Mrs Starling.'

Kate and Connie exchanged a glance.

'How do you know my name?'

'My brother – he was at the grandmother's funeral.'

It wasn't impossible that one of the men who had made up the quorum for the service had afterwards asked the rabbi who Kate was. But they'd all been elderly.

'Is your brother a good deal older than you?'

'That is so.'

Kate gave her the benefit of the doubt. 'Was it from him you learned that Yuli is without a home?'

'When he visited us, last night.'

'You haven't yet told us *your* name.'

'I did not write it with the address? Please to excuse. I was not always so forgetful. I am Natalya Rubinov.'

Kate noted the increased speed with which she was stitching the handkerchief, as if agitation was building up in her. 'It was risky for you to write down and hand to me your address, wasn't it?'

'In this case, no.'

So it *was* a set-up, and the little brown bird not what she seemed, after all. Had she accidentally blown it? Or was her admission, and what was to follow it, as cunningly calculated as Kate knew the KGB to be? It would take a more naturally devious mind than Kate's to work it out. Meanwhile how let-down she felt. Though she was far from sure this was the right foster home for Yuli, something about Natalya Rubinov had begun to engage her sympathy.

'I see,' she replied coldly to the woman Natalya had turned out to be.

'No! You do not see.'

The needle went on flashing in and out of the square of linen, in an atmosphere charged with Kate's suspicion and Natalya Rubinov's pent-up emotion. Connie fixed her gaze on a potted plant and held her breath.

'And I did not have to be honest to you. But if I am to have the child, I would not wish afterwards to live with that I gained a gift from God by a lie. What I am now telling to you is the truth, Mrs Starling. My husband, he was promised the promotion at his work. But this is not for why I do it.'

Natalya put down her sewing and busied herself around the room, as if she could not stay still, patting cushions into place on the armchairs, smoothing down the bobble-trimming on the chenille tablecloth, picking up ornaments and putting them down again with jerky little movements.

The outcome of this is as important to her as it is to me, thought Kate. This woman needs a child in her life. Any child. Yuli would be petted, fussed-over, and cared for by her. Nor would I have to contrive this solution, since I now know the KGB have contrived it for me, and will view it as their victory.

Not just over me, but over those from the West who dare to poke their noses into what's going on here, Kate registered, as the wider implications of this minor matter began seeping through to her. Minor to those who had relegated human rights to where it suited their purposes for them to be. Major for little Yuli Smolensky – but who, in the Soviet Union, gave a damn about him? Other than his own. Since Russians had hearts like everyone else, there had to be some who'd care if they let themselves. The Smolenskys' neighbour had, and Kate was glad she had met him. And the nice woman in the shop, this morning. That she wouldn't go home thinking all Russians ticked like the taxi driver, or like Mr Kropotnikov, who didn't tick at all.

Meanwhile Natalya Rubinov, who *was* one of Yuli's own, continued her agitated pottering. Kate's final thought, before Natalya came to rest with one of the photographs hugged to her breast, was that she would never know if Farringdale and Arbington had been in on the contriving that had got her here.

'Perhaps you think I have made for you the difficulty, by telling to you the truth, Mrs Starling.'

'I respect you for it.' Pity you too. Who wouldn't be sorry for a woman who had to lend herself to a dirty trick in the hope of fulfilling her maternal instinct?

Natalya gently set down the photograph she was clasping, and reverently was how she glanced at it.

'Is that a photo of your husband?'

'No. It is of my dear brother, but when he was a young man. In my family are just the two of us. And, to him, I am still the little sister he did not expect to have.'

'I always wanted a brother,' said Connie.

'And you do not know what you have missed,' Natalya declared. 'I did not have my parents for too long, and my brother, he took me into his home.' She paused pensively. 'Only once have I not accepted his guidance. My husband, he is not the one my brother wished for me. But he has not once reminded me of that.'

Kate got up to have a better look at this paragon, added a beard to his face, and froze.

'Your brother's a rabbi, isn't he?'

'A man of God,' Natalya answered with pride.

Kate was beginning to wonder whose side God was on.

'What is to be with the child, Mrs Starling?'

It was hard to discount Natalya's need, or the appeal in her eyes. Beware of pity on *all* counts, Kate! 'I shall have to think things over,' she said.

'And I shall pray for you and Him to look kindly upon me.'

'God is welcome to resolve this on His own!' Kate exclaimed to Connie in the taxi taking them to the hotel.

They had found the vehicle parked near to the flats, but Kate no longer cared if it was conveniently there by arrangement with the KGB or not, and had leapt into it still gripped by the anger the visit's final revelation had evoked. Nor had she spoken a word until now, but had sat silently seething.

Connie crossed herself, like the good Catholic she was. 'So it's God you're mad at, is it? I thought it was the lady. Everything seemed to be going fine, then wham! What in the hell happened to tighten your lips in the last two minutes?'

Kate told her. The heck with what those who might later listen to the driver's tape would make of it. She wouldn't say anything that could endanger Natalya Rubinov, but she'd had it with them and their dirty games.

'If you ask me,' said Connie, 'that pathetic little person is as much a fall-guy as it turned out that you are.'

'That's one of the things that's made me livid.'

'How do you know it isn't for her sake that her brother said yes to the proposition?'

'Since, by his own admission, he's a man of many compromises, the best I'm prepared to say about him is he probably looked upon it as a way of helping her out, and keeping in with those he sees fit, for whatever reason, to keep in with.'

'Could the reason be he's protecting those of his flock who're staying put voluntarily?'

'That would give him a good out, wouldn't it? But it had occurred to me.'

The driver butted into their conversation. 'You would like, perhaps, tomorrow a private sightseeing tour? I do very cheap.'

'No, thanks,' Kate replied.

'Tomorrow we're leaving,' Connie said thankfully, 'and I've done all the sightseeing I need to.'

But Kate had done none, unless being ferried by limousine and cab between one move in the game and the next could be termed sightseeing. She'd been kept on the go both mentally and physically, would return home exhausted – and for what? *I might just as well have sat in a chair with Yuli on my lap, till the crunch came. But if I had, his gran wouldn't have got her funeral. Nor would Irina have had the small comfort I was able to give to her. Nothing is ever for nothing, Kate. But there was still Yuli, and how would she manage to smile at him when he ran to her arms the minute she got back?*

'What things have finally boiled down to,' Connie said practically, 'is a straight option. The lady we just saw, notwithstanding the fraternal connection, or a place like the one you were invited to see.'

'It doesn't take a detective to work that one out – '

'Not if the person doing the figuring has their priorities right, and it sure as hell has to be the one I shouted down your ear. Want some gum?'

Kate shook her head, and Connie unwrapped a piece for herself. 'Chewing helps me think. But it's *you* I have to make sort the wheat from the chaff.'

Kate glanced through the window at some children pouring through the gates of a school, and thought how carefree they looked carrying their satchels, and jostling each other as they made their way toward a bus stop. Why couldn't life be as simple as that for Yuli, who was no less Russian than they were? If the Smolenskys and others like them were let alone, allowed to practise their religion openly, they wouldn't want to leave their homeland.

'That little woman obviously has marital problems, not to mention a hang-up or two,' Connie said thoughtfully, 'but you can't let that influence you, and you know it. As for the fraternal connection, and Yuli's mom's stated objection – '

'The last two on your list can now be seen as one,' Kate cut in. 'If anyone is likely to colour the kid's attitudes it's that man. Whose sister thinks he can't put a foot wrong.'

'I can see I'm going to have trouble with you, Kate!'

Connie's conclusion was also Calvin's, when, by ten o'clock that night, Kate was still racked by indecision.

Yuli had elected to sleep in Kate's room. Kate and Calvin shared the putting-to-bed ritual with forced smiles on their faces, the little boy's blissful ignorance of what tomorrow would bring affecting Calvin as it was Kate. And there was, to the last, the element of comedy. Yuli had insisted upon going to bed with Kate's red beret on his head; and fell asleep with the mirror they had bought for him in his hand.

Afterwards, Connie and Brad joined them in Calvin's room. What was left of the bourbon was consumed. And Kate was aware of the three-against-one atmosphere, though nothing was said since the things the others felt like saying to her were not for the ears of the KGB and reams of paper would be necessary to convey to her in writing what she knew they were all thinking. Though it could be condensed to just one sentence: Be thankful you've found Yuli a home.

But for Kate, there remained the moral issue. And a vision of Irina and Lev, years hence, suffering Yuli's bitter non-forgiveness for what their "foolhardiness" had done to him, was heightening the dilemma. Hadn't Irina suffered enough? It was possible she would be released, and get her child back, before sufficient time had passed for the damage to be done. But some refuseniks had been imprisoned for years, and still were. Kate couldn't count on that.

Eventually, Calvin sprang to his feet and strode to the bathroom, beckoning the others to follow.

'Oh, goody! We're going to have a shower party,' said Connie, when he turned on the water, full blast.

Kate wanted to giggle, as she had when she and Calvin resorted to writing their private exchanges on toilet paper, after the notepad ran out, such was her state of tension.

Meanwhile, she was subjected to a battery of straight-talking, American style, which changed nothing, since its content was what she herself knew was commonsense.

'Then why don't you just make your mind up, and we'll all go get some rest?' Calvin snapped when she admitted it.

What a long way we two still have to go before we really know each other, Kate thought.

'Maybe we should adopt Irina's policy,' Calvin said wearily. 'Leave the outcome to God.'

'Since right now His ways seem to me rather more weird than wonderful, I'd be scared to risk it,' Kate replied, watching Connie and Brad cross themselves as if it were a reflex action. Religion was ingrained in Catholics and Jews from childhood and remained part of their lives, unless they deliberately turned their backs on it. The choice was theirs, but having others make it was something else, and Kate had the feeling that Irina would die before she'd let that be done to her, with her faith still intact.

'Then you'd better start seeing things the way they are, instead of how you'd like them to be,' said Calvin.

Brad, who was seated on the lavatory lid, with Connie perched on his lap, said drily, 'If we told the folks back home where we held this conference, they wouldn't believe it.'

'Would they believe any of the rest of it?' said Connie.

Kate said, 'Most people have only the vaguest idea of what's going on here, but I don't intend to leave it like that.' She looked at Calvin. 'This isn't going to be a repetition of the stowaway. I shall make use of the gift that God gave *me*, and this could be why He did.'

'What stowaway?' said Brad. 'Will somebody tell me what Kate's talking about?'

'Leaving the stowaway out of it – it'd take all night to fill you in – the power of the pen is what she's talking about,' said Calvin, 'and I guess I'm happy to hear it. For more reasons than the one she has in mind.'

Kate recalled his saying he thought her worthy of better things careerwise – or words to that effect – and gave him a smile.

'Time for you'n me to hit the hay, honey,' Brad said to his wife.

'How am I going to sleep, without knowing the denouement?'

'I guess I'll have the same problem, since I've grown as fond of Yuli as you have. But could be we'll find a way of distracting each other which it'd do our friends here no harm to try.'

'We'll see ourselves out,' said Connie.

They were gone before the telltale blush had faded from Kate's cheeks.

'How did that advice of Brad's strike you?' Calvin inquired. 'It sure sounded good to me.'

'Sex as a useful therapy, you mean?'

'No, Kate. Sex because, goddammit, I love you. And if we don't resolve *that* problem tonight, tomorrow will be too late.'

'The shower is still turned on,' she said to distract him – and herself.

'It isn't the only thing around here that's turned on. Am I going to have to put myself under it to cool off what I feel for you?'

'If feeling were all it took, it would have been resolved for me by now.'

'May I have a minute to figure that one out?'

'I want you as much as you want me,' Kate levelled with him. 'But whether it's for ever is another matter.'

'I personally have no doubts on that score.'

'But I would have to really know the man for whom I disrupted my children's lives – not to mention Alun's – and I'm by no means sure I do. He certainly still has much to learn about *me*. There's also the factor that your marriage, from the little you've told me, probably never worked from the start.'

'Too true it didn't.'

'But mine is to all intents and purposes still very much intact.'

'And if you knew how enthusiastic that didn't sound, you wouldn't have said it.'

Kate stared pensively at the gushing shower. 'People don't stay madly in love, Cal. It turns to affection – if they're lucky – and your probable expectation of marriage – well, its not matching my not-unhappy experience of it is one of the things that worries me.'

'If there were nothing to worry about, you'd invent some worries, Kate!'

'I haven't invented those I'm listing. Another is that you leaving Sandy for me would be the second serious relationship you've walked out on. That doesn't fit my experience of living one-to-one with another individual – that it has to be worked at – '

'You know nothing about my life with Sandy,' Calvin cut in.

'But your being prepared to write him off so easily tells me something about *you*. Would you mind turning off the water, the noise of it is beginning to drive me mad. And why don't we get out of here?'

Kate moved to leave the bathroom, but Calvin barred her way.

'We are staying put, Kate, until we've had this out. And the hell with the water!'

A silence followed.

Then Calvin said, 'There are times when I wonder how Alun puts up with you, but you have your compensations, Kate – and I don't see myself ever walking out on *our* relationship.'

The telephone rang in Calvin's room, forestalling what might have happened had it not. When he looked into her eyes like this, Kate's legs were rendered weak, and her heart had begun thudding.

'Who's calling me at this hour?' he said striding to lift the receiver lest the ringing disturb Yuli's sleep.

What a way for me to learn he doesn't stay up late at home, which I do, thought Kate. It was not yet eleven o'clock.

The caller was Farringdale.

'I asked to be put through to Mrs Starling, Mr Fenner, but appear to have been put through to you.'

'What do you mean appear to be? You have been, haven't you?'

'One mustn't rule out the possibility of your answering the telephone in her room.'

'Or of our friendly eavesdropper knowing that she's in mine.'

'Paying attention to fairy-tales, are we?'

'Living them, you mean – and fairy-tales they're not. Two of the characters in this one are called Tweedledum and Tweedledee.'

Calvin handed the receiver to Kate.

'I say, has our American friend had too much to drink, Mrs Starling?'

'No, and there's none left in the bottle, or he'd be reaching for it after talking to you.'

'Oh, dear. This isn't my night, is it? What *have* I done?'

'It's what you *haven't* done, Mr Farringdale. Which, in a nutshell, is stop one of the citizens abroad you're supposedly here to represent from being made an utter mug of.'

'What can you mean by that?'

'Come off it. I've no intention of doing what you do.'

'And what might that be?'

'Pretending I don't know that you know what we bloody both know, sums it up nicely.'

'The only difference I have yet established between you and my mother is she doesn't swear.'

'With you for her son, I find that surprising. Now what the heck do you want?'

'I just thought I'd give you a call to ask what kind of a day you've had. Should you feel like telling me, I am downstairs in the lobby with Arbington, and Mr Fenner would be welcome to join us, too. It's a pleasant night for a walk.'

'If you don't know every detail of the day I've had, I'll eat one of my berets. You've been asked to discreetly establish if where I was hoodwinked into going had the desired effect – and don't bother denying it.'

'Will you join us for our walk?'

'No. I've reached the end of my patience, and you may tell Mr Arbington the same goes for Mr Fenner.'

'But please spare a thought for those who will still be here when you have departed.'

'Including, may I remind you, the child who has been, and still is, at the core of the matter. But it will soon all be over bar the shouting.'

Kate slammed down the receiver and stood glaring at it as if it were Farringdale.

'Feeling better?' Calvin asked.

'It was high time I told him a thing or two.'

Calvin took her arm and ushered her back to the bathroom, where the shower was still usefully pounding out water.

'He wasn't the only one you told, was he? It'll soon be all over bar the shouting, you said. In a room we know is bugged. And how do you suppose the KGB will interpret that?'

'I've reached the stage when I no longer care, Cal. And I'm still riven by indecision.'

'Does the indecision include me?'

'I thought I'd made that clear to you. And why does nobody but me appreciate the moral dilemma I'm facing about Yuli's future?'

'What makes you think I don't? I'm just not having the trouble you are in getting the scales to balance.'

'That could be because you haven't met Irina. Look what she's put herself through, so Yuli can grow up a Jew who's free to be one. The last thing Natalya Rubinov said to me this afternoon was she'd pray for God and me to look kindly upon her. Me, bracketed with God, Cal. I can't tell you how it made me feel. I don't want the destiny of a little boy to be up to me – nor the possible consequences of what I decide to alienate him from his parents in years to come.'

'But I guess that's the way it is, Kate. Bearing in mind the alternative to the rabbi's sister – '

'I'm not even going to think about that.'

'Then why don't you just stop having this struggle with yourself? The other one, too.'

Kate reached up to turn off the shower. 'I can't get this contraption to move. It seems to be stuck.'

'It's behaved temperamentally from the off – like a certain person I could mention – but I've coped with it, as I have with her. I'd offer to deal with it now, but why would I help you out with another of your deliberate digressions?'

'They're not usually deliberate.'

'Then you admit that one was?'

'Look – I'm getting soaked! And I'm determined to get this thing turned off.'

'Well you're no giver-up, are you, Kate? Not even when defeat is staring you in the face.' Calvin went to her aid. 'Move out of the way.'

'Not on your nelly, mate!'

He held on to the shower rail and leaned over the bath to clamp his hand on hers, getting as wet as her in the process. The flimsy rail crashed down.

'Now look what you've done!'

'And how is Mr Kropotnikov going to interpret it?'

They looked at each other and had to laugh. Both had water dripping from their hair, and though there was nothing particularly hilarious about that, the situation that had precipitated it could not have been more absurd.

'Okay, I'll leave you to deal with the shower handle. Also to dry off,' Kate said, picking her way through the mass of plastic fabric now on the floor. Then she tripped and fell against Calvin, and thoughts of shower handles and drying off departed their minds.

'What am I doing in your arms?'

'I caught hold of you to steady you.'

'That isn't the effect it's having.'

Their second kiss was as intoxicating as their first, and they made their way, like two drunks undressing each other, to the bedroom.

'This had to happen and you know it, Kate.'

They reached the bed. Had she known it? All that

mattered now was that it *was* happening. And a great surge of joy was carrying her away.

Later, when they lay peacefully together, Kate reflected wryly that accident, not design, was responsible, as if, as Cal had said, it was meant to be. If she hadn't tripped on the shower curtain, mind over matter might have prevailed. She hadn't *chosen* to commit herself to Calvin. And there was no more chance of deciding if she wanted to, in the short time left to them, than of finding the perfect solution for Yuli, was her last coherent thought before passion claimed them again.

CHAPTER ELEVEN

DAYLIGHT WAS flooding the room, and Yuli seated astride them, when Kate and Calvin awoke on their last morning in Moscow.

'Kate, Cal! Cal, Kate!' the little boy chortled, pointing a finger back and forth at their two heads side by side on the pillow.

His delight in seeing them thus was plain, and Calvin pulled him down to join them for the kind of family cuddle he could not have experienced since his father was arrested.

'This reminds me of the show Lori and I used to put on for Gary,' he said with the brusqueness with which he hid his emotions, 'to fool him that he wasn't going to end up in the same broken-home situation as some of the kids he played with.'

'It's been a long time since my two invaded our bedroom,' said Kate, 'but it was fun when they did.'

'Can you and I maybe look forward to family fun together?'

'Since I'm on the pill, not right now! And "maybe" remains the operative word.'

'I see.'

'But, as usual, only from your own point of view.'

'If that's what you call knowing what I want, you're right.'

'I hope our eavesdropper is finding *this* conversation interesting! But I don't mind him or her hearing that I am still a long way off knowing what I want to do with the rest of my life – and whether or not it's going to include Alun ought not to be decided by a one-week experience that included you.'

The sudden change in the atmosphere was such that Yuli

311

disentangled himself from them and clambered down from the bed.

'I guess this final showdown had to happen, too.'

'If that's how you choose to see it, Cal. But what it actually is, is me trying to explain why I have to take things one step at a time. I've not yet put myself together from taking the one I didn't intend to.'

'Is that why you've picked a quarrel with me in bed?'

'Alun and I have had some of our *best* quarrels in bed, and since both quarrels and bed are a feature of marriage, why not?'

'Unfortunately for this quarrel,' Calvin replied, 'though we're very suitably situated, deadline time is nigh and a very important third party is present, so kiss and make-up is out.'

Yuli was eyeing them questioningly, Kate's beret askew on his head, and the mirror clutched in his hand like a talisman.

'Why can't we make everything right for him, Cal?' Kate got out of bed and covered the child's face with kisses. Not that he would go short of them from Natalya Rubinov. Forget the rabbi, and look on the bright side, Kate. Your moral misgivings can't come first.

Meanwhile, she and Calvin still had their packing to do; Yuli's things would have to be put into carrier bags for the threeway parting that would be painful for them all.

There was still one thing left that Kate must say to Cal, but it wasn't easy to put into words. How did you tell a man who'd told you he loves you that his hopes might come to nothing? Haven't you already said that to him indirectly, Kate? But indirectly was neither fair, nor good enough. The best of men were capable of thinking that once you'd slept with them, if you weren't the sort who slept around, they'd as good as got you.

Another self-discovery was then added to the rest. No man, no matter how much she loved him, was ever going to really get Kate. She was always going to be her own person.

She plunged in. 'I was sort of straining at the leash before I set forth on this trip, Cal. But I thought it was just dissatisfaction with my work. Now, I know it goes a good deal deeper than that. You've helped me find out.'

'And this sounds like the brush-off.'

'Not necessarily. And, come what may, we have to stay friends. Will you promise me that?'

'From the other side of the Atlantic ocean, viewing you platonically might just be possible!'

'*I* have to be sure, among other things, that I'm not just bored with my husband and viewing *you* as an exciting replacement. And there's something else I'd like you to promise. That you won't see me as a reason to break up your present ménage the minute you get home.'

'You're a great one for not wanting things on your head, aren't you, Kate?' But Calvin felt as if his had been bludgeoned. How could the woman with whom, but a few hours ago, he'd shared not just a sexual encounter, but heterosexual love in all its glory, now be urging him to stay put in the gay groove?

'Hasn't it occurred to you that you've helped *me* find out something from which there's now no turning back?' he said. 'I guess if it isn't you I go forward with from here on, I shall have to search for your replica. And would it be too platitudinous if I told you I shall never stop being grateful to you? Now come back to bed, and we'll have another cuddle.'

Yuli was eyeing them uncertainly.

'You, too, little guy. We may as well round things off as the unlikely threesome we've been.'

The cuddle was short, but sweet, the atmosphere now devoid of undercurrents, if tinged with poignancy on the child's account.

'I'll call Tweedledum immediately after breakfast,' Kate said, to which Calvin made no reply, since he had known what her decision must be in the end. How Yuli would behave when the parting came, neither wished to contemplate.

They were never to find out. When they returned from their respective bathrooms, the little boy was gone.

'Why didn't you wait to take your shower until I'd had

313

mine, like we've been doing!' Kate lashed out at Calvin. 'Or take Yuli with you?'

'I haven't taken a shower yet. And the answer to your second accusation is I'm the kind of guy who has to have privacy when obeying a call of nature. They don't always come at a convenient time.'

If Kate had been capable of laughter at that moment, she would surely have laughed her head off at the absurdity of their having guarded Yuli as they had, and the KGB getting him in the end because Calvin had to go to the loo. But, at this stage, they'd have taken him even had Cal been in the room, and knocked Cal cold if necessary. The velvet-glove treatment was over.

Kate stood in her dressing-gown, trying not to look at the chunk of lemon and the little packets of honey on the coffee table, while Calvin went to ask Daphne if Yuli had again popped in to see her. The toys all over the floor were a reminder of the little boy who ten minutes or so ago had been playing with them, and Kate had thought then that several carrier bags would be required to transport them all to Natalya Rubinov's flat.

Calvin returned shaking his head, as they had known he would. 'If you want to blame me for this, Kate, I don't mind.'

'It's myself I'm blaming. Shall we go through the motions of questioning the floor-woman?'

'Anything that will make you feel better.'

'Nothing will.'

They trailed down the corridor without exchanging a word, to where Babushka was engrossed in inspecting the stack of bed linen on a trolley.

'There is something you wish? Assistance with the baggage departure, perhaps? For that, it is necessary you should call for a porter.'

Kate emerged from her numbness. Anger replaced it. 'Where is the child?'

'Which child, madam?'

'The one who's passed by you, with us, dozens of times since we brought him here.'

'I am not the noticing person, madam.'

Calvin grabbed Kate's arm and steered her back along the corridor, lest she take Babushka by her lying throat and throttle her, which he felt like doing.

'I guess we just heard the Party line on this, but what else did you expect? And I seem to recall your saying, the night we arrived back with Yuli, and had the brush with the girl at the desk, that his not being officially here meant, to them, that he wasn't. There's nothing on paper to say he was.'

'Exactly. But there will be when I get home to my typewriter!'

'We're talking proof, Kate.'

'And I don't feel like talking.'

She was hopping mad, her fists as Calvin had frequently seen them, and at the same time distraught, her expression grief-stricken.

'I knew I was going to have to part with him – and handing him over would've been hard enough – ' she said quietly, when they were back in her room. 'But it won't be Natalya Rubinov they've taken him to, will it? And that's down to me. Not only did I dither about what I shouldn't have, I shot off my mouth on the phone, to Farringdale – or the KGB wouldn't have got the wind-up that I'd make a last-minute public scene, with Yuli clinging to me. How am I going to live with what I've done?'

'Stop it, Kate.' She had put her head in her hands. 'Nobody could have done more to protect Yuli than *you* tried to. Even to the lengths of thinking ahead to his future relationship with his parents. It was that that kept you hoping for some miraculous solution unto the end, or you'd have called it quits last night. If you want to hold yourself responsible for what's happened this morning, I'm sure not going to help you embark on a lifetime's guilt trip.'

Calvin stood for a moment gazing down at the toys.

'I can't bear to look at them!' Kate exclaimed. 'And since we certainly shan't take them home for souvenirs, they will probably end up brightening the lives of Babushka's kids, or get sold on the black market.'

'I don't see the mirror we bought him, Kate – '

'He would have bitten through the hand clamped over his mouth if they'd tried to take it from him.'

But Kate's red beret was lying on the floor. She averted her eyes from it. 'Get through to your embassy, Cal, and I'll do the same.'

'Want to lay a bet that Tweedledum and Tweedledee are unavailable this morning?'

And so it proved.

'Nevertheless,' Kate seethed, 'Farringdale has not heard the last of this or of me.'

She was taken aback, on her arrival at the airport, to find him there awaiting her.

'Is this the equivalent of you seeing me off the premises, Mr Farringdale?'

'On the contrary, Mrs Starling, I shall be sorry to see you leave.' He would have liked to add that she had lightened his life.

Kate gave a straight answer to what had seemed to her another of his meaningless niceties. 'Without the living evidence, there's nothing I can now do to embarrass you and my country, is there? A physical tug-o'-war was neatly avoided – though there wasn't going to be one.'

She refused to let him carry her suitcase, or to fetch her a trolley, but could not prevent him from escorting her through her final experiences of Soviet officialdom, which his presence made a good deal less onerous. Daphne and her mother were having to queue their way through, but that hadn't been necessary for Kate.

'Why am I getting this VIP treatment?' she inquired coldly, when Farringdale seated himself beside her in the bleak departure lounge. Anything less like the busy international airport Kate had visualised would be hard to find, but she hadn't then related it to what a closed society meant. That only the fortunate few were ever allowed out, and welcome was not exactly written on the mat for the sprinkling from the West allowed to enter. Tourists arriving

316

here with pleasurable anticipation were liable to leave breathing a sigh of relief.

Calvin's party had not yet left the hotel, when Kate boarded the airport bus. He had stood with Connie and Brad, waving goodbye. Hardly a private leave-taking. Which was perhaps a blessing, Kate reflected now. What was there left for them to say to each other that had not already been said? The attraction between them was as strong as ever. As for the rest – Time would tell.

'Is Mr Fenner due for the same treat, before his plane takes off? And I'm still waiting to learn why this kindly gesture was made to me,' she prodded Farringdale.

'I have no idea how cordial their relationship is,' he replied. 'Arbington's and Fenner's, that is.'

Had the sarcasm gone over his head, or was he ignoring it? And if he thought he and Kate had a relationship of *any* kind, it was wishful thinking, she was saying to herself when he gave her a smile so warm, she almost believed it was genuine.

'But I couldn't let you depart,' he went on, 'without telling you how much I admire your spirit, Mrs Starling. To call it the John Bull kind would be underestimating it.'

He switched his gaze to his umbrella handle, upon which his folded hands were resting. 'Though you didn't get this from me, the embassies would have liked to see you and Fenner win.'

'If what you mean by that is get fair play for Yuli, I should damn-well hope so! But instead of putting your weight behind us, all you did was lecture us and pander to the other side.'

'Suffice it to say, Mrs Starling, that diplomacy is as diplomacy does. But were I to add a word or two of embellishment, it would be that terrain which appears firm ground to the untrained eye is all too often a veritable quicksand.'

'Wouldn't it be simpler if you just said, straight out, that the West is scared to take a wrong step, even when it would be in the right direction?'

'How well you put it. But given the currently changing climate – '

'Which I'm as aware of as you are,' Kate interrupted, 'but meanwhile the injustices are still going on. Fortunately, there are some ordinary folk who don't just sit at home saying how terrible it is. Two of them are the couple who got me into this and were themselves deported. And they and their kind are never going to accept that what they're fighting for is a lost cause. There's no need for me to tell you that the refuseniks who've already been let out of the Soviet Union are proof that it isn't.'

'Bravo!' Farringdale said, to her embarrassment.

'I didn't repay you for the flowers for Irina Smolensky – it slipped my mind till now, when I don't have any Russian money – '

'Then allow it to be my small contribution,' Farringdale replied. 'Unofficially, of course.'

Kate might have found the good grace to accept his gesture, but the ritual disclaimer attached to it had, in this case, made her blood boil. One of her most cynical remembrances of this eventful week would be of Farringdale's repeatedly telling her she 'hadn't got it from him' – as if the truth was the plague.

'No, thanks,' she said crisply. 'But I have neither my cheque book nor much sterling with me. I'll repay you when I arrive home. Could that be arranged?'

He took a card from his breast pocket and handed it to her. 'Why not do it with flowers, on my behalf? This is my mother's address.'

One way or another, his mother always entered the action, and Kate was not surprised that he carried her card next to his heart. What must it be like for his wife? Did Lady Farringdale know how large she continued to loom in her son's life? Kate pondered briefly on the effect of childhood influences upon the adult one became, and in her mind's eye saw Yuli standing beside Ida while she played the piano in the music room. The mirror was not in his hand.

'They've put Yuli in a Home, haven't they, Mr Farringdale? If you pretend you don't know, I'm going to scream, as I promised you I would on a previous occasion.'

'I'm afraid so. But if what I believe you would have done,

had they trusted you, is correct, it may console you to know that his stay with the lady you visited yesterday would have lasted no longer than the time necessary for you to see him there. That is what I wanted to tell you before you left. Off the record, of course.'

'This entire affair has been off the record. And I've been made an even bigger mug of than I'd supposed.'

'May I offer you my sympathy?'

'I'm not the one who requires it. Did you and Mr Arbington know about this in advance?'

'Please believe that we didn't.'

Kate would like to – but could she? Britain's firm stand on human rights, America's too, was well known, and when Kate got home and cooled down she might be able to view objectively all the pussyfooting around – but right now – 'I appreciate your telling me,' she said stiffly.

But some consolation it was knowing that Yuli would have finished up where he was now, no matter what she'd done. Nor that she had been led by the nose to the end. Not to mention how Natalya Rubinov and her need had been so callously used. The only good that had come of Kate's lengthy dithering was that Natalya had been spared the anguish of having a child fleetingly enter and depart her life.

Wily though Kate had, of necessity, found herself capable of being, she could not have anticipated that final twist. 'Nobody could be a match for them,' she said as her flight was called.

'Don't ever think that, Mrs Starling,' Farringdale replied. 'It's what they want us to think. And heaven help people like the Smolenskys if your sort falls for the bluff.'

They shook hands, and Kate went to board the plane fortified by the sole pearl of wisdom Tweedledum had uttered throughout their acquaintance. It was good to be going home, to know she'd soon be seeing the kids. Alun, too, though her self-discoveries, once made, would not go away; nor the disconcerting one, made via Calvin, about Alun and one of his female colleagues.

There was much that Kate would have to deal with one step at a time. And when she was back where freedom was taken for granted, the mother and child whose plight had embroiled her in all it had would continue to haunt her.

After take-off, she glanced at the two unoccupied seats beside her, and thought of the couple who had led her to see for herself that compassion wasn't enough. From now on, Kate would lend her strength to the cause in every way she could.

Meanwhile, she allowed herself a pipe-dream of the new Soviet leader standing with the other big brass atop Lenin's tomb, for the 1986 May Day Parade, declaring an amnesty for all political prisoners and that all the refuseniks could go to Israel. Give the man time, Kate! – that's only two weeks from now. Just keep your fingers crossed that he is what he seems, and the others will eventually let him; that this time next year, things could look better for the refuseniks.

She ordered a brandy, nibbled some nuts from the packet that came with it, and raised her glass to absent friends. Calvin. And the intrepid New York cops. Howard and Barbara. The Baptist preacher. Daphne, who was just a few yards away in the first-class compartment. Irina. And the little boy Kate had briefly been a mum to.

There were tears in her eyes when she swallowed the drink down. Even if Kate's pipe-dream one day materialised, nothing could wipe out what the refuseniks were made to endure. How did they *manage* to endure it? Remembrance of Irina's Sabbath Eve table again returned to Kate. What were those candles, burning bright in their poignantly makeshift holder, but a testament to an all-enduring faith.